BLACK RIVER

BLACK RIVER

Melanie Tem

HEADLINE
FEATURE

First published in Great Britain in 1997 by
HEADLINE BOOK PUBLISHING

A HEADLINE FEATURE hardback

10 9 8 7 6 5 4 3 2 1

British Library Cataloguing in Publication Data

Tem, Melanie
Black river
1.Thrillers
I.Title
823.9'14[F]

ISBN 0 7472 2060 3

Typeset by Palimpsest Book Production Limited,
Polmont, Stirlingshire
Printed and bound in Great Britain by
Mackays of Chatham PLC, Chatham, Kent

HEADLINE BOOK PUBLISHING
A division of Hodder Headline PLC
338 Euston Road
London NW1 3BH

DEDICATION

For my beloved son Anthony.
And for Steve, who took his own journey.

ACKNOWLEDGEMENTS

My thanks to the following for invaluable research assistance:

Kevin Black, Assistant State Historian, State of Colorado; Kenneth C. Gibbons; Karn Koske; Robert Ilsevich of the Crawford County (Pennsylvania) Historical Society; Wreatha McKinney; Roberta Robertson; Lois Werner-Gallegos.

. . . Every year
everything
I have ever learned

in my lifetime
leads back to this: the fires
and the black river of loss
whose other side

is salvation,
whose meaning
none of us will ever know.
To live in this world

you must be able
to do three things:
to love what is mortal;
to hold it

against your bones knowing
your own life depends on it;
and, when the time comes to let it go,
to let it go.

—Mary Oliver
'In Blackwater Woods'

Chapter 1

Life was good.

That is, life contained many good things.

Her life was a vessel, and she took pains that it held an abundance of good things. Or, her life was clay, and she worked to mold it into the size and shape she wanted. Waiting at the bus stop, Renata Burgess examined her life in some detail, as she often did – her marriage, her children, her social work and writing careers – and found the inventory enormously satisfying.

It was 5:15 on a bright blue-and-white March afternoon. A Friday. Friday, March 18, 1988. Life was good.

Renata was tired. The bus was late, a portent that there'd probably be standing room only. People paced and scowled. A young man jingled his change irritatingly; Renata shot him a warning look but he was oblivious. She leaned against the bank of newspaper dispensers and willed the bus to come *now*, visualized its gray-white hulk rounding the corner of the campus just over there.

There was a faint rustle on the courtyard side of the bushes that edged the campus. A rabbit, Renata thought. The idea of rabbits burrowing in the midst of an urban campus never failed to delight her, and a few times she'd brought her kids down here just to watch the bunnies.

But it was a snake. Renata watched in amazement, a little chilled, as the thin and rippling creature, not much longer than a pencil and nearly the same color as the concrete path, slithered out from under one row of bushes, across an open space, and into another hedge. She looked around at the other people who made up the small milling crowd waiting for the bus, but nobody else seemed to have noticed.

1

The bus came. She smiled at the young man who, still jingling his change, stood back to let her get on first. She smiled at the driver, who nodded. Surprisingly she found a completely unoccupied seat and piled her books and purse and lunch sack beside her to discourage anybody else from sitting there. She closed her eyes, stretched her legs under the seat in front of her, and leaned her head against the cool damp window. Allowing the rumble and grind of the engine, the sporadic chatter of the other passengers, the occasional ding of the signal bell, the repressed music from someone's earphones to meld into white noise, Renata set about tidying up the work week in her mind so she could put it aside for the weekend.

It had been a busy week. The campus was in the throes of mid-terms, gathering momentum toward spring break, and the disabled students that Renata's office served were as frazzled as the rest. She let herself worry a little about the sign language interpreter who'd quit without notice on Wednesday, forcing two deaf students to request extensions on their midterms until a substitute could be found. She reviewed with satisfaction the news that an accounting major, whose cerebral palsy made it impossible for him to hold a pen or work a calculator, had been named Outstanding Senior – not Outstanding Disabled Student, or Outstanding Student with Challenges, but just Outstanding Senior.

The bus stopped. Renata shifted in her seat and opened her eyes to smile at the pretty little Chicana, maybe three years old, with waist-length, nearly black hair who'd just boarded with her mother. The mother's hair was long and black, too; her features had thickened into a different sort of beauty. She didn't smile back but the child did, and Renata felt the little thrill that always came when she made unexpected contact with another human being.

Hating to waste time, she'd learned to use the bus ride to relax, and by the time she reached her stop she was somewhat refreshed. She stood at the stop for a few minutes after the bus had pulled away, making herself *notice* things. The particular city-evening slant of the light. The stocking-capped man selling marshmallow-colored carnations that looked as plastic as the child's bucket they sat in at his feet. The pigeon waddling across the Safeway parking lot, a slight burnish to its black and gray feathers. Her own competence, always a little surprising and gratifying as she went about the complex business of living; when she thought about it, it was astonishing that any human being throughout history had ever made it through a day, with so many interlocking details to attend to. She grinned when the 'Walk' light came on just as she reached the curb.

It promised to be a busy weekend, too. Vanessa was going to a birthday party sleepover tomorrow. Tim and his longtime girlfriend Shauna might be over for Sunday dinner; Renata liked Shauna a lot, resisted only with conscious effort thinking of her as her daughter-in-law. Ian would, as usual, clamor to have a friend over tonight.

Almost ten, she thought, and shook her head in disbelief. Ian's birthday was April 11, the same day as hers. He'd already made out his birthday list. For the first time, 'books with chapters' was on it. That brought a little buzz of parental self-satisfaction; all their children had been late learning to read, and now Ian was showing signs of becoming their only true reader. She thought again, because the thought gave her such pleasure, how glad she was they'd chosen to adopt, and to adopt older kids, how gratifying it was to help give someone a life who might otherwise hardly have had one.

She frowned. She tried to avoid thinking like that, but the image of herself and Glenn as rescuers was sometimes too tantalizing to resist. It was also, she knew, more than a little smug, and insulting to her children. She'd have to be more careful.

Sometime this weekend, too, once they found a sitter for Ian, she and Glenn had a date to try yet another of the tiny Italian restaurants in their northwest Denver neighborhood. Her sense of anticipation was acute. They tried to get away by themselves every weekend, even if it was only to Dairy Queen for raspberry malts, and after almost nine years of marriage, he was still the most interesting person she knew.

Life was full of good things, many of which she'd put there herself.

'You always get everything you want!' Tim had hurled at her once in a scattershot burst of adolescent hostility.

'Oh, right!' she'd shouted back. 'You think I *wanted*—' she'd stammered a little, searching for something to list – 'my first marriage to end in divorce?'

3

'But you always *end up* getting what you want. You don't hate him. You say it wasn't a mistake. You're not sorry it happened. Everything always turns out good for you. It's not fair.'

'You think I *want* you to be so unhappy? To spend time in jail before you were sixteen years old? To have a drug problem?'

'You wanted to adopt me and you did,' he'd snarled, as if that were the ultimate accusation, and stormed away.

There was a sense in which she knew what he meant. What she didn't understand was why she should have to defend herself against such a charge.

She stood on tiptoe to peer inside the light fixture on the outside wall of the fire station. Last spring, she and Ian and Vanessa had discovered, sheltered behind the bulb, a little pile of twigs and string in the back corner; it could have been nothing more than windblown debris, but they'd kept checking on it whenever they'd passed by and gradually the pile had been rounded and hollowed into a recognizable nest. Then three blue eggs had appeared – 'robin's egg blue,' she'd told the kids, delighted – then three tiny naked birds chirping and gaping. Renata had had to lift Ian up to see; Vanessa had been able to stretch her suddenly gangly legs long enough to reach it herself. They'd all been saddened and awed when one late summer afternoon they'd found the nest deserted. 'It's nature's way,' she'd told them. 'Baby creatures grow up and leave the nest and start lives of their own.'

'Doesn't it make the parents sad?' Vanessa had asked, shooting her one of those knowing glances.

'Sure,' Renata had answered carefully. 'But proud, too.'

'But it's like you're losing your kids.'

'All parents lose their kids into the world, one way or another. That's what being a parent is all about.'

Remnants of last year's nest still littered the fixture, but there were no signs of renewed habitation. Thrilled that their lives had intersected with the brief and alien lives of those birds, Renata stepped down from the curb, waved to the lone firefighter eating his lunch on the other side of the window, and went on her way home.

She turned off 26th into the alley. In the middle of the block, the red Chow waited till she was almost past its yard, then hurled itself against the fence, barked madly twice, and raced back to its porch again. It was a routine; Renata was startled, as always. She chuckled.

Across her path was a wavy line in the concrete and asphalt and dirt of the alley. When she scuffed at it with the toe of her shoe it peeled away, and she saw that it was a dead snake, flattened by innumerable tires, dried by the sun. Or maybe the sloughed skin of a snake that was not dead, only changed. At first that seemed a hopeful thought, but then the idea of a snake crawling around the neighborhood made her shudder.

She came up on the south side of her house. It looked like a castle, tall and red on its hill among its smaller, newer, flatter neighbors. It had been built in 1898 by one of two rivalrous sisters, the other of whom had built the exact same house catty-corner one block east. The 'twin house' was on much lower ground, had white trim instead of dark gray, had no thick veil of Engelmann ivy spreading over its porch and bay windows, faced east instead of west, and had a completely different feel to it. More open, lighter, neater. Had she owned the twin house instead of her own, Renata thought, she'd probably have found reasons to prefer it; as it was, she was very glad this one was hers.

Under the still-bare catalpa, which worried her every spring because it was the last tree to leaf out, Renata paused to gaze up at her house, to take in the strong sense of *home* it emanated. And *good fortune*.

For almost a decade – four years by herself after the separation from Vaughn, six with Glenn and then with Glenn and Tim and then with Glenn and Tim and Vanessa and Ian – she'd lived in a much more modest turn-of-the-century house two blocks south. Almost every day she'd happened past this house or deliberately altered her route to take her past it, and she'd fantasized about living in it. Much of that time it had been vacant, and sometimes she'd dared to climb the ten red granite steps up the front hill to peer over the black wrought-iron gate.

When Renata and Glenn had decided that their little house was too crowded for their expanding family, Glenn had been sure they couldn't afford to move. Renata had contacted a realtor anyway, a brittle and utterly single-minded young woman who had discovered that the house on the hill had been vacant and on the market long enough that the asking price could be nudged ridiculously low. Then she'd engineered, apparently effortlessly, a financing plan so 'creative' that Renata had found it impossible to understand and hard to believe. A scant six weeks from her first phone call to the realty, they were moving in, carrying boxes and boxes up those ten steep steps on an icy February weekend.

Sometimes Ian was waiting for her at the side gate, having seen her coming for blocks. 'Hi, Mom!' he'd call, his voice still childishly piping, remnants of the speech impediment still giving his *th*s and *r*s a babyish lilt. 'How was your day?' Just lately he'd matured enough actually to listen to her reply. Often Renata would save a funny or inspirational or educational anecdote to tell at the dinner table; lately Ian had been doing the same: 'I have a story for dinner!' he'd announce proudly before she was even in the yard. A squirrel had let him get this close, or a kitten had come to the window of his classroom, or a truck had run into a telephone pole right outside the corner store. Sometimes he tried to tell jokes; last week he'd taken the quantum conceptual leap to understanding the principle of the punch line.

He wasn't waiting for her today. Probably he was at a friend's; Ian was a very social child, far more so than either Tim or Vanessa, and seemed able to form relatively uncomplicated relationships. Vanessa tended to second-guess, often inaccurately, what other people wanted of her, and Tim had had trouble making friends until he was an adult, really until he'd met Shauna.

Renata counted the steps as she climbed them, in order to generate enough momentum to get to the top. She let herself in the back door and scowled at the disorder in the family room. Happily, she and Glenn had always shared a rather casual housekeeping standard, but she hated coming home to such a blatant mess. Smelly socks and tennis shoes under the couch: Vanessa's. Orange rinds arranged in fanciful scallops on the TV stand: Ian's, since currently Vanessa hated oranges. Popcorn kernels and the little white circles from computer paper perforations scattered across the worn red rug. Immensely annoyed, Renata was already rehearsing what she'd say to them about cleaning it up before dinner, working for just the right tone of displeasure and firmness without losing her temper over something admittedly trivial.

She went up the three steps into the kitchen. The dogs were in the kitchen all the time now instead of spending their days in the kennel beside the house, because Shaman was so sick. Renata set her things on the counter and crouched beside the old white dog. With a great sighing effort, Shaman raised her head and gave Renata's hand one weak lick.

Hastily, Renata sat down on the floor so that the dog's muzzle could rest on her thigh. She bent to lay her cheek on the soft snout, felt and heard the shallow rasping breath. Surely it wouldn't be long now. She couldn't read anything in the gold-brown eyes, though they regarded her steadily when she gently raised the dog's head.

Her throat ached, and tears welled. Gypsy, the high-strung younger dog – always the underdog, always dependent on Shaman or on a human being to tell her what to do – came to sit anxiously beside her. Renata put an arm around the sleek auburn neck. Gypsy was panting and glancing worriedly back and forth between her and Shaman. 'You'll miss her, too, won't you?' Renata murmured, and Gypsy wagged her tail because she was being spoken to, but Renata had no idea whether what she'd said could be true.

'Shaman's dying,' she'd told the kids yesterday, the morning after the vet had called her with the test results.

'Ohhh!' Vanessa's fingers around the glass of orange juice had abruptly turned white at the knuckles.

'There's a tumor in the lining of her heart. The vet says her heart just won't last much longer. It's been beating for a long time.'

'Operate,' Ian had suggested brightly, taking a third helping of the green eggs and ham Renata always made for St Patrick's Day breakfast. 'Give her some medicine. Do a transplant.'

'The vet says she's too old and weak for any of that, and it probably wouldn't do any good anyway. I guess it's just her time.'

'How do you know when it's your time?' That was Vanessa, who could always find something personal to worry about.

'You don't. Nobody does.' Renata had considered how to comfort without lying. 'But not very many kids die. Shaman's an old dog.'

'Grandma and Grandpa are old.'

'Yes. And chances are they'll die before you or me.'

7

'Shaman was just a puppy when you got her, huh?' Vanessa had asked, wanting the story again.

There'd been a curious, bittersweet pleasure in telling it. 'She fit in the palm of my hand. I've had her longer than either one of you has been alive.'

Their eyes widened and Ian exclaimed, 'Gee!' Not for the first time, Renata marveled at the egocentrism of children, how hard it was for them to believe that the world could exist both before and after them.

'But you'll be sad when she dies.' Vanessa still looked to other people for clues to what she should be feeling and how she should be expressing it. Her timidity was an ongoing test of Renata's ability to accept people as they were.

'Sure. Very sad.'

'I could take her for longer walks,' Ian had offered.

Renata had not pointed out that he protested walking the dogs as it was, that frequently he'd cheat and take them just on the other side of the block and wait until he thought enough time had elapsed that his parents would believe he'd gone the whole prescribed route, that she and Glenn had debated taking the whole job and its attendant increase in allowance away from him on grounds of irresponsibility. She said only, 'That wouldn't help, sweetheart. And anyway, the vet told me we shouldn't walk her at all anymore. Her heart's too weak. So just take Gypsy from now on, okay?'

'But she's got arthur-itis in her hips,' Ian had protested, parroting what he'd been told about the importance of those walks. 'Her legs'll get all stiff and she won't be able to walk at all.'

He was such a caring little boy. Renata had patted his hand, which still, she'd noted, fit whole into the cup of her palm. 'I don't think that matters anymore, honey.'

'Hey! I got a *good* idea!' Ian had plunked down his fork. 'Let's just turn her into a robot! Then she won't really be dead!'

'That's stupid!' his sister had declared, glancing at their mother to see if it really was.

'Oh, honey, this isn't a cartoon. When Shaman dies, when anybody dies, it's real. Death is *real*.'

Even as she'd said that, out of an instinct that it was an important thing for a mother to say to a child, she'd wondered uneasily what it meant. The truth was, death didn't seem very real. Her grandfather had died when she was fifteen; she and her parents had driven the hundred miles to visit him every two or three months all her life, and after he died they didn't anymore. That was all. She'd loved him; she'd have expected to feel more sadness, more sense of loss.

Her father, a man to whom feelings were enemies and talking about feelings a defeat, had told her that on his way to make the funeral arrangements he'd twice had to pull over to the side of the road. Like the horror writer who knows to break away from the goriest scenes for greater effect, or the romance writer who creates greater eroticism by suggesting rather than describing the sex, her father hadn't directly said what he'd done, but she knew he meant he'd cried. She could hardly believe it. She could hardly stand to think about it.

At her feet under the breakfast table, Shaman had lain sighing. 'What we can do for her now, I guess,' Renata had said to her children, 'is let her know how much we love her and keep her as comfortable as possible.'

'Is she suffering?' Vanessa had wanted to know. Both children studiously avoided looking at the dying dog.

'I don't think so. The vet said she's probably uncomfortable and weak, but probably not in much pain.'

'Can't the vet just give her a shot or something and put her to sleep?'

Renata had taken pains then to regard her children seriously, one after the other, and to speak as firmly and clearly as she could. 'If it gets bad enough, we'll ask the vet to help her die. But it won't be "putting her to sleep." I know a lot of people say it that way, but it's not sleeping. It's dying.'

Vanessa shuddered. 'I don't like that word.'

'But it's true. It's important to say what's true.'

Nobody had said anything for a while then. Ian had eaten the last of the green eggs in the blue bowl. Vanessa had stared into her juice glass, swirling the orange liquid dangerously close to the rim.

Finally Renata, unwilling to let the subject drop just yet, had added, 'I've been staying with her as much as I can. I sat here on the kitchen floor with her head in my lap until late last night. I don't want her to die alone.'

That was true. The other part of the truth was more selfish. She wanted to be present at the moment of death. She wanted to see for herself the change, one instant to the next, from 'living' to 'dead.' Since she'd been Ian's age or younger, she'd been terrified of dying; as a child she used to wake up screaming, 'I don't want to die,' and she still had recurring dreams of falling, drowning, being eaten by monsters, suffused with a terrible sadness and dread that, awake, she couldn't even imagine.

'What do you think it means,' she'd asked Glenn the other night as they'd stood in the kitchen enjoying their customary after-dinner hug, the dogs in brown and white piles against the wall, 'that Shaman's here now and when she dies – tonight, tomorrow, next month – then she won't be? What does that *mean*?'

When he'd shrugged and tightened his arms around her, the movement of his muscles against her had been comforting and steadying. 'I don't know. One of the eternal mysteries.' He'd chuckled a little.

'You must have *some* idea,' she'd said, somewhat accusingly. 'You write about death a lot.'

'I write about it. I don't explain it.'

'Well,' she'd sighed, burrowing her face into the hollow of his shoulder, 'I guess this will be a good lesson for all of us about death. Especially for the kids.' Ian had come in then and wriggled his way up between them so that they were all hugging each other.

Later, long distance to Jackie, her best friend since they were twelve, Renata had still been talking about it. 'I don't *understand* death, and I want to.'

Jackie, ever down-to-earth: 'Why? It's hard enough to understand life.'

'Maybe then I wouldn't be so afraid of it. I mean, it is kind of an important human experience.'

'Well, maybe it'll take the death of somebody close to you before you understand it. Our parents are all getting up there, you know.' And Renata had been vaguely agitated for hours.

Now she pressed her cheek briefly to the top of Shaman's furry snout, patted Gypsy so she wouldn't feel left out, got to her feet, and went on into the front of the house. She heard men's voices from the parlor: Glenn's still gentled by traces of the Appalachian accent, and the mellifluous baritone of their friend Sam Evans, also a writer. They were talking about editors and book deals, topics that had nothing to do with her yet, and she felt the familiar, ignoble stirring of jealousy. But mostly she was pleased. Glenn seldom socialized with anybody outside the family; for a man who loved his wife and children so thoroughly and willingly, he seemed oddly uninterested in friendship.

'Hi.' She smiled at Sam, kissed the top of her husband's head. His hair – the same red-brown as Vanessa's, as if she'd inherited it – was warm from the thin sunshine streaming in the arched front window. 'Where is everybody?'

She always asked that, first thing, when she came home from work; she always wanted an accounting, in as much detail as she could get, of where the kids were, what Glenn had been working on today, what he'd had for lunch, what had happened in school today. When she'd been out for the evening with friends, she always had to catch her breath before unlocking the door, and she'd be full of eager questions for Glenn, sometimes even waking him up to ask. 'Did everybody like dinner? What did you read for a bedtime story? Is Ian still mad at that kid in his class? How did Vanessa's social studies test go? Did your headache go away? Did Tim call?' She was always a little uneasy when she came home after being away, even for just a half-hour to run to the store, just as, to a lesser degree, she was always a little disoriented on her first day back at work after a vacation of even one or two days. Anything could have happened while she was away.

'Vanessa's at Wendy's,' Glenn told her now, 'and Ian's at Zach's.'

'Zach? Who's Zach?'

'A new friend. Looks a little older. But then, everybody looks older than Ian.' They both smiled. 'Zach lives on King Street, over by the store. I talked to his mother. She seemed mystified about why I needed to talk to her.'

Renata sighed. Sometimes she and Glenn seemed to be utterly alone in their determination to be responsible parents. It happened with all their kids: when Tim had started getting into so much trouble, not one of his friends' parents had been willing to admit that their sons might be involved, too, and so it had become much harder to

11

enforce restrictions. Last summer, when Vanessa was eleven, few of her friends had seemed to have much structure, several of them apparently away from home till well after dark with nobody knowing where they were. This, of course, had made Vanessa chafe under her own rules – 'Let us know where you are'; 'Be home for dinner' – even more than she would have otherwise.

'Don't you *care* when we get mad at you?' Usually it was Vanessa who asked that question.

'Of course I care. I don't like it. But I still have to do what's right for you. Being a parent isn't a popularity contest.'

'Do you *like* being a mother?'

'It's the best job I've ever had. The hardest, and the best.'

'He was supposed to be home at five,' Glenn was telling her. 'At 5:35, just as I was looking up the number to call over there, he called to ask if he could stay for dinner. He didn't even seem to realize what time it was until I pointed it out. I said no.'

Renata nodded. 'Was he upset?'

'Some. But he obviously didn't take it real seriously either, because he's late again. I told him to come straight home. It's maybe a ten-minute walk.'

Renata's watch showed 6:12. Worry stirred in the back of her mind, a primal parental response. Probably the cave mother had experienced that same uneasiness when she'd imagined saber-toothed tigers stalking her child who should have been home sooner. Renata imagined cars running red lights, kidnappers wearing stocking masks, and, in a vestigial sort of way, felt better for having given names to some of the terrible things that could happen while her child was away from home. 'I suppose we'd better make a point this time,' she said. 'It won't be long till he's a teenager, and you know what that means.'

Glenn nodded ruefully. 'Well, I think we say no when he asks to have a friend over tonight. Which he always does on the weekend.'

'That's fine. But let's not tell him till we're alone with him, if we can help it. No sense embarrassing him or making a bigger deal than it is.'

Sam – never married, no kids – was looking bemused. In a sense, he'd started it all; as a mail-order 'minister' of the 'Church of Universal Life,' he'd officiated at their mountaintop wedding ceremony. He'd been there, too, the day they'd met, at the local writers' workshop for which he functioned as mentor and lead critic.

The kids loved this story: Glenn, a graduate student living in a $35-a-week room in Fort Collins' Walnut Hotel, where not just on Saturday nights did you have to step over the drunks on the steps, and subsisting on spudnuts and Mrs Paul's fishsticks, had come to the workshop, which was at Renata's house that month. He'd sat in one of the ancient wooden chairs she'd dragged up from the basement. It had collapsed under him. Still blushing, he'd stayed to fix it, then asked to see her novel. He'd fallen in love with both the protagonist and the author and written her a letter to say so. Tim always chuckled at the part about the broken chair. Vanessa got dreamy-eyed at the part about the novel. When she was in Sam's company, Renata – who enjoyed contemplating that instant before which something did not exist and after which it seemed to be eternal – often thought about the beginning of her family.

The door banged open and Ian came in, yellow windbreaker muddied, blond hair tousled and dirty and, as always, needing a trim. Renata loved the range of hair color in their family, from Tim's nearly black through her own dark brown and Glenn and Vanessa's auburn to Ian's yellow. 'Hi, Mom!' He was followed by a taller, darker, quieter boy Renata hadn't seen before.

'Hi, Ian.' He came for a hug. Briefly nuzzling his sticky, sunny hair, she reminded herself that it wouldn't be long before he wouldn't let her do this anymore, and she forced herself not to hold on when he pulled away. 'Are you going to introduce me to your friend?'

'That's Zach,' Ian said promptly. 'That's my mom.'

Zach had sat down on the steps by the door, enough in the shadows that she couldn't see much of his face. She smiled in his general direction and said, 'Nice to meet you, Zach.'

After a moment, when Zach had said nothing, Ian admonished him, 'You gotta say something to my mom. She gets mad if you don't talk to her.'

As the other boy hastily muttered, 'Hi,' Renata felt herself blushing. 'I don't get *mad*,' she protested. 'I just don't like being ignored.' Some of Ian's friends had been known to sit through entire meals at her table hardly acknowledging her presence.

Renata had finally decided to protest being ignored. When she said hello she waited to be answered. When she asked at the table if anybody wanted seconds, she refused to pass the plate until she got a response. She complained loudly to Ian and sometimes to his friends themselves. The result was that, lately, she'd made contact, however brief, with every child who came into the house.

And last night Ian had looked up from his plate, spaghetti sauce charmingly all over his chin, and announced, 'I'm lucky I got you guys for a mom and dad.'

'Why?' Renata had asked, shamelessly.

'Cause you sit at the table and have dinner with me every night, and you ask me questions about how was my day, and you pay attention to my friends.'

Sam and Glenn came out of the parlor now, chatting about the implications of the latest publishing company merger. Sam said hello to Ian in the direct way he had with children, at the same moment that Zach suddenly announced in a stage whisper, 'You look a lot like your mom!' Renata suspected that the boys had been talking about adoption.

Looking at Sam rather than at the other boy, Ian said, 'She's not my birth mom, you know.' Renata noted with satisfaction that he hadn't said 'real.'

Sam grinned. 'I know that. I knew her a long time before you did.'

'You look a *whole* lot like her,' Zach repeated, surprised.

Ian and Renata exchanged a knowing, loving look. A shaft of clear sunshine turned the wooden floor a golden-brown, lit up Ian's canary-colored jacket, dappled the red wall. It might have been fleetingly encasing the scene in amber.

Glenn and Renata followed Sam outside and talked to him over the fence for a while. It was an exquisite spring afternoon, although officially the first day of spring was two days away, and Renata reminded herself to *notice*: the vivid blue sky; the sturdiness of her husband's arm under her hand; the pale cloudy greens of the trees across the streets in both directions, just budding, which pleased her even more since she'd read about the care and planning with which the Denver streets had been laid out in a grid and street trees planted at regular intervals along its axes; the yellow cat like a puddle of

14

sunshine herself in the greening grass; Sam's familiar friendly smell as she leaned over the gate to kiss him goodbye.

It was a lovely day, full of lovely details. If you noticed them, they weren't so likely just to slip away.

Zach must have left by the back door, because when they went inside, holding hands, Ian was sitting alone at the dining-room table tracing patterns with his fingertips across the dusty wood. 'Ian,' said Glenn, 'why didn't you come straight home like I told you to?'

'I *did*!' Ian's outraged innocence was a sure sign of his guilt.

Renata restrained herself from smiling at his transparency and said, 'It doesn't take forty minutes to get home from Zach's.'

'If you're going to be allowed to go places by yourself, we have to be able to trust you to be home on time,' Glenn told him, and left it at that. Ian stuck out his lower lip, a baby-faced caricature of displeasure.

Renata went upstairs to change her clothes, tired, glad it was Friday. Almost at once, Ian knocked at the door. She could tell who it was by the rhythm of his knuckles on the old wood, distinctive as footsteps. At her 'Come in' he stuck his head in. 'I'm going to walk the dogs now,' he said brightly.

'Just Gypsy, remember?'

He bobbed his head. 'Yeah.'

'Don't forget the pooper scooper. We don't want the neighbors complaining again about dog poop on their sidewalks.'

He made a face but didn't object. She knew what was coming. 'Then can I invite a friend over to spend the night?'

'No,' she said.

He looked shocked. 'How come?'

'I think you know why,' she said, amazed by the imperviousness of childhood. He stood there frowning, dangling the loop of frayed clothesline that he used as a tandem dog leash. She was afraid someday the clothesline wouldn't hold, but she couldn't seem to remember to buy leather leashes. 'Tell you what, Ian,' she said, exasperated. 'You think about it while you're out walking the dog and let me know what the reason is when you come back.' He opened his mouth to say something, but she made shooing motions with both hands and he went clumping angrily down the stairs, the rope hanging now like a tail from his back pocket. She winced

15

as every door in his path slammed, considered watching from the bedroom window to see that his anger with her didn't spill over into roughness with Gypsy, but decided it was too much effort.

As she struggled out of the business suit and pantyhose that had suddenly become unbearably confining, Renata allowed her mind to wander, creating a sensation of unwinding that was almost literal. Duties for the weekend: laundry, cooking ahead for the week, her share of the housework – domestic chores that both bored her and gave her satisfaction. A solution to a problem with the story she'd started that morning. Ian's state of mind.

No matter what self-help books, social work theory, and New Age dogma said, anger was not a pleasant emotion for either the sender or the receiver. But for their kids especially, learning to express anger cleanly and openly was important, as an antidote to their experience that when you got mad at somebody, when they got mad at you, they hurt you or you never saw them again.

Not long ago, Ian himself had been able to say, 'You know what? I used to think if I was really really good nobody'd ever send me away again.' They'd been reading *Little Miss Grumpy*; Renata had kept her arm around him and forced herself to be quiet so he could go on. 'But you and Dad won't ever get rid of me, no matter what.' Then he'd looked up at her from under those long dark lashes and demanded, in a voice not quite sure of itself, 'Right?'

'That's right,' she'd assured him. 'No matter what, we're stuck with each other forever.'

'Forever?' He'd liked the word.

So had she. 'Forever.'

Renata pulled on one of Glenn's old shirts over her T-shirt and slowly buttoned it, savoring the soft feel and cottony smell of it. She loved wearing shirts that belonged to either Glenn or Tim; much too big for her, they made her feel swaddled, protected, and close to the original wearer. She flopped onto the bed and turned on Tom Brokaw. It took effort to follow what he was saying; sometimes she found herself listening only to the tones and cadences of his voice, which were oddly comforting no matter what the content of the stories.

Hearing Ian climb the stairs, she knew before he spoke that he was furious. 'Mom?'

16

She rolled over, mildly resenting the intrusion. 'What?'

Ian's eyebrows were wrinkled, a sure sign of distress. Renata wondered if his wife would learn to take that as a clue, too, fifteen or twenty years from now, and if he'd still have the slight lisp that made his ugliest words charming. 'Is it because I was late?'

'Because you were late *twice* and you didn't call.'

He stomped to his room. She heard the knotted rope strike the wall in passing, and gritted her teeth when he slammed his door. When he started yelling she turned up Brokaw's volume. Tim had had world-class temper tantrums; neither Vanessa nor Ian ever kept up the pounding and shouting for very long.

Vanessa called, 'I'm home!' as she went past the door, and from his office next door Glenn answered, 'Hi, honey.' Vanessa went past her brother's door without pausing and into her room at the end of the hall; she shut the door firmly, and almost at once Renata heard the faint beeping on the phone by the bed as her daughter dialed the extension in her room.

Ian was complaining loudly about the unfairness of it all, and periodically objects thumped against his door, which rebounded with what must have been a gratifying rumble. Renata did her best not to hear exactly what he was saying. Brokaw signed off. The cuckoo clock in the living room struck 6:30 a few minutes fast. Commercials streamed past; milliseconds after they ended, Renata could not have said what they pitched.

She stretched and yawned. Already she was less tired. Unless there was a major hassle with one of the kids, coming home almost always energized her. The local news came on. There was such a steadying, ritualistic quality about listening to these particular anchors that Renata felt unsettled any time she missed them. Her attention drifted, to nothing in particular.

Larry Greene predicted a beautiful weekend, sunny and mild, and made one of those self-satisfied remarks about what a privilege it was to live in Colorado. Renata grinned; it was. She turned the TV off when Ron Zapollo began sports with a basketball story; that must mean there was no important news about the Broncos, which was the only thing she cared about in sports.

Groaning self-indulgently, she sat up on the edge of the bed and reviewed dinner: The salmon had been cleaned and mixed with egg

17

and breadcrumbs, ready to be made into patties. She'd cooked the potatoes in the microwave this morning, so they needed only to be peeled and mashed, and she'd checked that there was enough frozen corn, one of the last two bags she'd frozen from the Farmer's Market last summer. It would take maybe half an hour to get the meal on the table, and nobody was clamoring. With only a trace of guilt, she decided to read the paper first.

Carrying the folded paper under her arm, she went down the hall to the bathroom, almost unconsciously taking stock of where her family was. Once children left home, you couldn't play this little magic game, but it seemed a harmless self-deception with those who were left: Know where they were and what they were doing, and they would be safe. She could hear the busy whir of Glenn's computer. Ian had quieted again; she considered knocking on his door and decided against it, decided he had a right to his anger. Vanessa's telephone chatter was shrill enough through her closed door that Renata heard a string of boys' names.

When she came back to the bedroom, she sat in the comfortable old yellow wingback chair to finish the paper. She read Ellen Goodman's column, an article about Ayatollah Khomeini, Miss Manners, the comics. As she was chuckling over 'Rose Is Rose,' Ian started up again, kicking or pounding his door. Abruptly, Renata had had enough. 'Ian!' she shouted, through the two walls and across the narrow hallway that separated them. 'Stop it. Calm down now so you can eat. We'll be having dinner soon.' The thumping stopped.

Willing now to be domestic, she made her way downstairs, enjoying the nub of the carpet under her bare soles. It wasn't really warm enough to go barefoot, but she loved the feel of carpet, wood floor, grass, even gravel under her feet and was willing to put up with a little cold. The sky was completely dark now, and the tall stairway windows reflected her movements down the stairs, blurred and intensified the yellow lights, red carpet, brown woodwork that made the house so snug and homey. Sometimes squirrels took shelter between the Engelmann ivy and the south wall of the house; sometimes one or both of the cats sat on the broad windowsill and stared out at the unperturbed rodents. Right now the yellow cat was daintily eating from her red heart-shaped bowl; Renata stroked the thick fur with her toe, and the cat gave a tiny answering purr.

Although the kitchen, more than any other room in the house, needed remodeling, and the chipped cupboard doors and stained rug sometimes made it seem tacky, Renata liked being there. She turned the country-western station on loud and put wails and yodels into her voice as she sang along with Jessi Colter and Willie Nelson. It took just a few minutes to get the salmon patties into the electric skillet, the potatoes peeled and mashed and into the microwave for heating, the corn into the little enamel saucepan. The bright yellow kernels against the bright red pan pleased her, and the cooking food made her suddenly hungry. She liked to imagine good smells drifting upward to her family, to fantasize that someday her kids would tell their kids fond memories of Mom fixing dinner. The cuckoo clock struck eight. She went to put placemats and napkins on; sometimes she called either Vanessa or Ian on the intercom to help set the table, but tonight she could just as easily do it herself.

At 8:20 everything was ready. She turned the radio off, and switched the intercom dial to Station 1 which connected to both kids' rooms. 'Vanessa! Ian! Dinner!'

Vanessa's voice came through, tinny but clear. 'Coming!' Ian didn't answer.

'Ian!'

No answer.

She tried once more. 'I-*an*!'

Often when he'd been upset he'd just fall asleep. When he'd first come to them, they'd been concerned about this coping mechanism because it had happened so often, but over the years it had mellowed more and more until now it seemed no more than an idiosyncrasy.

She switched to Station 3 and called Glenn. 'Ian's not answering. He's probably asleep. Will you wake him for dinner?'

Still humming 'You Are My Sunshine,' she went back to the skillet to dish up the salmon patties onto the thick flowered plate, noting that they made a pattern not unlike petals themselves. She was carrying the plate to the table and wondering if she should cover it to keep the cats away when Glenn screamed. Just her name, hoarsely, over and over. 'Renata! Renata! Renata!'

She ran to the foot of the stairs with the plate still in her hand, screaming herself. 'What? What?' Only with great difficulty did she stop long enough to hear what he said next.

'Renata! Renata! He hung himself!'

Chapter 2

Dialing the phone, saying the words and believing them although they were unbelievable, marveling that she should believe them so readily on the basis of only Glenn's initial shouts – he was silent now – and the thumping from upstairs and Vanessa's shrieking. 'My nine-year-old son has just hanged himself.' Careful to say 'hanged' and not 'hung,' remembering Mr Gibbons's ninth-grade English class: 'Pictures are *hung*. People are *hanged*.' 'My nine-year-old son has just hanged himself. Please come!'

'What's the address, ma'am?'

Sirens before she even hung up the phone, sirens outside and on the phone and in her head, coming to help her and Glenn (oh, God, Glenn, to have found his son hanging, she should go up there but she couldn't, not yet), coming to help Vanessa (who had already been through so much, once children were adopted they were supposed to be safe), coming to help Ian but it was too late.

Cool smooth evening air, the security lights around the house glowing across and through the juniper bushes. Security was important to Glenn, and she'd always been glad of that, if a little bemused. Cars going by on the street and pausing at the corner as if nothing were happening in the house on the hill, red taillights, streetlights pink on the hoods and roofs. No snow. No moon, no stars, no clouds. No flowers yet, though there would be, and the air already smelled of spring.

She stood in her front yard and screamed and waved her arms, screamed and waved her arms, screamed and waved her arms. Under her screaming, a faint rustling. Among the frantic gestures of her arms, a faint serpentine motion.

21

A young man cut across 25th Avenue, calling to her before he got there, 'Is everything all right, ma'am?'

'No! No! No!'

'What's wrong? Can I help?'

'My son – hanged – himself.' Sirens and flashing lights just down the street. Were they coming closer? She screamed and waved her arms, screamed and waved her arms, screamed—

'I know CPR. Where is he? Can I help?'

'Up the stairs, first room on the right.' Ian's room. A stranger in her house, she shouldn't let a stranger in her house, a stranger already was in her house and would never leave again.

Ambulance. Red lights blue lights across the front hill, across her hands where they fumbled with the latch on the gate, she couldn't get the gate open, she stepped back and the first paramedic at the top of the steps opened it for her. Three of them, then she saw a fourth, all in dark uniforms, police cars and a white fire engine and the street and yard were filled with flashing lights – Ian would love this – and she felt a dangerous twinge of hope. Maybe everything would be all right.

She stopped screaming or thought she stopped screaming long enough to tell them, 'Up the stairs, first room on the right.' Ian's room. They raced past her, four, five of them, more, and she screamed and waved her arms, screamed and waved her arms, but nobody else was coming to help. She wanted to sink to the ground which would be wet and cold no snow no flowers and stay there until it was all over but it would never be all over and she had to go inside her house to Glenn and Vanessa and Ian they needed her Ian needed her she screamed.

'I did what I could, ma'am,' the young man said. He was standing in the darkness well away from her, panting, hands in his pockets, and she felt his sympathy and his awe.

For the first of many times that night, she asked, 'Is he dead?'

For the first of many times, someone dared not answer. 'The paramedics are here now,' the young man said, and ducked his head and hurried out the gate. 'I just had an accident myself and I got to get to the hospital.' From the sidewalk he called back, 'I hope everything turns out all right.'

If she could believe what he told her, if she could believe anything, he'd just had an accident himself and had to get to the hospital but he'd stopped to help. That a total stranger would do such a thing was wonderful. That something had happened in her house to require such a thing was terrible. She meant to call her thanks after him but would never know whether she had or not.

Up the stairs, hundreds of stairs, up the stairs and the cat came down mewing, out of habit she stroked the cat's head in passing, cupped it in the palm of her hand. She felt the silky fur and the hard little skull and the carpet under her knee when she stumbled, but those things had nothing to do with her.

Ian's room was crowded with people in black uniforms. Through them she saw Glenn, and she wanted to get to him, to shield him from all this, but she was afraid to move. She saw Ian's bunk beds, his clothes jumbled together with bedclothes, toys on the floor; she didn't see Ian, but a terrible silence emanated from a place on the floor at the foot of the beds, a silence as tangible as the skull of the cat but growing, the silence of absolutely no movement including no heartbeat and no breath.

A stretcher. Her son on the stretcher. She reached for him, but they were going too fast. She ran after them partway down the stairs. 'Is he dead? Is he dead?' She bumped hard into the newel post, slid against the banister to the first landing, collapsed. 'Is he dead?' The carpet and the wallpaper were bright red, bright red. Vanessa was crouched on the stairs with her uncle Charlie who must have seen the ambulance and police cars and fire truck from his apartment across the street or when he was coming home from work, she was sorry he had to come home to something like this. 'I thought it was Glenn,' he was saying now, 'had a heart attack or something.' He never would have thought of Ian, the youngest, the baby.

'Is he dead? Is he dead?' Vanessa was echoing. Charlie had his arm around her. 'Oh, God, he can't be dead!'

'You don't want to ride in the ambulance with him, ma'am. It can be pretty upsetting. They'll be cutting a hole in his throat.'

They had surrounded Glenn and were asking him questions, making him tell again what he'd found. Ian's gerbil was rattling in its cage; it might be distressed, or it might be playing. Glenn was shy, hated crowds. Glenn had just found his son hanging from the post of his top bunk. 'I lifted him up to get the rope loose and –

and—' Glenn was having trouble talking, having trouble breathing, they should leave him alone, she had to protect him, she had to keep more bad things from happening to him. '—and I finally got the rope off and then I tried to give him mouth-to-mouth resuscitation. I did feel some air coming out of his mouth and nose, but I don't know if it was his breath or if it was my breath coming back out. I don't know. I just don't know.'

He was crying, wringing his hands, looking around frantically. Looking for her. 'Leave him alone!' she cried, and put her hand on the arm of the officer closest to her, and staggered against him. 'Ask me! Talk to me! Leave him alone!'

Somehow then she was in their bedroom, separated altogether from Glenn, sitting and rocking on the edge of the bed, bent double over the pain in her chest and stomach, dimly and ludicrously embarrassed by the shabby old rug. They were going to completely remodel this room as soon as one of them made a novel sale, she wanted to tell that to the detective squatting in front of her with his notebook open on his knee, but he was asking her questions. What exactly happened tonight? Had there been any signs that Ian was suicidal? Were there family problems? Where was she when her husband found the child? She didn't hear herself answer. She didn't feel her mouth move. The bedside lamp was glaring in her eyes but suddenly she couldn't remember how to turn it off and when she fumbled for it the red metal base and gooseneck singed her fingers.

'Adopted?' The detective's face swam toward her, round glasses with black frames, thick dark moustache. 'Tell me about that.' His pen was poised.

She must have said something about the kids being adopted. Now he thought that was why Ian had done this, or he thought they didn't love him. Trying to back away from the detective, she fell backward across the bed and drew her legs up, heard herself wailing and wailing.

'You can go on to the hospital now,' one of the officers said. A woman, with tears in her eyes. 'We'll take care of your house for you.' The kindness pierced Renata, put down roots.

She said, 'The dogs haven't been fed.'

A stocky male officer stopped short. 'Dogs? In the house?'

'They haven't been fed.'

'You'll have to put them outside before you go.'

'I can't.' Her head was spinning. Ian was on the way to the hospital with a hole cut in his throat and no heartbeat, no breath. She was clutching the doorframe between the dining room and the kitchen; somehow she had gotten downstairs. The police were looking at each other. She managed to say, 'One of them, the white one, is very sick. She's dying. She can't be outside alone.'

The cop had his hands on his hips. Maybe on his gun or nightstick, she couldn't tell. 'Put them outside.'

'No.' She had no intention of being defiant, but she couldn't think of anything else to say.

On the way through the kitchen she paused, very confused. Then she took the plate of salmon patties out of the oven and dumped them on the floor, making sure Shaman could reach some without getting up. The yellow corn was burning black in the red enamel saucepan. Glenn turned the burner off.

She heard Glenn ask Charlie, 'Can you drive? I can't drive.'

The lights of the hospital were reflected in the lake. Questions: Ian's full name, his date of birth, insurance. Someone crying in the waiting room. Someone laughing.

A small windowless room with beige walls and beige-and-gray tile floor. Two couches. A lamp with a friendly yellow glow on an end table with a telephone. *A telephone*, she thought, and for some reason its presence in this room, where they would wait to find out whether their son was alive or dead, seemed particularly gruesome, particularly desperate. A portrait of a sad Jesus on the wall.

Waiting.

Voices in the hall outside, but not coming here.

Vanessa huddled in a corner of one of the couches. Glenn put his arm around her and she fell silently against him. Charlie stood with feet wide apart and hands in his hip pockets. Renata didn't know where she was, except that she was waiting.

The door opened. A priest came in. Very old, dressed all in black with a high black collar, very pale wrinkled face, very pale wrinkled hands, sparse transparent hair on a very pale wrinkled scalp. Seeing him, Renata gasped. He crossed straight to her and took her hand from her lap. She wrenched it away from him and whispered, 'My

25

God, my God, what are you doing here? You look like the Angel of Death!'

'I am here to be with you, my dear, in your hour of need.'

'Oh, God, is he dead?'

Forcibly now, he took her hand again in both of his, stroked and patted it. His skin against hers hurt. 'I can't tell you that, my dear. But it doesn't look good. It doesn't look good.'

Desperately she curled her hand into a fist between his, and finally he let her go. 'We're not Catholic,' she managed to tell him. 'We don't need you.'

'I will do whatever I can, whatever your faith.'

'Please go. We don't want you here.'

'You need me.'

'*Please go!*'

He hesitated, standing lonely in the open doorway, shimmering black in the fluorescent backlighting from the hallway behind him. A bent and determined old man, bewildered. *Evil*, she thought, though of course he was not evil. A doctor in white took his place.

The doctor had no face. He introduced himself, but he had no name. 'Are you the mother?'

'Yes.'

'Are you the father?'

'Yes,' Glenn said.

Renata cringed, dreading whatever they had just admitted to. 'I'm sorry,' the doctor said. 'He didn't make it.'

Renata screamed and flung herself onto the cold tile floor.

Vanessa arched her back and splayed her arms and legs and wailed.

Charlie put his fist through the wall by the door.

Glenn threw his head back, closed his eyes, called out over and over, 'My baby! My baby!'

The doctor had kept talking through their din. Later, she would worry that maybe she'd missed something he'd said, and at the same time would be certain that she had not, that she'd heard every word. His heart had stopped before the paramedics got there. He was already dead. 'There was nothing we could do.'

The cacophony continued. On the floor, Renata was still writhing and screaming. Vanessa wailed, 'No, no, he can't be dead!' Charlie pounded the doorframe, his own thigh. Glenn sobbed.

'You *do* need me.' Somehow, the doctor had gone and the priest had reappeared.

'Get *out*!' Renata shrieked, and pulled herself to her knees.

'Father,' Glenn began. His voice was shaky and he was short of breath, but his tone was utterly reasonable and polite. 'We know your intentions are good, but we don't share your beliefs, and your presence here is making things worse. Please leave us alone.'

Renata thought wildly: *Such a good man. Such a kind man. It isn't fair that this has happened to him.*

The priest still stood there, hands folded at his waist as though in prayer. 'Get the fuck out of here!' Charlie shouted at him.

'Listen, *I* didn't put that hole in the wall,' the priest said indignantly.

'No. *I* did.' Charlie took a menacing step toward him.

Somehow, Renata scrambled to her feet, pushed past them into the hallway, and grabbed the first white-uniformed woman she saw.

'He won't leave us alone! You better get him out of there or he's going to get hurt! Our son has just died and he won't leave us alone!' *Our son died.* She was trembling violently, panting, not at all sure what she'd said. But she thought the woman flushed and nodded, and when Renata went back into the room the priest was gone.

Now she was kneeling on the floor in front of Glenn and clutching at his legs. 'Don't leave me! Oh, Glenn, please don't leave me!'

He didn't open his eyes. His hand on the arm of the couch was white-knuckled; she was reluctant to touch it for fear it might be cold and dead, but she did touch it and it was cold but not dead. She didn't think it was dead.

'Oh, God, please don't leave me, Glenn! Don't go away in your mind!'

He turned his hand over and closed his cold fingers around hers. 'I'm right here,' he said. 'I'm not going anywhere.' She knew he wished it were otherwise.

Someone else was in the room. A woman, saying quietly, 'You can see him now. He's on a table, kind of a cold metal table. The oxygen tubes are still in his nose. He's kind of a blue color, and, of course, there's still a red mark around his neck.'

27

Of course.

What terrible things to have to say, Renata thought. *What courage and kindness to say them.*

'Whenever you're ready,' the woman said softly. 'My name is Barbara.'

A dim, echoing hallway. An elevator with all of them and Barbara in it. Renata could not hold in her mind the knowledge of why they were on this elevator all together, what they were on their way to see, except to think over and over: *Ian.*

Another hallway with dim brown light. Another room. Another sad brown portrait of Jesus on the wall. Curtains across the back, drawn shut.

Behind those curtains lay the dead body of her little boy. Renata moaned and swayed. Someone caught her – Charlie, swaying too. Glenn swaying, too. Vanessa rigid.

She and Glenn and Vanessa huddled together. She opened the circle, held out her arm to Charlie, who came. 'I don't want to do this,' she was saying, chanting. 'I don't want to do this. But we have to. Let's do it together. Oh, no, I don't want to do this—'

They moved together with small shuffling steps, arms around each other, toward the drawn curtains at the back of the room. Somebody opened the curtains.

Ian's small face was contorted, mouth pulled fiercely down on both sides, eyes shut unnaturally hard. His blond hair was matted and dirty. Oxygen tubes ran uselessly to his upturned nose. There was a raw red ring around his soft throat, inside the V-neck of his blue-and-white football jersey. The table was, in fact, cold metal; Renata was grateful to have been warned that it would be cold.

Glenn, sobbing, bent and kissed his dead son's forehead. A big man, a strong man, a kind man; *it's not fair.* She didn't want to, but she moved closer, too, and kissed Ian goodbye. His skin was cold and rubbery. His absence was utter.

'That's not Ian,' she said aloud. 'Ian's gone.'

The volunteer's last name was something Polish. Renata struggled to remember the last name, and Barbara held her hand so she wouldn't float away.

Barbara sat on her right side. Vanessa sat on her left, leaning her head against the window. Their thighs pressed against hers because it was crowded in the back seat of the police car. Their warmth seeped into her. She couldn't think of Barbara's last name. She'd been talking and was still talking, but most of the time she didn't know what she said, except that it was about Ian. Ian was dead.

'What's the address again, ma'am?' The policewoman on the passenger side of the front seat half-turned, her profile back-lit by passing cars and neon signs.

Renata said Tim's address again. The numbers vanished the instant they left her mouth.

The cops exchanged a few quiet words. From the radio came another man's voice, the dispatcher, one side of numerous conversations. The radio crackled. It must be a slow night; the voice was bantering, chuckling, soft and casual.

Renata leaned forward. 'Excuse me, but does the radio have to stay on?' She didn't know whether she said any more or not, anything about how horrifying and insulting it was to have this pleasant voice in the car chatting about things other than Ian.

She didn't hear herself put it into sensible words that anyone else would understand, but the policewoman understood. She glanced at her partner, said, 'We have to leave it on, but we can turn it down,' and turned it down. Gratefully, Renata sat back. The seat was cold against her back, as if she hadn't been leaning against it, as if she wasn't there now.

'Will you still come to my sixth-grade graduation?' Vanessa sobbed.

'Oh, honey, yes, of course.' Renata could not imagine how she would do that. Ian would never graduate from sixth grade. But Vanessa needed her to say 'yes,' so she did.

'Will you still be proud of me?'

Renata promised, 'Yes,' although it was ludicrous and offensive to think that she would ever feel anything but this anguish. 'Yes,' she said again. 'Oh, Vanessa, I'm so sorry that this has happened to you. After all you've already been through in your life, and you're only twelve. You were supposed to be safe now. Adoption was supposed to make you safe. I'm so sorry.'

Vanessa leaned her head back next to her mother's. In the variegated moving lights, her cheeks glistened. 'At least this time

I'm going through it with somebody who understands. Somebody who loves me.'

I can't love you came unbidden and whole into Renata's mind, a complete reeking thought. *I don't dare love you because you'll die. One way or another I'll lose everybody I love.* But aloud she said, 'Oh, I do love you,' and that was the truth.

'Will you and Dad ever be happy again?'

'I don't know.' *No. No.* 'I guess so.' That wasn't enough for Vanessa. She turned her face full toward her mother, vivified by an expression of abject terror. With terrible effort, making it up as she went along, Renata said only because her daughter so desperately needed her to say it, 'Yes. It will take time and it won't be easy, but we'll be happy again.'

Before she'd said it, it had been a disgusting lie. But, with the excruciating effort of forming the phrases and pushing them one after another out of her brain, came an undeniable swelling of love for Vanessa and the sense that what she'd forced herself to say to her might actually be true. She might someday be happy again. She might learn, whether she wanted to or not, how to live her life, in which, among all the other things that had happened and would happen to her, her beloved son had died.

The thought shamed her. She wrenched her mind away from it, and *Ian died tonight* immediately swelled to fill her head with fire. That was how things should be and how they would always be. Pain, which was right and eternal, made her groan and clutch Barbara's hand. 'I'm here,' Barbara said softly. 'Tell me what I can do.'

'Bring my son back.'

Calmly, the volunteer stroked her hand and told her, 'I wish I could do that, but I can't. Nobody can. I'm sorry.'

'Then just don't let go of me because I'll fly apart if you do.'

'I won't let go.'

'Vanessa, I'm scared. I'm scared that I don't know how to be your mother anymore. I want to be a good mother to you, but I don't know how.' The word *mother* was an obscenity now, but she didn't have a substitute.

'You're a good mother. You're still a good mother.'

'If I were a good mother, Ian wouldn't be dead.'

'It's not your fault!'

Vanessa was a little girl, too young to have to say such things to her mother. But because she *was* so young and so frightened and so undeniably *there* – warm, trembling, her pulse racing in the delicate wrist Renata held between her fingers, her breath faintly sour like a baby's – Renata didn't stop herself from going on. 'I'm afraid I'll never be able to say "no" to you again.' *When I said 'no' to Ian he killed himself. It's not fair. I didn't deserve this.*

Vanessa's eyes were luminous with panic. 'Mom, you have to say "no" to me sometimes. I'm only twelve,' and Renata's heart, already broken, threatened to burst again.

They were still on Federal Boulevard, heading north. Between 47th and 48th Avenues Renata recognized the series of little brick houses with peaked entryways where for a year she'd made home visits to a family who'd adopted a baby with spina bifida and Vanessa and Ian had sometimes gone with her, recognized the intersection at 50th where you turned west to go to the dentist. She recognized landmarks and knew where she was, and at the same time none of it made sense and she was wildly lost, floating in time and space. She thought they'd been heading north on Federal for a very long time.

A thought struck her, and she leaned forward again to talk to the cops in the front seat. 'You know, it's Friday night, and my son' – *my only son, my surviving son* – 'is nineteen and, uh, doesn't exactly walk the straight and narrow. He might be doing something – illegal.'

The officers looked at each other. Renata saw them both smile faintly, but they said nothing.

'Can you – overlook things tonight?'

The driver cleared his throat and shrugged. After a moment his partner said without looking around, 'Hey, we're Denver. This'll be Adams County. Outside our jurisdiction, you know?'

'Thank you,' Renata breathed. The magnitude of the kindness set her shivering, and Barbara held tight to her hand. 'He may not even be there,' she said, thinking she'd said it before. 'He doesn't have a phone. Where is Ian right now?'

Barbara didn't miss a beat; she'd been paying attention. Gently, she asked, 'Where do you think he is?'

Dimly feeling foolish, Renata nodded, laughed a little. 'That's exactly what I'd say if a client asked me that question.'

31

'It's an important question to be asking, but nobody can give you the answer. You'll have to find the answer for yourself.'

'I don't know, I don't know. I can't find him anywhere.'

For a while then she sobbed frantically, clutching Barbara's hand on one side and Vanessa's on the other, and between them reeling in midair like a balloon stretched to its limit with red-hot and hurting air. Vanessa wailed, 'Oh, Mom!' and the police officer at the wheel glanced worriedly into his rearview mirror, but Barbara murmured, 'You're doing all the right things. You're doing fine,' and nobody told her to stop.

The policewoman said something to the driver and pointed left. They turned off Federal onto a much darker side street.

Suddenly Renata found herself wanting to know how these strangers had come to be in her life at this most intimate of times. She couldn't think how to ask the police officers, so she asked Barbara, whose last name she still couldn't remember, 'Do you work for the police department?'

Barbara hesitated, probably unsure how much to say about herself and what it was Renata wanted to know. 'I'm a graduate student intern,' she said carefully.

'What program?'

'Psychology, at D.U.'

'Oh, I know somebody there,' Renata said, but couldn't think of his name and was appalled by her own impulse to make small talk. 'I'm a social worker,' she said. 'For all the good it's done me.'

Barbara smiled ruefully. 'We try all sorts of things to protect ourselves, don't we? But the truth is anything can happen to anybody, good or bad.'

'You're good at this,' Renata said. It didn't come close to saying what she wanted to say, and she was dimly afraid that it sounded cynical. 'You have good instincts.'

'Thanks.' The directness of Barbara's gaze was like a tractor beam through the half-light, for a few moments holding Renata steady. 'So do you. I hope you can keep listening to your instincts.'

'I've never done this before. I guess this is grieving. Over the years I've worked with a lot of grieving people, but I didn't know what the hell I was talking about, not really. Now I know.'

'You're doing all the right things. You're reaching out to other people – your husband, your son, Vanessa, Charlie – and you're also doing things to take care of yourself. You're going to be all right, Renata.'

Renata shuddered. She didn't want to be all right. She didn't dare. But, reluctantly, she nodded.

'There it is.' The policeman at the wheel turned the cruiser into the parking lot of a crescent-shaped, four-story apartment building. Several young men getting loudly out of a van a few spaces away stared suspiciously at the police car.

'I'll hurry,' Renata mumbled. 'I know you have other things to do tonight.'

'It's okay,' the driver said. 'Take as much time as you need.'

She thought he sounded impatient. 'I'm sorry,' she said, confused.

'It's *okay*.'

Vanessa got out of the car on her side and Barbara on hers. They both left their doors open. Renata was paralyzed with indecision, and she shivered as the cold air sliced down both sides of her body.

Then, suddenly terrified of losing Vanessa, she struggled out the left door, managed to stand upright on the swaying pavement, and reached frantically for her daughter. She could see the child, not far away; she could hear her ragged breathing, feel her violent trembling. But now there were multiple images of Vanessa, all of which her arms passed through. She choked out her daughter's name, and Vanessa came to her, put her arms around her waist, hid her face against her shoulder. Renata stroked the soft tangled hair. She was as afraid to touch this living child as she'd been to touch the dead one, but she couldn't stop herself.

The apartment complex was actually several separate buildings. Renata stared at them helplessly. Finally Barbara took the slip of paper with Tim's address on it. Several times she squinted back and forth between the paper and the numbers on the buildings. Then she led the way, and Renata and Vanessa, holding onto each other, followed her.

Along a dark narrow sidewalk between looming buildings whose lights looked like random shards of bone, white and newly dead. Renata heard voices in the thick shadows, and movement; it was her duty to protect her daughter from all sorts of unseen evils,

33

and she couldn't. Wisely, Vanessa was walking closer to Barbara than to her.

Down some steps. They shimmered and her foot went through. Not seeing that they'd ended, she turned her ankle painfully at the bottom.

Into a building whose tiny vestibule reeked of weed. Down more steps; watching her feet, Renata suddenly forgot how to negotiate steps, and stood immobilized halfway down until Vanessa came back to take her hand.

'Number Two.' Barbara gestured toward a door on the right, then discreetly turned away. Vanessa moved with her, leaving Renata alone in front of the closed, blank door of her son's apartment, which she was approaching now for the first time. To tell him that his little brother was dead.

She tried to take a deep breath, but an obstruction in her chest kept the breath shallow and painful. Insufficient oxygen made her light-headed and nauseated. She knocked, couldn't be sure the cold wood was there under her knuckles, knocked again.

No answer. She didn't know how long it had been since she'd knocked, so she waited, hands at her sides, swaying, not touching anything in the world. She knocked yet again, and had to make a conscious effort to stop after a few raps of her fist, which she couldn't feel and which, at the same time, sent pain ricocheting through her arm and ribs. What she wanted was to pound and scream and kick, to force Tim to come to the door and hear the unbelievable thing she had to say. Much as she dreaded his reaction, she needed to see it, the reaction of somebody who didn't know yet; she needed to comfort him, to help him understand what she would never understand. She wanted to be the bearer of bad news instead of the receiver.

No one came. 'He's not home,' she said miserably.

Voices were brazen from the apartment across the hall. Laughter, rap music. *Ian likes rap music*, and, before she could stop it, a vivid and detailed image: straight fine blond hair poufed into a semblance of an Afro or greased to resemble dreadlocks, small elbows and knees bobbing to an awkward beat, baby voice lisping the tough-guy words. She cried out and collapsed against the wall by Tim's closed door.

'Mom!' Not knowing what to do, Vanessa didn't do anything.

'I'm all right,' meaning *I won't die right now. I'll stay on my feet for the moment. I'll stay sane long enough to find Tim.*

The hallway was so narrow that she just reached sideways to knock on the door of Number One with the side of her left fist. There was instant quiet from inside, voices hushed, music turned way down. Renata straightened, brought herself around to face the door, knocked again. The motion of knocking was all there was: she had never done anything but move her fist back and forth in the air, strike her knuckles again and again on the wood; she would never do anything else, and she couldn't remember why she was doing this, what the purpose of knocking was.

'Mom?' Vanessa said fearfully.

The door opened just wide enough for Renata to glimpse black T-shirt, jeans, wary insolent eyes. A young man with longish dark hair. *Tim*, she thought in a surge of love and confusion, *oh Tim*, but it wasn't.

'Is Tim Burgess here?'

'Who?'

'I'm his mother. It's – an emergency. Please.'

'Who?'

'Tim Burgess. He lives there.' She gestured vaguely over her shoulder at Number Two.

'Never heard of him,' the young man said, and shut the door. There was a geyser of shrill laughter, and the music went loud and unkind again.

She didn't know what to do. She pivoted shakily, laid her palms against Tim's door, leaned her forehead against it. Barbara had gone to stand on the little landing, out of the cramped hallway. Now her voice came from behind and slightly above Renata, disorienting her even though she knew where she was, where Vanessa was, where Glenn was. She did not know where Ian was. *Ian is dead.* She did not know where Tim was. 'You could leave him a note.'

Tears welled in Renata's eyes at the impossibility of it. 'I didn't bring paper,' she confessed. 'Or a pen.'

Barbara handed her a pocket-sized spiral notebook and a blue ball-point. Renata didn't understand where they'd come from; Barbara wasn't carrying a purse. That bothered her so much that she almost put her hands behind her back and didn't accept them.

Then she was holding notebook and pen in her hands, staring at them blankly. Then she wrote, on a page she hoped was empty with a pen she hoped was working: 'Tim – please call home as soon as you get in, no matter how late it is. If there's no answer, leave a message where we can reach you. It's an emergency. Mom.' Because he had two mothers and she dared take no chances tonight, she added her name in parentheses and then the date: Friday, March 18, 1988. The day Ian died.

Ian has two mothers, too. His birthmother doesn't know he died. Do I have to try to find her? Do I have to tell her?

Yes.

It's not fair. I can't stand this.

She was suddenly enveloped in a cacophony of colors, textures, shapes, sounds, tastes in the back of her mouth, sounds utterly outside and disconnected to her, textures that raced on the underside of her skin where blood had once flowed to and from her heart, odors that bored like termites through her bones which were the bones of the world collapsing. The world was a dark, bloody, pulsing womb of loss. Things slithered in it, in her.

No no no no no I can't stand it.

Somehow then she was back in an enclosed and moving space (*police car police Ian died tonight Ian hanged himself is it hung or hanged? a picture is hung, a person is hanged*). Someone *Vanessa* sat on her left, holding her hand. Someone else sat on her right, holding her hand. She didn't know who that could be. *Barbara.* Someone named Barbara, who was in her life only because Ian had hanged himself. *That's not possible I can't stand knowing that. I hate her.* Renata clung to both hands although she could scarcely feel them, could scarcely identify what they were, her own hands or theirs. She was wailing although she heard no sound. She was being swept into, was becoming, the endless bloody pulsing tunnel of this night. Something coiled around her, then withdrew.

They took her back to the hospital. There was no point in going home.

But when they passed her house, she recognized it immediately, with an unpleasant burring in her nerve endings like electric shock. Lights were on in Ian's room. She frowned. It was way past his bedtime.

It isn't Ian's room anymore. What will we call it? How will we bear passing by that door, open or closed, for the rest of our lives?

Ivy covered the bottom half of his window. At this very moment it was sending tough little tendrils under the sash and around the frame. Ian hated it when they trimmed the vine. 'Can't we just let it grow in my room?' She could hear his voice, feel its sweet timbre in the back of her own throat. 'It could be my pet.' He'd laugh then, a string of perfect seashells, bubbles in a golden light.

Missing him exploded in her chest, swelled again, exploded again. She arched her back and clenched her fists against the pain.

Leafless for the season, the ivy hid nothing. Renata could see the brown bunk beds and blue wallpaper, police still milling, one of Ian's black-and-white pandas in a mound on the top bunk near where Ian had tied the rope.

She wondered how many passing motorists, neighbors in their own safe houses, kids skateboarding recklessly in the twilit street could have seen the little body dangling from the bedpost if they'd only looked up. She wondered how she hadn't known her son would do something like this, hadn't *known* the moment he was dying, why her own heart hadn't stopped, her own breath choked, her own brain exploded. Maybe they had, but too late.

She hadn't seen him hanging. She was grateful for that, and shamed. Glenn had seen him. (*Had his head been twisted at an unnatural angle? Had his eyes bulged? Had his cat-scratched, jelly-smeared, smooth-cheeked face already been turning blue? Had his helpless little fists been clenched at his throat, or already dangling at his sides?*) Glenn had lifted him down, fought to loosen the noose, pushed useless air into the small gaping mouth.

It was inconceivable that a father should ever recover from this. She had lost Glenn, too.

The glaring white-on-blue EMERGENCY ROOM sign almost made her laugh. It wasn't an emergency anymore.

But they pulled into the circle driveway and she got out because there was nothing else for her to do. She meant to thank the police officers but couldn't tell whether she had or not. Someone led her through endless and nonsensical corridors until she was once again in the terrible brown room where they told parents their children had died. The portrait of Jesus gazed, forever mournful, from the wall. The news of children's deaths thickened the air in the room, made it hard to breathe.

'He wasn't home,' she said. 'I left a note.'

'I don't want him to find out some other way.' Glenn's voice was near enough to familiar that Renata thought he was still alive, still sane.

'I'll call Shauna's father if we don't hear from them by tomorrow.' *Tomorrow.* The word was flat, with neither resonance nor sense, except for the knowledge that when she woke up, tomorrow and for the rest of her life, Ian would be dead. If she ever slept again. If she ever woke up.

'I called my parents,' Glenn told her. 'I called Danny; I figured he could tell the rest of Ian's friends. I left a message on Sam's machine.'

'Oh, God, what did you say in the message?'

'I just said, "Ian died tonight. I don't know what else to say."'

'God.'

'I tried to call your parents but there was no answer.'

'No answer? It's late on a Friday night.' *Friday, March 18, 1988.* 'Where would they be?'

'I'll try again in a few minutes.' Glenn gestured toward the phone which squatted, an evil brown toad, on the end table. His hand set up ripples through the air; the ripples reached her eyes and hurt her, hurt her throat. She shut her eyes, opened them, shut them again, and the ripples had stopped. Now the sight of his hand lying still hurt her eyes, her throat, her cramping belly.

'I'll call them. It's not fair that you should have to do that.'

'I think it would be better if I did.'

She didn't fully understand why, but he seemed to be right. 'What did your parents say?'

'Mom cried. Dad didn't say anything. I'm not sure he stayed on the phone.'

'What did Danny say?'

'I talked to his mother. I – I'm not exactly sure what she said.'

So the news of Ian's death was out now, made public, spoken aloud. Witnessed. It had demon eyes and tentacles that wrapped around her lungs and heart, but its body and head were in the world now, in human company.

'Hi.'

Vanessa gasped and wailed, 'Oh, Wendy!' Unable to get up, she leaned forward and held out both arms. Wendy was crying. The two little girls sat huddled together on the couch.

Wendy's mother came to put her arms around Renata. She was crying, too. 'I'm so sorry about Ian,' she whispered, and at the direct and sorrowful mention of his name Renata shuddered. Then she could not stop the spasms that raced through her body, and she knew she would come apart in chunks: head, heart, hands. Wendy's mother held her.

'How did you find out?'

'Vanessa called Wendy and asked her to come. I hope that's all right.'

Renata nodded, nodded again. 'Why would he do this? You knew him. Why would he—' More than ever before, it seemed important to use the exact words, to speak aloud precisely what she meant and in no way to obfuscate. But she couldn't do it. She could only repeat, 'Why would he do something like this?'

'Maybe there was something in his background none of us knew about.'

'Then Vanessa—' Panic blinded and deafened her, stopped her voice.

'No. No,' Wendy's mother crooned, but they both knew she couldn't give any real reassurance, and soon she was giving what she could. 'You know my sister died when she was the same age.'

Renata remembered having heard parts of the story. 'Tell me again how she—' the word stuck – 'died.'

'In a fire. They could hear her screams but they couldn't get to her. My dad broke his leg and suffered burns getting his wife out, but he couldn't get to Alice and his wife blamed him for letting Alice die.'

So that's one way to do it. You could blame each other. You could turn love for Ian into hatred for each other. She considered it. She was surprised by her ferocious desire to hear now about the deaths of other children and the lives of their parents afterward.

'They lost their only two children. A little boy to pneumonia and then Alice in the fire. His wife left him before he got out of the hospital and he never saw her again.'

'And did he survive all that? Did he—' she could hardly bring herself to say it – 'have a good life?'

The other woman nodded emphatically. 'He married my mother and had us. They had a good marriage. He was a terrific dad.'

'Did you grow up with a ghost?'

The nod was smaller and sadder this time. 'He hardly ever talked about his other family, but I found Alice's pictures and little by little he told me the whole story. She was his angel. Especially when I was a teenager, I felt I could never measure up to her. Alice would have been perfect.'

That's another way to do it. Make the dead child more important than the living. Renata considered that, too.

'But he's been happy for a long time now,' she went on, still holding Renata. 'He loves my mother and he loves us and he enjoys life. He has fun. The sadness is just part of his life.'

Against her will, Renata thought clearly: *So, this can be done. Other parents have lost children and kept it from consuming their lives.* Her stomach cramped and her head spun away from the blasphemous thought.

She flung herself free of this stranger's grasp. She collapsed, and the floor tilted with her, giving her an illusion of support as the world reeled. She spread her arms and legs, pressed her face flat against the cool tile, and willed herself to lose consciousness.

Instead, she gained consciousness. The terrible and wonderful thought completed itself: *Other parents have done this, it's part of human history, and I can learn to do it, too.*

Chapter 3

People were coming to the house. For some reason, Renata hadn't thought of that; every time somebody else came, she didn't expect it, and she had trouble holding in her mind a comprehension of why they were all there, although she knew it was because her child had died, Ian had died.

The doorbell had started ringing early Saturday afternoon, and it kept ringing most of the day. Because she didn't know what else to do, and because she was unexpectedly grateful that they were here, she kept opening the door to them, letting them in, and closing the door behind them. Once they were in her house she lost track of them, for her responsibility was only to let them in. They brought covered dishes. They brought relentless spring sunshine into the darkened house. They brought the comfort of human history, part of which was the unwavering acknowledgment that when one's child dies there is no comfort to be had. It surprised her that she wanted them there, and the surprise brought pain, brought comfort.

Neighbors came. The yuppie couple from the twin house brought an apple pie made with too much sugar but still warm from the oven; the wife's sister had died while they were growing up, she said, and Vanessa asked, eyes wide and glistening: How did she die? How old was she? How old were you? Comparing: Mine's worse. Did not ask: Did it ruin your life? Were you ever happy again? Comparing.

Teachers came. Some of them she wouldn't have recognized in another context. Teachers from previous years, including the elderly lady, now frail, who'd retired after Ian's kindergarten class. 'You wore her out,' they used to tease, and Ian would grin; remembering, Renata reached for the doorjamb, missed, clutched empty space. This year's teacher pleaded, 'He was having such a good year!' and

41

Renata hoped that someday she would tell this grieving woman how much Ian had liked her, how important an influence she'd been in his life. (*But what's the point of that now? What does it matter if you make a difference in somebody's life, once their life and yours are over?*)

'We've been talking,' the teachers told her. 'We'll never believe this was suicide. Among us we have over fifty years of teaching experience, and we've known a lot of children, and Ian was not a suicidal child.' (*What do they think it was, then? Do they think the rope got around his neck by accident? Do they think we did something to him?*) Despite herself, she saw that they meant for her to be reassured. Despite herself, despite the protests that jammed her thoughts, she guessed that someday she would be.

The principal came. Renata didn't know who he was at first; she'd never seen him outside school. He sat on the rigid-backed wooden deacon's bench in the parlor and, unbelievably, chatted with her father about Pennsylvania politics, and the state of American education. But he also took her hand in both of his and told her, 'This has hit all of us very hard. Sometimes we don't realize how much investment we make in a particular child.'

Am I expected to comfort him? She tried to withdraw her hand, but he held on.

'We've all been impressed by what good parents you and your husband are. This doesn't change how any of us feel about that.'

What's the definition of a good parent? Surely the bottom line is that your kids don't die, your kids don't kill themselves. But through the tympanic clamor of her unspoken protestations, she heard him, and saved what she heard.

'We'd like to have some sort of memorial service at school,' the principal said.

Renata shivered. 'I don't think we could come.'

He nodded. She could tell he was a little disappointed, and she thought perhaps she was supposed to find the idea of a memorial service comforting, and perhaps she should attend, the grieving mother strengthened by the support and grief of her child's friends. But she could think about such a thing only barely, lightly touching the image and wincing away: all those living children. 'I think it's important for us, though,' the principal was saying, 'for the kids and the teachers. Maybe we could plant a tree in his name.'

'That would be nice.' *That would be stupid. There are plenty of trees. And what if the tree dies? As it will.*

'I'll let you know.'

The gym teacher, who looked very different in street clothes, had come bearing stories about kind and funny little things Ian had done in her class. The stories were offered as gifts, but they seared when Renata tried to accept them. She didn't dare listen to eulogies. She already knew what had been lost. She listened anyway because she didn't dare risk losing anything else, and, of course, she lost it anyway.

Co-workers came: 'I'm sorry.' 'I'm so sorry.' 'If there's anything I can do.' 'Take as much time as you need. We'll take care of things at the office for you.' There wasn't anything else they could say. The paltriness of their ministrations – and their implausible but undeniable efficacy – enraged Renata, forced an inkling of another kind of understanding about the profundity of what had happened to her. People had been saying such things to each other for millennia. Such things never helped, couldn't bring the lost one back, couldn't change what happened and yet, such things helped profoundly, fundamentally. They were part of a safety net that stretched vertically through time and horizontally across space. Part of a map.

She had, in fact, called her secretary in the middle of the night he died. No. It was vital to be precise: She had called Theresa at 3:10 in the morning of Saturday, March 19. 'I'm not sure why I called you,' she'd said near the end of their brief, terrible conversation, and Theresa had assured her, 'I'm glad you did. You did the right thing.'

Friends came: 'Oh, God, Renata.'

'I'm going to need you,' she told her friends, and was surprised to hear herself say that, for it implied that there was a chance of getting through this, a chance of survival, when of course there was not. 'I'm going to need you a lot, and for a long time.'

'I love you, Renata. I'll be here. A lot and for a long time.'

A few of those who came, she was almost sure, were strangers, although it was possible that she should have known them from somewhere. Someone's husband whom she hadn't met before. Someone's children (*How dare they bring children into this house?*). She couldn't bear to look at the children and couldn't tear her gaze away.

A woman in her seventies named Daphne, with flat eyes and a flat voice, her body rigid against constant pain, her shadow thick and rigid across the dusty hardwood floor of Renata's house. Renata knew her, but couldn't think how. Out of some unfathomable urge, one among many, Renata found herself begging of Daphne, who could not answer, who apparently could not say anything, 'Why would he do this? Why would he do something like this?'

Another woman she thought she'd never seen before, who seemed to be associated with no one else here. Her own age, build, coloring; looking at her was like looking in a mirror, and Renata was afraid of looking in a mirror. The woman held Renata's hands in a grip steady and unbreakable because it could have been her own. 'My name is Belinda,' she said.

'I – Have we met? Did you know my son?'

'Yes.'

She's lost a child, too, Renata thought, incredulously but without doubt. *She's lost many children.*

'I'm so sorry that Ian died.'

The stranger said, 'Ian.' At the sight and sound of her dead son's name coming out of someone else's mouth, the feel of it forming again and again, Renata staggered. Belinda held her; Renata was enveloped in the other woman's body heat.

Out of the overwhelming nausea and vertigo, then, rose the head of a giant serpent. The creature was utterly familiar to Renata, and utterly mysterious. Its mouth gaped red for her; its fangs were sharp and hollow. It rose and rose on its thick undulating body, then began to coil itself around her. It was going to consume her. It was protecting her from being consumed. She was terrified, and she was not afraid.

'Ian,' said the stranger again, calmly. Now she seemed taller and stockier. There was gray in her hair, gray dust on her hands and neck. Her skin was weathered. Her clothes looked vaguely out of date. 'Betty,' she said. 'Grace. Frederic.'

Renata could only nod, though she didn't know what she was

acquiescing to or acknowledging. There was no snake in her house, of course, and she lost track of Daphne and Belinda and the other gray woman as people came and went.

Tim came home, her handsome troubled son, grown now but still troubled and still not safe, never safe. She watched him walk slowly across the just-greening side yard and up the front steps, Shauna beside him. He was a sturdily built young man with strong dark coloring, but she knew how vulnerable he was, and now he looked frail – almost transparent, she thought – in the pale spring sunshine of his little brother's death.

Renata longed to run to him. But by the time the impulse had coalesced into a thought and the thought into action, by the time she was fumbling with the door, he'd opened it from the outside and they were clutching each other, she and her only surviving son. 'I'm home,' he announced to her, his voice thick and trembling. 'I came home.'

'I don't think I can stand this.'

'You have to.'

'No. No. I don't have to. I can choose.'

'It wasn't your fault. You can't be blaming yourself.' He was holding her by the shoulders as if to look into her face, but when she put her head back to meet his gaze he looked anywhere but at her, a habit that had become ingrained long before he was her son. He ducked, turned his head, closed his eyes.

She'd tracked Tim and Shauna to Breckenridge and had left three frantic messages at the ski lodge before he'd finally called her back. Waiting, she'd imagined him coming off the slopes – his only ski weekend all season and here she was ruining it with bad news that wouldn't keep – finding the messages ('Call home right away! Emergency! Urgent!'), ducking his head and squeezing his eyes shut and heading back out for one last run before the world changed, half hoping that when he did call he'd get the answering machine and be spared for a while longer. Tim was used to receiving world-changing bad news, used to people leaving him forever. She was not. 'Oh, God, Tim!' she'd gasped after telling the operator she'd accept the charges. 'Ian's dead!'

'No,' he'd said, simply.

'He hanged himself because we wouldn't let him have a friend over to spend the night.'

'Jesus, he wasn't even ten years old.'

'I know.' *And he never will be.*

'It's not your fault,' he'd said then, too. 'You can't blame yourselves.'

She'd tried. She'd searched for a way this could be her fault, something she'd done wrong, something she'd missed. She could find nothing. The dawning comprehension of the extent of her own helplessness was far worse than guilt would have been.

'I should have been a better big brother,' Tim was saying now. Dully, she was surprised. The parlor was full of people he didn't know, and he was talking as much to them as to her, staring from face to face and gripping the arms of the rocking chair where she used to rock him, used to rock Ian. *Ian.* 'I haven't been home enough.'

Renata's careening attention came to focus on her son's need. 'He knew you loved him.'

Tim leaned his head against the carved back of the chair. 'I never spent enough time with him, and now it's too late.'

'You know that Masters of the Universe mirror you gave him for Christmas? He took it to school three or four times. He'd tell people, "My brother gave this to me."'

'That's not enough.'

'Look, Tim, we all do the best we can with each other, and I don't think it's ever enough.'

'If I'd been here with him, he wouldn't have done this,' he said flatly.

Renata put her hands on his shoulders and started to massage the tight muscles, but he pulled away. She lightened her touch then, stroked and patted, and he let her do that while she said, 'No. This is nobody's fault.' And then, because he needed it, she said the truth, although it sickened her: 'Ian made a choice.'

Tim shook his head, stood up, walked to the other side of the room. Renata saw that his eyes were squeezed shut. Sitting on the floor with her long knees drawn up, Shauna watched him, too, and brushed tears from her eyes.

The woman from the crematorium came. That might have been

before Tim came or after he'd left, before or after the principal came to pay his respects.

'Remember,' her father would say to her on the phone one Sunday morning months later when she still had no place in the universe, 'an anchor holds you steady when there is no solid ground. That's the point of an anchor.' The image would strike her with the thrill of an epiphany, partly because it was offered by her father who spent so much of his life avoiding all strong emotion, love or fear, joy or anger or sorrow. Renata immediately recognized the value of the gift and the price he must have paid to give it to her, and these things in themselves became anchors, too.

'I want to see his body,' Vanessa said.

Glenn and Renata looked at each other. 'You already saw it, honey,' Renata managed to say. 'In the hospital, remember? You kissed him goodbye.'

'I want to see it again.'

Glenn said, 'I don't know—'

'Maybe she knows what's right for her,' Renata said. *Maybe not. Ian didn't.*

'You understand there's been an autopsy.' The woman from the crematorium, who was very pretty and seemed to Renata very young, said the awful words gently and without fear, and, before they had to ask, explained. 'There'll be a scar across his chest, and one from one ear to the other across his skull.'

Renata clutched the disintegrating arms of the chair while the room reeled and nausea rose in her throat.

'What does that mean?' Vanessa demanded.

The woman from the crematorium was paying close attention to Vanessa, to all of them. Now she leaned forward intently toward the earnest little girl in her father's lap, and told her what she needed to know. Renata understood that she herself needed to know, and so she listened although she violently didn't want to, and was grateful to her daughter for asking. 'They cut open his head and his body,' the woman said carefully, 'to see if they could find any physical reason for him to do this, or any other cause of death.'

'They cut him *open*?' Vanessa was incredulous. Glenn buried his face in her hair.

'It's an empty body now,' Renata said, and against her own will

47

she listened to herself. 'He's not in it anymore.' *But I don't know where he is.*

'Whenever somebody dies under—' the woman graciously did not say 'suspicious' – 'unusual circumstances, they have to do an autopsy.'

'Did – did they find anything?' Renata asked. She didn't know what she imagined they could have found. Drugs? Demons?

The pretty young woman, who by now Renata thought was very good at her work, looked at her as intently as she'd looked at Vanessa. 'No,' she said quietly. 'Nothing.'

'I want to see him,' Vanessa said again, pleading, insisting.

It seemed a great deal to ask. Renata was suddenly enraged that parents were continually expected to do the impossible, such as accepting their son's death, such as allowing their daughter to see and talk about his mutilated body because it was right for her, such as having to decide whether it was right for her.

Glenn and Renata looked at each other again, and Renata said finally, 'I can't go with you, honey. I can't look at him again.'

'I'll help her,' offered the woman from the crematorium. 'I'll go in with her and explain things.'

'Thank you.'

'It's part of what we do.'

'You're good at what you do,' Renata managed to say. 'And it's important work.'

'How can you stand it?' Vanessa wanted to know.

'We try to help people understand that death isn't anything to be afraid of or horrified by. It's part of life.'

As if that helps, Renata thought fiercely. *It shouldn't be part of life.*

All afternoon and into the evening, her tension – already impossibly high – mounted.

She watched clocks, did not watch them, again and again tore her gaze away, *heard* them ticking.

She couldn't escape the lowering of the sun, the thinning of the light, even though she stayed inside her house, inside her room, and covered her head.

It was the day after Ian died.

It was dinnertime, although she didn't eat.

It was going to be eight o'clock. Something terrible was going to happen at eight o'clock. She had to do something to prevent it.

It was eight o'clock. Something terrible had happened. She hadn't stopped it. Consciousness imploded. She curled up on a floor somewhere. Nobody came to her, because nobody could. Ian was dead.

No.

Renata fell asleep and woke up. The worst part was waking up. Before she was fully conscious she would be crying out, 'No! Oh, no!'

For two full days Glenn shut himself in his office upstairs. Renata and sometimes Vanessa took him food from the dishes people brought. Because she forgot what was on the tray the instant she wasn't looking at it anymore, Renata couldn't keep track of whether he was eating, and that frightened her.

A few times she stood trembling in front of him, pleading wordlessly for an audience, or knelt on the floor and laid her head in his lap. He looked at her as if he didn't see her, or didn't want to, and he made no move to touch her.

'Where are you?' she asked him once. 'What are you doing?'

After what she thought was a long silence but might have been a split second, he answered, 'Being with it. Absorbing it. Making it mine.'

Understanding that she wasn't welcome, a feeling she'd never before experienced with Glenn, Renata forced herself to get up, go away from him, leave the room.

She was in Ian's room, amid the bright cloudy light through his big windows and the little-boy clutter of toys, books, clothes, school papers, various odds and ends with no particular purpose but still-obvious wonderment. Some parents never touched a dead child's room, or cleaned it every day. (*That was one way to do this: Create a shrine. Curate a museum.*) On the perpetually unmade lower bunk that did not smell of him, did not hold any imprint of him at all, clutching one of his gigantic black-and-white teddy bears, she rocked and keened. This must be keening, this serrated wailing that hurt unbelievably – almost but not quite unbelievably – as it cut new pathways for her mourning, but that hurt much less than not keening, than not having pathways.

She keened and shrieked. Hid her face in his panda and keened. Opened her face to the light and clutter of the world without her son and shrieked. Everyone would hear her. No one would hear her. No one would ever hear her. The phone rang. She rocked and keened, sitting in her dead son's room.

'That was Eric's mother. He wasn't in school when they told the kids about Ian's death,' Glenn said, and Renata shuddered violently, hated him for being able to say those two words together: *Ian's death*. 'She asked if she could bring him over.'

'No,' she managed to say, shuddering and keening.

'I said yes. They're on their way.'

'I can't—'

'I will.'

She rocked and keened, rocked and keened, until the rocking and keening were endless and without beginning, she had always been sitting in her dead son's room making this terrible empty motion and this terrible teeming noise, and she always would.

There was a long green serpent in the room with her, and then it was gone.

Dead son.

Ian is dead.

No.

'Eric just left.'

She didn't know he'd come. She didn't know Glenn had left the room. She didn't know time had passed. Time opened loosely on all sides and contained nothing. She didn't know who Eric was. Almost, she didn't know who Glenn was.

Ian.

'He just stood there not looking at me with tears running down his cheeks. Didn't sob, didn't contort his face, but those tears. His mother stayed in the car.'

That was one way to do this. Abandon your kids every chance you got. Let somebody else take care of them. Renata considered it.

'I just sat beside him and told him he won't always feel this terrible because his body and his mind won't let him.'

Suddenly very clear, Renata looked straight at her husband and demanded, 'Is that true?' He nodded. 'How do you know that?'

'I know about healing,' he said.

Teach me give me magic words tell me what's real lay your hands on me and heal me do this for me.

'He wanted to know if Ian's mom and I were mad at him.'

To feel any sympathy for this poor little boy who'd lost his friend would be somehow to deny Ian. Still, she breathed, 'Oh, why would we be mad at him?'

Glenn shook his head. 'I put my arm around him and turned his face to look at me and just kept saying, "You didn't do anything wrong. Nobody did anything wrong."'

Profound admiration for this man, for Ian's bereaved father, swept her. This man whose loss was so immense she could not bear to know it. He couldn't have it. He couldn't have this pain.

She raised her face and her voice again, keened and shrieked and rocked, and sometime Glenn went away.

A fragment of song she'd never heard played now in her head, tinny and crackly from an old-fashioned radio. The inside of her body swelled with impending birth and impending death. As though being given a gift, then, or instruction, she came into another time and place and was told a stranger's story.

Chapter 4

'Hello, little friends, hello.'

Turned sideways to gaze out the streetcar window at the jiggling green countryside, Daphne hummed Uncle Don's theme song. His show would be coming on about now, and she wasn't sitting beside the radio with piecework in her lap and Mike in the kitchen chair that didn't tip, on the other side of the room but close enough that their knees grazed.

Listening to the radio was just about all they did evenings. When Mike got home from work he was too tired for anything else. He accused her of not having enough to keep her busy in the two-room apartment since she'd taken a leave of absence from teaching in order to start a family, and she guessed that was true, but she'd have liked to go for a walk along Lake Erie once in a while, or maybe take in a show. Pregnant four times and no baby to show for it, no baby to fill her time, now she was pregnant again, nearly forty years old, her last chance, and all she had to do was listen to the radio while she waited for this one to die, too.

The pink console with its fluted front and chest-high row of brown knobs took up more space in the kitchen than the pot-bellied stove and was every bit as important. *Uncle Don* was for children, but both she and Mike enjoyed it, Mike maybe still dreaming about children they would someday have. Mike made fun of Daphne's stories, *Brenda Curtis* and the new one just this year, *The Brighter Day*, and the trials and tribulations of Stella Dallas's beautiful daughter Laurel. After a while she'd gotten browned-off and started making fun of his *Colgate Sports Newsreel*, never mind that she liked some of Bill Stern's interviews with athletes, too. Lately the jokes she and Mike made at each other's expense had taken on a mean edge.

53

He'd be home soon. The swell black DeSoto, a brand-new 1948 model they could not afford, would pull up grandly in front of the tall shabby white house where they lived. Mike would wonder where she was, until he saw her note that she'd taken the streetcar down to their property and his supper was in the refrigerator. Always before, she'd made sure to be home before he was. She supposed he'd listen to the radio without her. That made her feel queer, and adventurous.

Babies and pregnant women were everywhere. The couple in the other upstairs apartment had a new little girl who cried at night sometimes, not very loud but the wall was thin, and in the shared bathroom at the end of the hall the odor of diapers lingered until the cleaning woman the landlord hired had been and gone. On the streetcar was a girl all dolled up in her husband's uniform, the pea jacket pushed out in front into a shape for which it had never been intended. Daphne thought she ought to take offense at the disrespect; hadn't the Armed Services posted notices on college campuses warning that impersonating a serviceman was against the law? But the young husband kept grinning and patting.

People looked at her, too. Some smiled. Some averted their eyes, embarrassed. Instead of maternity clothes she wore loose chemises and shirtwaists, today a jitterbug skirt and a Sloppy Joe sweater, but still it was obvious that she was with child. Not so obvious to anybody but her -- not, apparently, even to Mike, though it should have been – was that she would lose this baby, too. When she stepped down off the streetcar, which kept swaying and clattering as though it barely deigned to stop, she almost lost her balance, and she thought maybe this was how it would happen this time, blood on the asphalt, the dead baby like a package sent to the wrong address. But a man behind her put out a steadying hand and before she knew it she stood firmly on her feet again.

From the streetcar stop in town she had to walk a mile and a quarter north along Route 19. Her legs and back ached. Trucks roared by on their way between Erie and Pittsburgh; some honked rudely, and their wakes puffed out her skirt. But the minute she turned off onto the dirt road, one of many without names that wound down toward the creek, and then off the road into the wooded two acres where they were going to build a house after the baby came because Edinboro, a small city as cities went and more refined than most because of the Normal School, was still not the place to raise a family, she felt better. 'Hello, little friends, hello,' she sang out now, supporting her pendulous stomach with both hands.

On the surface, the lot hadn't changed much since they'd bought it. It was as if everything that was going to grow there had already taken root, so that now it all just got denser down along the ground and, she imagined, underground, roots sending out runners, branches branching. This Keystone corner of Pennsylvania, smack in the middle of the Great Lakes' moisture belt, received more precipitation than almost any other part of the country; Daphne liked knowing that. So the low-lying ground here never dried out, was always springy and often swampy underfoot. A stream – a ditch, really – formed the far back corner of the property, and the black loamy banks were steep and slippery, sticky around her shoes or between her bare toes, accepting and swallowing up any footprints. In the spring there were pussy willows, and pink-purple wild phlox that sometimes carried strong sweet fragrance and, strangely, sometimes didn't smell at all. The water in the ditch sparkled brown; muddy but, she thought, not unclean.

Daphne pushed her way among the trees and brush into the clearing she'd discovered when the first baby had died while Mike was fighting Over There. By now there were four graves. She made no attempt to keep them from being overgrown, and there never had been any headstones to speak of, so a stranger – Mike, even – wouldn't have noticed they were there. Daphne sometimes wondered, without much rancor, whether Mike had ever thought of their dead children once they were dead.

Four graves:

Carla, the perfect little girl born dead although she'd had a perfect gestation and a perfect delivery. They'd kept Daphne in the hospital for seven days just as if she'd given birth to a living baby.

Raymond, so hideously deformed that the nurses hadn't let her see him, and so she'd imagined him with no face, with an extra arm sprouting from his chest or a horn from his forehead, with webbed hands and feet, but most often with no face because they hadn't let her see him. Both these graves were actually empty; she wondered and wondered what they'd done with the bodies.

Justine, dead after not quite seven months in her mother's womb;

Daphne had suspected she was dead because the quality of her interior presence had changed, but it took the doctors two weeks and a series of tests and observations to be convinced.

And then, with another tenant shuffling impatiently in the hall outside the bathroom door, the fetus floating in the bloody water of the toilet, not yet formed enough for her to tell its gender. So, with a certain self-conscious irony, she'd decided to think of this one as Lee, which could be either a girl or a boy. She'd buried Lee with the others, only this time she'd carried him or her in a shoebox on the streetcar so she'd actually have something to put in the little grave. She hadn't even told Mike or the doctors that there had been another baby.

Four graves in the wet woods, and soon there would be a fifth. There was something about her. She couldn't exactly call herself barren for it had turned out not to be hard at all for her to conceive, but her womb didn't seem willing to send its fruits out into the world.

Sometimes here in the woods she'd heard women's voices crying what she understood to be the names of children: *Stone. Frederic. Nathaniel. Eileen.* Sometimes she whispered with them, her own children's names or theirs. Lately a new name had begun to come up through the wet earth, down from the misty sky: *Ian.*

These other women, these other women's voices, made the same sound Daphne herself still sometimes made, which she supposed was how she recognized them for what they were. The deep raspy moaning was, apparently, supposed to take the place of breathing, but it didn't let enough air in or out.

Taking her accustomed position among the four little mounds in the clearing, she tucked her feet under her and hugged her arms to her chest, made herself as still as the graves, although her heart still beat in her ears and she was painfully aware of her breath.

She saw them, too, a long line of dark glimmering shapes, no less vivid for being indistinct. Sometimes the line extended as far behind and ahead of her as she could see, horizontally from past the island in the creek she could hear from here but not see, up across Route 19 and the railroad tracks well into the hills; and sometimes it stretched vertically from deep under the tangled ground high into the sky that hurt her when she looked up at it but mercilessly drew her eyes. She was in good company. It reminded her of the ration lines during the War: Whenever she'd see a line she'd get in it, asking only after she'd wended her way nearly to the front what they were handing out, usually accepting whatever it was – nylon stockings, sugar – because you never knew.

Other things lived and died out here, too. Microscopic moss, skunkweed whose noxious odor rose only after it had been trampled and so made her feel both sorry for it and superior, Queen Anne's lace high as her shoulder and smelling delicately bitter, forty-foot spruces bluer than the sky. Daphne walked, then crawled through the weeds and flowers and tree roots and brush. When her belly grazed something, the tender spot stung where her navel used to be and would be again when the baby wasn't pressing on it from inside. She brought her eyes very close to the fuzzy tendrils, serrated leaves, segmented or smooth or branching stems of the myriad plants. She touched her tongue to them, sipped their bitter or sweet or tasteless saps.

When her belly felt too full for her to crouch or crawl, she lay on her back on the ground and stretched out her limbs. She made herself minutely aware of every plant that touched every cell of her skin, every plant that she couldn't help crushing, every plant that sprang back when she shifted her weight and the weight of the baby she carried.

Once there had been panthers in these woods, and bison along the shores of the creek called by the early French trappers *boeuf à l'eau*, cattle of the water. Longer ago, there had been dinosaurs. Sea creatures. She liked knowing about all these forebears, though when she sat in her steamy kitchen listening to *The Green Hornet* she didn't quite believe in them.

Mice and rats scampered across her path or alongside it, no matter what path she took. Spiders spun webs that adhered to her skin and her very presence broke them; she encountered the webs far more frequently than the spiders themselves. Snakes, variations of the gold-green-dark brown woods itself, wriggled through the underbrush with her and sometimes – deliberately or obliviously – went right across her shoe or even her bare foot.

Sorrow raised detail. Everything was lovely, and everything hurt. The humid heat of August set the world to shimmering, as though she were moving underwater, breathing water, herself a fetus in some other mother's womb, or already encased in amber that had yet to harden. She thought this was how this last baby would die, suffocating in her womb because Daphne herself couldn't get enough air.

The first subtle touches of gold and red in the leaves made her eyes sting and swell, and she couldn't stop crying. She thought that maybe the baby in her womb would cry itself to death well before it was born.

All she knew to do was wait for it. Nothing more maternal was left to her now. She curled herself up around it, then thought better of that and stretched herself out on her back with the encased baby upward, as exposed as she could force it to be.

It came to her, with no sense of alarm and not much even of surprise, that she was sure to miss the last streetcar home. She'd miss Arthur Godfrey at 9:00. She'd just have to sleep out here.

She made herself comfortable among the mounds of her children's graves. Her stomach, where the new baby curled, made a new mound among them.

The gurgle of the creek rose in the night and the traffic sounds from Route 19 diminished. 'Hello, little friends, hello.' Softly she sang Uncle Don's theme song to the four small dead children and the living child mounded in her womb. 'I've many, many things to tell you, on the radio.'

Mike didn't come. If she'd heard the DeSoto rumbling down the dirt road, she'd have hidden, but she was hurt and frightened that he didn't come. The night wasn't as long as she'd anticipated. Maybe she'd slept. Now brown birds nesting in the trees over her head burst into chirping and fluttering and she realized she could see both birds and trees against the sky although the sun itself wasn't yet visible. It was to be the last really hot day of the season; tomorrow would come a cold snap.

A snake slithered across her bare foot, as if the foot weren't there, or as if the foot were part of the grass and ground, which, she mused, it might well be. For her part, she hardly saw the snake, had only fleeting though unnerving impressions of it. Dry, she thought it was; very fast; very light. Brown and gold. Maybe green. It seemed to be longer than it ought to be.

A seed pod floated onto the back of her wrist. It was the same color and texture as her skin, with complementary patterns. A light breeze blew like her breath across her lips.

Maybe, if she made herself very still, she could escape notice.

Daphne caught sight of someone else. She froze, squinted. It was a woman, her own age and physical type, hair the same color, and pregnant, too. The woman was moving along the edge of the empty acre, on the shoulder of Route 19, and Daphne thought sure she intended to come down into these woods.

But instead the woman crossed the highway and disappeared into the weedy ditch between the streetcar tracks and the railroad tracks. Daphne waited, tensed, for her to show herself again, but she didn't.

After a while, Daphne wended her way as far into the woods as possible, into what seemed to her its heart. It wasn't very far and didn't take her very long, but she seemed to be going deep, through layers. A grove of laurel grew in the middle, guarding sumac with deep purple leaves among green. Stella Dallas's daughter's name was Laurel. Smiling, taking that as a sign, Daphne eased into the grove, among the close trees, among the thin round knobby trunks of them, her feet among their roots.

Well aware that what she was about to do was nuts, Daphne was rather pleased, for such madness demonstrated several truths that were pleasing in their sheer enormity: How hurt she had been by her tragedies, by all those babies dead inside and outside her womb. How grossly unfair life – fate, God, the universe – had been to her. How she would not stand for it, would not accept, would never surrender.

She took off all her clothes, which weren't many: the loose beige flowered shirtwaist, the blitzie she hadn't been able to fasten between her legs for some weeks. Her white socks and brown loafers had already been discarded; somebody looking for her might stumble upon them, but she doubted she'd be able to find them on purpose. The clothes would have become too lightweight in tomorrow's cooler weather, but in the heat and humidity of today they'd been too much, hot, sticky, and she welcomed the exposure of her nipples and pubis. When she dropped the dress and undergarment, they didn't vanish, but the relationship between clothing and plant growth became clear – similar patterns, similar ways of billowing and settling in the breeze, and each showed itself to be part of the other.

Breasts swung. Belly swelled. Hair, bobbed just below her chin, trailed across her face like a spiderweb, like a veil of branch and vine. The baby moved visibly under the thin barklike layers of flesh and skin, a caterpillar boring, seeking its place, not dead yet.

Kneeling on the spongy ground padded by generations of ground-cover living and dead and decaying into life, Daphne waited for balance. The air shimmered like amniotic fluid, righted her. From between her thighs seeped fluid intended to prepare her body for the expulsion of the infant, living or dead, which would not be allowed, living or dead, to stay inside her much longer. The fluid pooled beneath her and sank into the ground, which she would have considered already saturated but which apparently could take more.

Her hands like fronds coated herself with grasses and grass heads and dirt, with insect carapaces and snakeskins and shreds of nests. Moisture was absorbed into all her surfaces, and moisture was exuded.

On the back of her neck, against her scalp, over her eyes, her hair acquired a certain leaflike quality, the strands veined, the follicles stemmed. Her arms bent and swayed like branches. She swayed. Something had made its nest in the pithy hollow of her throat, not to choke her but in order that they might live by consuming each other.

Soon her feet and knees, where her weight rested on them, were rooted fast. She synchronized her breathing – and, by extension, the baby's – with the tilting, rotating, revolving of the globe. She stayed very still. Dead or alive, the baby hid in her womb, where it belonged.

But Mike easily found them there, Daphne and the baby. She hadn't heard the automobile, or hadn't identified it. His footsteps and panting hardly registered until he was right there beside her, holding her elbows. His knees beneath the plaid Bermuda shorts might have been little animals, leaping and falling back. 'Oh, for cryin' out loud!' he shouted. The baby reacted not at all to him, and Daphne barely flinched. 'What are you trying to do, Daphne, get put in the bughouse?'

She spoke, but he didn't think she did. He heard her inhale and exhale, felt her quiver.

He put his arms around her. She raised her branching arms to fend him off, and he couldn't quite get through the tangle.

He kissed her. She willed her lips to feel like wood under his, and the wood recoiled. He spat, wiped his mouth.

He found her clothing, ground into the soil. Despairing of the blitzie, a garment he'd never understood, he tried to force the shirtwaist on over her head. But she seemed to have grown much larger and stiffer since she'd taken it off and it didn't fit anymore.

'Come home, Daphne, will you please come home? It won't be long until the baby's born.'

He tugged at her hands. He tried to pick her up and carry her. She was too heavy and rooted in place. Her feet didn't leave the ground.

More than a little frightened by her aspect and demeanor, which later he would tell people had hardly seemed human, Mike dropped his hands to his sides. 'Barbara Stanwyck's on the radio tonight,' he tried, not knowing if that was true. Daphne's body shivered in response, but she didn't move from her spot. Before long he gave up altogether, rested his hand briefly against her roughened cheek, and went away to get help, though he had no idea what kind of help to get.

Already the temperature was plummeting as the front came through. Wind blew cold, carrying cold rain, from the lake forty miles to the north. Before nightfall, the first snow of the season would speckle the ground and the things growing out of it, the four mounded graves, Daphne and the baby in the laurel grove, and before the night was over her last child was born.

A girl. Laurel.

Alive.

Needing her mother.

Needing to have the cord cut and tied, her lungs cleared, her heart adjusted to the rhythms of this world. Needing to have the blood of the birth canal washed away, the afterbirth delivered and discarded. Needing interpretation and buffer for the noise and light and cold rain and terrifying odors of this new place; needing help to understand her infinitesimal, indefinable, perfect place among its infinite horizontal and vertical axes. Needing the nipple.

Daphne didn't know how to cut the cord; a long thick snake came and bit it through. Didn't know how to wash her daughter, so let the rain do it, too cold and too hard. Had no milk, though her breasts ached and leaked, could not feed her child, and so the mice and rats came, and a long line of ants, each bearing a tiny gift, each taking something of Laurel away until she was gone.

Daphne stayed where she was, rooted, transformed, hoping to escape notice. Living, but stone; living mother stone.

Chapter 5

Ian is dead.

Renata woke screaming.

From a fireball of half-sleep into an infinite explosion of searing knowledge: *Ian is dead. My little boy is dead.*

Into the whirling razor-sharp truth of it, which gouged her and flayed her, again and again inflicting the same profound wound – almost but not quite unbearable. The wound was all she was now and all she would ever be.

Ian is dead. Dead.

Into the fangs and coils of it. The molting skin and fire-breath and razored thrashing tail of it. It fed on her throat, her groin, her heart. Her heart beat so wildly it took up all her insides. She couldn't feel any other part of her body, but she saw that it was all still there, splayed nearly naked on top of the bedclothes.

This thing that had happened, and now this grief, was a monster. It had turned her into a monster, for she had to say, had to think: *My son is dead.*

Renata screamed and writhed on the bed. Her back arched. The pain sank its teeth into the base of her throat, the nape of her neck. She curled up, knees against her chest and head between them, but the pain forced her open again, spread her ribs, pried under her fingernails. The pain was primeval, monstrous, and immortal: *My child is dead.*

'No!'

But the word had no power anymore, no meaning, scarcely any form. The terrible truth that had formed itself out of her life was the only truth, and the dizzying agony of it was almost but not quite beyond belief.

She shrieked, 'No!' again, as though it would make any difference. She arched her back, pounded her fists on the mattress, hardly knowing when she struck the headboard and bruised her knuckles.

She could hardly feel Glenn's arm around her, although she knew that it was keeping her from flying away, from disintegrating. His tears were on the skin of her shoulder. His ragged breath came across her neck, and his heart raced hard against her back, but some great distance away.

The house still stood around them. She heard clocks ticking, water in pipes. But the house made no sense anymore, had no purpose, for it had lied, it had promised them shelter.

She had promised them shelter. She had pledged to hold them all safe. She was wife and mother, woman of powers. Those had seemed lovely things to be, lovely names, but she heard them now as siren songs, ruses to make you feel powerful when you weren't at all. Ian was dead.

The names had failed. The powers had failed. She had failed; she had done something wrong. The thought brought a cool pinprick of relief.

But then the fiery helplessness, which was the utter truth, rose to consume her again. She screamed his name, as though she could call him back.

Ian!

Tunnel.

Here was a tunnel.

It gaped at her feet, at her fingertips, at the tip of her tongue. It followed and absorbed the wet curves of her eyeballs.

It led somewhere. From this place to another.

It had always been there, gaping, leading from one place to another. But now she saw it for the first time. Felt its magnetism for the first time.

She was being swept into it.

Ian was dead.

Ian is dead.

'Oh, God, no!'

Glenn's arm tightened around her and stopped her at the very mouth of the tunnel. At the very lips. She felt him sobbing. She managed to move back more snugly into the trembling curve of his body and hoped, desperately but distantly, that this would bring him some comfort, because it was all she could do. She couldn't imagine how to turn over, how to hold him, how to look at his pain.

Convulsions were racing through her. The walls of the tunnel were convulsing, pulling at her, a peristalsis drawing her in. The mouth and lips of the tunnel and as far as she could see along it, which seemed very far, were red and wet with overlapping membranes like petals, like scales – pink, scarlet, coral, burgundy.

Pulsing. Contracting. Propelling her into the tunnel.

If she went into that passageway, she would never come back.

If she went into that passageway, she would die. She would be transformed into something alien, something beyond recognition.

'Hold me! Glenn!'

Glenn pushed his other arm under her, flung his leg across her legs, and held her.

A long time passed, or a split second like the interval between Ian's life and his death. Whatever its dimensions, a lifetime passed. Renata could have lain sobbing in her husband's arms, afire with fresh grief for her child, trying to resist the sucking of the long red wet tunnel, for the blink of an eye or for the rest of her life.

Glenn sighed. He removed his arms and legs and tears from her and got up from the bed. Renata cried out.

'I'm just going to the bathroom, honey.'

With difficulty she did recognize his voice, did understand that he was telling what he took to be the truth. She heard his heavy footsteps down the hall past Ian's room, past Vanessa's, and each footstep didn't seem to be connected to the others, each was a single thud that just stopped. She heard the familiar creak of the bathroom door, the click of the latch, and the sounds were traitorous.

'I'll be right back,' he'd assured her before he left, but she knew now that no one ever came back. And she wouldn't be there if he did, because the instant he wasn't touching her the tunnel swelled up around her.

And there were monsters.

In the walls of the tunnel, just at the half-circle edges of her peripheral vision, there were monsters. Ready for her.

Long bulbous appendages, black and silver and colorless. Faces turning into other faces, inside out, backwards, upside down, full of eyes and teeth and sucking penetrating tongues. Bodies twisting, blooming, growing and shrinking and sloughing off layers of themselves, layers of her.

They were calling her name without words, singing a summons to her without a tune. They were chanting – evilly, and yet with kindness – *Ian is dead your child is dead.*

And other names as well: *Lee is dead Frederic is dead your child is dead Betty is dead Eileen is dead Nathaniel is dead your child is dead your children are dead dead.*

The striations of the tunnel walls wrapped themselves around her head, shoulders, neck, and pulled. Renata shrieked, perhaps out loud, 'All right! Take me!' and stopped struggling.

There was a great warm wind, a rushing of monstrous voices, a vivifying of the red and orange and burgundy light. The passageway widened and elongated. Hands and sticky tentacles and scaly tails attached themselves to her and propelled her along.

When Glenn came back into the room, as he had said he would, she wasn't there. She knew he thought she was asleep, and her rage at him for thinking that was unfair, for her body was limp, her eyes closed, her breathing shallow and regular. *Goodbye*, she called to him, but from an enormous distance, and it was clear that she made no sound that he could hear. *I love you.*

Glenn bent and kissed her, then tiptoed away. She had no thought to stop him. She had lost Ian and she would lose everything, everyone.

She left her body on the bed and hurtled into the warm and pulsating passageway.

Chapter 6

Without leaving the bloody tunnel, without leaving the company of either the monsters in the tunnel or the other mothers (more than just Daphne; more to be told; more stories to travel back into), Renata heard Glenn's heavy, sad, deliberate footsteps as he went to answer the door. The footsteps frightened her, and so did the sounds of the door opening.

She heard Jackie come into her house and, dully, she loved her. Something was out of the ordinary, something was very wrong, for Jackie to be here. She'd never been here before; it was fifteen hundred miles between their houses, and Jackie was raising three kids alone on a teacher's salary. Renata was confused. *She's here because Ian is dead and she's my best friend, she loves me*, she thought confusedly, and there was both incomprehensible pain and great comfort in that convoluted thought, and of course it didn't make any sense.

She heard Glenn and Jackie say hello to each other. Then their voices changed slightly when they hugged. The fact that they said hello to each other, the fact that they hugged, the fact that their voices altered when they hugged, the fact that she noticed any of this all terrified her.

She heard Jackie ask, 'Where is she?' and Glenn answer, 'Upstairs,' and she supposed they were talking about her. She supposed it was true that she was here, upstairs in her house, curled up on her bed. She supposed that this woman, this creature, was she.

Jackie was here. There was nothing odd about Jackie being here.

Then, horrified, she remembered begging her to come. She'd

known her since they were twelve years old. Since before any of this particular life which now seemed the only possible reality. Since before she'd had Ian. Since before she'd lost Ian.

Then she remembered clearly: *Ian is dead dead* and pain in her belly sent her catapulting from the bed.

She thought she was moving very fast. She would spin apart or fall, she was moving so fast. Or she would shoot past Jackie and Glenn and Vanessa and Tim and Ian (*Ian is dead*) and out the door and out of the house and off the surface of the earth. The world was a storm of snakes, and she had no place here.

But she must not have been moving fast after all, because Jackie was all the way to the top of the stairs before Renata met her. 'Hi,' said Jackie, and Renata went into her arms.

Renata's vision blurred, blackened. She clung to her friend, whose heart was beating, who was warm, who wouldn't let her fall down the stairs even if she herself didn't much care whether she fell or not. Who, for now, would keep her from flying off the face of the earth, even if that's what she most wanted to do.

Who was the same height and weight and coloring as she, both of them thickening and graying a little with middle age, neither of them caring very much most of the time. In their high school graduation picture, they'd looked like twins: Same hairdo, same smile, same gold tassel.

But Jackie had not lost a child.

Say it. Say the word. Jackie's son had not died.

Ian would never graduate from high school. Ian would never be thirty-eight years old, or even ten. Ian would never have a friend like Jackie.

Renata was outraged, very grateful, shot through with electric pain.

Ian would never race down these stairs again, risking his neck. He'd never do another thing endearing or infuriating or admirable. From now on, whenever Jackie talked about her son Brett who was a year older than Ian (a year older than Ian would ever be), Renata would have nothing left to say.

So she'd lost that, too. The precious, grounding exchange of experiences with someone she'd known and loved for twenty-six years. The easy bragging and easy complaining of parents; at Glenn's last technical writing job, he and his office mate used to swap cute stories about their kids, and he'd bring them home to tell at the dinner table. He'd never do that again.

Renata lost consciousness. Totally (consciousness utterly vanished and never retrieved) or parts of it (a category of experience gone, a piece of information altered enough to change its meaning, an angle of approach skewed, layers of perception sliced through and rearranged). Briefly (a split-second, so nobody else noticed) or for a long time (decades, centuries, the consciousness of others impinging). She lost and gained consciousness, lost and gained, tasted the feathery forked tongue of the serpent, felt stone, heard voices:

'That's not your world anymore.'

'Come down here with us.'

'Stay down here with us. You belong here.'

'I love you, Renata.'

Now she came upon herself trying to make up the sofa bed in the family room for Jackie. She should have had the room ready before Jackie came. She worried about whether this old couch would be comfortable enough, and whether the cat and dog dander throughout the house would make Jackie's chronic allergies worse. She had no idea what to cook while Jackie was here; she hadn't been expecting company.

Renata could not figure out how the corners of the bottom sheet were supposed to fit over the corners of the mattress. It seemed a fatally flawed design, an impossible assignment. She struggled and flailed, came close to panic. When she managed to get the elastic to hold on one corner, it sprang off another. She couldn't do this. She couldn't do any of this. It was all too complicated. There were too many interlocking tasks, too many steps to remember in a prescribed order, and her hands were violently shaking, her whole body was shaking.

She dropped the mattress and sheet, pressed her fists to the base of her throat where the pain had for the moment localized, and stepped unsteadily backward. 'I can't do this,' she gasped. 'I don't know how to do this. It's all gone.'

'It'll come back. You'll get it back.' Jackie took over. Her movements – quick, efficient, practiced – hurt to watch. Renata watched, in admiration and despair. Jackie smoothed the bottom sheet snugly over the mattress, tucked in the top sheet and blankets, fluffed the pillows. Each part of this single task involved hundreds of separate movements and decisions, each of which depended on all the others.

Panic rose. Never again, Renata knew, would she be able to do anything as complicated as making up a bed. Never again would she function well enough to get herself or anybody else through a day. Everything she would ever be required to do – eat, sleep, breathe, talk – was too complex and too painful, and she couldn't possibly hold all the details in her mind long enough to cook, take the bus to work, dial the phone, open a door with a key, love any other person ever again.

She refused to think. What she would think about from now on was only: *Ian is dead.* Anything else would be heresy.

She thought, though, about Daphne and all those babies dead. She didn't know who Daphne was or how she knew her story.

The room was tilting, pulsating, filling in with dark shapes at once growing and stone. Frantically, Renata searched for Jackie, who was lost among the dizzying colors and shapes. When she finally found her, her face was layered and fractured, floating, spinning, turning itself inside out to reveal the blood and bone underneath the features.

She saw something moving a great distance away, and then realized it was her hand, her separate fingers. There were no edges to things, no shapes that held. Colors were unrecognizable, unnameable, and so vivid they cut. The air was thick with a buzzing that tore at her inner ears, made her dizzy and sick. The world had turned psychedelic, alien; she had no idea where she was in it, or whether she was in it at all. It coiled.

All day, eight o'clock approached, doom recurrently announcing itself from a great distance, and still impossible to avoid. All day, Renata struggled to find a way to avoid it, but clocks progressed and the sun sank and dinner came and went and eight o'clock struck. She couldn't stop it. Again and again, she couldn't stop her son from dying, even when she saw his death coming every evening at eight o'clock.

Sometime later – the next day maybe, if light and then darkness and then light again meant anything – Renata sat in the spring mud of the dog run on the north side of the house and cradled Shaman's head in her lap. Shaman was dying. Ian was dead.

The living-room windows faced out over the dog run, but were too high and reflective for her to see back through from where she sat on the ground under them. Inside the house, on the other side of the glass and brick where she could barely imagine them, were Vanessa, Glenn, Shauna, Glenn's mother Mary Jo, Glenn's brothers Pete and Charlie, Jackie. But not Ian. Ian was dead.

Not Tim either, because Tim was here beside her. He squatted in the mud, not looking at her, not too close to her, and held his hand out to Shaman as he'd done so many times before that it had become a character-defining gesture. But now Shaman didn't lick his hand or blink her flat golden-brown eyes.

'Hi, honey,' she thought to say.

Although she hadn't been sure she heard her own voice, she heard him clearly when he said, 'How is she?'

'She's dying.'

'How do you know? Maybe she's just sick.'

It would have required a long string of words to tell him how she knew, and Renata couldn't remember by the time she got to the end of a sentence what had been at the beginning. She just shook her head. Her hands kept stroking Shaman's flank, which was barely moving with the animal's labored breaths. Her fingers kept burying themselves in the thick, familiar white fur, all the way to the softer undercoat and the body underneath that still pretended to be solid with bones and flesh.

'You should have her put to sleep,' Tim advised, full of adolescent certainty.

'It's not sleep!' She looked at him and suddenly he was in sharp focus, which didn't last. 'It's death. Shaman's not going to sleep. She's *dying*.'

'The vet should give her a shot.'

'It's not putting her to sleep, though,' Renata insisted. 'It's helping her die.' She hadn't realized she'd stopped crying until saying that made her burst into tears again.

It was too much for Tim. He petted Shaman's snout once or twice more, then got up and went back into the house. Now she could barely imagine him, either.

71

Renata crossed her legs under her and bent forward to lay her cheek against the top of the dog's head. 'Where are you going?' she asked aloud. 'Where is Ian?' But they were foolish questions; once she'd put them into words, it was obvious that they had little to do with whatever it was she so desperately wanted to know.

Shaman managed to lick her hand once. After that, although the dog didn't move again, she seemed somehow to withdraw farther under the massed, moving, leafless bushes, farther from Renata, already well on her way.

Afraid to leave Shaman even briefly, but knowing what she had to do now, Renata struggled to her feet and made her way out of the kennel and into the house. Gypsy met her at the door, whimpering; Renata paused to pet the anxious dog and to croon, 'Good girl. I love you.'

Renata's family was in the house, what was left of her family, but none of them came to her. That made it minimally possible for her to find the phone and sit down in the chair next to it with the phone book heavy and awkward across her lap. When it slid off, she had great difficulty organizing her thoughts and directing her hands to pick it up again.

Not being able to find a phone number in an emergency was a recurring nightmare for her. Now, for long terrible waking minutes, she couldn't find the vet's number because she kept forgetting her name, couldn't remember the sequence of the alphabet, and again and again lost her place among the wavering rows and columns.

At last she found the number, misdialed, dialed again, spoke to the receptionist. *My son is dead*, she wanted to cry, but surely this young woman would know that, would be able to tell. 'Dr Massingill, please.'

'She's with a patient right now. Can I take a message for her?'

'This is Renata Burgess. Could you tell her it's an emergency?'

'One moment.'

Renata waited. The room around her was obviously her dining room, but it was utterly altered, unfamiliar, because now she sat in it as a bereaved parent. A disengaged part of her mind hummed along with the Musak on the vet's 'hold' line – 'Do you know the way to San Jose?' She found her attention adhering randomly and purposelessly to one object after another – the table, the china

72

cabinet, the spider plant hanging in the bay window – and could not comprehend what they were, although she could have named them and listed their functions.

Vanessa was curled up in Glenn's lap on the couch, and they were both crying. Dully, Renata wondered why, then remembered and gagged. It was her fault. In some profound way that she was struggling to understand, it had to be her fault that Ian had killed himself, her fault that the rest of her family was suffering. It was her job, somehow, to keep them all safe and happy. She was supposed to bring happiness into their lives, not pain, not suffering. She must have made some terrible mistake, incomprehensible but specific, surely, and ultimately identifiable. There was an odd relief in that notion.

She heard Jackie talking to Pete about their respective divorces, Pete's desire to be married again, Jackie's disgust at the very idea. Jackie was here from Pennsylvania, Pete and his mother Mary Jo from Virginia. Vaguely, Renata wondered why, then remembered and doubled over the pain. Ian was dead. Pete and Jackie were actually talking about something other than the fact that Ian was dead. She hated them both, wanted them to get out of her house, and at the same time was intensely grateful that they were here.

'This is Donna Massingill.'

For an instant, Renata had no idea who that was, or why this woman's voice was interrupting the jaunty music on the telephone. Then she heard herself say, 'This is Renata Burgess. It's time,' and hoped the vet would know what she was talking about because she could not possibly organize all the words it would take to explain. *Shaman is dying Ian is dead.*

'I'll be right there.'

'Wait. There's something you should know before you come. Our son died three days ago.' What had she just said?

'Oh, God.'

'So we're all pretty crazy around here.'

'Oh, God.'

'I just thought you should know.'

'I'll be right there.'

When the vet got there, Tim brought her out to the dog run where Renata was sitting in the mud again with her hand on Shaman's head. A bird was chirping insultingly in the peak of the house, and a radio was spewing mariachi music a couple of houses down. She remembered that she used to find mariachi music stirring.

Renata looked helplessly up at Dr Massingill, remembering having sensed kindness under the crisp efficiency. The vet crouched beside her, touched the quiet white dog, and said in some alarm, 'All her systems have shut down.'

'Then it is time, right? I was right? It is time to – help her die?'

Dr Massingill was already preparing a syringe from her black bag. Without looking up, she nodded and said, 'Yes.'

'I want to be here. I want to say goodbye. I want to feel her spirit leave her body. I want to know the exact instant she changes from alive to dead.' Renata recognized her own hysteria but had no thought of controlling it. 'I want to be touching her when she takes her last breath. I want—'

Tim muttered, 'Holy shit,' and the vet said brusquely, 'That's fine. No problem. You just tell me when.'

Renata bent to kiss the dog's silky head. There was no response. Always so attuned to her moods, always so dependent on her for food and love and purpose, Shaman was now quite beyond her. Knowing it was pointless, Renata whispered, 'I love you, Shaman. I'll always love you. Thank you for – everything. For being in my life and letting me be in yours. For—'

This time she stopped herself. Words were no match for what was happening here. She straightened and nodded. The vet's needle glinted smoothly into the neck muscle. Shaman didn't wince or whimper. She just sighed once, relaxed, and was dead.

Renata threw back her head. Against her will and against any sense of rightness, she saw the sunny blue sky and the bird on the peak of the roof, and she sobbed, 'I'm sorry, oh, I'm sorry.'

The vet misunderstood. 'It's okay. Go ahead.'

'I thought this would help me understand what happened to my son, understand why he died and where he is now, but it doesn't, it doesn't help at all!'

Dr Massingill busied herself with putting her instruments away.

'Oh, God, what do we do now? With the body?'

The vet hesitated, then said briskly, 'I'll take care of her.'

Somehow then Renata was on the sidewalk along the base of the hill at the side of the house. She didn't know how she'd come to be there or why. She was watching the vet – a small woman with fine features and strong, deliberate hands – carry the big dead dog down the steep steps. Shaman's body draped heavily from her arms; the long white fur was caked with mud, feces, urine. Tim came earnestly behind her, obviously wanting to be involved and not knowing how. He walked beside her across the street and helped her lift the body into the bed of her pickup, although it was apparent that she could have done it herself.

Watching them through a rainbow film of tears, swaying with pain, grieving on a public sidewalk for all the world to witness, Renata recognized Donna Massingill's gift and Tim's, and she could not bear it.

Jackie and Mary Jo cleaned and cooked. Renata couldn't have done those things, but she wished they wouldn't, either. Wished they would stop fussing around her house, where there might be dirt in the back of the silverware drawer and where a child had died. Wished they'd see that such things didn't matter, food and laundry and dishes and mopping the floors, couldn't be allowed ever to matter again. Wished they'd go away and never come back. Wished they'd never leave.

Wished, *wished* her own mother would come. Wanted her mother: *oh, Mama, my baby died.* But her mother didn't know what to do. A betrayal. The best her mother could manage on the phone was, 'How are you feeling?'

'Don't be afraid of my pain,' Renata had pleaded, but her mother was.

'Where are the paper towels?' Mary Jo wanted to know.

Renata didn't know what she meant. 'I don't use paper towels. Because of ecology. I use rags.'

Mary Jo looked at her in blank amazement, and then she heard her tell Jackie, 'She doesn't use paper towels!' and both of them laughed incredulously, and Renata knew, fleetingly, that this was what she'd done wrong.

Jackie cleaned Ian's room. She must have asked. Renata must have asked Glenn, must have given permission. She didn't throw anything out, just put his things in bags to be gone through later. Renata could not imagine ever doing this. 'I found a lot of math papers under his bed,' Jackie said, laughing a little but clearly disapproving; she was a teacher, after all. 'He hadn't been doing his math.' That wasn't true. He'd always done his math. Those were extra papers, practice papers. Renata couldn't put words together to tell her, and her cowardice betrayed Ian. His room had black plastic trash bags in it now, and the skeletal bunk beds.

'I can't find the broom,' Jackie said. 'I want to sweep the kitchen floor and I can't find the broom.'

The one Renata managed to find for her was old and worn, bristles falling out. Vaguely, she remembered that Ian had swept the front porch last week. He'd probably left the good broom out there somewhere. She couldn't form sentences to tell this to Jackie. Helplessly, she just handed her the defective broom, symbol of her failure.

Jackie examined it distastefully. 'You need a new broom,' she declared. 'I mean, just look at this!'

Sometime later, Renata and Jackie went to the grocery store. Once outside, Renata couldn't believe she'd exposed herself like this, or that her best friend had allowed it. The fresh air was peeling away layers of her face. It smelled sweet. She was walking through a glittery cloud of her own dead skin. The cells hurt when they left her body, kept hurting when they were no longer attached to her. No new cells would form, of course; she was shrinking, thinning. Soon she would be nothing but the stone at her core, which would still hurt but maybe not so much.

The bright blue sky was a blade. The street trees beginning to leaf into a pale green-gold spilled acid onto her flesh, and could not possibly be responding to spring.

'What a gorgeous day,' Jackie said.

'It's my fault he's dead.'

'It's not your fault.'

She dared not accept false solace. 'How do you know that?'

'You didn't have him for the first four years. You don't know what happened then.'

'I was his mother.'

'What would you do differently?'

Renata tried to think. 'I don't know.'

They crossed a street. Renata knew, dimly, where they were.

Every year the tall white house in the middle of the block had a wonderful garden in the unlikely space between sidewalk and street. The house was iridescent now. The roof shimmered and might come off.

She didn't know the people who lived there. She'd always looked for them when she went by, wanting to tell them how much pleasure their flowers gave her, but she'd never seen anyone, just the evidence of their work. Now, dully, she was glad she'd never said anything, since it would have been proved a lie.

This time a man and woman were crouching in the garden space. She didn't say anything to them; they would know why. They would know by looking at her, even without looking at her, that flowers could mean nothing to her anymore. Thinking she saw a little snake slither rapidly among the flowers, she thought maybe it had some use in a spring garden, but then it wasn't there anymore. Two yellow crocuses and a purple one were blooming already. Renata stared at them as she and Jackie walked past, unsure what they were even though she knew they were crocuses in bloom.

'It's good to get out,' Jackie said.

'It's strange out here.' Renata was breathing hard. 'I'm glad you're with me.'

'I'm with you.'

'I hope they don't deliver Ian's ashes while I'm gone.' It astounded her that she was talking to her best friend about her son's ashes. 'Glenn didn't want to face that.'

'Do you want to go back?'

'No.' Once she'd started shaking her head, the motion seemed perpetual and she couldn't imagine how she'd ever stop. Once she stopped, she couldn't imagine how all those muscles would ever again work together to cause her head to move. 'No, we need milk, and Glenn can't drive.'

'Anyway,' Jackie said gently, 'it's good for you to get out in the world again.'

'*Why?*'

Her friend didn't answer, just put an arm around her waist.

Renata watched her own feet walking on the sidewalk and wondered how she did that, how anyone managed to put one foot in front of another. Someone called to someone across 26th Avenue and she flinched. A garbage truck turned the corner in front of them onto Grove Street. Renata was bewildered to see that garbage trucks were still dirty yellow, that Grove Street was still named Grove Street, and especially that people still cared whether or not their garbage was collected.

The rumble of the garbage truck made her teeth ache. When it turned into the alley, the beeping of its signal sent pointed, colored ripples through the air. She lowered her head and kept walking. Walking. She had no power and no reason ever to stop walking.

Jackie threw a protective arm in front of her. Renata winced at the sudden motion, then saw that they'd come to the busy intersection of 26th and Federal and a car was turning the corner at full-speed. She wished, although not with much energy, that she had stepped in front of it.

Jackie kept a hand under Renata's elbow as she said, 'Okay. It's safe now,' and started them across the street. Dizzy from the ludicrousness of the word 'safe,' Renata stumbled over the far curb. Jackie kept her from falling.

She was lost. The Safeway store looked like nothing she'd ever seen before. At the same time, it was ominous because it was so familiar. The big red letters pulsated. In each window panel across the front was a letter, too. The curve of the P slid over the back of her tongue, gagging her. The prongs of the L and the E stabbed at her inner ear. It took her a long, convoluted time to understand that together the letters spelled out L O W P R I C E S. It bothered her intensely that the P was with the L O W on the left side of the doors, instead of on the right side with the rest of its word where it belonged, symmetry chosen over meaning.

People in the store treated her as if she were just like them, as if she were the same as she'd been last week. People she'd seen here often before – the mustachioed produce man, the grandmotherly cashier named Irene – smiled at her and spoke. People she didn't know smiled more vaguely or averted their eyes. 'My son died three days ago,' she wanted to tell them, although surely they already knew that.

The fluorescent lights flickered purple, pink, blue, white. They captured her eyes and she couldn't look away, although the flickering and buzzing hurt. The apples were too red, the peppers too green, and she didn't understand what the bottles and jars on the right side of the aisle were for, although she read the labels: 'Chunky Bleu Cheese Salad Dressing,' 'Tomato Catsup,' 'Worcester Sauce.'

Here was a whole array of greeting cards with flowers on them. They held a message for her. She did her best to refuse it, but the cards and their flowers wouldn't let her go until she'd taken note. Pansies, roses, Queen Anne's lace, sunflowers, violets, buttercups, Indian paintbrush, gladioli. An infinite number of species in the world, an infinite number of individuals in each species, and she one of them, Ian one of them.

She didn't know what that meant, but it seemed a deliberate message *to her*, and it seemed important. She stood still.

She'd forgotten why they'd come here. 'Milk,' Jackie said.

Waves of cold sped out from the dairy case and enveloped her. She could see them, taste them, and she was shivering violently.

'Here's the milk,' Jackie said from some distance away. 'What kind do you use?'

'Two per cent,' Renata answered automatically, knowing it was the right answer but not comprehending it.

'Here's the two per cent. My kids won't drink anything but whole milk.' Jackie shook her head ruefully.

'My family doesn't notice the difference,' Renata had said before she could stop herself. It was a foolish, hurtful thing to say, since she didn't have a family anymore. She braced her shins against the cold half-wall of the dairy case and thought maybe she could topple into it.

Jackie was there to steady her. 'Are you all right?' That was a foolish and hurtful thing to say, too, since she would never be 'all right' again; the idea that anyone could be 'all right' was deceitful. But Renata nodded and let herself be led two steps to the right, where the milk was. 'Here's the two per cent,' Jackie told her again, and lifted a bright white gallon out of its bin.

She held it out to Renata. Renata stepped back, frightened. It got into her hands anyway, somehow, and she misjudged its weight and shape and almost dropped it. She wished she had; white milk pooling on the gray tile floor. But Jackie supported both her and the cold bottle and, finally, Renata was able to carry it herself.

'Do you need anything else?' Jackie asked.

'I – don't know.'

'I got paper towels. I don't know how you can keep house without paper towels.'

I can't. Ian died, Renata thought clearly, but said nothing.

'Do they have postcards here? I want to send the kids a postcard of Denver.' As if she were on vacation. As if Ian hadn't died. Renata's fury shocked her, made her teeth and bones throb, and then left her numb.

They made their way up one long, snaking aisle and finally joined the line at the checkout stand. In front of the cash register was a rack of picture postcards; after some deliberation, Jackie picked out three, and Renata thought she would faint. The milk was making her fingers ache, and the side of her thigh where she rested it for balance.

A very old woman was ahead of them in line. She didn't look familiar. She didn't, in fact, seem to have been there a minute ago; hazily, Renata thought there'd been two teenaged girls, a fiftyish man in a cowboy hat, a woman with a squalling baby she kept telling, without much interest, to shut up.

The cashier finished an order and started on the next, and the line moved forward one place. The old woman turned, levelly met and held Renata's skittering gaze. 'Hello, Renata. I'm Daphne.'

The old woman smiled and, before she could stop herself, Renata smiled back. Stopped where she was and would not go any farther, rooted herself like a tree.

That wasn't safe enough. Made herself stone. Layers and layers, like the rings of a tree, petrified.

But could not reach the core. The core still lived.

She slipped backward.

Found other bereaved mothers. Other lost children. Found and lived this same pain, stretching backward and backward, stretching forward through the generations to her. The seeds of loss. The roots of loss spreading underground, holding the ground together.

Living mother stone.

Chapter 7

That's another way to do it, Renata thought. *Turn yourself into something inhuman. Metamorphose into wood and stone.* Riding in her son's funeral procession less than a week after her son's death, she considered it.

It was strange, this experience she'd apparently had of the woman in the little wilderness, half a continent and almost fifty years away. She knew it was strange, but didn't care much whether it had been a vision, or a message, or a grief-fever dream, or some sort of collective memory. It was no stranger than anything else that was happening to her, such as, for instance, the fact that she was riding in her son's funeral procession cradling the box of his ashes on her lap.

Charlie was driving their car because Glenn still couldn't drive. Charlie and Glenn's mother sat in the front passenger seat. In back rode Vanessa, Glenn in the middle, and Renata with the box on her knees.

Simple and functional, the box was brown plastic and about the size of a shoebox, but more square than rectangular. The surface was featureless, except for the gummed name label on the lid: 'Ian Andrew Burgess.' It was inert. It emitted no energy, no heat or vibrations. But it contained the ashes of her son.

Two other cars followed. Tim drove his, with passengers Shauna and Jackie. Pete was behind the wheel of Renata's parents' car because they didn't like driving in the mountains; her father sat beside him in the front and her mother rode alone in the back.

Reviewing the positions of everyone in the funeral procession obsessed her. She went over and over the arrangement in her mind and ran her hands repeatedly across the smooth surfaces of the box. Tim driving. Charlie in front of her. Her mother alone in the back seat.

Suddenly she thought the ashes had spilled and, though she saw that they hadn't, couldn't stop wondering what would happen now that the ashes had spilled. She rubbed her fingertips together, brushed off her lap, peered out of the corner of her eye at any dust suspended in the sunny air. She couldn't imagine what a person's ashes would look like, feel like, smell like. She hadn't been able to bring herself to open the box.

The young woman from the crematorium had delivered the ashes to the house. Knowing that was an unusual level of service, Renata had struggled to thank her. The woman had pressed her hand and said it was the least she could do; she had a nine-year-old son herself. 'I wish I did,' Renata had said bitterly. Then she'd had to find Glenn and say to him, 'Ian's ashes are here.'

Glenn had gasped. For a terrible moment he'd stared at her wildly. Then he'd put his head on her shoulder and sobbed. A big man, he'd clung to her, and she'd supported him, kept him from falling, cradled him in her arms. It was all she could do, and of course it wasn't enough. She'd held him for a long time, standing in a patch of sunlight in the dining room. His mother had started toward them to comfort him, too, but Renata had waved her away; later, she would wonder why she'd done that.

The plain brown box holding their little boy's ashes had sat on the table by the window. That hadn't seemed to be the right place for it; she couldn't guess where a good place would be.

'Let's keep them here,' Tim had begged. 'I don't want to throw them away.'

'Oh, Tim, no. It wouldn't be good for any of us to keep them.'

'We could keep the box on the mantel.'

'Sweetheart, you have to let him go. We all do.'

'I can't. I don't want to lose him.'

'You have to. We all have to. The truth is, Ian's dead. He's gone.'

It was the second day of spring, a crystalline day. The sky was so blue that she needed words other than 'blue' to describe it: cerulean, azure. Trees were beginning to bud, feathery chartreuse on black branches against cerulean sky. She must have rolled her window down; the air was so sweet it hurt.

The rock face on their left, created by the cutting of the road bed, was dramatically striated red, gray, and a creamy pinkish yellow that she thought was quartz. The red was sandstone, part of the formation that ran along most of the Front Range and had helped to give Colorado its name. The gray was granite, or shale.

As if from an enormous distance or from another life, she remembered how eager she'd been to learn about the geology, biology, history of this place. Now, of course, she had no interest. The very thought of being interested in anything other than her pain made the pain worse. But she kept repeating the words to herself anyway, long after they'd become quite useless: quartz, sandstone, granite, shale.

In many places the rock strata ran at angles sharp to the horizontal, witness to tremendous and prolonged heat and pressure at that very spot millennia ago. *Heat*, she thought confusedly. *Heat. Tremendous pressure*. The narrow mountain road climbed steeply and twisted in tight switchbacks, falling away to their right in a sheer, high cliff, often without guardrails. In the front seat, Mary Jo restrained herself from saying anything, but she turned her head away from the windows and gasped audibly every few seconds. Charlie responded, every time, with a remonstrative, 'Mom!'

It offended Renata that anyone should be afraid of anything. Ian was dead. They were on their way to scatter his ashes. In a world where everyone loses everything, there's nothing to lose. While she didn't have the energy or concentration to will the car over the cliff, she wished, hazily, that Charlie would miss a turn, that there would be an avalanche at just the right time and place, that the road would take flight off the mountainside and carry them into the crystalline azure air, which would not support their weight.

Nearly nine years ago, Glenn and Renata had been married on top of this mountain. They'd thought about it carefully, planned so the setting would be just right, written their own ceremony. It had been perfect. It had been a beautiful afternoon in late September, blue and gold and crisp as apples, and all their words had said exactly what they'd wanted them to say.

But they'd never thought about where to scatter the ashes of their dead child, or what to say while they did it. Renata couldn't tell whether this mountain was the right place or not; it had been the only spot either of them could think of, and they couldn't bear to talk about it very much. There would be no service. There were no right words. This was beyond words, beyond thought.

Except that it was not beyond thought. It should have been, but it was not. Renata found her mind quite capable of encompassing the primal, inchoate knowledge of her child's death, as if the knowledge had already been there before Ian died, and was not hers alone.

Frederic came into her mind, and was no more bewildering than any of her other thoughts. *Betty. Grace. Carla. Eileen. Stone.*

A steep half-mile or so below the summit of the mountain, the road was barricaded, not yet open for the season. Snow coated the slopes, with brown patches of rock and winter grasses showing through raggedly. Another car was parked in the icy gravel off the side of the road. Renata wondered why these people were up here, couldn't imagine beyond a few lifeless words anyone else's wedding joy or funeral anguish, wondered whether the mountains and the cerulean sky and the shale, granite, sandstone, quartz would have room for what was brought to them today and nine years ago and a hundred years and seven hundred years ago.

Joy was a ruse. Happiness was a trick of mirrors and scarves. Peace made no sense. When she and Glenn had been married in this place nine years ago (she remembered, viscerally, walking up this road; she remembered the music, and the words, and the profound sense of being part of a miracle), she had not known what was real. Now she knew: anguish was real, and the continual coiling and recoiling of loss.

Behind the wheel, Charlie regarded the barricade across the road. 'What should we do?'

'Walk,' Renata said.

Alarmed, Mary Jo wanted to know, 'Is it far? Is it high?' Glenn said no, and Renata was insulted that she'd even asked.

The three cars parked in a row in the gravel, and the mourners got out into the cool blue spring sunshine. In pairs and small groups and one by one – Renata's parents and Glenn's mother together but not knowing what to talk to each other about, Jackie with Vanessa, Tim and Shauna holding hands, Pete and Charlie, Glenn by himself, Renata by herself but carrying Ian's ashes – they went around the barricade and started up the snow-covered dirt road, through the smell of pines and the high sound of wind. Shauna was wearing a bright pink scarf. Jackie's sweater was blue. Renata cradled the brown box in both hands against her belly, and wasn't sure from one step to the next that she could keep her balance.

'Vanessa,' she heard Charlie say. 'Come away from there.'

She looked over her left shoulder and saw only the jumbled landscape, trees and rocks, white snow and very blue sky. For long slow moments she thought she might already have lost everybody, might never have had them in the first place, might be alone here forever with the warm ashes of her child.

She looked over her right shoulder and saw Vanessa, also her child. Vanessa was off the road, stepping and leaping from boulder to boulder as if she were crossing a stream, keeping her balance with outstretched arms. *Playing*, Renata thought furiously. *At her brother's funeral.* But the girl wasn't playing. Her face was somber, and she didn't laugh when she slipped off a rock and landed on her knee in the icy dirt.

'Vanessa,' she heard Charlie say again. 'Come over here and walk with the rest of us.'

Scowling now, Vanessa turned away from him and jumped off the downslope side of a split log. Debris rattled down the hill and off the cliff, and Vanessa disappeared. Renata stopped and stared. Vanessa reappeared, circled back, and stepped onto the road apart from the others, head down and fists in her pockets. Against her will, Renata saw how her daughter's hair shone in the sun, and pain roared through her. Understanding that this kind of pain would always be as normal for her now as the blood in her veins or the thoughts in her head, Renata kept walking and carrying it with her.

Pete was walking alone just behind her. She'd met him only a few times before; he was nearly a stranger to her. From a pulsating and ringing distance, she saw that his shoulders were hunched, his steps were faltering, and he was crying.

To Glenn, who apparently had been silently beside her for some time, she murmured, 'I think Pete needs you.' Glenn started, stared at her uncomprehendingly for a few steps, then simply pivoted into his brother's path. The two men – strong, tall, kind, and profoundly helpless – stood weeping in each other's arms on the cold blue mountain road, now looking very much alike.

'Vanessa!' Jackie called suddenly. 'You're making me really nervous!'

Again Renata stopped and searched for her daughter. She was seeing double- and half-images of things, and objects that she knew to be stationary were moving wildly – rocks spinning, trees fanning in and out – so it took a long time for her to locate and recognize Vanessa.

Finally she found her, too far away and much too far down a rock-strewn slope. The child was frenetically setting up small avalanches, balancing on one foot and then the other, running haphazardly, crouching, pirouetting, clambering far too high.

The terror was incomprehensible, unbearable, and so Renata refused it. Deliberately she told herself: *She's okay.* Then: *There's nothing I can do anyway to keep her safe.* She turned away and kept walking up the road.

Her breath came short and shallow now, and she was light-headed from the altitude and exertion. Iridescent auras had formed around all objects that came into her line of vision, and she saw individual blades of grass, individual pebbles, individual snowflakes and grains of icy bark. The box was so lightweight and its edges so indistinct from her own that she thought she might not be carrying it anymore.

Then there were three deer on the ledge above the road. Four deer, five. They glowed brown and gold and white amid the white snow, glowing brown trees, azure sky. Renata gasped.

The deer presented themselves calmly. Their auras shimmered. Their breath made delicate clouds, and Renata's breath was warm across the tender insides of her lips. Their winter-coated hides quivered, and she felt their body heat on the underside of her own skin. Their eyes gleamed and their ears cupped and flickered in the pale wind; Renata saw the world from among them on the ledge, saw the funeral procession and the scattering ashes, saw herself and heard their five hearts beating with hers in her ears.

It was not that they had been sent; they had always been there, and were now making themselves known. It was not that they brought a message personally to her from Ian or from anybody else; their message was in the simple demonstration that they existed as did she. They had taken form out of the multiform universe, where she and they and Ian always were. From somewhere beyond her particular human consciousness, and having nothing to do with time or place, Renata understood.

She was still holding her breath. She was standing motionless in the wind and sunshine. A chill raced through her, then waves of radiant warmth, and her ears rang with a wordless and tuneless song. She'd never before been close enough to deer in the wild to see them clearly. Someone else saw them, too, and cried softly, 'Oh, look!'

For an immeasurable time the deer stayed, offering themselves, bearing witness. Renata's heart rose to them, then split open. She didn't fight the pain this time, but softened around it, sang with it, allowed herself to be torn apart, and answered to the deer, *Yes*.

One by one, unhurried, the deer went on. They turned and made their way along the ledge, back into the sparse alpine woods. She heard their small sharp hooves on the rocks and pine needles, smelled their scent, saw the dapple of their tails. Then they were gone. But they were always there.

Shaken, pain still coursing through her, Renata sank onto a fallen log at the edge of the road and stared at the ledge where the deer had appeared. She tried to convince herself that they'd never been there, that she'd imagined them out of her own desperate mental state or that only their absence was real, but she couldn't hold such thoughts.

The top of the mountain wasn't far now. Mary Jo had stopped again and was sitting on a boulder with her head down, panting and pale. Glenn stood beside her while she struggled to catch her breath. On her feet again and passing them, Renata saw him reach out a hand to the grimly cavorting Vanessa and pull her to him, heard him murmur something to her at once stern and gentle, saw her squirm to get away and then abruptly bury her face against him.

Renata kept walking. The deer drew her on. She was carrying her son's ashes, and the summit wasn't far. So she was alone in the terrible blue of the sky and the mountains' anguished beauty when the snake crossed her path.

It stretched from one horizon to the other. Its tail disappeared downslope among the rocks and scrub pine; its great flat head was somewhere upslope. Its head reached toward the high sun as if to devour it, as if to regurgitate it in its own image, as if the snake and the sun and she were made of the same elements, as if the snake and the sun and she were the same.

The serpent was as big around as she was, then wider than the road, then thinner than a thread of grass. Its scales were patterned in diamonds, spirals, waves. It hissed. It crooned. Its jaws gaped and its fangs dripped. Its mouth was as red and deep as a tulip. Its mouth was her own torn heart.

Then the snake wasn't there anymore, and she was at the top of the mountain, and the others were with her. She and Glenn were leading the way now to the amphitheater among the pines. Another group was having a picnic on the far side of the amphitheater; Renata had vaguely thought it would matter if someone else was there, but it didn't. The colors of their clothes and skin and hair in the sunshine, their voices carrying in the thin clear air, weren't real.

Without discussion, Renata and Glenn made their way to the border of the amphitheater where the pines closed in again and this mountain sloped away to other mountains, deep green and brown where they were, blue and paler blue in the distance. Birds sang. Squirrels chittered. Renata looked into Glenn's eyes and held out the box. He opened the lid.

Ian's ashes were gray. Trembling violently, sure she herself would disintegrate on the spot and be scattered among the green and blue mountains, Renata plunged her hand into the ashes. They were soft and fine in some places, coarser in others, with a few larger bits like pebbles, like teeth or bone.

'I don't know what to say,' she said desperately to Glenn.

'There is nothing to say.' He put his hand in the box beside hers, took a handful of their dead child's ashes, cupped it then in both hands and walked a few steps downslope. For a moment he stood still, his hands in front of him where she couldn't see them. Then she saw his shoulders move and his hands go up, and she knew he'd scattered Ian's ashes, although she didn't see them go.

Renata's father stepped up, took some ashes, and sprinkled them carefully among the roots of the trees. 'Here,' he said to her mother. 'Take some.'

'No!' Her voice choked and she took a panicked step backward. 'I can't!'

'Come on. It's okay.'

'No!'

'Daddy, she doesn't have to,' Renata said, and her mother all but ran to the far side of the amphitheater, as if to join the picnickers there.

Jackie and Vanessa came next. Jackie kept her eyes on Renata's face as she dipped her hand into the box of ashes. Vanessa wouldn't look at her. They walked to a spot off to the right a little, among the tall straight trunks of the trees. Renata guessed they must have said something to each other or together to Ian, and then they raised their hands and let his ashes drift away.

The sacrament, the communion, continued. Mary Jo, Charlie, Pete stepped up to Renata where she held the box, took a share of the ashes of the beloved child, and gave them back to the universe – where, of course, they already were.

Tim dipped his fingers into the box and couldn't take them out again. 'Jesus,' he whispered raggedly. 'I can't do this.'

'You don't have to, sweetheart,' Renata told him. 'You can say goodbye to him in your own way.'

But finally he lifted a very small amount of his little brother's ashes in both hands and stumbled away with them. Shauna hung back, watching him. Birds sang. Squirrels chittered. An airplane buzzed across the sky not very far above them.

Renata set the box carefully down on the ground and scooped up what was left of Ian's ashes. As she made her way to a place on the mountainside – any place, she realized; none was any more or less fitting than any other – some of the ashes trickled from between her fingers, leaving a trail that disappeared almost at once. She imagined Ian's ashes working their way into the ground, into the roots of the trees and the pine nuts the squirrels ate, into the pores of her skin and the air sacs of her lungs.

She rested her back against a pine tree like all the others and wedged her feet among its roots. In her cupped hands were the diminishing ashes of her child, which she could not hold. She ought to say something.

Finally she simply opened her hands, and Ian's ashes fell, drifted, blew away, and Renata was suddenly buoyed by a curious sense of harmony and evanescent sorrow.

'I think Tim needs you,' Jackie said gently to her some minutes later. 'He says he can't let go.'

'That will take time,' Renata managed to say, hoping the words she spoke had some relationship to each other and to what Jackie had said. 'It's hard for all of us to let go.'

'No,' Jackie told her. 'I mean literally. He says he can't let go of the ashes. He's still holding them.'

Renata nodded and went to sit beside her son on the warm boulder where he crouched and stared at the little gray-white pile in his palms. After a while he whispered, 'I don't want to leave him here alone.'

'He's not alone,' she whispered back, not knowing what she was going to say until she heard herself saying it. 'And he's not here. He's already part of all this. Part of the sky and the trees and the mountains, part of the deer, and part of us. He'll always be part of us.' *That's not enough*, her mind shrieked. But it was all she had.

Finally Tim nodded, took a long shuddering breath, and spread his fingers to let the ashes go. Most of them had already seeped out. What was left trickled onto the hardpack between his sneakered feet, forming a tiny gray-white cone that flattened immediately and then was gone. Tim raised his knees, buried his face in his arms and sobbed.

Renata put her arm around his broad young shoulders and held him. 'Tell me what you need,' she murmured to him, as she had, fruitlessly, so many times before. 'Do you want me to stay with you, or do you want to be alone right now?'

'I want you to stay right here,' he told her with uncharacteristic directness. So she stayed beside him for a long time and he cried, and around them birds sang, squirrels chittered, the mountain breezes blew pine needles and sandstone dust and Ian's ashes past and through them.

At last it seemed to be time to leave. Renata put the empty plastic box into a trash can, not knowing what else to do with it. She was wondering what someone would think who found it there when she saw Glenn go back, peel the name tag off the lid, and crumple it into his pocket.

'I need some time alone,' she said suddenly.

She climbed far enough down the steep slope that she was out of the others' line of sight, although she guessed that Glenn and maybe Jackie would come to the edge to watch her, to make sure she didn't fall or jump. They were right to do that. She sat down on the spongey layer of pine needles with her legs straight out in front of her, pressed her palms flat on the surfaces of the earth, breathed as deeply as she could bear of the mountain air, and said aloud the little ritual phrases she and her son had used every night since he'd been her son: 'Good night, Ian. I love you. See you tomorrow in the morning.'

Chapter 8

Ian was screaming and pounding on the door with child's fists, clawing at it with child's nails, not really producing much noise but nonetheless making a frantic commotion. Both Renata and Glenn rushed to let him in – there was no reason the door should have been locked in the first place. 'Bees!' he was shrieking. 'The bees are chasing me!' Indeed, clouds of yellow jackets swarmed around him, and Renata could tell, more from the periodically rising timbre of their buzzing than from the child's generalized panic, that they were stinging him.

Five years old, Ian was hysterical, as much, she understood in the midst of her own alarm, from the betrayal – creatures he loved were being mean to him – as from actual pain. 'Inside my socks! Inside my shoes!' he wailed, heartbroken.

They pulled him into the house and slammed the door shut, locked it this time against the bees. No bees got in. Glenn scooped up the sobbing little boy and carried him to the living-room couch, knelt and stripped off his grubby tennis shoes and socks stiff with dirt and sweat. Kneeling, too, Renata saw three or four tiny red welts on each little ankle, among the ribbed depressions left in the soft flesh by the tops of the socks.

'It's okay,' she was crooning, before she knew that it was, that he hadn't been badly stung and wasn't allergic. Glenn went to make a compress. She eased off the rest of her son's clothes to check, found no other stings, gathered him to her. He was breathing raggedly but sufficiently. 'It's okay, honey,' she soothed him, honestly now, 'the worst is over. You're safe now. It won't get any worse than this. You've made it through the hardest part. It's okay.'

He relaxed in her arms, found the place in her lap that was always

93

there for him. He nuzzled into her shoulder, still crying but more softly now. She could feel his fear dissolving, though not his hurt feelings. Love swaddled them both, tenderness, security.

She woke up. The incident with the bees had really happened when Ian was five years old, but this had been a dream. The dream said: You did take care of him. You did protect him. You were a good mother to him.

Renata lay trembling. She'd been afraid to have dreams of Ian, certain they would be stinging, poisonous hauntings. Certainly, the suicide by hanging of a nine-year-old held all kinds of potential for nightmare images. She hadn't been prepared for this message of reassurance. It was tempting to try to think of it as a message from Ian himself, but she couldn't quite manage that.

'Happy birthday, Mom.' Vanessa came in. Renata intended to welcome her onto the bed. Maybe she did, although she was unaware of anything direct she actually said or did, or maybe Vanessa simply assumed she would have a place there. She laid her head on her mother's shoulder.

It's Ian's birthday, too. Neither of them said that. How was it possible that their birthday and Ian's death existed in the same universe, the same field of consciousness? The only answer, of course – the answer that, in its countless permutations, had dislodged her utterly from the place she'd occupied in her own life – was that they did.

'Are you okay?' Vanessa asked that a lot now, and Renata never knew how to answer in a way that was both truthful and reassuring.

'I had a dream,' she began, then stopped.

'About—'

Renata waited. Stroking her daughter's perpetually tangled hair, she felt a distant stir of habitual maternal irritation: If you can't keep your hair combed and clean, I'm going to cut it short. I mean it. Maybe it would be good to re-establish that minimal level of normalcy.

Which was why last night, setting the table for only three, she'd suddenly lifted one end and swung it around. It was much lighter than she'd expected and she almost lost her balance and let go of it to fly through the bay window and out into the street. It was much heavier than she'd expected and she almost couldn't budge it at all.

But she managed to get the table perpendicular to the way it had always been, so that, instead of sideways in front of the bay window it now extended out into the room. She stepped back to regard it, as though this had been nothing more than a redecorating project.

This would work. There was plenty of room on each end, and this way the table was more nearly centered under the chandelier. They should have done this before. But then, when Ian died, she'd have had to move it parallel to the windows in order to exorcise his empty place.

'It's my turn to set the table!' Vanessa had looked heartbroken, and it was her mother's fault. Never mind that both children had routinely complained about the chore. Never mind that from now on it would always be her turn.

'I'm sorry,' Renata stammered, not surprised to find herself apologizing for this, too. 'I – thought you wouldn't want to.'

Vanessa stopped in the doorway as if unable to cross the threshold. 'The table's all different,' she accused.

No shit sprang to Renata's lips, but she modified it to the slightly less sarcastic, 'That's right.'

'It's weird.'

'Come and sit down.'

'Where am I supposed to sit?' Belligerent.

'Anywhere you want. You can choose.'

Vanessa had just stood there. 'I don't want to.' Her whine drove Renata crazy under the best of circumstances, and now it had been very nearly intolerable.

She should go to her. She didn't want to. She didn't want to touch this child, as loved as Ian had been, who, one way or another, would leave her, too.

She'd crossed the room to take the little girl in her arms. Vanessa had been stiff, just short of pushing her away. 'It's weird,' she'd insisted again. 'It's not, like, normal. Nothing's normal anymore around here.'

Renata had rested her cheek on the top of her daughter's head and said softly, 'Vanessa, honey. Our lives have changed. There's no sense pretending they haven't. We have to live our new lives now and see how that feels. We have to find a new normal.' But she couldn't bring herself to say or do anything other than to run her fingers from Vanessa's skull down, gently but pointedly tugging at knots. Vanessa was looking at her plaintively, whether for permission to say her brother's name out loud or for permission not to. 'About Ian,' Renata confirmed, and winced.

'I have dreams about him, too.'

It was an invitation, a plea. Renata was supposed to ask what the dreams were, to listen while Vanessa recounted them and encourage detail and interpretation and catharsis. A good mother would do that. She could not. All she could manage was a hug – and even that was truncated because Vanessa didn't lift herself off the bed or turn toward her or in any other way reciprocate. Yearning for Ian swelled inside Renata like a balloon, physical pressure, physical threat.

She felt like celebrating her birthday. How could that be? Dread of this day had sprung into her mind very soon after she'd known Ian was dead. Along with it had come a quicksilver, childish gladness – her birthday was hers again; she didn't have to share the spotlight with anybody – and then, of course, shame. And the realization that now she had to share her birthday with a dead child, who would get more attention than the live one had. *Shame.* And the anticipation of awful pain. What she had not anticipated was this sweet acknowledgment that she had, still, something to celebrate.

It was a lovely day, bright pastels and a breeze fragrant not with blooms yet but with the promise of bloom; she was glad for this sudden spring. How could she be glad?

Breakfast was hard. Ian seemed especially present to her at breakfasts they would have shared, and especially absent; especially today. They'd have said, 'Happy birthday' to each other at breakfast. He'd have said, 'You look pretty, Mom.' She'd have kissed him goodbye and he'd have said, smiling crookedly, 'Have a good day to work,' a turn of phrase he'd been using since he was four, when he'd first come to them, which had permanently been incorporated into the family's speech patterns.

'Maybe we shouldn't do anything for my birthday,' she'd said to Glenn, trying out the possibility, gauging her reaction by his. 'Maybe we should just ignore it.'

'If we don't do something this year it will be even harder next year, and for the rest of our lives.'

'Maybe we should just ignore my birthday from now on.'

'No,' he'd said sternly. 'It's still your birthday.'

They went to the Italian restaurant they always went to on her birthday. One year Ian had chosen Dairy Queen for his, much to the consternation of his brother and sister, because he wanted a banana split; most years – there had been only a paltry and pitiable five joint birthdays – he'd picked a pizza place with video games and a floor show by child-sized dancing and singing puppets. Those years they'd had two celebrations, and she'd thought they always would; she'd imagined going out to dinner alone with her grown son on a day close to their birthday, leaving the birthday itself for respective celebrations with everyone else.

She wasn't even sure the restaurant was her favorite anymore. Maybe Mexican or Vietnamese would be better. For a while she'd been entangled in the skeins of this dilemma, which loomed momentously: if she chose wrong, she would ruin something important. Then, abruptly, it came to seem ludicrous and ugly, under the circumstances, even to *have* a favorite restaurant, to take pleasure in homemade pasta and garlic cheese bread and the world's best minestrone soup, to eat at all. But she needed tradition: to reclaim it, to see what it would be like without Ian. Whether she could bear it. Whether anyone else could bear it. Whether they loved her enough to celebrate her birthday when it was no longer his.

The world was now fraught with such conundrums, ethical at the most fundamental level and intensely significant: Now that Ian was dead, was it accurate to speak of April 11 as his birthday anymore? Was it better – wiser, more loving, more honorable – to think of him as nine years old forever, or to keep active a mental calendar that marked how old he would have been this year and next year, and the next, and the next?

They trooped into the restaurant early enough not to need a reservation. On the way to the table, Renata counted, found one person missing, and thought she couldn't eat, she couldn't have a birthday, she couldn't sit at a family table at which Ian would never again sit. There would always be a person missing. Nothing would ever again be whole.

But they sat around a table with a red-and-white checked cloth whose colors hurt her eyes and whose crisscross pattern trapped them so that again and again she had to wrench her gaze away and then had nowhere else to fix it. They ordered; Renata asked Glenn to order for her, but he wouldn't. Lasagna, then; waiting for it.

Tim, sitting beside her, big and broad-shouldered and warm, was teasing Vanessa, across the table beside her dad, small. The tone of it sounded mean to Renata, dangerous, but Vanessa was giggling and blushing with pleasure at her big brother's attention.

The taste and texture of the lasagna made almost no impression. She could tell she was taking food into her mouth, chewing and swallowing it, because of its weight and mass, how it obstructed her airway and then dislodged to lie heavy in her stomach. The salad was individual pieces, slimy, no taste. She hadn't dared to order wine. She couldn't eat the garlic bread; when she brought it to her mouth she couldn't bite into it, put it down on her plate.

Vanessa, ever vigilant: 'Are you okay, Mom?' This was one of the myriad ordinary questions that were no longer answerable. Renata managed to nod, which was neither the truth nor a lie.

Warmth suffused her. She checked to see that she was not drinking wine; it was water in her glass, and she had drunk almost none of it. To Tim she said, not knowing she was going to, 'I'm happy.'

Of all people for her to be saying this to, her son was the least likely – this young man so strange and so dear to her for whom strong emotion was an alien substance, talking about it an activity worse than pointless, and the very idea of intra-psychic processes laughable. But here they were, their lives having intersected and flowed into each other, sitting beside each other on her birthday and having lost Ian.

So she said to him, through a haze as if she were drugged, 'I can't believe I'm happy.'

Tim frowned. 'Don't worry about it.'

'I can't believe there's so much love in the world. Still.' She put her hand on his knee.

Feeling him stiffen, she thought he might ignore her touch or brush it off, and it would be as if she had never touched him, they'd be shown to be more strangers than not, and she'd lose him, too, someday – but in the midst of her surging despair Tim took her hand in both of his and looked at her squarely. 'Don't think about it too much, Mom. Just happy birthday, you know?'

A few days before he died, Ian had given her his birthday list, pale smudged pencilled quasi-cursive with approximate spelling, that she hadn't yet tried to decipher and now wouldn't. With pride, though, she had noticed that, for the first time, he'd asked for chapter books. He'd known it was a milestone: 'books *with chapters*,' he'd emphasized with wiggly underlining. She didn't know where that list was now. She should find it and destroy it. The thought of it lying in wait for Glenn or Vanessa or Tim to stumble upon and detonate made her frantic by the time they got home. But she didn't know where to begin the search.

She had to open presents – a jacket from Tim, the new book of Valerie Martin stories and a mint-green cotton nightgown from Glenn (both surprises; before Ian died, she might have given him hints); personalized envelopes Pete had printed at work; a bouquet of tulips made of looped construction paper from Vanessa; nothing from Ian; nothing from Ian.

She had to blow out the candles. She had no breath and certainly no wish fit to make. The flames sputtered and the thought occurred to her that maybe they were trick candles that would keep relighting and relighting so she'd never get her wish. But Glenn wouldn't do that this year and she wouldn't get her wish anyway, and the sediment of wishes and denied wishes was thick in the birthday room.

She had to cut her cake, chocolate with white frosting the way Glenn knew she liked it. Ian had liked white cake, so they'd had to have two cakes, too. One by itself looked puny now.

As soon as they got home, Vanessa went to bed. When she was more or less settled, Renata and Glenn both went to check the answering machine. No messages. Renata dared to say, with a brief bitter laugh, 'Jesus, I was hoping there would be a message from Ian.'

Glenn nodded. 'I had the same fantasy.'

They looked at each other.

Then they were in each other's arms, clinging, desperately kissing, crying, holding each other on top of the covers, working at each other's clothes. Shivering. Not letting go of each other, they struggled under the quilt and made love. Renata scarcely felt it, hardly was there, but the fact of the lovemaking was balm.

But then there were still hours left in the day without Ian, and hours in the night. It wasn't even eight o'clock yet. Something bad would happen at eight o'clock, birthday or not, and it was up to her to stop it, or, failing that – as, of course, she would fail – to throw herself in front of it before it struck anybody else. Everyone drifted away. Renata drifted away, too.

The idea sprang alive, and with it excitement, that what was required of her now was to learn how to live in a new kind of relationship with Ian. Gratitude swelled.

Then bitter skepticism: Was this a 'real' revelation, or merely the pitiable expression of psychological need? How would she ever know?

'You can't do it this way,' she heard Glenn say.

She stood stock still, not knowing where he was. He might be, might always have been, speaking only from inside her head.

Ian, though, was real, and everywhere. He'd been dead (*oh, God, Ian is dead*) for twenty-four days now, and memories of him bombarded her constantly, never letting up, from every direction and filling every waking and sleeping moment, so that she couldn't remember anything else alive or dead:

Singing at the top of his lungs on his way to a friend's house early on a Saturday morning, to the great annoyance of a neighbor who worked nights and had just fallen asleep. Ian, bewildered and a little hurt by the man's scolding, protesting to her, 'But I was only *singin'*!' She heard that over and over now: 'But I was only *singin'*!'

His laughter like seashells. His exuberant obscenities, so creative as to be nonsensical. His nearly wordless rage at her the night he died. A child's normal anger at his parents. Healthy, even; a sign that he felt safe, a sign that he knew Renata and Glenn, unlike other adults in his life, weren't going to hurt him or leave him. It should have been good for him. It shouldn't have been lethal.

Ian had been mad at her when he died (*died*), which negated all the love and tenderness and happiness she'd always thought they shared. His last thoughts of her had been bad. He'd hated her at the moment he put the rope around his neck and jumped off the top bunk, whether he'd done it on purpose, exactly, or not; he'd been trying to hurt her. No matter how much of the rest of his short life he'd loved her, he'd hated her when he died (*died*).

He'd died because he was angry with her. He'd killed himself (*he was nine years old*) because he was angry with her. He was dead (*dead dead*) because of her. It was her fault her son was dead.

Renata cried out, but no one heard.

'It'll kill you this way,' Glenn said from somewhere, not to her.

Stumbling over the green chair – which she'd owned for fifteen years and which now was utterly unrecognizable at the same time that it was bitterly familiar – Renata made her way through the parlor to the big front window. After a moment of gathering her courage, she raised her head and looked out.

Sudden sunlight glazed her eyes and hurt from inside her skull. The pane shimmered with so many grotesque rainbows, thickly overlapping, that she couldn't decipher what she was seeing through it.

Whatever was out there would hurt her; she didn't know how. The buds on the rosebush looked wrong – the wrong shape, the wrong shade of red. Each was swollen and quivering with the fat evil thing it hid, until the moment it would burst out to attack her. And wasn't it too early for roses?

Charlie was sitting on the porch swing, doubled over. Glenn stood in front of him with his hands in his pockets. The erratic motion of the swing left poisonous ripples in the air, and Renata tried to back away from them but couldn't be sure she had.

Charlie said, in a voice within a voice that wasn't his, 'This is the only way I can do it.'

'Look at you. Trying to push it down, to keep it in. It'll eat you alive, from the inside out.'

Charlie was gasping for air. A beer can at his feet cruelly reflected the sun; Renata tried to avoid the flash but couldn't figure out which way to tilt her head. Charlie wasn't crying. His arms were crossed over his abdomen, and he bent farther and farther forward until she was certain he would fall off the swing at his brother's feet.

Then he raised one fist, leaving the other buried in his belly. For a moment Renata imagined he was threatening Glenn, and she thought she would leap through the glass and it would do no good.

Charlie's voice was calm and taut as he told his brother, 'If I let any of it out it'll destroy me. It'll destroy the world.'

Glenn sighed. The sound was sad – almost but not quite unbearable. Even from this distance and through all the distortions, Renata could see the enormous sorrow in his eyes – the tightness of the skin around them, the furrowing of the brows, the pulsing and shimmering of the beautiful hazel irises and the extreme dilation of the pupils as though they couldn't believe what they saw, had no hope of believing it unless they took it *all* in.

Renata reeled from her husband's eyes. She would never be able to look into them again. It was bad enough that she had lost her son; Glenn's bereavement was surely more than she could bear. She backed away from it, flailed her arms to fight it off.

She ran hard into the far wall of the parlor and, instead of recoiling from the bruising pain of the impact, pressed her back and the back of her head against it, hoping the wall and the pain would part to let her pass through. Even so, she distinctly heard Glenn ask Charlie, 'What did you do with the ball?'

'I didn't touch it. It's still in the backyard under the lilac bush. Where he left it.' Charlie groaned.

The lilacs would be blooming soon. Renata wished urgently for a late hard frost, or for drying chinook winds that would kill the buds on the bushes before they could open and do more damage.

'Do you want us to keep it?' Glenn was asking.

There was a silence. Unwillingly, Renata listened with Charlie for what Glenn would say next, because she didn't know what he meant, either.

'We'll be keeping some of his things, but probably not all,' Glenn explained.

She hadn't thought of that. Now she thought of Ian's glasses, so tiny they fit in the palm of her hand, and couldn't bring herself to imagine touching them, let alone deciding whether to keep them or throw them away. She thought of his collection of black-and-white 'generic bears' from the supermarket – 'junior bears,' he'd called them, even after he'd surely known better. She thought of his socks.

His head between his knees by now, Charlie choked out, 'I – gave him – that ball and – bat – for his – ninth birthday.' But he didn't say any more.

Renata's skin hurt. Dangerous love for her husband made her heart swell and race. Her mind protested so wildly that she knew it was not her mind; some alien consciousness was taking possession of her.

She willed it to do so, quickly, but it made no difference what she willed. Tentacles with hot suction tips and poisonous bristles attached themselves to her heart and mind, shielding her from this life-threatening love. Renata turned and ran back through the house and down the basement steps, knowing all the time she couldn't get far enough away. The floor opened and then dissolved. Hot, sticky, crosshatched tentacles pulled her underground, under the house *the house where Ian lived, the house where Ian died Ian died*, under the alien and dangerous city where she now lived and would live for the rest of her life, where she had always lived and had not known until she'd lost her son.

Chapter 9

She was in the tunnel again, then through it. She had dismissed the tunnel with its guardians and guides, labyrinthine under the house, city, family, body of her daily life, but whether she acknowledged it or not she was hurtled through it. Gales across the opening swept her breath away.

The mouth of the canal ripped; she'd torn it pushing through. Viscous fluid oozing from the wounds she'd caused was diluted by driving rain; where it adhered to her skin it was sticky, briefly, and then it washed away. She lay where she'd landed, flat on wet ground, stunned, but the hard rain hurt her skin and flesh, and she curled up as if to protect herself but was still exposed.

Letting her mouth fall open, she used what might be the first or last breath in her lungs to wail. All around her was wailing and shrieking. Her voice flowed into the other voices of the tempest, gained power from them, and was lost.

She managed to sit up. Rain drenched her, pummeling her bent head and cascading down her shoulders and flanks like a torrential veil. Her weighty clothes had become all of a piece, engorged and odoriferous woollen sweater nearly indistinguishable from soaked shirt from jeans clinging to her skin whose fabric absorbed enormous quantities of the downpour and sluiced enormous quantities of it off into her shoes. She cast off her shoes.

She struggled to her knees, fists sinking again and again wrist-deep into mud, knees sinking. Rain and tears coated her eyes, ran down her cheeks into her mouth. Her dripping hair was plastered against her face, then whipped across it, stinging. Lightning cracked, huge incandescent gashes, and she lost count before the thunderclap but knew it was very close, maybe already having struck.

She tried to stand, but wind threw itself against her like an open hand and her legs went out from under her. As she fell, she slid, and thick water rose over her, covered her nose and mouth. She gagged, managed to hoist herself high enough to breathe, spat. The current was fast and hard, wind blew, and things flew through both water and air, battering her, forcing her along.

Fighting both the forward and the downward motions of the elements, she didn't know what she fought against or why. If not forward – tumbling, scraped, clutching at objects that seemed hard and fast but that bent or dissolved in her grasp – then where did she think to go? If not downward – into mud, underwater – then where?

She could see now – only dimly, but this place was not pitch black. Blue and gray and purple streaked past her, steel-colored to cloud-colored to misty, and in the current were undulating creatures, fluttering creatures. Brown things, probably in some way alive, tugged at her with suckers and pincers. Branches like a woman's hands slapped her in the face and clawed at her arms and chest, thin and thicker black twisted lines against a sky and ground that were not quite black.

As one such branch swung at her, like the negative image of a lightning bolt, she grabbed it and pulled herself up a slippery bank. The branch strained at its body-like trunk, and the trunk threatened to pull up its own roots, which were, after all, only the feet of a bereaved mother frozen in place by defiant terror.

Renata's feet dredged deep trails back downslope, the branch gave, and she fell. Wind peaked gritty water into a geyser and tossed it over her.

Her heart plunged. Vertigo took hold, spun her in a fierce whirlpool, slammed her into rocks. A slimy creature insinuated itself against her. A furred creature half as big as she was, soaking wet and chittering frantically, clawed its way across her belly toward the outcropping.

She blacked out.

She regained consciousness. The storm still raged.

She clambered up another embankment, this one studded with gravel that painfully pocked her hands and knees, and did manage to extricate herself from the swollen river, only to enter more directly into the tempest itself. A drenched bird clung to a skeletal branch; when lightning crackled across the sky, the bird and branch seemed very close. The bird squawked faintly. Renata heard human voices but saw no one.

Crawling, stumbling, forcing herself step by step by grasping and then releasing branches, rocks, hands, she made her windblown way along what might have been a path. Shelter. She needed shelter.

She was violently unsteady from cold and wet, and violently dizzy. But she stayed on her feet and kept moving. Finally, suddenly, in the wild gloom the path opened and squared, and she saw herself surrounded by looming shapes.

They were monstrous. Beautiful. They were absolutely motionless, but they leaned over her. She was frightened, but she noticed that when she stood among and under them the storm was deflected, the wind seemed almost playful and the rain – though still loud outside the cluster of statues – here inside was only a drizzle. *Shelter*, she assured herself, and stopped.

Chapter 10

Incredibly, there had already developed a history, brief because its beginning was still so recent and not because its end was anywhere in sight or in the least conceivable. In the first days and weeks after it had happened – not allowing herself refuge in the euphemism, she forcibly rephrased it: after Ian had died – the extremity of her revulsion at speaking the words that would describe the event had led her to speak them again and again, obsessively, learning their shape and substance and their feel coming out of her, and the way they dissipated once she'd spoken them, needing to be spoken again.

She had called friends, some in the middle of the night. She had written an anguished note to her former mother-in-law, who had called and written back. There were people she had met as a direct result of Ian's death – other bereaved parents, mostly – who were already part of her past, because the commonality of bereavement had not been enough to sustain a relationship; she'd have thought it would be.

Incredibly, too, a future without Ian had begun to form. She had already started to compose their Christmas letter – 'Our son Ian died this year' – knowing it would take all year, at least, to get the words even approximately right. And Christmas cards. The dilemma brought small, acute panic. No pre-printed sentiment would say what she had to say, even if she knew what that was; the prospect of sending generic holiday wishes made her skin crawl; using blank cards would mean she'd have to write whatever she decided to write over and over again.

How would she bear Christmas anyway? How could it be that there were eight months between now and then, and that in all those eight months – how many days? how many hours? The computations, which seemed essential, were beyond her – she would never see Ian?

She woke from a dream – though neither 'woke' nor 'dream' was the right term – about sojourning in a garden of statues in which she was invited to become a statue herself. Over and over she cried to Glenn, 'I'm going to forget he's dead, and then he really will be dead! I'm going to forget he's dead! Then he really will be dead!' Worse than nonsensical, it hurt Glenn; she could see that it hurt Glenn, offended him. But she couldn't break the perseveration until it ran down under its own weight. 'I'm going to forget!'

Jeffrey had been her friend for nearly fifteen years, since before she'd met Glenn, since before she'd even wanted children. In graduate school – and a few times since then, each time with less passion and more comfortable affection – they'd been lovers. They'd seen each other through respective divorces, the vicissitudes of career development, his thinning hair and her thickening waistline. Jeffrey gave her a sense of continuity, of the possibility that her identity would again consist of more than 'Ian's mother,' 'bereaved mother.'

'I'm going to need you a lot for a while.'

'I'll be honored,' he'd promised.

'I won't be very good company.' It was a test.

'I love you, Renata. Let me know what you need. Anything. I love you.'

'I need Ian back.' *Okay, Jeffrey. Prove your love. Let's see you do that, since you love me so much. If you can't do that, what good is your goddamn love? What good—*

'I know. I'm so sorry.'

'I won't be able to reach out.'

'Then I'll reach in.'

And he had. She'd seen him every few days for a while; she'd rambled and raged, wept and lain stunned on his couch first tolerating and then craving his touch as he massaged her shoulders, her scalp, her eyes swollen from crying and still crying, the space over her heart that she could barely stand to touch, the prickling soles of her feet.

Pain so intense she flailed and howled and curled herself around it and it still didn't ease. It was too much. She couldn't do this. 'I

110

can't stop!' she moaned. 'I don't want to stop! This is the only thing I should be doing for the rest of my life!'

Jeffrey wasn't afraid of her pain. He stayed with her. He hadn't loved Ian. This wasn't his loss. She clung to him. She walked straight ahead, *into* the pain. Jeffrey couldn't go with her, but he sent her on with provisions.

Now here he was, sitting on Ian's bed beside her while she went through Ian's things. She and Glenn had agreed – she thought they had agreed – that they could not do this together. That scared her. She didn't know how Glenn would do it, or had done it – by himself, probably, which broke her heart. She didn't know where Glenn was right now, or exactly what he was feeling. She ought to know. She ought to be making it right for him. She dared not stop being vigilant, even though vigilance had proved itself disastrously inadequate. But since she could not reliably gather or organize information, anything she did or didn't do was likely to make things worse.

'Oh,' she said, 'his brown cords. I wondered what he did with these.' She snatched her hand back from the small pants as if they would burn, then forced herself to take them from Jeffrey. They didn't burn, but the individual wales of the corduroy trapped and scored her flesh, and the overall softness of them was an affront.

Watching her, Jeffrey suggested gently, 'Tell me about his brown cords.'

No, I can't. 'He didn't like them. They were brand new. He had to have them. Then he said they were ugly and he wouldn't wear them.' She waited for the explosion of agony in her chest, the scouring sobs. They didn't come. The old annoyance over the pants was resurrecting itself, mildly. 'By now they're too small.' Catching her breath, she insisted on making the obvious correction, which for Jeffrey's sake could have gone without saying but for hers could not. 'They *would have been* too small.'

Jeffrey nodded and smiled a little. She was touched by the care with which he weighed how much to say, how little. 'He was his mother's son. He had a mind of his own.'

Renata arched her back against the pain, which now came hard. Jeffrey didn't apologize or do anything to soothe her; he sat beside her, solid, steady, direct, and did not go away from her. When she could speak again, she said, 'He hated shirts that button, too, and mittens.' *That's all, that's all, no more.*

She stood up, leaving the pants to Jeffrey, and crossed the cluttered room. It still had the air of Ian's room. There was no sign of a struggle – for there had been only the few minutes it would take a small person to die of hanging, and her little boy had gone through that alone.

But much was different. The top bunk, from which her child had jumped or fallen with the rope around his neck (or been pushed? Renata entertained the notion that someone had sneaked into the house and murdered her son, and along with the revulsion came a tempting and terrible relief), was no longer stacked on the bottom one. The bunks had been disassembled; the footboard with the post shaped like an ice cream cone around which Ian had looped the rope whose other end he'd noosed around his neck (the effort of forcing her attention to this image until it was done left her shaking) was leaning against the wall. She had a vague memory that Glenn had said he was going to do that, but no memory at all of him having done so, and it was further proof of her alienation from the world that she hadn't been aware of hammering and carrying, or of this detail among the many of her husband's grief.

Her gaze, her hands, wandered haphazardly over the jumble. Jackie had put things in piles and boxes and drawers. Renata was fleetingly but fiercely seized with the conviction that Jackie might have thrown away the one magical object that, used correctly, would bring Ian back. There was still an overwhelming amount of stuff to go through, an impossible number of decisions to be made about what to keep and what to throw away and what to give to whom.

Behind her Jeff asked, 'Do you want to keep the brown cords?'

'No.' How could she let anything go? 'Yes.' Why would she need any tangible reminder of Ian? 'I don't know.' She was doing this wrong. She had to make decisions. Her hands went to her throat, which was closing.

'That's fine,' Jeffrey assured her. 'There's no hurry. This can take as long as you need.'

'Your time—'

'I have all the time you need,' he said, and although he didn't move from his place on her dead son's bed, Renata felt embraced.

'His squirt gun,' she said, recoiling from it, grasping it. 'The latest in a long line.' She took a deep breath and made herself say it right. 'The last in a long line.'

'Tell me about his squirt gun,' Jeff said quietly.

'He loves squirt guns. He loved squirt guns.' That said, she warmed to the subject as though it were not a dead child she was talking about. 'He'd squirt bees. He'd try to squirt airplanes and clouds. He loved it when the cats clawed the furniture and he got to squirt them officially. He'd hide around the side of the house and squirt Vanessa in the face. I thought she was going to kill him.' She heard what she had said and shuddered at the irony, but rushed on. 'One time Tim got so tired of it he hung Ian on the fence by his belt loops.'

Watching her, Jeffrey laughed, openly and easily, at the antics of her children, and now she was laughing, too. Laughter in her chest and throat was a peculiar sensation, but she allowed it and it didn't kill her.

But the laughter whipped out of control and spun her off into hysteria. The sound of it cut loose from its source. She was shaking, disassembling, and she couldn't stop laughing. Jeffrey was there. He caught her from behind and held her until she wasn't laughing anymore. 'Shall we stop for now?' he murmured against her hair.

'No.' She pulled free. 'I guess I want to keep the squirt gun.' Jeffrey nodded against her, hugged her, and put the squirt gun into the box they'd designated for things she wanted to keep – placed it carefully, she noted gratefully, rather than just dropping it in. It was a plain cardboard box; shouldn't it be special somehow? Draped in black or decorated with pretty hearts? There was something both right and wrong about keeping mementoes of Ian in a plain, sturdy cardboard box that didn't pretend to be anything but what it was, a container for things that had belonged to her little boy Ian, who had died.

She scanned the room, touched things, caught up now in the need to tell little stories about her son. 'Here's one of his Herbie books.'

Jeff responded at once. 'Tell me about Herbie. Who's Herbie?'

'I can tell you don't have a little boy,' Renata said before she thought, and was struck: *Neither do I.* She rushed on, headlong, holding the thin blue book in both hands. 'Herbie's a Volkswagen who has adventures. He catches criminals and gets his owner together with the woman he has a crush on and saves stranded kittens. Ian would *giggle*!' Her inability to convey the lost sound of Ian's delight was tragic.

Jeff had been rummaging through the bookshelf, which contained all manner of things in addition to books. It seemed an awfully personal thing for him to be doing. She supposed that was all right. 'Here are a couple of other Herbie books.' He held them out to her. She didn't take them. 'Do you want to keep them all?'

Here was a decision to be made. She could keep everything. She could render everything associated with Ian sacred, construct a shrine. She could insist that everything in his room be kept exactly the way it had been when he lived here and shut the door, or keep it open so every time anybody passed in the hall they'd have to look in and be reminded that Ian Burgess used to live here. Then the neighborhood kids who said this house was haunted would be right, and the grief would move away from the real child – Ian chortling over the adventures of Herbie; Ian wearing this muddy yellow windbreaker; Ian racing these matchbox cars across the kitchen floor and banging them into the baseboards and leaving them for somebody to fall on – the real child who would never do these real things again. The grief would have become symbolic and symbolized, once removed, demanding more and more nourishment to keep itself going.

'I'm starting to heal,' she said to Jeff. 'My God, I can feel it happening.'

'I love you, Renata,' Jeffrey said.

'Is that okay? That I'm starting to heal?'

'Yes,' he said. Gravely, she nodded.

In the end, she put aside only a few things. Maybe later she'd wish she'd kept something else; maybe the reasons for keeping these particular items would be lost. She thought about them as carefully as her disheveled mind would allow, and, to fix them in place, she told Jeff:

The yellow windbreaker. 'He was wearing it the last time I saw him. The last time I saw him alive.' Protracted shudders were triggered by the shape of these sentences in her mouth, but she

114

went on anyway. 'He wore it a lot the last year or so.' Jeff nodded and looked at the crumpled little garment with a certain fondness of his own. 'Oh, but maybe that's wrong, because he was already growing out of it, the sleeves were already too short, maybe it's wrong to keep something forever to remember him by that didn't really fit him.' If Jeff had told her it was indeed the wrong thing, or if he'd presumed to suggest a substitute, she'd have been horrified. If he'd told her it was fine, it didn't matter whether the jacket had fit or not, she'd have suspected he was trying to rush her, losing patience. If he'd said there was no right or wrong here, she'd have known he didn't understand, because there was.

She was not the first mother to have stood paralyzed with her dead child's possessions in her hands. She would not be the last.

Mary Shelley had lost all but one of her children, not to mention her husband, before she was thirty, and she'd lived many more years without than with them; legend had it that she'd kept Percy's heart in a box beside her bed, but Renata had never read what she'd kept of her children.

Mary Todd Lincoln had clutched her dead son's cap to her breast while she'd paced the White House hallways, ghostly herself late at night, deepening her husband's grief.

And she knew, would soon know, the story of someone named Willa. She didn't understand how it was that these stories were being revealed to her, nor the underworld accessed through the bloody tunnel, but their reality was no more questionable than the central fact of her existence: *Ian is dead.*

Renata shook herself out of the intense reverie that had overtaken her. The sensation remained, though: another story of terrible loss strung on a long line of such stories, which she could grasp to inch her way along.

Jeffrey made no comment. He waited with her. 'I'll keep it,' she said in a rush, and he waited a beat or two more, then respectfully folded the jacket and put it in the box. 'I'll wash it,' she explained, talking too loudly and too fast, making gestures too broad with her hands. 'I'm allowed to wash it.'

A smallish Junior Bear, this one predominantly white with black ears and a black nose like a polar bear. She buried her face in it. It smelled only of plush, not of Ian. There were five Junior

Bears in his room, two of them enormous. The big ones were especially appealing, and in a sudden burst of hyper-clarity she considered keeping one of those, rejected the impulse because of how awkward it would be to store a toy that size, how hard to keep it clean. And there wasn't any reason to think that he had liked the big ones best.

She would keep this small one. Or that one, mostly black with a white mask and vest. Which one? She held them both at arm's length, then in against her, immobilized by the sorrow of having to choose one of them to keep, having to choose any of them.

'This one.' Without looking, she gave one of the bears to Jeffrey and consigned the other to the giveaway jumble on the floor.

He nodded and smiled. He didn't drop the bear into the box like the inanimate object it was, but set it very carefully upright.

'I love you,' she told him, shocked to be feeling such a thing, shocked to be saying it.

She froze in place while a thought played itself out, clear and bright in her mind: She would think of this grief as a tribute to Ian, however hard it was, however long it took. Healing would be a tribute to Ian, too.

Matchbox cars. Not so many when Jeff had gathered them from all their hiding places, deliberate and offhand – under the dresser, in the bedclothes, inside shoes, lined up in a miniature traffic jam across the top of the door frame (What had he climbed on to get them up there? That wasn't safe. Had he been looking at them when he died?). It took Jeff a while to arrange them for her in the lid of a box, and fondly Renata watched him act out the same small-boy impulse Ian would have had.

'Okay,' he said, with satisfaction, and she started to get up to go survey them and could not. Could not get up. Could not bring herself to look at her dead son's cars. Bent over with pain. Didn't cry. Didn't make any noise that she knew of. But couldn't move for a long time.

Jeff rubbed her back. 'Whenever you're ready,' he told her gently. He didn't say, 'You don't have to do this,' because he knew she did. He didn't say, 'Come on, I'll help you,' because he couldn't. He said, 'Whenever you're ready, I'll be right beside you,' and eventually she was able to straighten her body and strengthen her legs enough to walk the four steps to the box lid and look down on all Ian's cars.

She wished she knew which had been his favorites. That would have changed from day to day and mood to mood. She wished she knew which had been his favorites when he died, as if that moment in freeze-frame had more significance than any other moment in his life. The truth was, she would never know. It was important to act on the truth. So she chose two cars, not knowing for more than a few seconds what color or make they were, and passed them to Jeff to put in the memento box.

And his rock collection. When Jeff handed her the oatmeal box almost full of stones, Renata knew right away that she would keep it, and she knew why. Not because of any strong association with her son; Ian had collected all sorts of things at one time or another, like a lot of little boys, but none with any particular fervor or dedication.

Not because of any interest of her own intrinsic to the rocks themselves, though she liked rocks, too, liked to learn about their geologic features, liked their shape and weight in her hand; when she poured Ian's rocks out onto the floor, she found them generally uninteresting and was ashamed, was briefly frantic to know what had been in his mind when he made each specific choice, and never would know. Other than a few bits of quartz, a few flecks of shiny mica in otherwise dull gray, and one faint ovoid depression that maybe could have been a fossil footprint in a slab of shale that would have been about as big as his small hand, she couldn't find anything about these rocks that would have caught his attention.

But she recognized an incipient ritual, and that she would need a ritual. Something small, simple, private. She would keep his rock collection on her desk, and every year on March 18 she would add one more rock to it. Not necessarily a rock Ian might have chosen – there was no way to guess at that – but something she liked, a conglomerate with an interesting array of shapes, quartz with a rose streak through it, a tiny octagonal pebble. One every year for the rest of her life – why? In memory of Ian? She didn't need anything tangible to remember Ian. To mark the passage of time? She doubted there would be any impulse to count the years without him. To commemorate his life or his death? She didn't know why. But she told Jeffrey, 'I'll keep his rocks,' and he held the box for her while she gathered them up. He knew not to touch them. She didn't know why she wouldn't have wanted him to touch them, and she didn't know how he knew that, but he was right.

The sound of the rocks tumbling into the cylindrical cardboard box – clunking against the bottom, thumping and clattering on top of each other, ricocheting briefly from the sides – was so intensely aversive that she thought she would not be able to bear it. But when it stopped there was no echo, and she wished terribly that there would be.

Her focus, though, had slipped. Incredibly, she was distracted. Jeffrey wasn't with her anymore. She must have kissed him goodbye. She must have thanked him. She was in the company now of the woman named Willa, in another time and place.

Chapter 11

A gaunt brown New Mexico jackrabbit hopped through the bear grass and mesquite on the other side of the fence row, its camouflage ruined by the sun that turned the points of its fur golden. Willa paused in the cramping rhythm of her fist up and down the rub-board, forced her fingers to straighten in the hot soapy water, and watched the rabbit until she couldn't see it anymore. Then she countered the small pleasure by reminding herself that who knew what would live out this next fall to see 1930, rabbit or child or Willa herself?

Her husband Clarence, her son Frederic and her sister Mattie's twin girls would be home any minute, expecting supper. The twins were seventeen now, the age Betty would have been.

Willa scrubbed again at Clarence's heavy coveralls and in her mind re-counted the roasting ears she'd picked this morning before she'd known the twins were coming. Two more mouths to feed for the week. There'd be enough, she decided again, uneasily. If Grace were alive, she'd have sent her to the field to pick half a dozen more, just to be on the safe side. But Grace had been dead a year.

The sun was slanting lower, the dusty air of the high plains summer a little bit less hot. Willa lifted the sopping coveralls out of the water and held them up to the sun, frowning, her shoulder muscles straining. Might be she'd have to boil them with the whites to get them clean.

She scowled and shook her head. Not this time. He could wear them the way they were. They'd just get filthy again anyway. At least Grace's shift, which her mother washed every week only to fold back under her own underthings, didn't get dirty. At least Betty's nightgown stayed its faded blue. Guilt over the things she did wash

119

and the things she wouldn't made Willa welcome the stinging of the lye across her scraped knuckles.

The shade of the peach tree – though better than that of the cherry, which was the only other tree on the place – was too sparse to protect much from either the blazing afternoon sun or the storm gathering on the northern horizon. A sheer edge of gray-blue-black across the otherwise cloudless sky, the storm was building fast and moving this way fast. If Clarence and Frederic and the cousins didn't get here in the next few minutes, she'd have to gather two or three tow-sacks of cow chips herself. Deliberately she thought of rattlesnakes, whose protective coloration wouldn't be spoiled by sunshine; some might still be shedding their skins, blind and irritable, striking at anything, jackrabbits or human beings, whether or not you meant them harm.

They'd wanted her to go with them, swimming at the dam. At least, Frederic and the cousins had; Clarence had just stood there, as was his habit now. Willa had snapped, 'There's work to do around here. Somebody has to stay home and do it,' which was true but wasn't the whole truth.

The rest of it was that she looked forward to the rare peace of a few hours by herself, even admitting the price of such peace: Two daughters dead. A husband with whom she'd exchanged barely a civil word in twenty years. A barren little homestead shack in the middle of the barren New Mexico prairie, with nothing from here to Fort Sumner but rattlesnakes and mesquite and her brother Elmer's homestead shack on the other side of the barbed wire fence.

She and Elmer never had gotten along. 'But, Mama, I don't want to go all the way out there with Elmer! I want to go to the Normal and be a teacher!'

'Why, Willie, what are you saying? It's your Papa's desire.'

Twice on the long dusty train ride she'd actually gotten off the train and stood on the platforms of towns whose names she'd sworn she'd never forget but had, thinking she would not do this, surely Papa's desire couldn't reach this far. Finally, both times, at the very last 'All aboard!' she'd climbed back on and sat turned from the window so as not to see the landscape sliding by, changing its skin like a rattlesnake in spring.

Back wrenching now from twenty-one years of daily wash, the

more tiring the heavier she grew and she grew heavier by the season, Willa wrestled the heavy coveralls into the rinse water and wiped sweat and soap off her forehead with the back of her wrist. Though she took care not to get soap in her eyes, just the smell of it made them water. She used the puncher to stir the coveralls. Then, grunting, she lifted them again to hang them over the fence, the barbs scratching her fingers before they finally pushed through and secured the thick rough cloth.

The wash water was still just hot enough, she decided; at least she would be spared one more trip with the heavy black kettle from the kitchen stove. Hastily, she bundled one of Frederic's gray shirts into the tub and thrust at it with the puncher, harder and harder till the bitter water splashed on her, wetting the front of her dress. Even then she didn't stop, for she was suddenly enraged by the memory of how Grace had done that when she was twelve.

Poking with the puncher so fiercely that the precious water sloshed, Gracie had cried because the work was so hard, she hated her life. Then she'd cried because the soap had stung her eyes. Then she'd cried because her mother had slapped her for wasting hot water and to teach her that a woman's tears in this life were nothing but another waste. 'You better get used to it, girlie. You'll be doing it the rest of your life, till you're so old your children have to do it for you.'

When Gracie'd wiped at the red slap mark, soapsuds had streaked her cheek like caustic tears. 'Oh, Mama,' she'd whispered in a rare fit of insolence, 'why didn't you get off that train?' Less than a year later she'd been crumpled on the hard red ground like a corn husk, pushed off the windmill platform when the becalmed big blades had suddenly started moving in a gust of wind you couldn't even feel down below. Willa wondered sometimes if Grace might have fallen off the windmill on purpose, so she wouldn't have to do the wash.

Thinking she heard voices, shouts, from the direction of the dam, she shielded her eyes with a wet lye-smelling hand and gazed off across the prairie. She didn't see anybody. As usual, her yearning for a break in the flatness came strong and hard; a mesa, she wished for, like the one behind Mattie's house near Albuquerque, or a break of cottonwoods. From the other side of the house she'd be able to see the rise with the two scrub pines forever coming down it like marching figures. Strangers, and threatening, for all that they'd always been there and likely always would. When Grace was a little girl she'd been afraid of those trees. That still made Willa mad. A woman didn't dare give in to foolish fears when there were plenty of real things to be afraid of, and so she'd set about mocking the fear out of her daughter. All along, Grace had been right, which didn't mean Willa hadn't been right to try to knock it out of her. She should have tried harder.

She saw movement. Flickering, between sky and ground, but she didn't think it was really as far away as the horizon. A flash of silver and of shiny brown. Diamonds and curves going on and on.

A ghost, she thought against her will, and chilled in the hot afternoon. Grace's ghost. Betty's ghost. Frederic's ghost, though he wasn't dead yet. *Ian's ghost.* She didn't know anybody named Ian, wasn't even sure it was a name.

It wasn't a ghost. A huge rattler had risen out of the prairie, out of the storm. Willa sucked in her breath and clutched her son's dripping shirt to her, not caring that she was getting soaked. The snake's rippling back broke the flatness of the prairie and brought color to it. Its rattling was part of the storm, or it was bringing the storm, or keeping it away.

The first raindrops struck the back of her neck. She put her hand there, but otherwise she didn't move. The snake was coiling up higher and higher, and she could see through its body. The things she saw she barely had names for: tall shiny clustered buildings reflecting a sunset and then reflecting the sunset again from each other, reflecting a child's face distorted in death and a mother's glowing tears; a country of so much moisture that it floated, a wide fast deep river on one edge and water oozing from ground and sky; rooms carved into sheer red rock, walls covered with paintings and carvings of gods taking human children for their own. Then the snake was gone.

For a long time she'd known she was crazy. In a way, she was proud of that. Raindrops struck her face now like individual cold fires.

Frederic's shirt was as clean as it was likely to get. The stubborn dirt angered Willa, just one of the things in life that she couldn't do anything about. As she lifted the shirt onto the fence, she heard the voices of the swimmers again, louder than they should have been all this way. And harsh, as if something was wrong. She could almost hear words. In fact, she thought she kept hearing her son's name.

That frightened her, and she stood still for a minute to catch her breath, wasting precious time as the stormclouds took up more and more of the sky, her heart beating painfully in her throat. She was convinced something terrible was about to happen, but she knew she couldn't trust her own instincts. Fear had become her way of life in this place, and, anyway, she'd had no premonitions when Grace had died, or the baby Betty.

A bitter winter morning. Snow that had blown in the cracks of the house days earlier still white on the floor. Betty dead in the bed between them, with no warning. No cause or reason, either, the doctor from town said when he finally got there through the drifts; 'these things just happen sometimes.' Willa had not asked whether she could have suffocated the child; she was a big woman. He hadn't said.

Clarence wouldn't get out of bed, wouldn't let her have her child's body all day long. Since then Willa had not shared a bed with him, sleeping instead with Gracie, a big girl, not enough room on the narrow cot for them both, until Gracie died, too. Since then, for the first time in her life, Willa had been sleeping alone.

'Frederic!' she heard again. Sounds could carry long distances just before a storm, and she also heard Grace's voice raised in complaint, and the baby Betty eternally wailing. Knowing these voices were in her head didn't make her doubt them; for the most part, she just tried to pay them no mind.

She fastened Frederic's shirt as securely onto the fence as she could, hoping the barbs through the collar and shoulders would keep it from blowing away. The wind was already flinging the sleeves at her, whipping her hair across her face and her skirt irritatingly around her ankles.

Bucket by bucket, she dipped the rinse water out of the galvanized tub and carried it to the cherry tree on the other side of the house. The peach tree had been watered from yesterday's rinse. Thunder rumbled. She put her shoulder, hefty but not as agile as before, to the washtub and dumped the water onto the hardpack; it aggravated her every time she had to waste water like that, but lye made it too caustic for any use. The soap-filmed pool would stay there for hours before it soaked in, unless the rain was hard enough to dilute it and wash it away. There'd been no rain for weeks after Grace fell from the windmill, but Willa, hard as she searched, never could find even a trace of her daughter's blood.

Trying to straighten, Willa groaned and pressed her hands to the small of her back. The ache was there all the time now, worsened by her weight. She leaned back against the stiffness and then suddenly found herself giving in to a rare foolish impulse: turned around in a slow circle with her heels scrabbling into the hard gritty dirt and her face lifted to the sky.

To the north, the sky was deep blue-gray, shot through with lightning. She could see sheets of rain, silver and slanting, and feel the freshness of it coming, energy arcing toward her through the dry air.

To the west, south, and east, the sky was still purely blue. Sunshine fell like a curtain, a boundary she had the feeling she could almost see through between one world and another. A lark sang.

Willa gasped. Despite herself and the circumstances of her life, the beauty of the time and place in which she lived made itself known to her. Her cheeks were wet with tears.

She was wasting time, acting the fool. She hardly knew herself. But she lowered her gaze, lifted her arms out from her sides, though they would not go far, and made another slow pivot. She was crying in earnest now: for everything she'd lost and would yet lose, and for the beauty of the world anyway, the wonder. She didn't want ever to stop turning, even though she was getting a little dizzy and feeling more than a little silly.

Each scene she saw as she turned and turned was all by itself, yet clearly connected to every other scene she'd ever noticed and to those she hadn't yet. Each was oddly distorted, too – by the storm, she thought, the way it changed not only the light but the nature of the air; by her spinning head and rotating body; by the fact that she was so tired and mad. Lightning crackled and, right away, thunder boomed. Willa started, wiped her face.

Rain was falling steadily now, and there was almost no blue left in the sky. She hurried to get two empty tow-sacks – no, three, she could manage three – and headed with them to the north pasture closest to the house.

Still some ways away but very clear, Clarence was yelling for Frederic. Bending and scuffing with her toe to find the cow chips in the grass and dirt, worrying about rattlesnakes, Willa listened to him calling and calling. He sounded mad. *About time*, she thought; *he spoils that boy*. The cousins' shriller voices seemed to be coming this way, but there was no chance now that they'd get here ahead of the storm, so it was up to her to save a week's worth of fuel from melting into the ground. Leaving one filled sack in the path she was likely to take back to the house, hoping it wouldn't be too dark to find it by then, she started on the second one. *They better at least get home before it's time to bring the cows in for milking. I can't do everything*.

Her hand brushed against something dry, scaly, soft. She jerked it back. Trying to catch her breath, she bent to see. A small rattler lay in the dirt, half out of its skin. When she nudged it with the sack, it didn't move. Dead. Stuck.

It was raining hard when she struggled back to the house with the three bulging sacks. They weren't heavy, but they bumped against her thighs and made her stumble. She was very aware of her own bulk. She'd come out farther than she'd intended, and the shapes of the homestead were blurred – the four houses made into one house, the windmill spinning so fast it might never stop this time, the two spindly trees and the clothes flapping on the fence and Clarence and the girls running toward her. One of the twins was carrying Frederic's shoes. Clarence told her, 'Frederic drowned.'

'Mother!'

Three days later, Willa was still hearing the cry, although nobody else gave any sign that they did. She hoped she didn't give any sign, either, and she did her best to ignore it; she would never be called by that dangerous, insinuating name again.

The call had first sounded on the day of her son's funeral. Blinding brown earth and flat blue sky so hot it looked white, meeting at a horizon so far away it had nothing to do with her. The windmill picking up speed and then slowing almost to a stop, all day long going faster and then slower and then faster again, making a distant threatening clatter.

Puffy white creature laid out on Frederic's bed, in Frederic's good shirt and pants that she'd scrubbed as clean as she could; her knuckles would sting for days and bleed again when she bent them, and always after that, for the rest of her long life, would stiffen whenever she used them much. The clothes didn't quite fit because he'd grown. No, because the body was swollen with pond water.

This couldn't be her son. It had taken them hours to find the body in the dam pond. Willa had stood on the shore and watched, her hem and shoes getting wet, unable to believe she was doing this thing. In the shade of the cottonwoods around the water, it was a horribly beautiful day, the storm passed. Birds sang. Birds wouldn't sing if her Frederic was dead. Maybe they'd found somebody else's body. She felt sorry for that boy's parents.

Yet she carried the body inside her as if she were pregnant with it, her dead son, her dead daughters floating and swelling in her fluids. She would carry them like that for the rest of her life. She would never let any of them go. When she died, she would be carried like that, as she had been carried before she was born.

Born and unborn, alive and dead, she carried her children: Frederic not yet two and Grace a babe in arms, Betty years from being born and none of them dead yet, none of them dead, Willa'd been alone and had had to carry water from Elmer's well because theirs had gone dry that summer. It was a long ways. Frederic, sick with the croup and just barely steady on his feet anyway, couldn't walk it. Willa couldn't carry both children and the water pails, too. She had to have water. Finally, desperately, she'd left the little boy fitfully asleep by himself and rushed to the well with the baby on her hip, rushed back with the two pails too heavy and sloshing water alarmingly over her skirt and shoes, checked on Frederic, jostled Gracie who was fussing, rushed back the long ways to the well again. On the second trip, halfway between the well and the house, she fell. The baby wailed. One of the buckets tipped over and the wasted water spread fast across the rock-hard ground, soaking her skirt, making her hands and knees slip as she tried to get up. The baby wailed. Back to the well, to the pump that blistered her hands and put a crick in her shoulders as she tried to work it hard and fast without dropping the baby, who was screaming by now. Back to the house with the too-heavy buckets and the too-heavy baby, hearing Frederic crying for her ('Mother!') long before she could get to him, seeing the rattler slither across the road.

The snake hadn't poisoned her son. She hadn't dropped Grace and killed her. She'd protected them both that awful day. And then later, no matter what she did, Grace died, and the baby Betty, too. And now Frederic.

'Corn don't growe,' she wrote home to Rachel Jane, penning the letter on her knees while she sat beside the body that was not her son's, waiting for them to come and take it away. Laid out on her son's bed in her son's good clothes that she never had been able to get really clean and now never would. 'Nothing growes. This land was not ment for things to growe.' Oklahoma was a long ways away, a long time ago.

A man from town came in a wagon to take the body away. Willa didn't try to stop them, but she didn't help, either, the way Clarence and Elmer did. The boy's own father and uncle, carrying Frederic's body past her, out of the house, onto the wagon where the horse snorted and twitched its tail against the flies and a stench rose already in the heat before the body ever got there.

Then there was more waiting. Willa didn't know what for. She imagined them digging the grave in the churchyard in town, imagined it from where she sat by the empty bedside, from the hodgepodge screened porch that never had kept snow or heat or snakes out of the house, from under the thin cherry tree and the windmill dangerously turning, dangerously stopping. Mere shovels would not persuade the ground to open the required six feet, so they'd have to use picks, the blows ringing out.

Willa was sick with grief. 'I have felt puerly,' she wrote to Rachel Jane, but didn't say why. Her vomit stained the crust on the ground before it finally sank in, to travel eventually into the roots of the scraggly corn, or evaporate into the air that all of them had no choice but to breathe.

'Mother!'

The cry came from some secret place. Against her will, her head jerked up in acknowledgment, and she listened through the ringing in her ears. She heard nothing now but two bitter notes of a birdsong, repeated twice. It wasn't a song she recognized, but that didn't mean anything. This was not a message from her dead son. Resentfully, she saw Clarence – sitting in the direct sun with his back to the house – raise his head to listen as if it might be.

On purpose she wrapped her hand around the barbed wire of the fence, because Clarence, the father of her dead children, had no right. The pain was hers. The craziness was hers. Her hand bled a little but didn't hurt. It ought to hurt. 'Mother!' Apparently Clarence didn't hear that, which gave Willa some satisfaction.

The cry was not the voice of her son, either, nor of either of her daughters. Could not be. But she stumbled back inside to stare at the place where the bloated body had been, still so recognizable as Frederic though she'd tried to convince herself it didn't look a thing like him, couldn't be him. Now that she was back inside the house, she could tell the call was coming from outside, but she was too weary to go looking. *Outside* meant anywhere in the whole huge world. All the way to Fort Sumner. All the way to Albuquerque where the insane asylum was, or Denver.

Outside also meant the past and the future, her own and everybody else's. Willa tried to think that the past and the future had nothing to do with her anymore, but the truth was she was in a tunnel that went both backward and forward, and the clear cry, 'Mother!' came from somewhere along it. If you did nothing else, you had to face the truth.

She got into the buckboard when Clarence and Elmer said to, and they rode the nine miles into town in silence; she had nothing to say to them. The brown church still looked raw and new compared to the ones she remembered from back east, but her other children were buried here, too, and she walked right to the place.

People came. Willa didn't know how people knew to come. She stared at them and wished them all dead where they lined up around her son's grave.

A minister she hadn't seen before did the service. At least, he claimed to be a minister. Willa doubted that in the same way she doubted the reality of her own feet on the ground that would leave no footprints, the body of her son in the coffin. She never did hear the so-called minister's name. The words he spoke over Frederic she might as well never have heard before, for all they meant to her. His voice was a steady drone. *He* hadn't lost *his* child.

Later, she would carefully cut out and save the obituary the so-called minister wrote for the Fort Sumner paper: 'Died, May 28, 1929, son of Clarence Stearns and his wife.' He'd obviously forgotten both her name and Frederic's, or hadn't thought them worth including in the announcement.

The minister stopped talking. Eighteen years of a life he didn't know anything about, and he'd run out of things to say about it in minutes. Clarence, Elmer, Mr Malick, and Mr George bent to hoist the coffin. Clarence stumbled. Rage at him sent Willa stumbling, too. Her son was in that box, the dead body of her son in the good clothes not washed quite clean.

The men lowered Frederic's full coffin into his grave. Clarence backed away, holding his hands in front of him in a queer way. *Let him go*, Willa thought fiercely. *Let him just go*. The minister (he claimed to be a minister; he claimed that her son was dead) was talking again.

Willa collapsed. It seemed to her that she lay for a long time on the hardpack dirt of the churchyard, eyes dry and fixed open, body flinching skinlessly when the dusty wind bit. Right past her face a very faint wriggling line had been etched in the dirt.

Christina Malick knelt beside her, stroked her tangled hair, put hands under her elbows to urge her to her feet. 'You must get up, Missus. You cannot stay here.' Willa didn't see why not.

Mrs Malick kept talking, softly and quickly, urgently; Willa thought it must be in German, since she didn't understand another word of it. Finally the other woman put her arms around Willa and lifted her; the warmth and closeness of her sturdy body loosened the pain in Willa's chest, for a moment made it seem bearable, which of course it was not.

Frederic is dead Grace is dead Betty is dead Ian.

'Mother!'

A huge rattlesnake stretched among the bear grass on the far side of Frederic's new grave. Through the shimmer of heat and tears she couldn't tell how far away or how big the serpent was, but she'd have said it made the horizon, for above it was blue sky and under it was yellow-brown earth.

Diamond shapes along the thing's back glowed black and dark brown on lighter brown. The patterns and the outline of the sinuous body itself were blurred here and there, especially toward the tail, and Willa realized with a start that those blurs were layers of dead skin, translucent and almost colorless, and that the new skin of the snake was shiny like the skin of a newborn babe.

At the tail were the rattles. Big as her fist, they looked. They weren't shaking now or making any noise, but she knew that at any minute they would.

The other end of the creature was a head bigger than her own. The snake had fangs; Willa could see white poison dripping from them like mother's milk. The snake had eyes.

It could not, of course, really be there. But then, Frederic and Grace and Betty could not, of course, really be dead, either. The snake moved, causing the horizon to ripple.

In a distant sort of way, Willa was terrified. Vaguely, too, she felt foolish being afraid of anything now that the worst she could ever have imagined had happened. Had happened three times.

Deliberately, she tried to picture what a rattlesnake this size could do. Its fangs and their poison: hot puncturing pain, and then a swift numbness that paralyzed you so all you could do was stand there and wait for it to finish you off, stare death in its scaly, slit-eyed face and wait. Which, really, was what everybody did every day of their lives; most people just didn't know it. Most people were fools.

Deliberately, she tried to picture the serpent's gaping mouth, and herself being sucked in. Being swallowed whole into the body that was not much more than an elongated throat, by contractions not that different from labor pains in reverse. Dissolving in the body fluids of the beast, becoming a smaller and smaller lump as she was used by the snake, which was a long dark wet tunnel, a conduit, a passageway.

But none of that was very clear in her imagination. Willa had no doubt that the snake and the danger were real, at least as 'real' as the terrible sun and the terrible blue sky and the bitter two-note birdsong punctuating the hymns sung by this pitiful handful of mourners on this vast empty plain. But the snake and its very real danger didn't matter to her any more than the rest of it did. The only reality that

130

mattered, that would ever matter, was that her children were dead
Frederic Grace Betty Ian Justine Stone
  'Mother!'
  Nobody else heard the cry, either, and for her part Willa ignored
it. It had nothing to do with her.
  Now men were trying to fill in Frederic's grave. She winced when
a clod thumped and rattled across the lid of her child's coffin. She
heard her own hoarse cry, and, now just starting, the ominous buzz
of the giant snake's rattles. All from a vast distance. All from a
place so deep inside herself that she'd never known it was there.
  'Mrs Stearns?'
  Willa straightened and managed to turn around without falling.
A woman her own age and build and coloring stood there, a
stranger.
  'My name is Belinda. I've come to tell you how sorry I am that
your children have died.'
  'Thank you,' Willa said automatically, certain she would faint.
  'Frederic,' the woman said calmly. At the sound of her dead son's
name from someone else's lips, Willa thought of the snake's piercing
poisonous fangs. 'Betty. Grace. Ian.'
  Willa stood very straight and still. She would not give in to
hysteria in front of this stranger, who was on purpose making the
pain worse.
  The woman held out her hands. Over this stranger's shoulder,
Willa saw that the horizon was as empty now as it had always
been, blue sky above and barren gold-brown dirt below, the rattler
gone again. She must have accepted Belinda's hands, because now
they were in her own, neither smaller nor larger, neither weaker nor
stronger. Delicate skin scales came off into her own skin, but it was
a steadying grip. Willa didn't think it right that she be steadied, but
Belinda wouldn't let go.
  They stood there together for what seemed a long time, Willa
and this woman who looked so much like her. She didn't know
where Belinda could have come from. It would have been hard for
her either to have mingled unnoticed with the group of mourners,
which was as sparse and gave as little shelter as the shade of the
fruit trees by the house, or to have come across the open prairie
unseen.

Willa managed to say, 'Thank you' again, and Belinda nodded. Willa felt her own head bob and, concentrating fiercely, stopped it.

Clarence and Elmer and the others were coming toward her now.

Quickly, quietly, Belinda said to her, 'Two things I know. How much pain there can be in a person's life, and what a miracle it is to heal.'

'*Heal*?' Willa thought she must be shrieking the insulting word. Then she thought it was too obscene for her to say at all. Belinda's grip on her hands, hers on Belinda's, hurt. 'You don't know what you're saying! How can I heal from this? Why should I? All my children are dead!'

'I do know,' Belinda insisted. 'All my children die, too.'

Only a few steps away, Clarence said, 'Oh, Willa!' and reached for her, and Willa broke and ran.

She had run all the way home, through the clear heat, through the shimmering glare of panic and grief, through the bear grass that had cut her ankles. She'd stumbled over holes and lumps and ridges made by prairie dogs, made by rattlesnakes, made by the frantic footsteps of parents for years and years searching for their lost children.

She had fallen many times. 'Mother!' she'd heard, whether she had fallen or not. She hadn't understood why nobody came after her; they could have caught her easily in the wagons or on a horse. She hadn't known where Belinda was, or the gigantic snake, or any of her children.

When she'd reached the homestead shack, the afternoon sun had been shining full into her eyes from over the ridge where Grace's trees marched, and the two-note birdsong had been sounding rhythmically from somewhere out there and from somewhere inside her because there'd been no distinction anymore: 'Mother! Mother!' She'd stumbled into the empty, windblown house and locked the door.

Now it was two days later. Frederic had been buried two days. *Frederic, buried.* Willa paced through the unfriendly, hodgepodge house, from one to another of the four rooms that should have stayed unconnected, but were fastened clumsily like people who had no business being together.

The door was locked. On some of her pacings past it she must have moved things in front of it, because chairs and a table and the two big cast iron kettles and Frederic's bed (*no use for it anymore no use for anything Frederic is dead*) were piled against it. The door was locked and barricaded to keep Clarence out, and there was hardly anything left in any of the four rooms except dust; there hadn't been much to start with.

Clarence came to the window in the south room. 'Let me in!' She could hear him through the glass and dust. She put her hands over her ears and backed away, but she could still hear him. 'Willa! You're acting crazy! I'll get the sheriff! Willa!'

'*Mother!*'

Papa, she thought suddenly, and knew what she'd been hearing.

Her father, Thomas Beals, a frightened and weary young man in the Oklahoma wilderness long before Willa or any of the others was born. (There'd been two before Elmer who'd died on the trip west, two whose names were never spoken in the household but which Willa had discovered: Elizabeth and Samuel. *Frederic Elizabeth Grace Betty Carla Ian Samuel.*)

Her father, not yet her father, standing by the doorway of his dusty and cold little shack. Her father the lost child. Thomas, staring eastward and calling out, not to God, but to his mother whom he'd left without a word when he was fourteen, who might well have believed for the rest of her life that her son was dead. Calling out across the prairie for comfort: '*Mother!*'

Willa longed to be the one who answered. But it was too late for that. She thought she heard a dim rattle, clearly heard the woman Belinda's voice. 'Let him in, Willa. Let him in.'

Clarence had gone from the window and was banging on the door again, shouting her name and cursing. Willa backed as far away as she could get, against the east-end wall, which wasn't very far, and did not answer. Never again would she answer.

Then the storm that had been gathering for days, since the afternoon Frederic drowned in the dam pond, broke at last. Lightning lit up the prairie, throwing its barrenness into barren relief. Thunder shook flat sky and flat land, warping them to its purposes. Rain drove through chinks in the walls and roof into the homestead house, which in the flashing metallic light stretched and narrowed into a tunnel.

Clarence had left, fleeing the storm, but somebody else was in the tunnel-house with her. A woman. Reaching for and missing her hand. Both of them crying. 'Do you know why my son is dead?' the woman pleaded. 'Do you know why Ian died?' But Willa, of course, did not.

Chapter 12

Renata was sleeping through the night, and not dreaming about Ian. But then every new day, forty-six, forty-nine, fifty-one of them since Ian had died, required her to wake up. This morning there had been a very long transition between sleeping and waking, awareness gathering and gathering and gathering that Ian had died, Ian was dead, she would never see Ian again. Even now, the awareness continued to accumulate; even now, she didn't think she was fully awake.

She remembered the other women's stories – not details; not names or circumstances; only that there were stories other than her own – but now she didn't believe them. Maybe this had happened to countless other women and men throughout human history and would happen to countless more, but she and Glenn and Ian were the only ones who mattered. Maybe there was a tunnel leading to another dimension, but Ian had died there, too, so of what use was it? And she wasn't in the tunnel now.

Crying in Glenn's arms again, bright spring sunshine in the kitchen making rainbows through the prisms in the window, Renata knew then that she would kill herself.

Did not know, though, that she would say so to her husband, who had already lost a son and now would lose his wife, too: 'I can't stand this! I can't live with this! I want to die!' She didn't quite say, 'I'm going to die. I'm going to kill myself,' but he would know. She intended him to know.

He had been crying. His eyes were red and the skin around them stretched taut. He held her – but not too tightly; not tightly enough – and said, 'It won't always be this bad,' as if he were counseling an impulsive adolescent: This, too, shall pass. Suicide is a permanent solution to a temporary problem.

She railed at him. 'How do you know that? You haven't been through this before, either. How can it not always be this bad? This isn't a temporary problem. Ian will always be dead.'

Maybe it was a cruel thing to say to him. After her child's death, Renata had no standard for judging other events – all of which were fundamentally insignificant – as kind or unkind, wise or foolish, sane or crazy. If saying such a thing to Glenn would make him hate her and agree that she ought to kill herself, so much the better.

Her head was spinning, but she didn't lose consciousness. Her stomach was roiling and her skin clammy, but she didn't throw up. There would be no easy escape.

He didn't say anything. He didn't stiffen or collapse against her. It was conceivable that he hadn't heard her. It was conceivable that she hadn't spoken aloud. It was conceivable that they were not in their kitchen talking about the death of their son. It was, however, not conceivable that Ian was still alive; Ian dead was the single thing she was sure of.

She had sunk onto the floor between his knees. Now his hands were only on the back of her head, and slipping off. She sobbed, 'I don't want to live anymore.'

'You have to.'

'No, I don't have to! I can die! I can kill myself! Ian did!'

'You don't have a right to do that.'

'Did he? Did he have a right?' She was probably shrieking, although it was hard to tell.

'Renata, he was nine years old.'

'You think I don't know that? You think I don't know how old my own son was when he killed himself?' She covered her mouth with her fists. Glenn was just sitting there. He wasn't crying; he wasn't outraged, as he should have been.

'I'm sorry,' she breathed, and it wasn't that she didn't mean it but that regretting anything other than Ian's death seemed specious. 'It's my life,' she said. 'I don't have anything to live for anymore.'

'You have us. You have me and you have your other children.'

'And I'll lose all of you! You'll all die! Why should I live for that?'

'We need you. Vanessa and Tim especially need you. Vanessa especially.'

'I let their little brother die. They don't need me. I'm dangerous to them. They need a mother who can keep her children safe, like mothers are supposed to do. I let him die. I killed him, somehow. I—'

'Renata. Stop it.'

His anger frightened and angered her. She scuttled backward across the floor, which was sticky in places and gritty although she thought she'd mopped it just yesterday.

He bent and reached for her, but it seemed critical to avoid contact with him now, and she backed up until her shoulder was against the stove. Gypsy whimpered and moved just enough to press herself against her thigh again. 'I can't stand this pain. I can't. And I don't have to.'

'Please. Renata.' He rested his forehead on the heels of his hands. She ought to comfort him. The impulse to comfort him was sharp, for she was his wife, but it was also quick and easy to deny, because she knew her comfort would be poisonous, her love lethal.

Fine. I won't say anything more about it. But I'll do it. I'll kill myself, and they'll all be better off.

It was not, though, a need to die. It was a need not to be alive. Not to take part in a world in which nine-year-old boys could die, could kill themselves, could hang themselves. She couldn't breathe. That was fine. She would suffocate. She couldn't breathe. She fought to breathe. She didn't want to live, but her body would not give up its breath.

'You lost him, too!' she shouted, and her breath flooded back to support these awful things she should not be saying. 'How can you want to live, either?'

Enunciating carefully, Glenn said. 'The rest of my life is all around me. You and Vanessa and Tim and the writing and all the rest of it. It's not a matter of rebuilding, or starting over. All I have to do is reach out and touch the rest of my life. And I'm going to.'

Beginnings and ends of scenes were vague to her now, and she didn't know where she was, then realized she was still in the kitchen but alone now, didn't know where Glenn and Vanessa were. Then remembered that Vanessa had gone to school; they'd had breakfast together, Renata refusing the easy relinquishment of routine that would have become its own neglectful routine if she'd let her daughter go to school for breakfast. She could not remember a single detail of the meal, which, according to the clock, had taken place less than an hour ago. On the stove was a pan with congealed oatmeal in it; they must have had oatmeal. It seemed to her that one of the kids didn't like oatmeal, but she couldn't remember which one; she could only hope, distantly, that it wasn't Vanessa. It seemed to her that this was important and she ought to make more of an effort, but she didn't. She couldn't remember what Vanessa had been wearing this morning; if she came up missing and the police asked for a description of what she'd been wearing the last time her mother had seen her alive, Renata wouldn't be able to say. She'd have to make something up, so the police wouldn't know how negligent she'd been with this child, too. She couldn't remember whether Vanessa had combed her hair, brushed her teeth, cried, kissed her goodbye, taken her homework or her lunch. Not only had she lost her son; she was losing her daughter, breakfast by breakfast, day by day. That seemed only fitting.

It came to her that she was going to work today. It was not her first day back; the first day back had been no more or less a milestone than every day since.

As much as possible without looking in a mirror, she inspected herself, and she seemed to be dressed for work. The idea of caring what she looked like – presenting a professional image, coordinating pantyhose with skirt and earrings with blouse, gauging how dressed up she should be by what meetings she had today with whom – was ludicrous, offensive. She thought she had combed her hair. She thought she had brushed her teeth.

She found her purse and briefcase, although she had no idea what was in them and no way of finding out. She couldn't figure out how to know whether she'd need a coat, so she didn't get one, then waited some more. She was waiting for Glenn to drive her to work, because she was afraid to take the bus.

They went out into the May air. As they walked across the frosty yard, equal parts green and brown, she saw in some alarm their shadows, fuzzy and flat because the sun was still low in the sky, it being morning and spring. They went through the back gate, which stuck, as always, and which Renata wouldn't have been able to open and close by herself though it wasn't that hard. She stood in the bright cracked alley by the trash cans, where someone – she – was required to bring the kitchen trash on Monday mornings – an impossibly complex assignment – and she waited while Glenn unlocked and raised the garage door; her flesh crawled with the anxiety of waiting.

He pulled the car out. She got into the car. Out of long habit she fastened her seatbelt; once she realized what she'd done, she would have unfastened it again if it hadn't been for Glenn, who would have noticed and objected.

They drove along streets where other vehicles traveled. They passed the fire station. They passed the convenience store at 18th, and she distinctly heard her son say the line that had, in the few weeks before his death, become a funny little family in-joke because he'd said it every time in the same wry tone, half under his breath so you had to collude in the mischief by anticipating what he'd say or you'd miss it, 'There Mini-Mart is.'

Glenn pulled into the parking lot behind her building. Renata sat there. After a while, Glenn asked, 'Should I come in with you?' There didn't seem to be an answer to that. She got out and shut the door. He started to pull away, and she realized in sheer panic that she didn't know whether she'd kissed him goodbye. She managed not to scream after him, but she waved wildly, and he stopped, and somehow she maneuvered the long sequence of individual and cumulative motions required to get to his side of the car, signal him to roll down the window, lean inside, kiss him and say she loved him. She would kill herself, very soon.

The student at the front desk chirped, 'Good morning, Renata. How are you this morning?' It seemed an impudent query, sarcastic and unkind. Seething, Renata barely replied. She took messages out of her box on the desk but didn't even look at them, knowing she wouldn't be able to decipher them.

It was not a long trek from the front door of the office complex to her own office, but the fluorescent lights flickered and buzzed sickeningly, the white walls pulsed, the gray carpet rose and fell and had inscrutable patterns in it, and she had too much to carry. She needed Theresa. If she could make it to Theresa she might be okay, until she killed herself. She wouldn't have to be okay for very long.

Theresa said very gently, 'Good morning, Renata,' and Renata grabbed the file cabinet to keep from fainting until her head cleared enough – a very slight thinning of the black fog – that she could edge herself around the corner of the door cut into the partition that didn't quite reach the ceiling and therefore didn't sound or feel like a real wall, and then around the sharp corner of her desk and then into her chair, which, on wheels, swiveled in arcs she couldn't possibly have anticipated.

Theresa wheeled her own chair back against the wall and tipped it so she could look through Renata's doorway. 'Can I get you a cup of coffee?'

'No. Thanks. My stomach's a little upset.'

Theresa nodded. She gazed at Renata a second or two longer, then disappeared from her view, presumably to go back to her work.

The opportunity to be served a cup of coffee apparently lost forever, Renata suffered a long moment's acute sorrow and frantic second-guessing: She should have accepted. Coffee might have tasted okay; the warmth of it might have eased her throat. It might have been nice to be waited on. Now that she'd refused, Theresa might hate her, might never offer her anything again, and she would need things though she couldn't think what. She calmed herself by reasserting that it didn't matter, nothing mattered, she wouldn't need anything from anybody much longer, including good will.

She sat at her desk and tried to decide what to do first. Her attention didn't focus directly on having lost Ian, but the mental quicksand also swallowed every other thought, allowing her only a glimpse before pulling it under. Everything was brown and heavy and thick. She tried to decide what to do first.

At last she settled on the scatter of messages. She read through them, some only once, some several times, some in an endless repetitive loop that she could break only randomly and with extreme conscious effort.

Finding that in some cases she knew how to respond, she responded: Another copy of the budget report routed to her boss, the report prepared – fortunately, appallingly – before Ian had died. The day of the weekly staff meeting changed from Tuesday to Wednesday, which necessitated other changes in her datebook as well; she was horrifyingly tempted to turn the pages back to before

March 18, just to see what it would feel like to look at the record of events that had taken place while she'd still been Ian's mother.

On the spindle at the corner of her desk, where Theresa and other staff stuck notes for her, was a piece of pink paper with something heavier taped to one end. Renata sat and stared at it, afraid. Then, cautiously, she moved her hand until it came into contact with the object, turned her hand over to grasp it with unwilling fingertips. A Tootsie Roll.

Before Ian died, she'd loved Tootsie Rolls, especially the bite-sized ones like this. Tears welled in her eyes. She removed the pink paper from the spindle and rubbed her eyes clear so she could read the message, in Theresa's erect hand: 'Because I care about you, and I wish I could make the pain easier to bear.' It did, in fact, make the pain easier to bear. Renata could not allow that; she'd already decided to commit suicide because she could not bear the pain. She unwrapped the candy and took it into her mouth. Although she could scarcely taste it, the chewiness of it was comforting. She didn't choke.

Theresa came in to tell her someone was on line one for her, and she realized gratefully that her own phone was still on cover. Ordinarily Theresa would have rung through to tell her, and Renata was also grateful that she hadn't. 'Thank you,' she said to Theresa, and indicated the message on the pink paper, tried and failed to look up, hid her face with the flat of her hand.

Mercifully, Theresa didn't touch her. 'You're welcome,' she said gently.

Renata understood the caller's name and what he was likely to want, though the recognition was delayed. Half a dozen times or more they'd exchanged information about a particularly troublesome student. Would he say anything about Ian? If he did, she wouldn't know what to reply; he was a virtual stranger. If he didn't, she'd feel obliged to bring it up herself, a powerful, principled need not to interact falsely with anyone during these last hours of her life.

Thinking she was going to ask Theresa to take a message or to handle it, instead Renata heard herself say, 'I'll take it.' As long as she worked here, as long as she was alive, it was her job to take it.

He said he was sorry to hear about her son. She said thank you.

That was all, as sufficient as anything could be. She was surprised by how simple it was. They went on to discuss the difficult student.

The morning passed of its own accord, whether Ian was alive or dead, whether Renata did any work or not, whether this was her last morning alive or one in an endless desolate stretch. Students came in with problems about classes; none seemed especially complex, which made her suspect she was missing something, but she did what she was supposed to do.

Many of these people she hadn't seen since she'd come back to work; others she saw virtually every day. Some treated her as though they didn't know who she was now; although that was a reasonable attitude, Renata disliked it. Some treated her as though nothing had happened, as though what they needed – recorded textbooks, untimed exams, an advocate to deal with an instructor who'd made an offhand comment in class to the effect that people with mental illness shouldn't be out in the world – was the only thing worth attending to; her urge to declare, 'Who cares? My son is dead,' was easy enough to circumvent.

A few of the students mumbled awkward sympathy. A few already had and now obviously didn't know if they should say it again. One man she'd always especially liked, an art student paralyzed in a diving accident twenty years ago, had sent a sympathy card. Now, when she mentioned it, he held her gaze longer than she was willing and said again how sorry he was. His aide stood in the background.

Someone asked Theresa about donations. Renata and Glenn had agreed, virtually without need for discussion, on the absurdity of flowers, and he hadn't objected to her suggestion that people send donations to a local adoption agency. But overhearing Theresa now – saying Ian's whole name, spelling it, giving the address to send money to in his honor, explaining why an adoption agency – had such potential for horror that Renata froze and made herself listen carefully and with only the barest of emotions, as though to a weather forecast when she hadn't had any particular plans for the weekend anyway. Being able to do that horrified her even more.

'Renata.'

Renata had some difficulty finding the source of the voice. Ellen Hughes had opened her door enough to poke her head in.

'May I come in?' Renata must have given some sort of assent, or else Ellen came in without it. A heavyset, stylish woman, one of the university attorneys, she had for a time interested Renata as a potential friend, but she'd never made any response to social overtures and, although their paths crossed professionally several times a month, they scarcely knew each other. Now she strode into the office, clearly having decided on a strategy beforehand, and leaned across the desk to take Renata's hands. Shaking them a little to punctuate her words, she said almost crisply, 'I am so sorry about your son.'

The words and touch started tears again. Ellen held onto her hands and made no move either to come closer or to shy away.

'Is there anything I can do?' Not everyone asked that question. Most people who did intended it as rhetorical. Renata understood why. Really, the only thing that would help would be Ian's resurrection – better, the erasure of his death altogether. Suspecting that, people felt dwarfed by the magnitude of the event, afraid their very offer of help would offend and wound, which, in fact, was often the case.

But this time there was something. Afraid she wouldn't be able to say it clearly and quickly enough, Renata gasped, 'I need someplace to go during the day.'

Instantly Ellen assumed an alert, eager manner; problem-solving was her forte. 'When during the day?'

'Over lunch.'

'What do you need it for?' Not prying, only gathering data.

'To cry.' *And maybe that's where I'll kill myself.*

The attorney's expression flickered, but she nodded. 'I'll work on it,' she pledged. 'I'm sure we can come up with something.'

'Thanks.'

'Is there anything else?'

Weeping steadily and making no attempt to hide it, Renata said no. Ellen squeezed her hands once and left.

Lunchtime. Renata was aware of being hungry but the sensation was disconnected from her. She hadn't packed a lunch, of course, and she wasn't up to the demands of going anywhere to buy food, even to the little campus restaurant around the corner, even to the vending machines at the end of the hall. Maybe this was to be the method of her suicide; maybe she could starve herself to death while continuing to go through the motions of her life. There was a certain dull, grim satisfaction in the possibility that she could die without much effort, by omission rather than commission.

Theresa asked, 'Do you have lunch plans?'

Renata said, 'I'll just stay here.' After saying so many words, intended to convey meaning, she was short of breath.

'Can I bring you something?'

'No. Thanks.'

'Are you sure? You have to eat something.'

Renata managed not to say the obvious: 'Why?' She said, 'I can't. Not right now. My stomach's a little upset.'

Theresa stood there for a while longer, hands in her pockets, head cocked sympathetically, and then she wasn't there anymore. Renata hadn't been aware of her leaving and didn't know how long she might be gone.

Very carefully, as though contact with a solid edged object would hurt her – or, worse, as though it wouldn't – Renata performed a series of actions which brought her into relentless sequential contact with solid and edged objects: She pressed the button on the phone that would route her calls to the front desk. She exerted upward pressure against the window so that it closed. She arranged her hands on her desk in such a way that the mitered and chromed edges of it pressed into her palms in two distinct lines. She constricted her thigh muscles so her feet were lifted off the floor. She pushed her chair back until it collided with the wall behind her. She pushed down with her right foot against the floor to pivot her chair to the left. She bent her knees. She leaned far forward. She sank until she was on her hands and knees between the desk and the wall. She lowered herself face-down onto the floor. She lay still.

Almost at once, she was hearing: 'Mother!'

Chapter 13

She had expected to move horizontally back through time. Instead, she traveled vertically, and was under the world again.

Lightning flashed auburn. Wind tore at Renata's breath but couldn't quite capture it intact, tore it apart instead. Rain fell, much of it deflected by the red rock formations that made up this place: slabs arched like backs, flat-fingered slabs and striations like tangled hair, rectangular protrusions held out like sheltering arms under which she could huddle. She could take shelter here if nowhere else.

The sky was gray behind the red rocks, but behind the sky was light. Features had been carved into the rock by wind, rain, ice, the heat of the sun, by plants that had forced in roots and by animals that had scratched and burrowed. Renata opened her fists slightly where they had been folded into the small of her back, and her nails scratched lightly across the surface she leaned against; it flaked, powdered.

Here was a mouthlike orifice, twisted wide open by pain and protest. Renata clambered up on a shifting pile of rubble and stretched until she could press her own mouth against it, taking some of its grit onto her own tongue, adjusting the shape of her own lips to match although the rock-mouth, far bigger, could easily swallow hers. The position expressed anguish solidified, given form.

The stone lips moved in speech. 'Welcome.'

'Where am I?'

'This is the Stone Garden. My name is Daphne. Welcome.'

A faint echoing chorus seeped from all sides, and Renata turned her head to look around. As sunshine began to break painfully through the quivering membrane of cloud cover, she identified dozens of other humanoid shapes formed out of the red rock. Curious and oddly excited, she moved among them, peered into their deep and narrow crevices, rested her hands on their sharp edges and eroded slopes.

Here were half a dozen hands, clawed and open to the sky in endless, pointless supplication. Renata bent her wrists like that, stretched and bent her fingers, and the bones of her hands stopped aching for the first time since Ian had died.

Here was a figure on its metamorphic knees. Its hands had no detail, were only the suggestion of hands clasped behind its bent neck. Its torso made an agonized arch under which Renata herself fell to her knees. She flung her head forward, clasped her hands behind her neck, arched her body in satisfied agony.

'We are all parents whose children have died,' Daphne explained.

Renata nodded. Her body trembled in an ecstasy of belonging.

'We refuse to stop grieving,' Daphne said, 'and so we are turned to stone.'

That seemed right. Here were others like her, and a clear, fixed way to do what she had to do. Sunlight from behind the clouds had brightened to the very verge of breaking through, and out of the diffuse glare more and more of the stone figures organized themselves. The Stone Garden was densely populated, and Renata assured herself, 'I can stay here.'

She struck a pose: Head thrown back and mouth gaped to emit a soundless shriek that would never be forced to quiet because it was made of stone. Arms flung out, palms out, in endless hardened anguish. The cells of her flesh and bone, of her blood, fossilized from the sustained heat and pressure of grieving, and their new weight fastened her in place. She bent backward into an arch, and felt her vertebrae fuse.

Daphne invited her, 'Stay.'

The other statues crowding the Stone Garden echoed, 'Stay. Stay.'

Renata stayed. She would stay forever.

Time passed like glacial rock, like stone only barely molten. Renata did not move. Eventually, though, she became aware of a slithering across the rock-hard surfaces of her body, and then of the serpent Belinda sunning on her upturned heart. 'You can't stay here,' Belinda hissed to her, coiling and uncoiling.

146

'Why not?' Renata's mouth didn't move as she spoke to the snake. 'I belong here.'

'No. There's more.'

Belinda dropped her massive coils down the length of Renata's torso. One by one, Renata's legs and arms were encircled, her head masked by the writhing serpentine pyramid, her eyes and nose and mouth covered over. Then Belinda began to constrict.

At first, there was no pain through the many hard strata Renata had acquired. But the pressure was merciless, the long muscles of the snake's body were powerful, and Renata became aware that there was danger. With enormous reluctant effort, she stirred herself to resist.

Trying to hold her position, she struggled to exert pressure outward in answer to the inward constriction. The coils rippled in response, but did not ease.

Renata exhaled deeply, hoping to make her body sufficiently smaller that the snake would lose her grip. The coils readjusted themselves and squeezed again.

Renata moaned. Belinda hissed, and Renata felt a stream of tingling air. Belinda tightened herself again, and with a cry Renata toppled off the rock slab that had formed as a pedestal under her feet.

Slowly the serpent unwound herself, and out of the conical space that had been made by her stacked coils Renata collapsed in softening pieces. 'It's time to go on,' Belinda insisted, and undulated her enormous body between statues, through holes in statues, around the frozen feet of statues toward the boundaries of the Stone Garden. Renata had no choice but to follow.

Chapter 14

Again, the next morning and every morning for the rest of her life, which was why she could not live much longer:

Waking into the searing knowledge *Ian is dead Ian is dead no! Ian is dead.* Wailing.

Getting up because she couldn't hold the image of herself as stone and so couldn't bear to lie in bed wailing, hurting, knowing Ian was dead and lying there with the knowledge. Then over and over, losing track of what she was doing. Holding toothpaste in her mouth until she gagged. Combing her hair and putting on minimal makeup without looking in the mirror, because she forgot and then because she couldn't face her own image. Finding no clothes clean and ironed so wearing wrinkled clothes, worn clothes, clothes that didn't fit – or maybe they were fine and it was she who didn't fit, was worn, was soiled. Missing a shoe; wearing the wrong shoes for this suit.

Worrying suddenly about the plant in the room Ellen Hughes had found for her. Ellen had insisted on giving her a chipper little tour: desk, chair, apothecary jar full of hard candy, chrysanthemum plant. Bronze flowers. Was she expected to take care of the plant? What if it died? Surely it would die.

Calling Vanessa, who was already awake and crying. Taking too long; she should have responded right away to her child who still needed her. Finally, sitting beside her on the bed and stroking her hot forehead, stroking the tears, able to say only, 'I know, honey. I know,' and that was too much, not enough, the wrong thing, she would harm Vanessa just by touching her, speaking to her, loving her, just by being in the same world with her.

Going to work. Trying to take the bus; going to the bus stop, navigating the three blocks to the bus stop in discrete steps, each one of which she had to force herself to think about, but getting there without noticeable problem, waiting for the bus, seeing it approach. Terrified, choking, backing away. Turning and running home and waking up Glenn to drive her to work again. Saying sorry, she was sorry. Thinking but not saying – because she wouldn't be able to hold her own in the argument that would surely result – that she wouldn't be a burden on everybody much longer.

The morning passed. Renata hardly spoke, even to Theresa. She kept her door shut. Her calendar was clear; distantly she wondered whether Theresa had done that for her, or whether people didn't want to see her in her grief, didn't trust her to participate in normal human discourse. They were right not to trust her. They were right that this unspeakable thing had made her unfit for anyone to look on.

She was supposed to be reading and preparing comments on the proposed campus accessibility plan. She turned the pages, scanned the lines, could retain none of the few meanings she managed to extract, didn't care.

All morning she didn't move from her chair. She seemed to have no bodily functions to attend to such as hunger, thirst, kinesthetic restlessness, or the need to excrete. Occasionally she would find that she was staring off to her right as if out the window, although the blinds were closed and only thin interrupted stripes of light came in, thinking featurelessly about suicide.

Then, sometime in the early afternoon, she didn't want to kill herself anymore. The overwhelming, decisive need not to be alive simply vanished, as though she'd been led away from it, and anguish returned full force.

She laid her face in her folded arms on the desk top, but that wasn't enough support. She lowered herself again onto the harsh gray carpet. As long as her weeping was quiet, lying on the floor of her office with the door closed was all right, but very soon it was apparent that she needed to sob and rail and pound something, and in this office complex sounds like that would travel. She stopped, sat up. She could go to the empty room; Ellen had given her the key. But she couldn't imagine how to get herself there from where she was now.

Her skirt had pulled up above the tops of her thigh-highs, and there was something fascinatingly repulsive about the dark brown bands pressing into the winter-pale flesh. She stared, had to shake herself out of the hypnotic half-trance to clamber back into the wheeled desk chair.

She left work early without calling Glenn to tell him she was coming home. That seemed a reckless thing to do. She took the bus. She didn't speak to the driver; he didn't seem to expect it. Before Ian died she would always have spoken to the driver, on principle if not out of actual friendliness, and look what that had gotten her. This early in the afternoon, there were seats, and she didn't have to touch anyone. Surely they could all tell she had lost her child.

She got off at the right bus stop at 26th. It was the right stop – Safeway was in the right place, and the fire station diagonally across the intersection – but everything was slightly skewed, so that for a minute after she stepped clumsily off the bus she was afraid to move and afraid not to move. She moved, though, got out of someone's way, turned right and walked to the corner.

The light changed twice and traffic started and stopped and crisscrossed twice before it dawned on her that she was supposed to step off the curb when the light turned green. The curb was too high, its gutter too deep, but then the pavement hit the bottom of her shoe with too much force and she stumbled. No cars waited to turn; she wished furiously for a drunk driver to careen around the corner and smash into her, so that she could die right here and now in a way that wouldn't have been her fault. The pedestrian light turned yellow and then red before she'd reached the opposite curb, and that scared her, but it had always done that. She and Glenn had warned all their kids about this light. Ian hadn't yet been allowed to cross this street alone. Because it wasn't safe. Because he might get hurt.

Then she was at her garage, her back gate, and three little boys were playing on the apron of the alley where it opened onto 25th, and without warning Renata saw them run over by a car speeding around the corner, their laughter shattering and elongating into screams and then silence, child's blood staining the alley, *now, now*; she stood still and gaped at them and willed it. Nothing happened, and the fervid desire swept away, leaving her gasping.

She made it across the yard, though the bar-like shadows from the fence threatened to cage her, and into her house. The house in the middle of a weekday afternoon was alien; she wasn't supposed to be here, wasn't welcome, had no place. She didn't call for Glenn, but he heard her and came downstairs, alarmed, while she was struggling to make her jacket fit on the hanger. 'Are you okay?' he asked her, and the query was so ludicrous that she nearly couldn't answer.

'I don't want to commit suicide anymore,' she informed him, defiantly, almost nastily. The jacket slithered off the hanger again and she let both the garment and the hanger fall. They made no noise on the closet floor, and her impulse was to pick them up again and throw them, smash them, insist that they declare themselves.

'Good,' Glenn said, and turned and went upstairs again.

She was alone in the stark sunny living room, where she had answered the phone that must have rung. 'Renata, this is Kari Dennis.'

Renata had known this woman for a long time but barely, just enough to be aware that they had little in common and didn't really like each other much. But she knew why Kari was calling her. Years ago – before Ian and Vanessa had come, a perspective that set Renata to shuddering – Kari had lost a child, too, an infant son, born on time and apparently healthy, dead of something like SIDS in less than three days. Renata had only a dim recollection of that time, and the sudden comprehension now of what it must have been like for Kari was profoundly unwelcome. 'Hi,' she managed to say through the cold suicidal fog which she tried with only limited success to wrap protectively around her, resenting the forced penetration of even that monosyllable.

'I heard your son died,' Kari declared in her brash East-Coast accent, 'and I'm so sorry.'

Something about the clarity of those two statements, their straightforward refusal to pretend to be anything but what they were, was refreshing. Barely able to move her lips, Renata whispered, 'Oh, Kari.'

There was the sound of inhalation and exhalation through narrowed lips, and Renata remembered that Kari had always smoked too much. She was bitterly distracted by the image of Kari doing something else, anything else, while she was talking about Ian's death. 'I can't say I know how you feel. Nobody knows how you

152

feel. But I can say you'll feel shitty for a long time, and it's possible to live through this.'

'Why?' Renata had sunk into the couch pillows, drawn up her knees, hidden her head in the resulting cavity of her body so that her barely audible voice echoed, and still felt exposed. *Why would I want to live through it? Why bother?* She couldn't put enough words together to say all that. Which was just as well. The thoughts came to her in questions but they were stolidly rhetorical; she did not want answers. Besides, if Kari didn't understand that without being told, she wasn't worth talking to. She wasn't worth talking to, anyway. Nobody was.

'So what happened?'

Renata's mouth kept moving as if getting ready to say something, but no words were anywhere near ready for speech.

'He hung himself, right?'

'He hanged himself,' Renata muttered.

If she'd really been correcting the grammar, which seemed incredible, Kari didn't take notice. She sucked in smoke and loudly tapped her cigarette against a metal ashtray which clattered on a hard surface somewhere near the phone. 'Goddammit, you know, my kids have been that mad at me. Hell, *I* was that mad at my folks a lot of times. I remember.'

Renata didn't say anything. She clutched the receiver, though not out of any conscious desire to keep the connection open; her hands were unable to assume another position without deliberate rearrangement, of which her brain was incapable.

'But your son *did* it. That's the bitch,' Kari said, and took another drag.

Renata nodded miserably. 'I keep being somewhere else, you know? I keep going to another time and place, or into some other dimension, or something.'

Kari said, 'The shit we think and feel and do when we're grieving would get us certified psychotic any other time.'

Renata pressed, 'Did you have that experience? Of actually being someplace else?'

'Not exactly that, no. But believe me, I had plenty of crazy – Hey!' Kari must have turned only slightly from the phone to yell, 'Hey, you little snots, cut out the crap! I told you, I'm on the goddamn phone!' The commotion that had risen in the background subsided a little, and Kari said in her flippant conversational tone, presumably to Renata, 'I bet you wish you had Ian to yell at right now.'

Renata might have nodded again. She might have produced a more or less inchoate sound. The matter-of-factness of Kari's ongoing everyday life and her commentary on it, the fact that she made no effort to conceal or mute her parental activities while talking to a newly bereaved parent was invigorating, a bright hard splash of cold water. Trembling hard now, Renata rejected the thought of being invigorated.

Kari said other things. Renata huddled, nodded, said a few wooden words. Kari gave her some phone numbers of people to call; for some reason, Renata actually did write them down. Toward what turned out to be the end of the conversation, Kari said, 'And the thing is, there's no reason to think this will be the last bad thing that ever happens to you. It's not like we pay our dues or something and then that's it. You know?'

Renata unwillingly felt her attention brought into abrupt, disorienting focus. What was this woman saying? And why was it, of all things, a relief?

Determined, Kari went on. 'It might not even be the worst thing that ever happens to you. We say that. But it might not be.'

Something lifted, threatened to lift.

'I'll call you again,' Kari stated without bothering to ask whether that was okay. Renata wouldn't have known whether it was okay or not. 'I gotta go now,' and she was yelling at her kids before she'd hung up the phone.

'Mom?' Renata hadn't heard Vanessa come in and certainly had had no inkling that it was time for her to be home from school, although now that the time of day had imposed itself on her it was obvious. To have missed that appalled her. She sat up, ran her hands hard over her wet face, thought about Ian coming home from school, never again coming home from school, was fiercely glad to see her daughter and fiercely missed her son. 'How come you're home from work already?' Vanessa didn't come close, as though her mother were someone to be afraid of.

'I had a bad day, honey. I expect I'll have a lot of those.'

Looking stricken, Vanessa backed away.

Anger spurted, and Renata said sharply, 'Why do you avoid me? When somebody you love is hurting you're supposed to go to them, not away from them.'

Vanessa said in a very small voice, 'I don't know what to do.'

'Hug me,' Renata said.

There was a long pause. Renata didn't know what to do next. Maybe she'd done the wrong thing already; maybe it was unfair to expect a twelve-year-old who'd just lost her little brother to reach out to someone else in the same mourning. But she had the conviction that this moment was a crossroads, that if she and her daughter turned away from each other now they might never find each other again.

'Vanessa,' she said. She'd have expected to say it gently, even as a plea, giving the girl a choice, appealing to her good-heartedness and her need to please. Instead, so sure was she that this act was crucial to her daughter's psychological survival and, then, moral development, that she gave it as an order. 'Come here and hug me. You're not the only one in pain. We need each other now.'

Very reluctantly at first and then in a rush, Vanessa crossed the long room to her mother and threw her arms around her. 'Mommy, Mommy.' Renata fought her strong instinct, which masqueraded as self-preservation, to flinch away from her daughter's burning touch, forced herself not to break the contact. The pain of it eased, became comforting. Vanessa rubbed her back, small tentative hands applying almost no real pressure but smoothing, soothing. Renata sobbed into her child's shoulder, and Vanessa tensed, but did not beg her to stop crying, sat in her lap and held her with thin arms around her neck. When Renata could look up, she saw that her daughter's face, tear-stained and sorrowful, was also radiant.

They fixed dinner together, pork chops and applesauce and cornbread. Setting the honey out, Renata was seized by a memory of the Christmas dinner when Ian, then about six, had spilled the honey all over the poinsettia tablecloth just minutes before the assembled company was to be called to the table, his mortification, her own and Glenn's calm on which her mother had commented, with disapproval masked as praise, 'You're so patient with these children. I would never have that much patience.'

The memory was bittersweet instead of terrible, which astonished her. For a moment she held onto the edge of the counter, not so much to steady herself as to stay still while the whole scene played itself out in her mind. Vanessa came to her and hugged her. 'I love you, Mom.'

Renata hugged her back, then got out the silverware for Vanessa to put on the table. She was bent over the open oven door, spearing the pork chops on the broiler pan to turn them over and paying close attention to the hot coils and racks whose position relative to her hands and forearms she couldn't quite determine, when she heard Vanessa putting things back into the silverware drawer. Dangerously distracted, she glanced over her shoulder. Quietly, Vanessa told her, 'We don't need four of everything anymore. Only three.'

'Oh, God.' Renata lowered herself into a crouch, face still swathed by heat from the broiler, and waited for the wave of horror and anguish. It came, but instead of hardening herself against it she let it pass through her and it didn't, after all, kill her. She turned the chops over and shut the oven door, straightened. 'I'm sorry, Vanessa,' she said, but Vanessa was back in the dining room by then.

The clock struck seven while they were eating dinner. Studiously Renata didn't look at either Glenn or Vanessa, who were conversing, in a manner so gentle that the rhythm and tone of the exchanges gave the pedestrian content – Glenn asking about her day, Vanessa telling about playground squabbles and a B on a social studies test – an almost holy aura.

Renata found she couldn't eat the pork chops; no matter how much she chewed, the meat stayed thick and sharp in her throat. But she managed applesauce and cornbread and milk, not tasting anything but able to get it down. Vanessa and Glenn ate well enough; one of the countless knots of anxiety in Renata's chest loosened at the sight of their emptying plates.

After dinner Vanessa and Glenn settled in at the table for their nightly homework struggle, and Renata cleaned up the kitchen, fed Gypsy and the cats, missed Shaman. In awful anticipation she watched time pass until it would be eight o'clock.

While she was unloading the dishwasher, moving slowly so as not to break many of the glasses, the phone rang. It was Jackie, who'd called almost every day since she'd gone back to Pennsylvania. 'How are you?' Jackie asked, as she always did.

From anyone else that might have been a stupid, even insulting query, but to Jackie Renata could say, reaching to shut the door between the kitchen and the dining room where Glenn was explaining another algebra problem and Vanessa was already crying in frustration, 'Well, I don't want to kill myself anymore.'

'Good,' Jackie breathed. 'I'm glad. A lot of us are glad. Does Glenn know?'

'I don't know.'

'Make sure he knows.'

'Okay.'

'Are you sleeping?'

'I think so. I wake up a lot.'

'Are you eating?'

'Some. Enough.'

'There's no reason for you to suffer like this. Why don't you ask your doctor for a sedative?'

'There *is* a reason for me to suffer like this. My son is dead.'

'But there are medicines that will take the edge off the pain and make it a little easier.'

'The pain is mine,' Renata declared, confused, not sure what she was saying but sure of its truth. 'The suffering belongs to me. I don't want to miss any of it.'

Jackie paused. 'I guess maybe I'd feel the same way. But it's hard to sit here and not be able to do anything and know how much you're hurting. I love you.'

'You are doing something. You call me. You listen to me.' For some reason, the next thing she had to say was hard, and Renata swallowed. 'You love me.'

'I guess that's all any of us can do for each other.'

'It's a lot.'

157

'We go through things alone, when you come right down to it, don't we?'

Racked now by pain for her lost child, Renata sagged against the open dishwasher and clutched the receiver in both hands. 'Yes,' she whispered.

'But little things can help,' Jackie said. 'Like the teachers paying my airfare. You know?'

'What?'

Jackie hesitated only a split second before she explained, and Renata understood both that she had already been told about this and that it was all right that she had no memory of it. 'When I got back from your house there was an envelope in my box at school. The faculty had taken up a collection to cover my airfare. There was a note with the money that said I was doing something for my friend and they wanted to do something, too.'

'That was nice,' Renata managed to whisper.

'It was a gift to you, too,' Jackie said firmly, and Renata did see that it was.

When she got off the phone with Jackie and finished loading the dishes, this time having broken only one glass against a plate and having cut her fingers only slightly on the shards, it was past eight o'clock. Shocked, she searched for the visceral sensations of disaster that should have accompanied the advent of that hour. For long moments she couldn't understand their absence, and there was an urgency about her need to find or generate them that she didn't understand, either.

Then she realized that the difference was in the quality of ambient light. Since Ian had died – almost two months ago now – daylight savings time had gone into effect, and twilight through the kitchen window was an hour brighter than it had been on March 18. Like a flower opening and closing to the rotation of the earth around the sun, this particular aspect of her grief apparently was triggered by cycles in the physical world, of which, like it or not, she was still a part. Now, probably, the horror would come at nine o'clock.

From the dining room Glenn yelled, and Renata, terror-stricken, fumbled with the doorknob to get to her husband and daughter. But Glenn was applauding, and Vanessa's face was flushed with pleasure, a sheet of completed algebra homework between them. Heart pounding wildly as the adrenaline still surged, Renata made herself applaud, too, and after she'd started it seemed, in fact, a good and worthy thing to do.

Chapter 15

Now she couldn't stop crying. Memories assailed her like hail:

She'd called to say they were ready to adopt a daughter. 'Well,' said the social worker, excitement just slightly warming her careful voice, 'we have a seven-year-old girl who's available right now, and she has a little brother.'

Ian had loved pancakes. Banana pancakes. Strawberry pancakes. Pancakes with yogurt and wheat bran in them. Oatmeal-peach-raisin pancakes. Always with too much syrup.

Ian's laughter had sounded like seashells. The image made no sense, really, but it was the image that stayed. Ian's laughter had sounded like seashells, and she could hear it now.

Ian had almost always cocked his head to the right when he smiled.

Renata covered her head against the onslaught of slashing memories, realizing yet another level of loss: Not only her son himself, but also any pleasure in remembering details from their life together. Pancakes would forever be a source of pain, and seashells, and the color yellow because of his windbreaker. There was the overwhelming sensation of having been cheated, and more memories threatening:

lullabies—

marbles—

roly polys in the small palm of his hand nested in her hand so she could see—

the yellow windbreaker, never zipped, clean for no more than a few minutes at a time—

hair smelling of sunshine—

socks and shoes soaked by the time he got to school and the teacher calling her—

a fat red tricycle, then a tiny two-wheeler with training wheels, then a red bike too tall for him but he could ride it fast and hard—

he never could skip, galloped instead with the same foot always forward like a colt—

'There Mini-Mart is'—

She all but leaped from behind her desk and all but ran out into the open central area of the office. Theresa, organizing textbooks to be sent out to readers for blind and dyslexic students, looked up. 'Are you okay?'

Renata nodded and pushed among desks and chairs and pairs of people talking, through the open area off which a dozen or more offices opened, out into the hall. The patterns of floor tiles made her chest hurt. Echoes swirled in her head, students talking and laughing, footsteps, snatches of art and accounting lectures through open classroom doors, from somewhere the whine of a power tool. Odors – paint, potato chips from the vending machines in the lounge, spring air when the outside doors swung open – brought thick nausea.

When she got this job, Glenn and the kids had posted a 'Congratulations, Mom!' sign on the back door, and there'd been a happy little family celebration, as though this was good news, as though it would matter.

She found the restroom door and stumbled against the wall, had to stand in line with half a dozen students complaining vociferously and in some cases with real bitterness about exams and boyfriends, thought she would faint, didn't. Finally she made it into a stall where she sat down and lowered her face to her knees. She stayed there a long time although there continued to be a line of women waiting; she could hear their voices and the impatient stirring of their bodies, see their feet.

There came a time when she couldn't stay there any longer. Struggling to rearrange her clothes in the cramped stall, she grazed the door with her elbow and it swung open. Apparently it had never been latched; anyone could have walked in on her at any time.

She washed her hands. She took cold water into the cup of her hands and lost it in dribbles between them, took some more and lost it again, repeated this process innumerable times before she finally managed to bring the water up against the flesh of her face and neck. The shock of it was profoundly unpleasant and she grasped the edge of the sink until the shudders subsided. Women washed at all the other sinks and stood in tiers before the mirror combing and making up; no one took notice of her distress.

When she left the restroom she turned, without any conscious will, right instead of left and went on outside. An area the size of a narrow city block not far from the building had been given the appurtenances of a park, grass and trees and benches, squirrels, flowers. She went there. It wasn't lunch time yet and there weren't many other people in the park, although somebody was playing a radio too loud and she wished it gone, silenced, broken, thrown against the cobblestones and shattered.

The sky was eggshell blue, with scattered clouds like the squirrel's tail. She understood that it was beautiful. The sunshine was warm, the breeze soft and fragrant. The flowers made a rickrack border around the park. She knew these things were pleasurable, but pleasure and beauty skimmed off her surface, were locked away from her in a diorama behind curved glass. Ian's death had robbed her of pleasure and beauty, too.

From the steeple of the old church used now for meetings and overrun classes, the carillon struck the quarter hour. She had an appointment at 11:30. She roused herself, got to her feet, made sure she was facing the right direction. When at last she reached her office, Theresa started toward her with a stack of papers in her hands and a somewhat urgent look on her face. But Renata said quickly, 'Give me a minute,' and shut her door. Theresa's exasperated sigh was audible through it.

She called Glenn again. Again, he didn't answer. Fear prickled, and she seriously considered going home to find him. She left a message. 'Just calling to see how you're doing. I – It scares me when I can't reach you. I love you.'

If he said he was in great pain over Ian, she would panic. She could not stand the thought of Glenn suffering. She wouldn't allow it.

If he said he was okay she would wonder frantically at the disparity, for she was decidedly not okay. Or she would not believe him, and then would be convinced there were lethal secrets between them – he was insane, his mind shattered by grief; he was dying, or planning to die; he was preparing to leave her and Vanessa because he couldn't bear to stay in the family where his son had died, or he had already left and there would be a note for her on the kitchen table, or there would be no note. Scenarios like that had an undeniably histrionic quality, but so did a nine-year-old hanging himself, and such things happened.

In her purse were the names and numbers Kari had given her. Renata was surprised, even awed, that she'd put them somewhere safe and that she knew where they were, proof of a self-preservation instinct she'd thought suppressed or eradicated. The three names were those of parents who'd lost children, members of a nationwide support group with a local chapter who'd volunteered to talk to newly bereaved parents on the phone.

Renata stared at the names, thought about all those children dead, dialed the first number. No answer. There was something chilling about the phone ringing and ringing in what she imagined to be an empty house, and it mesmerized her; she must have let the phone ring twenty times before she roused herself and broke the connection.

Without pausing she dialed the second number, and an elderly woman answered in the middle of the second ring, breaking the elongated buzz with a click that jangled Renata's nerves. 'Is this Althea Ford?'

'Yes.'

Overwhelmed by the enormity of what she was about to say Renata said it: 'My – my son – my son died!'

'Oh.' Althea must have heard the same words countless times, even with the same hesitations; there were only so many ways to say, 'My son died.' But she sounded as though she were struck afresh by the pain of it, as though this pain were new. 'I'm so sorry.'

There was nothing more to say, no way to get past this endlessly repeating moment. 'My son died.' Renata clutched the receiver in both hands and shook with sobs.

'What happened?'

She couldn't think how to start. She couldn't form the first word. She wept and gripped the receiver, afraid this stranger – who must have lost a child, too, though that was hard to conceive – would lose interest and hang up if she didn't say something soon. She couldn't say anything.

Althea asked gently, 'What was his name?'

Renata did not think she could say it. But she had to. She opened her mouth, shut her eyes hard, and forced the two small syllables past the thick constriction in her throat. 'Ian.'

'Ian.'

Violent shudders sped like whitewater through Renata's body at the sound of her son's name spoken by someone who knew it only because he was dead. *Ian is dead.*

'How old was he?'

'Nine.'

'Oh, my. So young.'

'He'd have been ten by now.'

'Children are always too young to die, no matter how old they are.' Althea gave a soft rueful chuckle. 'But then my mother died not long ago and she was a hundred and one, and I wasn't ready for her to die, either.'

Tears had soaked Renata's collar and were pooling inside it now. Tears were flooding the receiver and would surely ruin it. She fumbled in her drawer for the box of tissues, making a bleary mental note to bring more, and wiped her face and neck and the telephone, but tears kept flowing.

'How did he die?' Althea asked, leading her through it.

But that was too much. She could not say such things aloud. Instead she asked, 'Have you lost a child, too?'

'Two. A daughter and a son.'

'Oh, my God.'

If she'd been asked, 'Do children die? Could more than one child in a family die?' she'd have said yes, of course, but without any bones and flesh to it, without any detail or substance. A question on a social work exam. Before Ian died, she'd have wondered how parents survived the loss of a child. After Ian died and before this conversation with Althea, she'd have found it inconceivable that anyone could lose more than one child and live to tell about it.

Now, of course, the possibilities were more than obvious, the permutations endless, and terror swept her. It would not be enough to learn to live with Ian's death. She was also required to face fully the knowledge that Vanessa could die, too, or Tim. *Would* die.

'How old were they?' Renata asked, breathlessly. Astonished by the query, she was beginning to understand how this was done. 'What were their names?' And, incredibly, 'How did they die?'

Althea replied calmly. For the first time Renata wondered, with both relief and horror, if someday she'd be able to answer like that. 'They were both young adults. Susan was twenty-four when she was murdered, almost fifteen years ago.'

'*Murdered*?'

'Somebody kidnapped her from the grocery store and raped and stabbed her. She was dead for almost a whole weekend before we even knew she was missing.'

'Oh, Althea.' Althea was not a name Renata had ever used before, but it seemed familiar already. 'How did you survive?' *And then another one*, she remembered, *another child*, and held her breath to hear.

'I don't know.'

'Have you – have you just survived? I mean, has life been worth living since?'

'I was just getting my feet back under me after Susan's death when my twenty-two-year-old son Allen died in a skiing accident. An avalanche. They were skiing off-trail. The two he was with barely made it. They were buried for four hours.'

Renata was afraid to ask, driven to ask. 'But you survived?'

'There didn't seem to be much choice.'

'You could have killed yourself. You could have been miserable forever. You aren't miserable, are you?'

'No.' There was a pause. 'I get really sad sometimes still, but it's softer. It's not harsh anymore.'

'Not even about Susan?'

'No.'

'My son hanged himself!' Renata cried.

Althea caught her breath. 'Suicide! So young!'

'Maybe. Maybe he meant to kill himself or maybe he didn't know he'd be dead forever, or maybe it was an accident. We'll never know.'

'Had he been depressed?'

'No. He was a happy kid. He was mad at us that evening because we wouldn't let him go to a friend's house, but he'd never had an especially bad temper.'

'So maybe it was an accident.'

For a long moment, Renata felt herself swaying on the cusp of a choice. She could believe that it had been an accident. That would be easiest. She could believe he had intentionally put the noose around his neck and jumped, but with the caveat that he hadn't been old enough to understand the finality of death: something like, 'I'll kill myself, and then they'll let me do what I want.' She could believe it had been deliberate, despairing suicide, which would be the hardest explanation to bear but would, at least, be an explanation.

But it was important to stay with the truth. And the truth was, she repeated, 'We'll never know.' There was a cool satisfaction in being able to stay in that delicate position, on that thin trembling wire of not knowing, never knowing, and knowing that never knowing was the truth.

Althea took her number and promised to call her tomorrow. Renata thought she might well call Althea before then. She hung up, opened her door, read and edited and signed the letters and forms Theresa put in front of her, noting with distant guilt and gratitude that some of them were due today but none was past due; every grieving person should have a secretary like Theresa. As scheduled, she discussed with the man in the next office, director of another program, a problem between his staff and hers over use of the shared computer; they easily reached a compromise and he, whether out of his own slightly obsessive nature or out of an accurate intuition that she would not be able to retain any of this, said he would write it up and distribute it. She was absurdly grateful, absurdly relieved to have this task done.

At noon, pressure building, she hastened across campus to her empty room to cry. She almost didn't make it. The sensation was vividly that she almost didn't make it, although there was no image of what would have happened if she hadn't.

A street person in a long frumpy black coat, probably here for the Wednesday soup line, shambled into her path and stopped. 'A penny, mum? A penny for a sick auld woman?'

Intent on her mounting pain and its imminent relief, Renata was able to bring the woman more or less into focus but didn't comprehend what was wanted of her.

The woman reached out and took the front of Renata's silk shirt in both hands, boldly but not roughly. Her breath reeked. 'Can ye spare a penny, mum, so my children might eat supper?'

At the mention of children, tears flooded Renata's eyes. The woman stepped back in obvious revulsion but held onto the shirt with one hand. Renata fumbled in the back pocket of her jeans, pulled out a handful of change, quarters and nickels by the feel of it, and upended it into the outstretched gritty palm. The other hand came loose from her shirt then to cup around the money, too, and the woman gasped, 'Oh, oh, God bless ye, mum!'

Sobbing in earnest now, Renata made no effort to hide her face, but turned it up to the bright blue sky as if to show off her grief. She breathed, 'He already has,' and the woman, staring at her as if she were the crazy one, scuttled away.

Renata stumbled up the steps of the last building, unlocked the door with so little difficulty that she feared it hadn't actually been locked, all but fell inside, got the door shut as her sobs heaved. She actually sank to the floor, spread-eagled, sobbed. When after a while the weeping lessened, she called Ian's name softly, which brought deep sobs again. She moaned and writhed and gave herself over almost entirely to the wild grief, retaining only enough connection to the exterior world to check her watch now and then; she had until one o'clock to do this.

At quarter till one she knew she ought to get up, rearrange her clothes, comb her hair, wash her face, get herself together. But she wanted more, craved more. Deliberately she invited his face, the scent of his hair, his perpetually dirty sneakers into her mind, and anguish pinned her to the floor.

At ten till one she pushed herself up onto her hands and knees. Shaky, she couldn't stand upright without support, and she crawled over to the desk to clutch the edge of it and haul herself up. The chrysanthemum had been watered. The gift of it, the mercy, steadied her enough to stand and to leave the sanctuary.

Theresa looked at her. 'Are you all right?'

Knowing her face was swollen and her eyes red, Renata held her head high. 'I'm okay. I've been crying. That's what I'm supposed to be doing.'

168

Theresa smiled gently and nodded. 'Do you still want to go swimming after work? We don't have to.'

She hadn't exactly forgotten about it, but now her attention swiveled back with a certain dull disbelief. Swimming. She thought about it. 'I'll go,' she said, wondering why. 'My suit's still here.'

'You don't have to,' Theresa repeated. 'If it's too soon.'

'The longer I wait the more impossible it will be,' Renata said. 'Not just swimming.'

When she called Glenn to tell him, he answered after four rings. She was relieved until she realized how harried he sounded. 'Consultation,' he said, which had long been their code word for the need to discuss some child's infraction of some rule and what the consequence should be. Now that Ian was dead, Renata didn't think she could do it, but Glenn went on as though she could. 'Vanessa didn't bring her spelling words home. Again.'

At first Renata had trouble comprehending why this should matter anymore. Then, her indignation was out of all proportion to the offense. 'Shit,' she said.

'Well, we're all having trouble focusing,' Glenn said.

'But we can't loosen the standards. She really will feel insecure.' This seemed as likely to be true as anything else – more likely, in fact, because it demanded a course of parental action harder than just letting it go.

'You're right.'

'I'm sure you can come up with a nifty list of words for her to write ten times each.' This was scary, this going about the business of being careful, attentive parents to a surviving child, being required to make a decision about what was best when it had been proved in a way impossible to avoid that some things were out of their control. It was not terrifying, though, she noted; it was not impossible.

But later, when she went with Theresa and a couple of other women from work to the gym, she froze at the side of the pool. Submerged to her shoulders in the water that looked aqua but was actually clear, clutching the slippery tiled edge as if she would drown if she let go although her feet were flat on the bottom, shivering although both the water and the air were warm, she couldn't get out and she couldn't go in. Theresa kept an eye on her, but neither she nor anybody else said anything. Renata stood there, shivered, clung, until finally it was time to go home, and then she had no choice but to move to the steps, grab the slimy silver handrail, and put one foot after another to climb out. Because she had no choice, she did.

Chapter 16

In front of Stewart's, one of the finest department stores in New York City which Maggie Flynn had never been inside and never would, a veteran with no legs – a Confederate veteran, she thought, which was queer – held out his tin cup. It had a coin in it, one dull silver coin like a dollop of spit.

If it had been eyes he didn't have, Maggie could have taken the money. She'd done so once before and the blind beggar never knew, a sweet memory.

She made sure he didn't touch her. Seeing who and what she was, he didn't try to touch her. But she still felt begged from, soiled.

Soldiers, they were, in rags of uniforms. From the War between the States. Not her war; over well before she and Jock had come to this country from green, misty, starving, landlord-ridden Ireland in 1867, a long seven years ago. Not her States; she'd seen none of them but New York City, where she thought the war had not been, and resentfully she didn't know why the beggar veterans should be here.

Not her money, either; she was too weak anymore and too tipsy whenever she could manage it to run out of reach of their sticks. The big glass windows of the store reflected back mostly gray sky and gray New York streets, reflected back the ragged soldiers, too, but not Maggie Flynn. She was still quick enough on her feet and with the turn of her head never to have to see herself in the glass.

Traffic was heavy, wheels and hooves spattering filth on her. She didn't flinch, and it was a minute or two before she rubbed at the fresh streaks on her face with the heel of her hand, knowing she was only making the dirt worse. Horns of horsecars blatted, and something on their undersides clanged against the tracks. Omnibuses started and stopped with much shouting of reinsmen and neighing of horses and bustling of passengers. Wires hummed overhead, not far enough overhead; Maggie mistrusted the wires because they carried messages in some way she could not comprehend, from and to people she could not imagine, and she kept ducking, covering her head, avoiding their thin swaying sinuous shadows.

The bottle was empty. She let it drop. It broke, and she told herself with bleary sternness to pick up the pieces. But she didn't. If she bent sideways she'd surely fall over and she surely wouldn't be able to get up.

Maggie shied away from the beguiling thought of herself lying like dirty newspaper against the dirty building for the rest of her life, which, please God, wouldn't be long. Like whiskey, the picture was charming and poisonous as Satan Himself.

Anyhow, the bits of brown broken glass looked a bit pretty scattered amongst the grime of the gutter which Maggie was part of. A street rat – a girl, Maggie thought, but you couldn't really tell and it didn't matter, nothing about these children mattered, there were so many of them and none to care for them – crouched to play with dirty little fingers in the chunks and slivers and half-cups and rings and bracelets of broken glass. Maggie growled and swatted at her, wanting the pretty sparkles for herself. The child ran off.

Her children were street rats, or would be soon enough. Already Seamus was running the streets with a rowdy gang of boys. Sean, a newsie, fought with fists and teeth and sap for his corner, and little as he was he won as often as not, but her pride was discolored by how often and how bad and how willingly he got hurt. She didn't like to think where Eileen got the money she sometimes brought home, more than you could earn scrubbing floors. Unless she was really besotted, she couldn't look her daughter in the eye when she accepted the money, because she shouldn't be accepting it, and because she'd have to spend some of it on drink, and because she didn't like to think where the money came from, and because she guessed Eileen was holding some back for herself and that hurt Maggie's feelings.

None of them had enough to eat. Michael, especially, wasn't growing the way he ought to be growing. Seamus looked like a wraith. Maggie was always hungry, and it made her feel sorry for herself, as if it was something new, as if she hadn't been hollow-bellied all her earthly life.

And Rosemary was sick, fevered probably. Had the sickness, probably, such as had taken her Da not so very long ago, a few years but how many was beyond Maggie. Jock was the only thing in the world besides Ma that had ever been steady for her and ever would, and he died. Drink and Satan made it so much of the time she could scarcely remember him.

But the drink and the Devil did not always properly do their job. Every once in a while something got through, like a flea bite or like a knife. A stranger's voice would catch the hem of her attention like bits of a broken brown bottle, sounding like his. Rosemary would giggle. One night some weeks ago Seamus had come home with fresh bakery rolls all around – stolen, no doubt, or paid for with ill-gotten gain, but still warm and flakey. At times like that, Maggie would remember – or, worse, feel here and now – a sharp stray sliver of happiness or hope, and that would put her in mind of Jock, and that would make her cry and drink and cry some more.

A snake slithered out from under the stoop Maggie'd been squatting on. Thick as her thigh, brown and glittery as if the broken whiskey bottle had stuck into its skin. Maggie gasped, which made her cough. A ragged girl, older than Eileen and taller than Maggie herself, jumped out of her way, as if it were Maggie she had to fear and not the snake.

Maggie heaved herself to her feet and ran into the street, across the path of a speeding hansom whose driver cursed and flicked at her with his whip while the horses' hooves flashed and kicked the cobblestones loose. Maggie shook her fist. Danny'd been struck by one of those carriages when he was six. Now he was thirteen, and he still wasn't right, would never be right again in the body or in the head. He hadn't died. She hadn't lost him yet. She would.

The snake had, she was sure, been quite long enough to stretch across the street. Perhaps the hooves and wheels would kill it. Perhaps it would be cut in half and then there would be two snakes, each with a baleful eye, each with dripping fangs. It wasn't true, of course, that Ireland had no snakes; Saint Paddy hadn't been all he was said to be. But she'd never seen a snake in New York City, and she shouldn't have seen one now. Nobody else seemed to see it. When she got to the other side of the street and looked back, she didn't see it either. She must be daft. She must be even drunker than she'd thought.

She stopped on a street corner, any street corner that wasn't already too much occupied by whores and beggars half- and full-grown, newsies and preachers. She backed up against the grimy brick building, slid down it, and sat on the sidewalk with her skirt spread mostly over her crossed legs to make a catchment for coins somebody might drop. It would be better if the children were with her, especially Rosemary who always looked sick whether she was or not, or crippled drooling Danny. People gave more money to sick children than to drunk grownups. Maggie saw no snakes now.

Nobody dropped money into her skirt. Before long she got up and stumbled in the direction of the West Side shanty where she and Jock had lived with their children, just until they could get someplace better, and where now she and her children would always live until her children were gone. If she was now seeing serpents appear and vanish on the city streets, she had no business being out and about herself. Eileen and Seamus would bring home money, and no matter the source they would have enough for boiled cabbage and perhaps a bit of potato tonight. Her children would not yet starve.

It was the worst kind of winter day, gray and damp and cold but no snow. Snow was worse for the body because it made the cold stick, but no snow was worse for the soul. Crossing 23rd Street, she slipped but managed not to fall. In the mud and slop of the street, where if there were going to be serpents anywhere in this city there should have been, there weren't any snakes. Maggie snorted derisively. Next she'd be conversing with the little folk.

A group of rich people was coming toward her. She scuttled into the gutter, her proper and accustomed place, and the rich people went past her laughing, and not a one glanced her way. Maggie stared brazenly at them. 'A penny, sir? A penny for a sick auld woman?' thickening the brogue, staggering more than she had to. They didn't refuse her; they simply paid her no heed.

But behind the revelers, separate from them, came along a single lady. Maggie looked her over but could not tell who or what she was, rich or poor, from where. She had on trousers. Her hair was short and uncovered.

'A penny, mum? A penny for a sick auld woman?'

The woman looked around dazedly. She wasn't crying, but she had been and would again.

Maggie made so bold as to grab a fistful of the woman's shirt, too thin for a New York City winter day. She'd learned not to come too close to a mark while there was still a chance she might be given something, money or food or drink; her breath, fresh-whiskeyed or not, chased people away before she was fairly done with them. But she held onto the shirt. It was soft between her hands, not a kind of cloth she was used to, and her skin snagged it.

'Can ye spare a penny, mum, so my children might eat tonight?'

Tears flooded the woman's eyes and spilled over her cheeks with such force that it was Maggie who stepped back in revulsion. *I know her*, she thought, but she did not.

The woman was fumbling in the pocket of her trousers. Maggie had never seen clothes like this on anyone, male or female. She watched the shirt raised, the fingers inside the tight hip pocket, brass buttons at the corners where red thread had been stitched across dark blue heavy cloth rather like canvas. Then the woman was pressing money into her hand, so many coins Maggie was afraid to count them and closed her fist before she even really looked, let go of the shirt to wrap her left fist around her right in which the money was clutched. Heavy coins, heavier than pennies, and more than several of them.

'Oh!' she gasped. 'Oh! God bless ye, mum!'

The stranger had turned her face up to the gray heavens as if to show off her grief. 'He already has.'

It was a daft thing to say, weeping as though heartbroken and in the same breath proclaiming the blessings of the Lord. Too close to something she did not want to encounter, Maggie made to free herself.

But the queer woman was not yet done. She grasped Maggie's shoulders and Maggie could barely control her instinct to kick and claw. 'My son died,' the woman cried. 'Ian. My son. He killed himself.' Her eyes were wild.

Don't tell me yer troubles, mum, was what Maggie wanted to say. *I got troubles of me own.*

Maggie bared her teeth as the woman shook her. 'Why would he do such a thing? He was only nine years old!'

Maggie could think of plenty of reasons why a child of nine should want to leave this world, and rightly, too. She twisted away. 'You're his Ma,' she growled. 'If you don't know, who does?'

She meant to go straight home, after stopping at the butcher shop on the corner for a soup bone because Bridget loved soup and it would be good for Rosemary's throat, at the greengrocer on 19th for carrots and maybe a few apples for Sean who was saying just the other day – she thought it was the other day, but it might have been longer ago – that he could almost not remember how an apple tasted, and at the dairy for milk and eggs. A little giddily she wondered if she still knew how to cook eggs. Eileen would know.

She meant to spend her money on food for her children's supper and her own, maybe keep just a little of it for drink later, to celebrate her good fortune. Even as she slowed her steps outside Jimmy's, she was happily picturing herself struggling with her arms full of groceries through the alleys and pathways that weren't even big enough to be called alleys which smelled either like piss and rats or like the briny soap Eileen used to scrub the square she tried to call a stoop outside the door to their shanty. Just one drink to fortify herself, then it's off to the market and the dairy and the greengrocer and the butcher, and then home. She ordered a stout ale. The barkeep demanded payment in advance. Maggie made a show of indignation, extracted one coin slowly after another from her pocket until the exact amount made a neat row on the bar. Now that she saw it straight, the money looked not quite right, and Maggie glanced furtively at the barkeep, but he seemed more or less satisfied. The acts of holding and releasing money were supremely satisfying. Her pocket was noticeably lighter then, but it still had a nice heft to it.

Sometime later, when the barkeep gathered her up in his arms in what Maggie could almost pretend was an embrace, and she clung to his neck giggling and weeping as long as she could, which was not very long, there were still people left in Jimmy's Place and she didn't understand why she couldn't stay a while, too. It was dark outside and cold, the streetlights so still they looked hard and giving off only small streaks of light. The barkeep dumped her onto the sidewalk well away from the door of his establishment, half in the street. It was damnably late. The butcher would be closed. The greengrocer and dairy would be closed. The crippled flower girl might still be in the park with a flower to sell.

But Maggie had lost her money. Somebody had robbed her. Dully at first, then frantically, sick, she turned all her pockets inside out, jumped up and down as best she could, took off her broken shoes and shook them out, even stuck her fingers into her mouth and ears. The coins were all gone, all. Somebody had stolen the money she'd been going to spend for her children's supper.

The tragedy of it, the meanness of one human being to another, flung Maggie face-down against a rough building, where she stayed for a long ugly time. Exploding now with nausea and the need to rid herself of something poisonous, Maggie managed to pull herself up onto her hands and knees. Her cheek pressed against the curb, broken and slimy.

Sometime later, stomach long since emptied into the gutter but still cramping, determined to purge itself of even its own insides, she staggered to her feet, which she could not by now quite feel. The city stretched under her and folded as she made her long way home. She fell. She got back up.

New York City teemed with children. Was alive with them in the way a pallet on the floor was alive with fleas. Children for the taking. So late at night and still they roamed the streets, singly or in pairs or packs, quicker than she was, smarter.

Maggie passed among them, head down, meaning to keep her fists balled but losing her grip again and again, meaning to take up a weapon, thinking to look for her children among all these children and then forgetting to. They left her alone. They knew she had no money. They had stolen it. Her own children had stolen her money.

Sodden rage brought her to her knees, and two or three of them running – chasing each other in a child's game, or more likely, escaping from a victim or a policeman – tripped over her. Feet in her ribs, curses in her face, they went on their way hardly noticing her, and so did she.

She was getting into the latest burned-out section of town now. The feel of it was nice, more open space, never mind the cause, never mind that it was grimier down here even than the rest of the city and still smelled of fire. Because of the ash and soot floating, dancing, settling, rising again, the place had a lilt to it; Maggie thought of leprechauns, angels, demons. Her thin and leaning little house hadn't burnt, though close; next time perhaps it would.

The alley wasn't hers, just the more or less lined-up crack between shanties where she happened to live. Pitiful how people tried to call things their own when the truth was they owned nothing in this world. At the second bend, where Danny swore he'd been bit by a rat but Maggie had never found bite marks anywhere on him, she heard children howling from somewhere in Micktown. Could be anywhere, anybody's children. Maggie's head ached. Her stomach hurt from hunger. Seamus or Eileen had better show her some earnings from today. Sean was getting old enough to earn his own keep, too. Even Bridget could sell flowers in the park.

It was her children crying. She could pick out Rosemary's sickly wail, and the funny little hiccupping Danny made when he was upset. They fought a lot. They hurt each other sometimes, and even when she was there she couldn't stop it. Their Da could have stopped it, but he was dead, wasn't he now?

Almost she didn't go in. Almost she would face old fire and serpents and street urchins and cold without snow rather than the crying of her children which she could not do a thing about.

They let her get all the way in and close the door behind her as much as it would close before Seamus told her. 'Eileen's dead, Ma,' and in that instant Maggie knew exactly, terribly, what she'd do.

The Children's Aid Society was in a brownstone that used to be a mansion on the Upper East Side; one small part of this huge city Maggie knew deep, but that morning she had to swallow her pride and mask her fear and make her grief for Eileen into a weapon so she could ask directions of a series of passersby, all of whom looked at her knowingly. Perhaps there were street rats here, too, though likely that preacher famous for his good works on behalf of the homeless, fatherless, motherless children of this great city didn't dare have his office among the very people he served, for fear they'd overrun him in protest or supplication.

Miss Kate Abernathy was much the same age as Maggie herself, but surely she had not so old a soul. She was rounder, kinder, cleaner for sure. There was not a speck of judgment in her treatment of

Maggie, and sweet Jesus there ought to be. For that, and for her power to grant Maggie's unholy request, Maggie hated her with a certain sinful and glorifying passion. At the hands of women like her, angels of a hard mercy, children vanished. Word on the street was that they were taken on the Orphan Train to the western states and farther western territories, to be given to families there. Word was that they would be better off out west, fed good food, set to honest work in pure clean air, taught good Christian morals, even educated. But there was something sinister about the plucking out of these children from their places in New York and their utter disappearance, never, so far as Maggie knew, to be heard of again.

When the girl who sold apples in Central Park – every day in summer and in winter, never any bigger though years older than the first time she must have been there – was not in her place one morning, there was no way to know whether she'd gone west on the Orphan Train or at last been beaten to death by her Da. When the band of little hooligans who lived under the stairs in the office building Eileen and still sometimes Maggie cleaned was one day less by two or three, nobody knew or would say what had happened to the gone boys.

Miss Kate Abernathy looked at Maggie across the desk in the parlor. Maggie saw papers, lists, train schedules, things the Children's Aid Society used for this end of its work, sweeping up unwanted brats who had no Mas worthy of the name. Here was another difference between Kate Abernathy and Maggie Flynn: Maggie Flynn did her best never to look at anybody, least of all this woman whom she was begging to take all her children away from her.

All except Eileen. Eileen was dead these five days, broken like a bottle still with good sweet wine in it under the wheels of a dray. The driver had stopped. They didn't always. Seamus had said he had trouble with the horse rearing and shying, as though it had never seen a dead child in the gutter before. The passengers, a gentleman and a lady on their way to the theater, had stepped out into the street. 'Where is this child's mother?' Eileen's blood had soiled the lady's gloves, but she hadn't seemed to mind.

Miss Abernathy said, 'I assure you we will do our best to find

179

good homes for your children out west, Mrs Flynn.' As if she'd asked. As if she had any notion what 'good homes' might be. As if she could even try to imagine what lay in store for them. That was the point; if they stayed here in New York, with her, she could imagine every instant of their futures.

'When d'ye take them?' *The sooner the better.*

Miss Abernathy consulted a long paper on the desk. The desk was dusty. Cobwebs silvered the faded brown wallpaper. The floor badly needed scrubbing. 'A train leaves tomorrow.'

Tomorrow. So soon. 'Fine.'

'They will go first to St Joseph, Missouri.'

Maggie didn't like the sound of that. A town named for a saint. Neither the saints nor our Blessed Virgin nor the Lord Jesus himself had ever made themselves felt in her life. Anger turned into raging thirst before she even really knew it had been anger.

'Some may be chosen by families there. Others will board other trains for points farther west.' Miss Abernathy looked up. Maggie had already safely turned her eyes somewhere else, but not before taking bitter note of the way the winter sunlight through dirty windows played on the woman's glossy black hair, the same color as her own in name only, and on the steely sad righteousness in the set of the woman's shoulders. Maggie's shoulders always drooped; now she deliberately hunched them more. No point in pretending to stand upright.

'Tomorrow, then.' She got herself out of the chair. Nowhere in the room did she see any evidence of liquor. Had there been a bar or a likely cabinet, she'd have asked.

Miss Abernathy didn't stand up, but her blue gaze followed Maggie's motion. 'I'm afraid I cannot guarantee that we can place them together, Mrs Flynn. I've known of no families willing to take six children.'

'Seven,' Maggie had corrected before she thought. She waved her hands, too hard, nearly lost her balance. 'Six, six, yes. Fine.' She should have left it at that. She badly needed a drink. But she heard herself asking, fairly spitting out the question, 'And tell me, Miss Kate Abernathy, why would anybody in their right mind take on brats not their own?'

Miss Abernathy answered readily. 'Farm families need someone

180

to help with the work. Childless couples or those who have lost a son or daughter of their own want a child to love. Some do it out of Christian duty, because they know there are children in need.'

Well, Rosemary was too sickly to work, should she even live until St Joseph, Missouri, and Michael only a puny child. Danny was a wee bit daft, or slow; something. Seamus could make the most Christian of Christians doubt their duty. No one could love them as she had once done, and what good had love been to her or to them? She said none of this, for fear Miss Abernathy would declare her children unworthy of the Orphan Train.

'Here is the address where you are to bring them. The train departs at ten o'clock tomorrow morning.'

Maggie did not look at the paper but did not drop it, either; stuffed it into her pocket. Seamus could read, if he would, and Eileen – but Eileen was dead.

'On the back is a map.' Her kindness struck Maggie full in the face.

On a hook beside the door hung a lady's coat, not fine, not fancy, no fur collar, no wide cuffs, just a long warm black coat. It would fit Maggie. She grabbed it as she staggered out of the room and down the stairs. The heavy wool wound around her ankles and she tripped but managed this time not to fall. Miss Abernathy said not a word, took not a step after her. Maggie readied herself for a fight, and she would fight, but nobody apprehended her in the foyer or at the street.

Infuriated and somehow vindicated, Maggie stopped on the curb outside the building to struggle into the coat. She took childish pleasure in how it kept the wind and snow from her and in the fact that she had stolen it from Miss Kate Abernathy of the Children's Aid Society. Her six children for a good wool coat. A fair trade.

She had to find a drink. Then she would go home to gather up her children, who had not a Ma worthy of the name. Her luck held. A drunkard had passed out in the gutter, where Maggie had been not a few times herself and would be again this night if she did not get home soon. He would freeze to death here, for certain sure – as would she, if it came to that. It could come to that tomorrow, when her children were on the train headed west; not tonight. The bum's hands, past red from the cold to bloodless white, held upright, even in his stupor, a bottle still nearly full of lovely thick red wine. Maggie simply lifted it. He hardly stirred. His hands stayed in their loose fists, holding his phantom bottle. Maggie sat down straight-legged beside him to drink his wine, then, in a boozy sort of tribute, threaded the empty bottle back through his frostbitten fingers. He'd think he'd finished it off himself. Or he'd think she'd been a heebie-jeebie out of his own besotted mind.

Holding onto a lamppost, she heaved herself to her feet. Snow was falling hard now, filthy with coal dust coming down, grimy slush in the streets, frozen blocks of soupy garbagey sludge in the gutters. But here and there on a ledge or a lamppost it glimmered white. In her new wool coat, belly and head slosh-full of wine, Maggie could have liked the snow. It quietened the city. It prickled through the soot on her skin.

But tonight the wine had tricked her, betrayed her. Rather than fuzzing the knowledge that her eldest daughter, her firstborn child, was dead and tomorrow she would lose, by her own hand, all her remaining children, it made that knowledge only more sure and certain.

By now they would have buried Eileen in a potter's field. Maggie had no idea what that was, let alone where; for all she knew, they'd done no more than scoop the poor child out of the street with the rest of the city's waste. In the vast shit of New York City, what was one small Irish lass wanted by nobody?

Or perhaps they'd just left her there; blearily, Maggie bent to inspect the mess at her feet, tipped, caught herself, saw nothing of her daughter but was not reassured. She'd never know what had become of Eileen. There would be no grave for her to visit. Not that she would have. Hard enough it was to keep herself alive, and for no purpose that she could ever see.

She'd never know what became of the rest of them, either. Whether Rosemary had The Sickness. Whether Danny got more or less daft with age. Who Seamus killed; she was sure he would kill somebody someday.

She had thought, sentimentally, to make a list to send along with her children of sweet little things nobody but their mother would know – a favorite food of this one, a song that would bring sleep to that one, another's tiny endearing habit. But she didn't know any.

It seemed to her that once upon a time she had, but no more. Indeed it was hard to sort one particular child out from all the others, except for Eileen, and that only because Eileen was dead now, dead. Maggie was crying. Her eyes streamed. Her nose ran. It all froze on her face, stinging.

A lady stood right in front of her. Unaccompanied ladies should not be out on the streets of the city this late at night. Maggie swerved not to collide with her, muttering aloud with the bravado that drink and losing all her children gave her, 'Watch where yer goin', mum,' which, with better diction and somewhat different name-calling, was what upstanding citizens of New York were always shouting at her and her kind.

But the lady blocked her path, as though she intended to address Maggie directly. Maggie cursed. If she ran into trouble tonight, she would surely not get home. Tonight of all nights, tomorrow of all mornings, she had to be with her children.

The lady was looking at her. She had on no coat, nothing covering her head, but the snow didn't seem to be falling on her. A trick of the eye; a joke out of the bottle. Her face, though, looked frozen in place, ice-covered, and Maggie could tell she'd been crying, too.

Hastily Maggie broke her stare and looked down. Confusedly, flailing for some explanation that would make enough sense to let her get away whether it was true or not, she decided that it was Miss Kate Abernathy from the Children's Aid Society come to take the children tonight. *Take them.* Come to reclaim her coat, which was heavy now and smelled like a tenement stairway as it soaked up the dirty falling snow. Maggie clutched it around her and prepared for a fight.

But the lady was a stranger among all this city's strangers. What could she want of Maggie? Perhaps to arrest her for losing her children. Perhaps to give her clothing or food. A few winters ago there'd been ladies from some mission walking the worst neighborhoods with baskets of food and piles of coats and bags of shoes, looking for the poor and finding them readily; their bounty had not been nearly enough, and after two or three cold weeks they had not been seen anymore. Maggie still remembered the oranges, three of which she'd peeled and separated into sections to divide among her children, taking more for herself because she was the grownup, after all, she was the Ma. None of them had tasted an orange since. That is, she had not. Maybe Seamus had. Maybe Eileen. Eileen was dead. Maybe she'd died with the juice of an orange on her lips.

Here was a memory. Maggie stood stock still right in front of the lady, who hadn't spoken to her but wouldn't let her pass. Close enough to touch but neither of them touching. Maggie was all but knocked off her feet, as if in a crowd of pedestrians surging across an intersection, even though there was just this one lady and they weren't touching. Here was a memory.

Bridget in a little blue shawl from the baskets of the mission ladies. Maggie could see her in it, red hair, blue eyes like all the Flynns, blue fringed shawl. It hurt her to see it; it gave her cold pride. She wondered if Bridget was still wearing it, was a bit shamed not to know. She wondered if Bridget would wear it on the Orphan Train to St Joseph, Missouri.

Pushed roughly, meanly, by the need to find out whether Bridget still had and still wore that pretty blue shawl – which, if truth be told, Maggie had coveted for herself but had let her daughter have, a motherly thing to do – she set her jaw and advanced. The lady didn't move, and now that she was closer to her Maggie could see that she wasn't actually looking at her, either, for the brimming eyes didn't shift or re-focus as Maggie approached. Unsteadily she raised both hands to shove the lady aside. She'd done that before, been arrested once and spent a night in jail for it. This time her hands passed right through.

She knew, then, who this was, and awe welled up in her through the cloying wine haze and the bitterness accumulated and still accumulating in her like dirty wet snow. Our Blessed Virgin Mary.

'Holy Mother of God!' she breathed. She couldn't remember the last time she'd said religious words as anything other than blasphemy. But this was a greeting, an acknowledgment of this vision visited upon her, Maggie Flynn, lowliest for certain sure of all God's creatures.

She slipped to her knees, finding herself then in an unintentional posture of worship. Snow stabbed her bare neck inside the upturned collar of her coat when she bent her head. She could feel herself swaying but when she put out her hands couldn't find anything steady, no ground, no lamppost, no building within reach. Nothing solid about the Virgin, either, except that she still was there, not looking at her, while Maggie's cold and clawing hands passed through her and passed through again.

'What d'ye want?' she blurted, badly slurring, brogue thick as the wine coating her tongue. 'What is it ye want with me?' Our Lady only wept.

Then Maggie remembered: Mary had lost her Son.

'Holy Mother of God, I canna do this! I canna send my children away!' Maggie howled, and flung herself into the Virgin's arms.

The Virgin didn't catch her, didn't hold her up; she should have expected that. Ever the fool, though, she was shocked by the dizzying tumble through the body of the Virgin, the cold face-down crash. She just stayed there, even stretched out one cramped leg. If there was any reason for her to be getting up, the Virgin Mary would say so. Nobody said anything.

From some distance she felt in her hurting bones, especially in her left cheekbone which had struck something ungiving, the rhythm of a horse's hooves and the steady rattle of carriage wheels coming. Maggie's wine- and cold-soaked brain got stuck for a while on the oddity, which she'd never noticed before, that when a horse trotted fast there were three hoofbeats and a pause, *one*-two-three-pause, even though the beast had four feet. *One*-two-three. *One*-two-three. *One*-two-three. The hoofbeats and the wheels and the missing hoofbeat thundered inside her head, as they must have thundered inside Eileen's.

Perhaps a carriage was approaching and if she stayed where she was she would be crushed like Eileen. She stayed where she was, not out of any coherent desire or decision but because it seemed easier and more fitting than anything else she might have done – moving, praying. She had tried to do something right. She had tried to send her children away on the Orphan Train, and here she was instead, besotted, seeing drunken visions of the Virgin Mary as she'd seen the huge serpent that other time, about to freeze to death or be crushed under the three hoofbeats of a trotting horse. She had tried to throw herself on the mercy of the Virgin, and had passed right on through.

After a while Maggie didn't feel the hoofbeats or the buzz of the wheels anymore, didn't feel the hard street or the cold snow.

185

Perhaps she was dead. She raised her head. It was still pitch night. The same night, she presumed. The night before she would lose all of her children. Unless it was the night after, and she had already sent them away and just didn't remember.

Miss Kate Abernathy's wool coat did cut the wind, but it was soaked through now and frozen stiff at the hem and cuffs and all along one sleeve, making it harder than it would have been anyway for her to get her footing. Maggie's feelings were hurt. Miss Kate Abernathy could at least have had a decent winter coat.

Slipping and sliding, giggling and crying, waiting for the sickness in her belly to turn into vomit again so she could get it out of herself, Maggie started down the middle of the street. The flickering gaslight from the streetlamps didn't reach out here, and the wires overhead were still and empty. A pack of street rats scuttled past, and she stopped, waited, silently dared them. But either they didn't notice her or they were intent on other bad business. Orphan Train, she thought meanly. A curse upon them and their Mas and Das. Ought to be on that Orphan Train tomorrow, every last one of them. Let the fine farm families out west do their Christian duty with such as these.

She waded through broken glass, frozen garbage, mud. She raised one foot to step over a body – still alive, probably – wrapped in newspapers; lost her balance, brought her foot with most of her weight behind it down on the side of the soft belly, almost fell, cursed. Crawled into her shanty, the wool coat dragging her down now, her hands bleeding even though they were so cold.

When she sidled into the room where she lived this one more night with what was left of her children, five of them were asleep. Seamus wasn't there; now that she thought of it, she hadn't expected him to be. One by one, her children were vanishing.

But the others: Bridget, Danny, Rosemary, Sean, Michael. Maggie Flynn braced both hands against the doorjamb and looked at each of them, these few of all her lost children still available to her though not for long. Danny, Bridget, Michael, Sean, Rosemary. Maggie was stone cold sober, sweet Jesus truly like a stone.

If it hadn't been for Seamus, Maggie wouldn't have waited till morning. Morning was, anyway, not but a few hours off, and the train station likely would have been warmer than their shanty with the snowy wind blowing in right through the walls, not even needing any chinks or cracks to get itself in.

But who knew where Seamus was or when he'd be back. She'd wait for him, her eldest son – her eldest child now – until the first light of dawn. Until dawn, Seamus. No longer.

She didn't dare to sleep. She vomited a few more times; even when all the wine was gone, even when what little else was in her belly was gone, the snow outside the door kept steaming where her insides fouled it. Not enough came up.

From one of her sleeping children to the next and next she kept herself moving. Were they indeed asleep and not dead, not frozen to death, not dead of The Sickness? Would she know the difference? No harm must come to them her last few hours as their Ma.

There was a commotion not far down the row of shanties, men shouting, the thumping and grunting of punches thrown and landing, a bottle breaking hushed against the snow-padded ground but breaking still. Maggie laid Miss Kate Abernathy's black wool coat over Rosemary. Wet and frozen as it was, silver as it was from ice right in among its threads, it was better than none.

But perhaps not, Maggie thought then, confused; perhaps the soaked wool brought cold closer to the sick girl instead of keeping it away. Maggie didn't know. A Ma ought to know such things. Finally she left the coat on the child, realizing that, as usual, she was as likely as not doing a wrong thing.

Fire wagons clattered by fast, horses huffing, the heavy rubber slithering of hoses. Maggie thought she smelled smoke and heard flames, but perhaps not. Over Michael she bent low, braced herself on shaky elbows so as not to fall onto him, and held her breath to listen for his. Just when she could not stop herself any longer from taking in a bit of air, she heard his faint snore, and she backed unsteadily away before her gasping and staggering would wake him.

Between Danny and Sean stretched a serpent. Then not. Maggie rubbed her eyes and looked again. No serpent, only splotched shadow already changing like a snake shedding its skin, maybe, but really not much like a snake at all. She slid her hand there, to be sure. Nothing but cold air and the cold pallet on the cold floor. Should there not be body heat between the two boys? She laid her hand on one's shoulder and then the other's, trying to keep her touch light but disturbing them both, though not much; they stirred and Sean swore under his breath and Danny said something that might have been, 'Ma,' might have been calling for her, but they didn't wake. Both of them were warm, but their body heat together didn't fill the cold space between them. Maggie took her hand away and without thinking tried to stuff it into the pocket of the wool coat, which she was not wearing because she'd put it over Rosemary, which would have been wet, had been full of snow, but would have been warmer by far than the icy space between the two sons she was about to give away, the empty spaces her flailing hand kept shying away from.

Bridget woke up first. It wasn't even light. Maggie wasn't ready. She was sitting against one bowing wall with her knees drawn up for warmth but hadn't laid her head down on them for fear she'd doze off and she didn't dare do that. She saw Bridget rise, eight years old, tiny, blue shawl over her head. Even later today and then forever after that, when she wasn't Bridget's Ma anymore, Maggie would think of that blue shawl, lost.

Barely awake, Bridget looked at her in alarm that knew too much for her years. It made Maggie both annoyed and sad; it made her ashamed. 'What's wrong, Ma?'

Maggie frowned and said, 'Sshhh' and stayed where she was. It was too soon to say about the trip westward on the Orphan Train. Bridget and all of them would know soon enough, when it was time, when she decided it was time. She was still their Ma, and she was doing her best.

A lie, that was. People said that – 'I'm doing the best I can' – so they wouldn't be obliged to try to do better. Still, imagining these brats of hers going west on the Orphan Train in just a few more hours to start a grand new life, Maggie was actually excited for them, even a bit proud of herself for thinking of it in the first place.

Bridget stepped over and around the sleeping forms of her brothers and sister and went outside. Maggie had a flash of panic that she was on her way to disappearing, but she was only going to pee. Maggie had to pee, too, but she didn't dare to leave the room. She considered doing it right here. It wouldn't be the first time and for certain sure not the last. With her children all gone she'd be able to do anything she pleased.

But now they were all waking up. *No, it's not time.* But Michael was sitting up and rubbing his eyes, and Rosemary had started that whining before she was even awake, and now Sean stood up and was almost out the door before Maggie could say, 'No, Sean, wait.'

He turned around. Bridget came up beside him. They were silhouetted in the doorway, which was how Maggie realized the sky was getting lighter, morning was on its way.

'We're going somewhere,' she said, struggling to her knees and then to her feet. 'All of us. Get yourselves ready.'

'Not all of us,' Bridget said sullenly. 'Not Eileen.'

Rosemary's whines turned seamlessly into a wail. 'Eileen! I want Eileen!'

Danny woke up cursing. Maggie doubted he knew what was meant by the awful words he said, but he said them a lot and loudly and all strung together. She'd said such things herself and worse, would again, but she didn't like to hear a thirteen-year-old lad say them, and especially not now when he had to be nice or no family in St Joseph, Missouri, or anywhere else would have him. 'Shut up, Danny,' she snapped, and he did, though it wouldn't last for long.

'Where we going?' Sean was suspicious. Boys ought to trust their Mas. Ought to mind.

Maggie was rough getting her children ready to leave her. Physically rough with the little ones – pulling Michael's shoes on hard so he kicked at her, shoving him away from her when she was done, even slapping Rosemary to stop that whining and snatching away the black wool coat, setting her to crying in earnest. Rough with her words to Bridget, Danny, and Sean because they wouldn't just do as she said, they had to ask questions, Sean had to stand there scowling with his fists clenched and defy her, say he wasn't going nowhere till his brother Seamus came home. Maggie didn't know what to do about Seamus. Sean wouldn't shut up about Seamus. She'd have slapped him, too, if she could have moved fast enough.

She hadn't planned to be rough with the children this morning, this last morning. She'd meant to be especially tender and loving. But there were so many of them, even with two missing. They were all complaining that they were hungry and cold – as if that was her fault; as if she wasn't doing the best she could – and more and more scared as the sunny winter day broke over the city and she started hurrying them because she was afraid they'd miss the Orphan Train. She didn't know what she'd do then. She didn't know what any of them would do.

So, after waiting that whole long night for the right time to get started, now of a sudden Maggie thought the smudged sky entirely too light between the plumes of black coal smoke standing up straight as broom handles because now there was no wind, the city hubbub already too loud, too many people awake and going someplace, the day too far gone. And also of a sudden she wasn't for certain sure how to get to the train station. Eileen was dead, and Seamus might well be or just run away which as far as she was concerned could amount to the same thing, and none of the rest of them could read. The drawn map from Miss Kate Abernathy made little sense to Maggie this morning, wet and smeared as it was, flat on a piece of paper like that, streets with names that she hadn't thought about having names, no alleys pictured on it at all that she could tell.

She made the children practically run, Rosemary whimpering the whole time and Danny cursing wrong, calling her a bastard which in her nervousness almost made her laugh, which she should have cuffed him for but didn't take the time.

Once she picked up Michael but he was too heavy to carry, a fine big lad, and she set him down again. He howled and clung to her. She stumbled, kicked him without meaning to but it served him right, the little bugger, knocked him down in the snow which was a hard layer now over the hard city ground. He howled and she had to help him up, roughly, impatiently, swatting at him through his thin wet pants but barely connecting.

Bridget kept crying, 'Ma? Where we going? Ma?' Maggie had no breath to tell her and no words.

Through Micktown they went. At some point, Seamus joined them. Maggie didn't see or hear him come, but one time when she surveyed her brood and counted heads he wasn't there and the next time he was. She felt neither relief nor anger nor any additional sorrow or triumph for losing him, too; putting him on the Orphan Train, too; sending him off to what might be a better life or might be the end of him. Sean moved to walk beside his brother. Hunched in a torn and dirty but very serviceable jacket Maggie had not seen before and now instantly coveted, hands in

190

pockets, Seamus said nothing to any of his brothers or sisters and for certain sure nothing to his Ma. But he brought up the rear like a sheep dog, ready to stop any of them from straying, and that was a great help whether he meant to be or not.

Milk wagons rattled by, leaving mounds of fresh steaming stinking horse dung like stepping stones behind them. For a while both the sun and the streetlamps shined, gas flames flickering against spreading blue-gray glow. As Maggie and her lost children traveled farther into Manhattan's heart, store windows on one side and then on both sides of the streets glowed, some under awnings. A milliner was setting out umbrellas on the hardpacked snow in front of his shop; Maggie was just thinking how foolish it was to try to sell umbrellas on a winter morning when a lady stopped with the clear intention of buying one.

The morning air did have a freshness about it, but it was sharp with coal smoke. Rosemary kept coughing. Maggie thought she'd heard that out there where her children were going, in St Joseph, Missouri, or even farther west, there'd be clean air, but she didn't know whether to believe that or not. Coal out west would burn dirty, too, wouldn't it?

A locomotive chugged and hooted down the middle of the street. Though this had become a not uncommon occurrence, it still outraged Maggie and made her want to curse at it for its rudeness. Now she also had a moment's panic and actually raised her arm in what would have been a futile attempt to hail it, then told herself this could not be the Orphan Train for she saw it every morning of her life that she was awake and sober and out. Some of her children – Danny, Bridget, one she couldn't quite see who it was – waited until the very last minute and then scattered before it, hooting back at it, their childish voices piping against its monster call. Its whistle and the umbrellas of smoke from its stacks and the long clatter of its wheels on the track rattled Maggie's already rattled nerves.

When the locomotive had passed, and left only the echo of its terrible commotion and its bad smell and its tracks like twin dead snakes through the dirty snow, Maggie collected her children again. There were more of them than there ought to be, and the number kept changing. Eight, she counted; then eleven. Momentarily, Maggie was confused: how many children did she have? How many children would she lose when she lost all her children?

Then she recognized the newsie Sean and Seamus most often fought with, a black-haired, baby-faced, mean-eyed lad. She recognized the little crippled flower girl from the park, who limped along and held onto Rosemary's hand for both their sakes.

There were others, more every time she turned around. Many of them didn't look as if they could have come out of New York City in 1874. An older child carried a dark-skinned newborn babe. A tall strong-looking boy, almost a man, walked barefoot; his clothes were dripping wet. A boy about nine years old with dark blond hair and a bright yellow jacket streaked with dirt chased Michael; both lads shrieked with laughter, and Maggie found herself thinking a daft thing: 'Laughter like seashells.'

Maggie didn't guess it mattered if she delivered more children up to the Orphan Train than Miss Kate Abernathy was expecting. St Joseph, Missouri, and Out West were big places, and New York City wouldn't miss a few of its street-rats. By the time they got to mid-town, she felt like the Pied Piper of Hamelin, a whole crowd of urchins following her, running on ahead, dodging drays and horsecars as the day's traffic thickened, holding hands and fistfighting, crying and shouting and some walking along silently as if they knew something wonderful or terrible was about to happen to them.

Now instead of buildings, hills of mud rose around them, soupy tops running down onto still-frozen lower layers. Trenches cut like alleys pretending to lead somewhere, like streets with phony names. At first Maggie didn't understand what this place was, a dug and piled and buildingless place, big, in the middle of Manhattan, but then she remembered that this was to be a park, the biggest park in the city, The Central Park. Trees there would be, grass, streams and lakes, flowers. Pavilions. Space for children and grownups to play. Not her children. For certain sure, not her.

Trees there were already, one tree anyhow, suddenly sprung up in front of her. A laurel tree, the first she'd seen in the city. It surprised her that she knew what kind of tree it was; maybe there'd been laurel trees in Ireland, these many years ago. Shiny leaves, with serrated edges; smooth bark inviting her to touch it, insisting that she touch it; the tree not much taller than she was, a bush, really. Its tenacity was startling: it clung to the slick unsteadied earth and to Maggie, leaves tangling in her clothes and hair.

She lost her precarious balance and tumbled into the tree. It wrapped its thorny branches around her and pulled her close. She struggled, could not free herself, and none of the children came to her rescue or even paid heed to the trouble she was in. Then the laurel tree let her go. Just like that.

Some of the children were trying to scramble up the mounds of mud but slid down or sank in, getting all filthy. Children could make a game out of anything. Maggie thought she ought to tell them not to do that, but it was too much trouble. She was barely going to be able to get them to the train station where she could get rid of them. Families out west could put up with a little mud. She needed a drink. She needed food and sleep. She needed to be done with this and starting on the pain of having lost all her children, which, she knew, would last the rest of her life but would be better than this fear.

The Central Park was huge. She'd had no idea. The sun was rising dangerously high over the tops of the buildings. Maybe they'd already missed the Orphan Train.

But they made it. The depot was half in weak sunlight and half in weak shadow. Alongside it on the tracks, the train that must be the Orphan Train was not nearly as long as Maggie had imagined, and too quiet, couldn't possibly contain all the children she'd brought it, couldn't possibly carry them out of Manhattan let alone to St Joseph, Missouri, and points beyond, to new lives, better lives.

Miss Kate Abernathy stood on the platform studying a list. When she looked up and saw Maggie, she smiled faintly. Maggie walked right up to her. 'Here's your coat,' she said, thrusting it at her. 'Here's your brats, too. Lots of 'em.' She laughed. The children gathered around her like blown garbage in the streets.

The Orphan Train let out a terrible whistle, which made some of the children scream and some of them laugh, made Seamus draw himself up straight and stride toward it, made Maggie's heart break. 'Ma?' asked Bridget beside her. 'Ma, where we going?' Maggie turned and ran. Not a single child followed or tried to make her stop.

Chapter 17

She woke.

Her thoughts organized themselves.

Ian is dead.

She groaned and curled around herself, arms crossed tightly in the fiery hollow of her chest, head drawn down over her burning throat, fists clenched, knees up hard. The yellow cat Cinnabar came at once and stretched out flat and long on her flank, purring, sending warm vibration and kneading gently with her claws.

His face rose before her, blue, actually blue, in a frozen grimace, with the raw red ring of the noose scored into the cold flesh of his neck. She tossed and turned to escape it, and the sound of Glenn screaming her name, moaning, 'My baby! My baby!' rang in her ears. She cried out to drown it.

Beside her Glenn stirred, and she was stabbed by guilt that she had awakened him out of a rare sound sleep, but also by urgent need for him to awaken and hold her and keep her from being utterly lost. She moaned, then pressed her fists to her mouth and thought surely she would draw blood, but such self-martyrdom proved harder to accomplish than she'd imagined.

This time Glenn started awake, gasping before he was fully conscious, 'What? What's wrong? Are you all right?'

'Magic words,' she begged him. 'Please. I need some magic words.' She tried to laugh a little to show that she was being ironic, that she knew there weren't really any words with magical properties to help her.

But there were. She had begun to collect them, in a purple folder, scraps of paper which she shuffled and touched and re-read obsessively: Lines from a poem about the necessity of loving profoundly and then

195

profoundly letting go. Passages from Kubler-Ross and Stephen Levine. Bits of reflection from other mourners.

The stories of other bereaved parents throughout history.

A paradigm of grief as a hero's journey through the underworld; in order ever to emerge, you must find and face the dragons.

Magic words from Glenn were the most powerful of all. He could say things that functioned like spells, altering her perception of reality just enough to make it not only bearable but luminous. But he had to repeat them for her; when she said them to herself – even using his exact words, his inflection; remembering them in his voice – they had no power anymore. So, several times a day now, she pleaded, 'Say something to me, Glenn. Something magic.'

He didn't always do it. Sometimes, out of the depths of his own grief, he couldn't marshal anything to say. Sometimes he was just too exhausted. Renata feared she was using him and maybe interfering with what he needed to do for himself. But she couldn't help it. She would not make it without him.

Now he hugged her clumsily, mumbled, 'I love you,' and plunged back to sleep. She lay beside him for a while, hoping she could draw comfort, if not magic, from just the warmth and substance and proximity of him. But her mind skittered from one awful image to another: The bitter cold silence in Ian's room while his body lay on the floor. The damp spring grass under her knees and the damp iron of the fence where she knelt and clung and screamed, waiting for the ambulance. His small contorted blue face, actually blue. The near-weightlessness of his ashes in the plastic box, and then the heavy solidity of them when she held them bare in her hands, first struggling to keep them from drifting between her fingers, then turning and opening her hands. The icy silence in his room while his body lay on the floor. His blue face. The lightness and heaviness of his ashes.

Finally she flung herself out of bed, leaned precariously back to tuck the covers in around Glenn, and fled the bedroom. When she was upright, the panic wasn't so strong, the images dimmed. She went downstairs, where Vanessa was looking for something to eat. She made French toast. Vanessa ate five pieces with too much syrup, and drank two tall glasses of orange juice. Renata felt like a good mother.

Dishes cleared away and hamburger thawing in the sink for dinner, she dressed in a jittery state of clarity, feeling almost exotically efficient. Today she was to start therapy. She dreaded it. She also could hardly wait.

She'd known Cheryl Warner for some time but very slightly and distantly. It was a surprise to think of her now, the retrieval of information she hadn't been aware of storing.

Warner, a psychotherapist, specialized in work with families of children with what she called 'attachment disorders,' especially adopted children. She had six or seven children of her own, some born to her, some of various racial mixes adopted as infants, some Vietnamese refugees adopted as toddlers or preschoolers. She had a great deal to say about bonding, intimacy, and authenticity – how to recognize their absence, how to foster them, what the consequences were likely to be if they did not develop.

None of that was important to Renata now. What had surfaced was that Cheryl Warner had lost a child. Renata barely remembered the story, and her own inattentiveness appalled her now – a daughter, she thought; a young teenager. If she had ever known the girl's name, the manner of her death, when it had happened, she'd forgotten. She had no actual memory of Warner ever telling the story, and didn't know how she had come to know about it, whether Warner had made allusions to it in other contexts or whether other people had talked about it. It was just one of Cheryl Warner's characteristics: She had straight fine silky blonde hair in a page-boy cut; she lived and worked in a toney mountain suburb; she talked about attachment disorder; she had lost a child.

Now Renata craved the whole story. So she'd tracked down Cheryl Warner's number, called and left a message, received a wary return call and managed to remind the therapist who she was.

'I'm not a bereavement counselor,' Cheryl had demurred. 'Grief work isn't my specialty.'

'I'm desperate to talk to somebody who's been through this. I have to find a role model for how it's done.'

Across the line there'd come a sound of indeterminate nature. Not a laugh, really, and not a sob, but an outrush of breath that seemed to express both bitter mirth and ironic sorrow. 'Well, then, I'm definitely not your woman. I don't have a clue how it's done.'

Unbelieving, Renata had persisted, and finally she'd been given an appointment. Glenn made the hour-long drive into the foothills with her, but he wouldn't come in. For this of all things, he declared with more certitude than before, he did not need to talk to anybody else.

Renata sat in Cheryl Warner's classy waiting room, surrounded by books and magazines about children whose covers she didn't dare allow into her field of vision, and waited for deliverance. The hour of her appointment passed. Her anxiety mounted. Glenn would come back to pick her up when he'd said he would and she wouldn't be ready. He'd have to come into the therapist's office, or he'd have to wait in the car. The idea of inconveniencing Glenn, who'd lost his son, was intolerable.

She chafed. The clock on the wall showed the passage of the quarter hour; it occurred to her, not without a certain wryness, that it was probably not wise for someone who did not keep to a schedule to display a clock so prominently.

Resentment gathered, along with a sullen conviction that Cheryl Warner was correct: Renata's grief was not important, her sanity was not important, she herself was not worthy of much notice anymore. She recognized the absurd self-absorption – most likely the client before her was in crisis, too, and couldn't be cut off according to schedule – but the longer she sat alone waiting for the bearing of witness she'd scheduled and hired, the less absurd such thoughts showed themselves to be. If she could have left, she might have. As it was, she sank into the miry impossibility of ever healing, the banality of caring whether she healed or not, and by the time Cheryl came out of an inner office – alone; yawning languidly – Renata could hardly penetrate her own despair.

'I'm so sorry your child died,' Cheryl said gently almost the moment they sat down. 'Your daughter, was it? Or your son?'

Taken aback, for she'd said on the phone that it was her son and even repeated his name, Renata said again, 'My son. Ian.' Her throat closed, and she forced out, clutching the arms of the chair, 'It *hurts*.'

Cheryl nodded, looking down at her hands. 'It's the worst pain there can ever be.'

Validation of the client's suffering, Renata thought, recognizing the therapeutic technique. Next would come showing a way toward healing. Desperate, she waited, shoulders so tense her arms and hands trembled, breath stopped. But Cheryl, rubbing her thumbs rather vigorously across the backs of her hands, did not go on. So Renata stumbled through a prompt. 'But there are stages, right? There's movement toward acceptance?'

'Not that I've noticed.'

'I've – I've been suicidal.'

'I still have suicidal thoughts. I still long to join Laurie.'

'It's hard for me to pay attention to my other kids.'

Cheryl passed a hand down her hair, smoothing and fluffing it. 'I used to think, I still think, if I had to lose a child, why couldn't it be Eric? He's the one who's caused me so much pain. Why did it have to be Laurie? She was a perfect child.'

'I read a story,' Renata said cautiously, gauging the other woman's reactions, 'where a woman whose sister had died when they were growing up wrote that she'd always believed her sister's death was more important to her parents than her own life.'

Cheryl nodded. She had still not looked up. 'I can understand that.'

Renata's head had cleared. She stared at the therapist and said, 'But that's not right.'

Cheryl shrugged. She lifted her eyes and distractedly glanced around the room, sweeping past Renata as lightly as past the furnishings, the window, the door, the light and shadows on the rose-colored carpet. She rummaged in the desk drawer, came up with a yellow plastic bottle, and applied lotion liberally to her arms and hands. The ablution occupied nearly her full attention.

Amazed, Renata pressed her point, mostly now out of curiosity. 'I can't let that happen in our family.'

Cheryl shrugged again, but her attention was clearly still on the off-white layer of lotion slicking her creamy skin.

Renata's head swam with incredulity. 'How long ago did your daughter die?'

'She was eleven years old. She died twelve years, three months, and twenty days ago. At 2:14 in the afternoon.'

'How?'

'Of a brain tumor.'

'So – so you knew she was sick for a long time.'

'Almost a year.' Cheryl's face had taken on a haunted look.

Renata nodded, kept nodding, the motion of her head quickly becoming involuntary. Simultaneously, her thoughts were suddenly perseverating, too, ferociously stuck in trying to decide whether it was harder to lose a child without warning, the way she'd lost Ian, or slowly. Did you prepare yourself when there was a long dying? Or was there just more room for more variations of grief – the worry and then terror of the first symptoms, the shock of the diagnosis, the long time of watching your child slip away, the loss at the end still monumental? Would it be better to have had a chance to say goodbye? Couldn't you say goodbye to a person already dead? Would that be as good, as real?

There was a solipsistic quality to this rumination that struck her as not quite honest. With an effort she pulled herself out of it. 'It hasn't ruined your life,' she pleaded. 'You've gone on.'

'There isn't a day that goes by that I don't cry for her,' Cheryl insisted. 'I'll never heal from it. Neither will you.'

Renata sat there for a while. Neither of them spoke.

When she came out into the waiting room, leaving Cheryl still almost dreamily massaging lotion into her plump pale arms, Glenn wasn't there. It was like encountering a brilliantly transparent pane of glass which had no visual presence, did not distort the world seen through it, but was hard and shatter-proof and stopped her thoroughly: He had run the car off a cliff. He had forgotten about her and gone home, and he wouldn't notice she wasn't there.

She sliced through the waiting room as if through a brittle picture, barely even one-dimensional, painted on thin glass, and of course he was in the parking lot, sitting in the car right outside the door where she couldn't miss him, a magazine spread open on the steering wheel and sun on his hair. Love for him made her dizzy.

When she got in beside him, he turned to her and his sad face lit up. 'Hi, honey. How'd it go?'

'She says I'll never heal.'

'That's helpful.'

'She says she's never healed from losing her daughter almost thirteen years ago. Thirteen years.' She shuddered, astonished both that anguish could last so long and that there might well come a time when she would say that her son had died thirteen years ago.

'How old was her daughter?' Glenn wanted to know.

'Laurie. She was eleven.' She told him the story.

'Jesus.'

They drove in silence for a while. Between the mountain suburb and the actual outskirts of Denver was a long stretch of four-lane highway through a nice canyon, and Renata had been watching the striations in the rock, the ripples in the creek, the play of light across the mountain faces for some time before she realized what she was doing, and only then did the pain return.

She shook herself, wrenched her eyes from the hurtful pleasant scene through which she was traveling. Without her conscious will, her gaze fastened on a peak ahead of them and far enough to the right of the road that they wouldn't seem to pass it for a while, perspective having altered relative position and motion. The peak caught sunshine: golden, with spring snow silver and blue. Wisps of cloud gauzed the outline, then parted to show it in clarity more exquisite than if they hadn't been there.

Awareness exploded of Ian's presence in the mountain peak, in the clouds and sunshine, in the interconnections among mountain peak and cloud and sunshine peak. Quite literally unable to contain herself, Renata rose to meet him. In the flowing of the clouds, particularly, she immersed herself in him, and the exultation of it was nearly as painful as loss.

Eventually, though, they did pass the peak, and the sensation of Ian's presence subsided. Breathless, Renata waited a while, then said to Glenn, 'I've been thinking,' which wasn't actually true since she was aware of only just having had the thought she was about to say aloud, tentatively, probing the pain it would bring to her and Glenn. 'Probably we should try to find Judy.'

She saw him start to inquire, 'Who?' with his usual fuzziness about names, but then he remembered. 'Ian and Vanessa's birthmother,' he said wearily.

'She should know. Otherwise someday Vanessa may have to tell her. She shouldn't be the one to have to tell her.'

There was a tense pause. Then he sighed. 'I guess you're right. How do we do that?'

'Remember that class I took about how to be a private detective? The woman who taught it specialized in adoption searches. I could call her.'

He nodded.

The relief and pride Renata felt that they had discussed a potentially agonizing subject openly, come to a consensus, and made an honorable plan lasted a few seconds. Then horror thundered in upon her. They were talking about the need to find their son's birthmother to tell her he was *dead*.

She twisted in her seat to face him. 'Is it true? That we'll never heal? That this really has ruined our lives?'

'It can't be true,' he answered. 'We can't allow it to be true.'

'You don't believe what Cheryl said? That I'll always feel like this?'

He might have said he couldn't predict what would happen for her. Strictly speaking, of course, that would have been accurate. But he said deliberately, 'No. It's not true.'

She was not to be easily placated. 'How do you know?'

'I know,' he said firmly. 'We'll get through this.'

'The pain,' she said, pressing the flats of her hands to her chest where the pain was worst, 'just goes on and on.'

'It won't go on forever.'

'But it takes so *long*. I've never felt anywhere near this bad, and I've never felt bad for so long.'

'In the overall span of our lives, it isn't so long.'

And there they were: Magic words. She was aware of a smug little triumph, as though she'd tricked him out of a treasure. She laid her head back against the seat and turned what he'd said over and over in her mind, an amulet.

By the time he pulled the car into their garage, though, the amulet had lost almost all its sheen, and already she needed another. She put her hand on his arm before he got out of the car. 'Say it to me again,' she ventured. 'I need to hear it again.'

He frowned impatiently. 'What?'

'What you said before. About it not being so long in the overall span of our lives.'

'Yeah. That's it. You got it.'

'You say it. Exactly the way you did before.'

'I don't know exactly what I said before. And I have to go to the bathroom.'

He didn't quite shake her hand off, but he hurried to get out of the car and out of the garage and into the house. Away from her. She followed slowly and sorrowfully behind, feeling cheated.

Vanessa wasn't home from Wendy's yet and there was no message from her on the machine. There was no message from Ian, either.

Glenn went into his office and shut the door. The floor under Renata dissolved, and the ground. She sank.

Chapter 18

The path went steeply, steadily downward. Mud soaked and filled Renata's shoes, softened and enlarged her footprints and then filled them in. Nothing was higher than the ankle-high fetid mud. There were no railings or walls, no trees or bushes or boulders, and she could see no sky or roof overhead although there was the strong feeling of being closed in from above, even pressed down. The path, though, was plain, a glossy light-brown band through darkness, wide enough for her to walk on and very slippery, going down.

Others were in the near and far distance, some climbing downward, some sliding, some squatting by the side of the path. She had an impression of one wrapped in a heavy black coat, another with red-ochre streaks across her cheekbones, a third with hair the color of milk. But they did not pretend to be her comrades, and she went on alone.

Someone, though, was beside her. In front of her, walking backward, facing her. She saw the eyes. She caught the slight gleam of the skin, the faint outline of the form. She heard the light breath, felt it, gasped at it because she couldn't get enough air in here, took in its odor which she identified as decay but which was not in the least offensive.

She didn't ask who it was. 'I'm Jordan. I'll take you down.'

Her hands were grasped. She spread her fingers so Jordan's could work their way in. 'Do you know why my son killed himself?'

'No one knows.'

'Did he mean to die? Did he understand that death is forever? Can you understand that when you're nine years old?'

'You'll never know.'

'I have to know. Don't I?'

'It's beyond knowing.'

Jordan's grip tightened, but Renata wasn't pulled or steadied or guided. There was no need. She was descending, not precisely of her own volition but inevitably and without resistance. Even if she lost her footing or her mind she would descend, and there was no other way to go, no choice.

Down. Her feet slid, ankle-deep. The trail stretched and contracted like a wide elastic, and she went where it led her, down, where Jordan took her. Jordan – androgynous, perhaps hermaproditic – stayed with her, holding her hands, but there was no sense of comradeship here, only of efficiency, of somebody doing what needed to be done.

Renata hadn't fallen, and the road hadn't risen or deepened, but now she was covered with mud. Slick, it coated her eyelids, her eyes themselves, the pads of her fingertips, the insides of her arms and thighs. Her flesh was damp and slightly oily, redolent of decay and of soft swift descent.

There were no abrupt turns in the path and no drop-offs. It just went down. Until Ian died, Renata hadn't known there were such depths under the infrastructure of everyday life, such long slopes, such steep declines. She knew nothing about her guide – gender, size, coloration, origin, intent – except what mattered: Jordan was taking her down.

They were neither picking up speed nor slowing. There were no obstacles in the path, no bumps or rough spots. Smooth, it went down. She slid on its shiny surface, swam effortlessly just under its surface, made no motion beyond descending and descended through deep slime, went down.

She couldn't see through the layers of mud over her eyes. She couldn't speak around the mud insinuating itself between her lips, sealing her lips. She couldn't breathe out of the mud that packed her nostrils. She couldn't stop going down. She didn't want to.

Jordan whispered, 'Here we are.'

Things swarmed over Renata, had been swarming for some time before she'd become aware of them, swarming buzzing voices saying, 'Welcome.' The sweet mud was sucked from one of her eyes and she saw, very close, quivering antennae, furred insect legs, wings cold and blue as a dead child's skin, a bulging and faceted black eye. Mandibles clicked. 'Welcome.'

Revulsion skittered just under her skin. But if she brushed these creatures off and ran away, where would she go? And why were insects and stinking, drawing mud worth trying to escape when her child was dead?

'Jordan?' A reflex, saying the only known thing, but she wouldn't know how to use anything Jordan might say in response.

'Welcome,' Jordan whispered, and kissed her. Lips adhered to her lips and then pulled away, taking flecks of her fragile skin, leaving a residue.

Renata sank, floated, sank. Mud bubbled and pocketed around her, covered her, exposed her.

Some of the insects were as big as her two clasped hands while others, tiny, were only just visible. Pale and translucent at the head end, thick at the thorax with pale dry wings, the creatures were swollen at the abdomen and the color of blood in shit. Their six feathery knees bent up higher than their backs.

There must have been millions of them. Nests. An immense colony. A peculiar muddy light came now from no source and illuminated multifaceted eyes on stalks, shiny red carapaces, dust or pollen or clouds of seed. Renata shuddered, then went limp.

They were in her hair. The sticky cilia that furred their feet pulled at her scalp and at the roots and shafts of her hair. They were in her ears, swirling, burrowing. Attaching themselves to her tongue and teeth and the roof of her mouth, they fed and invited her to feed; in the soft slippery ruts leading from both wing-ends of her pelvis to her genitals, they bred and laid their eggs.

The long hollow needle of a proboscis pierced her skin, flesh, bone just at the corner of her eye. She saw it coming for a long time, didn't blink or turn her head. There was pain, a tubular aching with a sharp flanged point at the end. Then liquid was siphoned out of her, and some other liquid – hallucinogenic, poisonous – pulsed in.

Another needle, much longer and thicker and very firm, was inserted through the tender tissue of her breast straight into her heart. Her heart clutched and then relaxed as fluid was drained out of it, its own pulse setting the rhythm and pace, and a viscous, tingling, numbing fluid was pumped in.

'Welcome,' came the whispering again, and a hissing, chittering, 'Stay. Stay.'

Renata was nearly paralyzed by now, and euphoric. 'Yes.' She felt, saw, tasted herself metamorphose, transformed by grief and ministration into other forms of life and half-life: A swine, rooting, devouring her own dead young. A tree, sapped and wooden. An imploding star.

Jordan held her, and the insects came.

Chapter 19

Renata hung back. Althea, who'd been coming to these meetings for many years, went into the room smiling and greeting people, and when Renata came along she introduced her, but only by name. She didn't say, as she could have, 'This is Renata Burgess. Her nine-year-old son hanged himself.'

Though she didn't allude to anyone else's story now, either, she'd told Renata before they'd come about some of the parents she would likely meet here. Renata searched their faces, wondering with a peculiar, intent curiosity which went with which. Was this the couple whose kindergartner had been run over by a school bus? Was this the father whose teenager had failed to beat a train at a crossing? Where – this with some bewilderment – was the mother who'd sent her surviving children west on the Orphan Train? Of course she couldn't be here. Yet Renata found herself looking around for her.

The room was alive with mourning. Every person in this small crowd had lost a child, and the purpose of gathering was to say so. She belonged here. That was a terrible thing to admit, and her nerves buzzed painfully. At the same time, relief was immense at being with her own kind.

People were making small talk; she was amazed, offended and encouraged. People were drinking coffee and eating chocolate chip cookies; she wouldn't have been safe holding a cup of hot coffee, and she wouldn't have been able to taste or swallow a cookie, but it was a revelation both welcome and repugnant that these people, whose children had died as hers had died, could do such things and in such a gathering.

Laughter rose from one group; Renata's was not the only head to turn, and the revulsion that made her flesh prickle registered in the expressions of others. The new ones, she guessed; the initiates.

Althea was engaged in a conversation with two other women by the refreshment table. They were talking about gardening. Acutely self-conscious and slightly nauseated, Renata couldn't stay so near the food, couldn't insert herself into the banal conversation and couldn't just stand there by herself. She drifted toward the side of the room where a table held printed material – books about grieving, books about children's grief, recommended reading lists of alarming length and density, a flyer announcing a convention; the idea of a national convention of bereaved parents struck her as ludicrous, blood-curdling, and wonderful.

Unable to bring herself to pick up any of the materials, she just stood with her hands behind her back and looked down, scanned. Cliched phrases rose to meet her: *no greater sorrow, broken heart, lost child* – now rendered brilliantly true. She'd have liked to be staring without seeing, but she saw.

'Is this your first meeting?' Renata jumped and turned. 'Sorry.' The woman very lightly touched her elbow. 'I didn't mean to startle you.'

Struggling to extract some usable oxygen from shallow, ragged breath that skimmed only the surface of her lungs, Renata nodded, a disorganized gesture intended to mean *yes, it's my first meeting, my son died two months ago*, and *it's okay, almost everything startles me these days*, and *pleased to meet you but I don't want to know you, I don't want to have to know you.*

'This is a good book,' the woman said, tapping her finger on one of the stacks. The fluttering motion and the tapping noise made Renata flinch. 'It was really helpful to us.' Renata tried to read and retain the title. 'You can check it out,' the woman said helpfully, and proceeded to show her how.

She signed the proffered card. The letters that made up her name formed easily and legibly, though being aware of them individually was uncomfortable. The list of other readers filled one side; her name, starting the list on the back of the card, appeared both dangerous and endangered, and she had to drag her gaze away.

Not long ago she'd been utterly unable to sign her name. Naming herself publicly and in writing had seemed an invitation to dreadful things. Then, painstakingly drawing each line and loop, she'd been nearly paralyzed by the thought that the last time she'd made a capital *R*, the tail of a *g*, Ian had been alive.

Now she signed her name all of a piece. That was an improvement; it made her sad, made her pity herself. She saw even more pitiable progress when she had to think about the date, still used March 18 as the starting point for calculation but didn't automatically know how many days it had been, how many hours.

The book was warm and slightly sticky against her forearm. Under the mentor's protective gaze, Renata slid the book out, placed it horizontal on her palm, and opened the cover.

The sense of the words was apparent at once, and she plunged into them. This was the journal of a father whose daughter had died. He wrote about psychedelic grief, the structures of the mind and heart exploding, dissolving. He wrote about suddenly comprehending what had always been meant by 'despair,' by 'a broken heart.' Almost from the beginning, too, he wrote about a strange, persistent feeling of *rightness*, of things being as they should be though they were so far from what he wanted. Renata gulped in the words like air, and her chest hurt, her head swam.

'Shall we start?' called a man's voice.

Renata's stomach lurched in protest as though she were strapped into an open car on the lip of a roller-coaster hill which now, vehemently, she resisted going down. People were moving toward the circle of folding chairs.

Althea came up beside her. 'Let's go find seats. Do you need a cup of coffee?'

Reluctantly sliding the book into her purse, Renata shook her head. Her hands were trembling as it was – mostly, she realized, in anticipation of imminent relief.

The man who'd called the meeting to order introduced himself as Rob Torres, this year's leader. 'We're sorry that you have to be here,' he said, looking around, and Renata was touched by his graciousness. 'This is not a brotherhood and sisterhood anyone chooses to join. We're so sorry that your children have died. But we welcome you.'

Althea patted Renata's hand. Several people caught her eye. She felt welcomed.

Rob took a deep breath. 'My wife and I lost two children.' There were a few gasps, presumably from new people. Rob paused for them, then went on doggedly. 'Our baby daughter Cassie lived to be only four days old. Our daughter Amanda was four years old when she died. They both had a rare lung condition which is probably hereditary. We have two other daughters and a son. They're all teenagers now, and so far they're all okay. But sometimes I feel like my whole life could be devoted to just waiting for something bad to happen to them. Sometimes I think it *should* be. A lot of bereaved parents feel that way, even when they've lost only one child, even when there's no pattern or anything.'

Women flanked Rob, but both of them were obviously attached to the men on their opposite sides. Renata looked for his wife, then remembered that Althea had told her about the Torreses: they'd come to the meetings together for a while after Amanda's death, but then the wife had left – left the group, left Rob, left their other children, left the state. Althea said Rob had told the group that she couldn't stand any reminders of the family's curse. Rob had said he didn't hold it against her.

From the far side of the circle, the woman who'd been at the book table spoke next. Renata listened, rapt. 'My name is Brenda Henemann,' she began crisply. 'Three years ago this November 5, my son Colin was killed by a hit-and-run driver on his way back to his dorm from an evening class. He was twenty-one. He didn't have any identification, and he was riding his roommate's bicycle, so when the police traced the registration they called the other boy's mother. She thought it was her son who had been killed, but it turned out to be mine.'

She stopped. She had obviously said all this many times before; it had an incantatory ring, the rhythm of a ballad familiar even before it was told and structured so as to gather emotional momentum from the repetition and repetition of its refrain. In the quiet that followed, people were nodding, touched by the profound pathos of it, satisfied by its neatness and symmetry.

Renata tried to take Brenda's measure, to get a feel for what kind of person this could have happened to. About forty, slight, fair-skinned and blonde, wearing glasses and a tailored shirt with pressed black jeans, she gave the impression of meticulousness, even fastidiousness.

The next woman in the circle, one place closer to Renata, was older, dumpier, tired. 'I'm Jean McIntosh. This is my husband Arnie. Our son died eighteen years ago. Of leukemia.'

'Bill,' said Arnie, a fat man in a flannel shirt. His gruff bass underlay her soft soprano in a melody they'd obviously reprised countless times. 'He was fourteen.'

'I didn't know children died,' Jean said, and there was a ripple of assent around the circle, bitter chuckles and grunts.

'We have four other kids,' Arnie said.

'And four grandchildren,' said Jean.

'But we've never gotten over Bill,' said his father.

'You don't,' said his mother, looking around the circle with the confidence of a veteran. 'You don't get over it.'

The next man, who looked to be no more than twenty-five, could not speak when it came his turn. He shook his head once. The pale young woman beside him glanced at him with palpable resentment and spoke loudly, shockingly. 'We lost our daughter. Three months ago. She was two years old. She drowned.'

Renata waited for her to say their names and their daughter's name, but she didn't. *That's not right*, Renata found herself thinking indignantly. *You didn't do it right.*

Someone said, with appreciative sibilance, 'Three months. It's so soon.'

Someone else said, 'It won't get any better.'

'But it does change,' the first person said. 'It does – I don't know. Soften.'

Beside Renata, Althea spoke up. 'You don't get over it. You don't forget. But you do sort of get used to it, I guess.'

Renata looked at her gratefully, thinking, *Here. Here's how to do it.*

But a thin woman was talking, loudly and out of turn. Unadorned, her face would doubtless have been haggard; Renata couldn't believe, though, that the ghoulish effect of the heavy makeup was unintentional – layered pancake with edges clearly visible at her hairline and under her chin and ears; violet eyeshadow extended well beyond her lids; mascara thick and clotted as black jam; glistening

213

pale lipstick; blush pale and glistening in pools exactly where the hollows of her cheeks were deepest, deepening them. She was fairly shouting. 'Well, I'm not used to it. My name's Patty Devereaux, and my son Cory died six years ago, and I'm sure as *hell* not used to it, and I never *will* get used to it. It would be a dishonor to my son if I ever got used to it.' She glared at Althea.

'Oh, I don't think it's honoring—' Althea began, but several people, including the leader, were already talking.

'We don't criticize how each other grieves.' It wasn't clear whether this mild reprimand was addressed to Althea or to Patty.

'Whatever works for you is okay. Whatever you need.'

'Nobody knows how you feel. Nobody can tell you what it takes to get through something like this.'

'There's no right way or wrong way to grieve.'

Renata, a novice at this, found herself wondering whether those things were true.

Patty hadn't stopped talking, and even now that the other voices had died down she didn't stop shouting. Her remarkably sustained stridency, the jagged and exaggerated gestures of her hands and expressions on her face, were striking. 'They tell me at work, they say, "If you ever need somebody to talk to, you know I'm here." Especially my boss. How dare she say something like that to me? I wouldn't share my grief with *her*, for God's sake. My grief's too *good* to share with her.' Her silvery pink upper lip was curling away from her white teeth, and she was actually spitting in contempt.

'I think,' said the leader, very carefully, 'that we can learn to accept what others offer us—'

He was obviously going to say more, and Renata wanted to hear it, but Patty had leaned forward in her seat, half-risen, and was shaking her finger at him. 'Why should I? Why should I accept *anything* from *anybody*? *My son is dead!*'

There was something seductively liberating about such vitriol so expansively expressed, and for a few moments, in the silence that followed, Renata gave herself up to it. Something dangerous, too; she pulled herself away and turned beseechingly back to Althea, who was next in the circle and who began again to speak, to tell her story, the stories of both her lost children, which she must have told countless times here and elsewhere. 'My name is Althea Ford, and I've lost two children.'

Consternation again; revulsion. Renata was sharply reminded of an incident Althea had related to her: A woman had come up to her at a national convention, had sought her out to grasp both her hands and peer close into her face and declare, 'You're bad luck. You and others like you. You're proof that lightning *does* strike twice and I *could* lose another child, and I'm sorry, it's nothing personal, but I don't want you here.'

Now Patty let loose with a short, raucous laugh, close to mockery. She got up from her chair and took two steps toward the young couple whose daughter had drowned three months ago, extending her skeletal arm and pointing her pink-clawed forefinger at the husband in particular. 'Don't you let anybody tell you it ever gets any better. Because it doesn't.'

The leader said – rather mildly, Renata thought – 'Patty, let's let Althea tell her story.'

Patty held her bent, clawed position for an eerie span of several moments, while the feverish gaze of the young newly bereaved mother stayed riveted on her and the father sank lower in his chair with his legs out straight, ankles uncrossed and soles turned out, arms crossed over his chest as if to hold it together. Finally Patty said, venom diluted despite herself, 'Oh, hell, we've all heard *Althea's* story. She's been telling her story a helluva lot longer than I've been telling mine, and what good has it done her or any of the rest of us? I want to hear *new* stories. I want to hear about *new* dead kids. That's why we're here, right?'

Shocked, ready to spring to the protection of her friend, Renata nonetheless acknowledged that, in a way Patty did not intend, she was right. Hearing about other people's dead children was helpful – not consoling, for consolation wasn't the point and would have been a lie, but instructive, somehow; mentoring. Fondly she thought of Maggie, of Daphne and Willa, of Elspeth whose story – one of whose stories, the story of bereavement, which did not tell about the whole of her life – Renata had not yet been told but would, soon. Older stories than those in this room, they provided a context, a current, and in the midst of her panic she trusted them. She didn't think Patty Devereaux knew that, or would care.

But she did go back to her seat, pulling her feet up under her and wrapping her arms around one knee and burying her head so that her stick-thin body suggested a praying mantis in waiting. No one said anything else to her. No one addressed any remarks to the young couple, although looks were cast in their direction.

Outraged, confused about the mores of the group but certain that this could not be right, Renata reached for her friend's hand. Althea's answering grasp was firm but not desperately so; the older woman's fingers went between hers, and the bones of their palms lined up nicely.

Althea told her stories plainly. She didn't cry, though clearly she had and would again. She didn't adorn. Some people in the circle fidgeted; some were insulated by their own grief from hers; some seemed to pay close attention.

Renata paid close attention, and was struck by the difficulty of mourning directly such an enormous loss. Mourners caught and held themselves on details that gave the appearance of mattering but, really, were irrelevant: 'She had been dead the entire weekend before we even knew anything was wrong,' as though knowing right away would have made things better. 'His roommate's mother thought it was her son who'd been killed, but it turned out to be mine,' the same words in the same order with the same inflection every time: 'It turned out to be mine.'

There were plenty of hooks like that in the story of Ian's death:

'He would have been ten years old in three weeks.'

'The last thing he felt for us was hatred.'

'He was in his own home. He was right across the hall.'

'If only I'd had dinner on time. If only one of us had gone in to check on him fifteen minutes earlier. If only he hadn't had the rope in his pocket. If only he hadn't had bunk beds.'

It was true that fixating on such specifics, framing the grief in that way, was purposeless self-torture. But it had another, subtler, more profound effect that brought her up short: like all masochism, it was a perverse sort of self-aggrandizement, and it diverted attention ignobly from the thing itself, the terrible loss itself, Ian's death *itself*. She had to stay with the thing itself.

So when Althea was done and there had been a silence into which even Patty didn't speak, and it was her turn, Renata began with care. 'My son Ian died.' She paid close attention to the words of her own story and, though they seared, she wasn't destroyed by the pain.

When she finished, too, there was silence. Althea patted her knee. The woman on her other side took her hand. Someone across the circle said gently, 'Well, Renata, we're sorry you have to be here, and we're glad you came.' Maybe because it had been said so many other times to so many other parents, it seemed the perfect thing to say.

On the way home, Althea told about the bereavement of parents who hadn't been at the meeting tonight – the variety of causative events: car accidents, unmistakable suicides, illnesses, a fire; the range of parental response: marriages destroyed, marriages renewed, lives gutted, lives unpredictably enriched. Renata listened avidly.

Althea talked, too, about her dead children, anecdotes such as Renata could not bear to tell about Ian, and she listened in awe as Althea told them. Another car cutting in front of them made her relate how Susan had been an inveterate backseat driver, which reminded her of Susan teaching Allen to drive, which led to a description of the big red dump truck that had been Susan's favorite toy when she was about eight, which segued into problems Susan had had with her second-grade teacher. 'She was a feisty little kid,' her mother said, sadly, proudly. 'For that matter, she was a feisty adult, too.'

So automatic was her expectation that the next thing Althea would say would be, 'You'd have liked her,' that when it wasn't she found herself saying, for Althea's sake, 'She sounds like somebody I would have liked.'

'Yes. A lot of people liked her.' Then, 'But who knows? Maybe you wouldn't have liked her. And most likely you never would have met.'

They were both silent, in deference to the importance of saying only what was true and not what was merely easy, reductionist and therefore disrespectful. 'Does it hurt to think about your kids?' Renata ventured to ask.

217

'Sure, it does. But it makes me happy, too. They're happy memories, mostly.'

'Does it break your heart?'

'Not anymore.'

Hoping she wasn't being impertinent or unkind, but driven, Renata pressed. 'What would you say you feel when you talk about them now?'

Althea was quiet for a few minutes, considering. 'Bittersweet,' was what she came up with. 'Thinking about Susan and Allen is bittersweet.'

Renata sat back in her seat. Bittersweet. She could tolerate bittersweet for the rest of her life.

They were almost to her house when Althea said, casually, as though it were hardly worthy of note, 'Oh, I need catfood. Do you mind if we just stop at the store for a minute?'

Renata's throat constricted. But it had the slightly dishonest air of a habit rather than an immediate response, and she thought, *I can do this*, and she said, 'That's fine.'

Already pulling into the supermarket parking lot, Althea glanced at her. 'Are you sure? I can take you home and come back—'

'It's okay,' Renata insisted grimly.

Althea got out first, leaving her there. Renata was afraid to get out of the car. When she'd forced herself to do it – to put her feet on the asphalt, to shift from a sitting to a standing position and from an interior to an exterior space, when she'd locked and shut the door, she knew she'd be afraid to get back in again.

She was afraid to cross the parking lot, afraid of the cars and of the spaces where there were no cars. Althea was beside her.

She was afraid of the doors, and of the bright lights onto which they opened, closed, opened again as she hesitated in the beam of the electric eye.

Then, standing in the pet food aisle while Althea interminably compared prices, she was inundated by a peculiar comfort in the form and substance of an epiphanous thought: She had the rest of her life to mourn Ian. She didn't have to do it all at once. Relief flung the colors on the catfood bags at her, bright as balloons, and for a few minutes the renewed possibilities of life pleased her, thrilled her, made her giddy.

But before they had crossed the vast undulating parking lot, her skin was crawling. Althea opened the passenger door for her, settled her in, shut the door carefully. While Althea was gone, in the scant seconds it took for her to pass through the double proboscises of the headlights to, presumably, emerge on the other side, the bottom of the hollow space made by the dark vehicle dissolved, and Renata went down.

Chapter 20

Renata was awakened after another long period of unconsciousness – day or night, days or weeks, the period of time in which Althea moving through the headlights of the car in the parking lot left her alone – by huge crawling movement around and against her. At first she thought it was the world itself, this underworld, expanding and contracting with her inside it, writhing and pulsing against her so that she writhed, too, after having been limp for so long, and she felt her own pulse start up again, as Ian's would never do.

Behind her, the creature she knew as Cecily moaned in twilight sleep and pulled her closer. Renata snuggled back into her. The six slender legs, furred and suction-tipped, parted for her, folded comfortingly around her belly and chest, and where they touched, she didn't hurt anymore. The long silky abdomen massaged the radiating tension between her shoulder blades until, once again, it went away.

'You can't stay here.'

Hurt that Cecily would be saying such a thing to her, sending her away when she'd just found a place she could live and company she could keep as a bereaved mother, Renata whimpered. Cecily's legs and satiny wings folded back over her. 'Of course you can,' Cecily hissed. 'You can stay as long as you like. Forever. There's always a place for you here.'

'Thank you,' Renata breathed, and the pain of breathing was bearable. It wasn't Cecily who was trying to send her away.

The pressure and slithering motion of the dim world, a sinuous earthquake, resolved itself into coils, one on top of the other, each so massive as to be almost of a piece with all the others. In the soothing half-light to which Renata's eyes had gratefully become adjusted since she'd been down here, the coils gleamed, the skin

221

taut and flawless as if it never would be shed. Patterns of diamonds and stripes and coils within coils floated by, very close to the surface of her own skin, as if they weren't imprinted somewhere else at all but had a dimension of their own.

'No.'

'Renata,' came Cecily's seductive whisper, shushing the other voice. Something tender that carried a hidden sharpness brushed the back of her neck – Cecily's beak, with its beguiling poison. 'Stay. Stay here with us.'

'Yes. I will.'

'No. Renata.' A head rose out of the coils. Flat, triangular, reptilian, and fully as big as her own, its jaws slung open until they were nearly vertical, revealing double rows of fangs and a flickering forked tongue. Each prong of the tongue was longer than her arm; her own appendages seemed to have become vestigial, all but useless down here. The tongue insinuated itself on either side of her face, a slithering collar of thin flesh, from actually inside the snake. 'You can't stay here. I won't allow it.'

'Oh, but it doesn't hurt here,' Renata protested dreamily.

'But it *does* hurt. The truth is, it does hurt.'

'It doesn't have to.' Cecily caressed her from behind. The beak scanned Renata's flesh just above the surface, found and painlessly penetrated the soft spot behind Renata's ear. Instantly the sweet numbness was renewed, and Renata thought dimly what good friends Cecily and the others were, how lucky she was to have found them and their safe haven. The woman whom Cecily had turned to stone. The woman drinking Cecily's poison straight from her mouth.

'If you stay here you will lose yourself.'

'That's fine.'

'If you stay here you will lose your life.'

'I don't want it anymore.'

'If you stay here Ian will still be dead, and you will lose everything else, too.'

The pain started again. Before Renata even cried out, Cecily gave her a long, powerful injection, but it wasn't enough. The pain spread. Renata groaned.

'This is *yours*,' Belinda hissed. 'This pain is yours. Don't give it away.'

Renata cried out. Cecily's sticky tentacles were all over her, soothing, caressing, drawing the pain out of her and leaving only numbness in its place. Suddenly repulsed, Renata twisted and pushed, and realized she was trapped.

Urgent, deafening chittering rose. Cecily was joined by, then inundated by, then lost among the others, a few settling from distant corners and from intimate crevices nearby, then hordes. Bulging eyes bent on limber stalks to take her in. Tri-segmented bodies encased in hard shells slid across her soft flesh, making her think about the liquid inside their bodies and the hard bone inside hers. They attached themselves to her with the suction pads on their feet, and the cilia on their legs made her itch. Proboscises probed. Beaks punctured her skin and spurted anesthetizing fluid into her tissues to keep her from feeling pain. Pain that was hers. They sucked pain out of her. They sucked her soul out of her. In order to keep her here among them, they would dissolve and devour her.

'Belinda!' she cried. But the serpent had vanished.

Renata rubbed her hands roughly down her arms, which were fully formed as ever. Dozens of the fat red insects flew off. They made ticking sounds when they struck hard surfaces, little pops when they burst. But many of them still adhered to her, and clouds of others came.

At her right hand, half-submerged in the muck in which she now realized she was lying, was a stick. A thin and splintery cylinder, it might be a handle to something she could use as a weapon.

Struggling to breathe in the stench she'd stopped noticing long ago, struggling to breathe through the insect bodies and parts of bodies that had lodged in her mouth and nose, she worked at the stick until it dislodged. It was indeed a handle, attached to a brush with very stiff bristles that came out of the mud with a sound like cloth tearing and tore the skin on the inside of her wrist where it grazed.

Renata managed to turn the bristled side of the brush toward her, but the handle kept sliding out of her grasp. She gripped it too hard and nearly lost it altogether, loosened her fingers and eased them down through the layers of caked slime until they found wood. Then she brought the brush against the flesh of her belly and pulled down hard.

223

Skin ripped off and stinging pain replaced the itching, but the insects were dislodged only for a moment and then came back, fewer of them but much fiercer. They swarmed around the brush itself and tangled their sticky feet and hairy legs in its bristles, so that she couldn't use it against them anymore. It had in fact been turned to their advantage, her weapon into their tool.

One of the insects – a big one with a soft underbelly; it might be Cecily – had settled itself onto her face. When she tried to pull it off, her fingers stuck to it, forcing her to extricate them one by one and coating them with a viscous, foul-smelling film.

Flailing, her hand found a pliable sheet of some thin substance, like metal leaf. It stuck to her palm. She brought it around and inserted it between the insect's exposed underparts and the exposed flesh of her face. The metal pinged against the bridge of her nose and smelled like rust. With it, she skimmed the creature loose. Her face felt peeled. Awkwardly she swung her arm, intending to toss the odd weapon with its clinging cargo aside, but it still stuck to her.

Defeated, she let her arm and hand fall limp into the mud. The metallic sheet simply floated away on the surface water, but the insects were still attacking.

They swarmed around her feet and legs, abrading her with their wings, biting. Her ankles swelled. She kicked at them, but her frantic movements only increased the force binding her to them, and stirred up more of them.

She did not want to stay here. She wanted to go home. She fought hard. But the stronger her attempts to escape, the more ferociously the insects clung to her, and they multiplied, more and more of them fastening themselves to her everywhere, wings flittering, proboscises exchanging her fluids for theirs.

At last, she collapsed. Mud and excrement burbled up around her. She sank but would not drown; now she could feel the bottom and the firm sides.

Cecily hovered over her, bent-stick legs forming a cage, mushy underbelly reeking of her cloying poison. In the many facets of her globular eyes, Renata saw her own face reflected and reflected, her own eyes. Cecily's wings were torn, and blood oozed out of a rent in the shell covering her engorged abdomen. Her beak drooped. Her proboscis trailed across Renata's lips but made no attempt to enter.

Renata was swept by a bittersweet affection for this creature, who had loved and comforted her, whom she had loved. She put her arms up, smaller insects hanging from them like fruit, and embraced Cecily. 'I can't stay,' she told her gently.

The creature's bulbous head bobbed. 'I know.'

'But I thank you.'

The head bobbed again, this time wordlessly. The two segmented front legs quivered against Renata's cheeks.

'You're in charge of this place,' Renata whispered. 'Guard it for me.' Cecily buzzed softly.

Then Renata got to her feet. The insects fell or flew away, letting her go. She took a step and then a less tentative step forward, along a solid pathway which she recognized as the back of the serpent Belinda, laid down for her through the mire, taking her farther back into another story.

Chapter 21

The air was gray-green, and dripped. Elspeth Mary Broadt, who had now lived in the western Pennsylvania wilderness through the last winter of the eighteenth century and most of the first of the nineteenth, had yet to see a day here when the air did not exude moisture of some sort, gray-green or silver-white, black or brown or golden.

Although the winter snows could be fierce and there were occasional thunder- and hailstorms, usually the weather did not so directly declare itself, and, as now, the wetness could not properly be said to be falling, for there was no suggestion of downward motion. The air, the leaves or the leafless trees, the muddy or grassy ground, the cabin walls and dirt floor and the canvas hung over the single window opening to keep the weather out simply oozed excess water, as did her own skin and hair and clothes, as did the flesh of her boys, sticky where she had laid her hands upon them getting them ready this morning for the trek into town.

Preparing for Frank's absence from home, which he had estimated would be three weeks, they'd gone for provisions together the day before he'd left, and it had been tiring but enjoyable, a family event. He and she had thought the things they'd bartered for, with nearly the last of the corn and the men's shirts and women's dresses she'd sewn over the winter, would last until he returned, and their next such expedition would be a celebration of the family's reunion.

But it was coming up on five weeks now, and no word from Frank or about him. They could do without tea, coffee, and sugar, used up a week or more ago, and without chocolate, too, though the boys thought they could not. But now the flour barrel was nearly empty and she had broken her last needle. The dried apples she had guarded and apportioned – both boys adored them and she suspected Nathaniel of having raided the bin at least once – would be gone before the early spring carrots were ready. She'd stewed the last stewing chicken Sunday, leaving only four laying hens.

It was true that she'd begun to see unmistakable signs of rabbit and squirrel, and woods bison were moving shaggily among the ragged shadows again. Nathaniel had lately been pestering to be allowed to hunt. In her opinion he was far too young, barely four years old, but Frank would doubtless disagree; he'd already started showing both boys how to clean a gun. Certainly she couldn't teach him even if she'd been so inclined. She knew enough about shooting to protect herself and her sons, maybe, but she'd rather risk the trip into Cussawago than venture into the woods with a loaded gun in her hands and her children with her, Arthur at her heels and Nathaniel always beyond where she ought to let him go.

These woods might hold anything, might conceal and might grow anything. Indians. Poisonous plants. Animals whose very nature it was to stalk and kill. Witches, though Elspeth had no clear idea what form a Pennsylvania woods witch might take. The Devil, even; it was perfectly possible that she might meet the Devil on this road into town.

She'd not slept much last night for fretting. It had been a quiet night, as had every night since Frank had been gone – as, indeed, were most nights – but the threat of unquiet was constant. The boys seemed to have slept soundly. Elspeth, though, had eased out of bed half a dozen times to pace the tiny cabin, ramshackle and primitive, just enough to meet the requirements to claim the land under Pre-emption; Frank said they'd build a better house come spring, but Elspeth knew to doubt him.

Again and again she'd reviewed in her mind, until they had all but lost their sense, potential threats to the safety of her children and defensive measures she might take. In her husband's absence, keeping the children safe was her sole responsibility, a duty impossible to fulfill.

The truth was that she was incapable even of imagining all the dangers that could befall them, for the world was full of dangers, the frontier especially, and many would never occur to her until they came to pass. But during the long quiet night she had dispatched floods and hailstorms, typhoid and Indian raids, panthers and hydrophobic cats.

And horses, which she seldom thought of as dangerous but which, of course, under the right circumstances, sometimes mysterious and quite unforeseeable, could well be; as could anything in this world. Recently she had heard tell of a young girl from a family down near Conneaut who'd been kicked in the head by her own horse as she bent to pick a wildflower and had been dead, they said, with the still intact stem between her fingertips.

Snakes. Staring out her window into the wet moving dark, Elspeth had once more recounted to herself the story from last winter, before she'd known anybody around here by name or the names of any settlements other than her own, and so the tale retained the anonymous, universal quality of legend: A trapper had stopped for a night's shelter at a cabin at the very edge of the creek, on what was quite obviously a floodplain. The place was abandoned, but had not been long, for in the one filthy bed he had discovered a living baby, swaddled in a nest of hatchling water moccasins, the parents of neither the human infant nor the serpentine anywhere to be found. At some risk to himself, they said, the trapper had extracted the baby from among the snakes, noting dozens of tiny bites on its body, and had managed to transport it still alive to Dr Kennedy in Cussawago.

The tale, retold, always stopped there. Elspeth had never heard what had happened to the child.

Even when the dangers were thus easy enough to conjure, Elspeth had not been able to devise theoretical protection from most of them, only how to go on with life, her own and the others for whom she was responsible, after: How to construct another tarred bark roof to replace the one ruined by hail; how to rebuild the cabin and replant the corn when the floods receded for the season; how to bury the body and how to bear leaving the grave behind the next time they followed the frontier westward as so many graves marked and unmarked were left every day. How to wait out the storm until it calmed, the fever until it broke, the Indian attack until one way or another it was over. Elspeth understood this to be her strength, the strength of the true pioneer woman: going on, after.

She came from a long line of pioneer women. Her first memory

229

was of moving, so long in the covered wagon from Connecticut to upcountry Pennsylvania that by the time they reached the little rough hill-cupped settlement she had lived more of her life in transit than stopped anywhere, and certainly never settled.

Intertwined with those earliest memories of perpetual movement were memories of her mother crying. Her mother never forgave her father for wrenching them out of their lovely home, away from friends and family to go west, where she was never to be at home. That was because her mother never learned to see herself as a pioneer, insisted on regarding herself until the last unhappy day of her unhappy life as a high-born lady forced to consort with savages, whom she was always able to civilize only slightly before her menfolk flung her among savages again.

For Elspeth's mother, the journey westward across the Atlantic Ocean from the Old Country to the New had been meant as the end of her travels. For Elspeth's father, it had been neither the beginning nor by any means the end. Elspeth had been conceived on that rolling ship, already moving westward, already a pioneer.

The older she became and the deeper her faith, the more Elspeth's mother had come to blame God for her lifelong rootlessness. The grievance had grown intensely personal by the time she'd died, a bitter and devout old woman; God had been far more present to her than her husband, than the children and grandchildren she never saw once they had moved on west.

Born, raised, and married a staunch German Baptist – what people here called Dunkards, for their practice of total-immersion adult baptism, or, with no less scorn, Harmonites for their preachment of universal harmony – Elspeth still would have said she believed in God, but her faith was not now of an easy-going sort, nor did it transport her. God was present in her life in the form of floods and typhoid fever and Indian raids, in French Creek flooding and flowing and in the inhabited woods, in the eternal absence of a home.

Sometimes she felt a certain bitter pride in this condition, sometimes a contentment that seemed genuine although the moving on had never once been her idea. She'd have stayed. She'd have stayed even here.

Early this morning she'd kissed the boys and tousled their hair, Nathaniel's red like his daddy's, Arthur's almost white like hers and

230

hers had not darkened much with the years so perhaps his would not, either, yellow-white as fresh milk. Both boys were by nature hard to rouse. At last they'd stirred and Elspeth, relieved, had sung their names to a tune she made up.

Arthur had awakened crying. Elspeth had cradled him against her for a moment or two, then sat him up on the bench by the table and proceeded to get him dressed. 'Mama!' Wide-eyed, he'd stared over her shoulder. 'Mama! Papa's home!'

She'd looked, seen nothing, waited for her heart to still. Nat had said, with heavy scorn, 'Papa's in Pittsburgh, Artie. Don't you know nothin?'

'I seen him!' Arthur had whined, so insistently that she had turned her head again, fearing Indians, who, even if they were intending no harm, had been known to materialize inside one's house with neither warning nor by-your-leave.

This morning no one had been there. No Indian, no Frank. Arthur was a child and he told tales.

As she'd bustled around the dank and crooked little house, fearing that she would forget one of the errands she must do in town, she'd thought resentfully that the moment they were boys no longer but men – perhaps before that, even – they would be wanderers like their father. They would announce that they felt crowded and move on, or they would move on without saying anything, as their male natures demanded, taking with them wives and children, and she would never see any of them again.

One lost one's children. It was a fact of life. The sudden kick of a good-natured horse, the encroachment of a nest of snakes, the inexorable westward pull – there were countless ways to lose one's children.

As her mother had lost her, had never seen her again. As her grandmother in the Old Country had lost Elspeth's mother.

Elspeth's throat, always tight and aching, constricted further with the pain of this lineage of loss, then with anger that she should still feel such pain when this was, after all, the way of so much of the world. Among the families of her acquaintance, more mothers than not lived so far away from those of their children who had survived into adulthood and their grandchildren, any one of whom might well not survive – fifty miles, two hundred miles, a thousand miles across land, or across an ocean that defied any such measurement – that they never saw them. It seemed to Elspeth especially cruel, both as a daughter and as a mother, that the mother, so central to the happiness, security, and very survival of the child during those early years, could so summarily be dispatched, condemned to rely on months-old news from the occasional letter that made its way to her. It also was cruel that such inevitable separation should hurt so much.

This morning neither boy would stop playing, help her get clothes on him, eat his breakfast. Restraining the strong urge to box their ears for disobeying – really, for leaving her someday – she'd pulled Nathaniel's shirt roughly over his head. He'd protested, 'Myself! Do it myself!'

Elspeth had hardly heard him at first, so intent was she on mourning his future loss. But when he'd begun to squirm, actually to fight her off in his baby-man way, she'd stepped back with her hands raised in exaggerated surrender. 'Fine,' she'd said to him, and from his look had known he wondered at the sternness of her tone. '*Do* it yourself, Nat,' and turned her attention to Arthur, eighteen months older but still her baby. When Arthur had been ready at last and she'd trusted herself to glance at Nathaniel, he'd been dressed, shirt slightly askew and hair on end but dressed for the first time by himself, a milestone that broke his mother's heart. 'Good!' she'd told him, hugging him to her as long as he would allow. 'You're such a big little man.'

She'd finally managed to get Bobbitt hitched to the wagon, her finished articles for the clothier folded into the basket, and the boys tucked under the damp quilts in the wagon bed, where she knew they would not stay for long. They'd started out mid-morning, much later than she'd planned, which caused her grave worry.

This road had once been an Indian trail. A century and a half ago, George Washington and his troops had traversed it. Frank had amusing and hair-raising tales of the road north to Waterford, where he must go to pick up the salt delivered by barge from western New York State; in places, he'd declared, opening his arms wide and making the boys giggle, the road was four miles across where teamsters had swung their rigs to avoid sinkholes that could swallow up a wagon. When he got home this time, he'd sworn, he would join the group of men pressing for that road to be planked.

Elspeth had felt the familiar stir of uneasy excitement. The planking of the Waterford Road was another of those events that would gratify Frank for a while, but then too many trips along it would make him chafe at the inroads of civilization, and he would begin to say again that he was being crowded, it was time to move along. West, of course. She'd already heard the names: Ohio. Kentucky.

On Elspeth's right, all the way from Alden Mills to Cussawago, French Creek ran deep and fast. Not so deep, though, that she didn't know what lived in it, snakes and leeches and the harmless horrifying creatures the children called mud puppies, which looked more like mud than like any dog she'd ever seen and felt when you stepped on them, as you could not avoid doing if you ventured into the water, like the insides only of some living thing, because, in fact, they had no bones. The creek could seem to be the western edge of the world. But she knew there was plenty beyond it; there was always more world westward.

Behind her, her sons now lay flat on their stomachs atop the quilts, unsheltered from the mist. Elspeth worried over whether that risked illness. In concert and at arrhythmic intervals, they let noise out of their mouths that the jostling of the wagon turned into a kind of song. Elspeth found this extremely annoying, but it also served to let her know that her children were all right while she had to keep her attention so fixed on the horse and the road.

The current flowed in the same direction she was traveling, but faster than her horse could pull the wagon along the muddy trail and stronger by far than she was. This was the spring freshet Frank had been waiting for and she had been dreading. Frank was on it somewhere to the south, shepherding the coveted barrels of salt downriver. Extra money, he'd declared, not so much avoiding her gaze as passing through it unawares, and in cash; a man couldn't pay his taxes with barter, no matter how good his harvest, nor with service, no matter how strong and willing he was.

She tried to think that Frank was somewhere on this very water. But it would not be really the same water, only an extension of the channel through which water flowed. She felt quite apart from him.

Perhaps he was in Pittsburgh, spending some of their money on

Monongahela Rye, the best whiskey a man could buy anywhere in this country or, he swore, any other. Perhaps he was on his way home; the opening of the fields as the snow melted brought her both hope and despair, for she could not plant the corn alone and surely he would be home soon.

Perhaps he had drowned, or been captured by Indians, or caught between the Senecas and Delawares, both friendly tribes to white men but rumored to be on the brink of conflict between themselves.

All around her was gray and dark green: low gray sky above high gray creek, woods so dark green they might be termed black and made more so by patches of bright snow and brooding moss on north sides, water black dripping off bare chestnuts and sycamores, off pines bare now of snow, all but black where it pulled and pooled under Bobbitt's slurping hooves. Rich farmland, liquefied.

Nathaniel and Arthur were making rude noises with their armpits and other unmentionable parts of their bodies, their giggling uproarious but muffled as though by quilts over their heads. She had allowed this uncouth behaviour as long as she decently could, as their mother, and was on the verge of warning them over her shoulder to stop it this minute, perhaps would even have brought up the wagon to turn and emphasize her disapproval, perhaps would even have climbed down from the seat and gone around to the back of the wagon to cuff them both for good measure, though this would have been a self-indulgence and a waste of time she did not have – when Bobbitt shied.

Nathaniel whooped. Arthur whimpered. The wagon slid sideways, but mercifully stayed upright, and though both wheels on the creek side sank two inches or more in mud, Elspeth had some reason to hope they were not truly mired. The horse whinnied, and Elspeth could feel through the tautening and loosening reins – which, though they were slick, she had not dropped – that he was about to rear. But he did not, perhaps because of her steadying hand and voice, a delusion since she did not feel steady in the least.

Like a perpendicular rut across the rutted road lay an enormous snake, its brown and silver body disappearing into the cold weeds on the creek bank and wide as two wagon tongues, though curiously flat. Elspeth stared. Behind her, Arthur screamed, 'Mama!' Not as far behind her as he ought to have been, Nathaniel shouted, 'Mama! Look! A big snake!' and started to clamber over the side of the wagon, into the slung jaws of the beast.

The serpent quivered oddly – perhaps ominously, perhaps not; responsible for the well-being of her children, Elspeth couldn't take time to be certain of its reptilian intent. Nathaniel had one knee on the edge of the wagon bed and was hopping on the other foot in hopes of propelling himself up and over. Sheets of drizzle seemed to be moving sideways and upward as well as down. The horse snorted and stomped, jangling his harness, making the wagon sway, the sound of his hooves sucked down and swallowed by the mud.

Elspeth managed to transfer the slippery reins, which were buzzing with fear transferred between her and the horse, into her left fist and, in the same motion, to catch the X of her son's suspenders in her right. He had already started his jump, and the suspenders stretched alarmingly and twanged, but held.

Nathaniel hollered and flailed. Elspeth heaved him over the seat and thumped him down onto the floor at her feet. Immediately he tried to scramble up. Twisting his ear hard, she pushed him back, raised her hand in serious threat. He yelped satisfactorily. 'You stay there!' she hissed. 'Don't you dare move!'

Although his grimy little face contorted in outrage, he did, for once in his life, as he was told. But he did not keep still. 'Mama, it ain't a snake, it's a snake*skin*. Can I have it?'

Elspeth looked again at the dreadful thing blocking their path. Nat was correct; it was not a snake but the discarded skin of one, and somehow that seemed even more horrible than if the skin had been inhabited. The end of it with irregular eyeholes torn black in the silvery fabric rested in the brush on the east edge of the road, to her left, a flattened arrow shape. The west end of it – presumably its tail, though there seemed no real end to it – was not visible among the skunkweed and pussy willows on the creekbank.

Now that she forced herself to examine it more closely and steadily, she saw along it diamond shapes nearly but not precisely the colors of the rest of it. Its uneven edges looked frothy, delicate, against the dark ground.

The astonishing thought struck her: *It is beautiful. This is a gift.*

Nathaniel had wrapped his arms around her leg like beans around a pole and was squirming upward, exhorting, 'Mama, Mama, I want that big snakeskin! Mama, let me get the snakeskin! Mama! To show Papa when he comes home! Mama! Please! Let me!'

From under the pile of quilts in the back of the wagon, Arthur was calling for her. 'Come up here with Mama,' she told him crossly, and, ever the obedient child, he did so. Nathaniel was roaring in the wagon box at her feet, and abruptly, as if flinging up her hands although her hands remained on the reins where they belonged, Elspeth snapped at him, 'Oh, all right, Natty, go get it. Hurry, though.'

The words irretrievably out of her mouth, she could scarcely believe she had given permission for such a thing. But she would have no peace all day if she rescinded it now, for Nathaniel was nothing if not tenacious.

Pushing against his brother's knees and making him screech, he scrambled over the side of the wagon and down the wheel spokes. Once on the ground, he slowed and almost reverently crouched to lay his hands one under and the other atop the skin.

Elspeth found she was holding her breath, fearing the skin – delicate for all its enormity, beautiful for all the horror of it – would tear. But her small and normally incautious son seemed this time to know what he was about.

Slowly he rose, hands at shoulder level in front of him. She could see the outlines of his sturdy forearms through the membrane, which draped like a bolt of cloth on either side of him and trailed at some length across the ground. Face rapt, Nathaniel took a step or two toward the wagon, and with a faint hiss and rattle the skin loosened here and there from the undergrowth, like seams ripping. But the tail of it, its source, stayed fastened somewhere.

'*Hurry*, Nat,' she urged. Her bonnet was dripping in earnest now, and Bobbitt's withers glistened. She wrapped Arthur in a horse blanket, which would keep off the rain better than a quilt, but only just. He'd catch his death.

Nathaniel would not be hurried, though. Very carefully, he approached the wagon with his treasure over outstretched hands. Elspeth thought he must be leaving a trail in the road that, if the rain did not wash it out, would confound any tracker: a child's footprints softly brushed over.

Arthur suddenly tugged at Elspeth's damp sleeve. Unwillingly,

Elspeth looked once more where he was pointing, as when he'd insisted his father was home. In the deep wet woods, some distance off the road away from the creek, was a dark figure. Indians, Elspeth thought at once, and grabbed for Nathaniel.

But her younger son was well out of her reach, for he had abruptly changed course and was headed toward the creek, already a few steps down the bank so that he looked smaller than ever. 'Nathaniel David Broadt, you come back here this instant!' The dark figure, when she looked for it again, was gone, but the dread of it remained, and rain fell harder.

Nathaniel called something long and complicated in response. Elspeth caught only the word 'snakeskin,' but she understood with a sinking heart that he meant to have the whole thing, had taken it into his head to drag the tail end out of the mud or water or whatever other substance was trying to keep it from him.

For one long moment, Elspeth was paralyzed by indecision. Beside her on the seat, Arthur was crying now, and, through the blanket which smelled like a wet horse, clinging to the bodice of her drenched frock. She could not leave him alone in the wagon while she went to retrieve his brother. Bobbitt was stomping and snorting, shaking his harness. He might well bolt, take the wagon and Arthur off down the road without her.

And whoever had been watching them from the forest must still be nearby. It chilled her to think how prized were white children among the Indians; one never heard of Indian children being stolen by whites – the very notion was laughable. But either of her boys would be a temptation, creamy-blond Arthur if she left him in the wagon unattended, redheaded Nathaniel alone on his foolish child's errand in the woods between the road and the creek.

She shoved Arthur toward the side of the wagon. 'Get out!' she shouted at him. 'We must get Nat!'

But he was too terrified to let loose of her, even hid his face in her bosom. 'No! No!'

Dragging the boy like an extra appendage, whose weight and imbalance she could ill afford to contend with now, Elspeth managed to get herself off the seat and plant her feet, shoes sliding, on the slick curve of the wheel. Then Arthur, wailing, transferred his desperate grip to the edge of the wagon box. The blanket slid heavily off his shoulders, leaving him completely unprotected from the storm.

Clambering down, wet skirts tangling around her legs and wet sleeves goosefleshing her arms, Elspeth reasoned with him, threatened him, cajoled, tried to pry his cold fingers loose. All this time, Nathaniel was heading toward the French Creek torrent, perhaps was already in it, perhaps was already drowned. At last, she braced herself and brought her fist down hard, perhaps harder than necessary, on Arthur's little hands, one after the other in quick succession, until he, all but hysterical now, let go.

She stretched on tiptoe and reached up and over as far as she could, could reach only the back of his shirt and pulled on that. He came over, chin scraped and bleeding, reproachfully holding his fingers up to her.

She took no time to inspect or comfort or even to steady him before propelling him into the weeds. Just ahead, behind a screen of trees and bushes thin and bare but close together, the creek rushed, and she could both smell and taste it, wet, full of slimy boneless things.

Again she called for Nathaniel, but this time there was no reply.

Brush came to Elspeth's waist, well above Arthur's head, scratching and streaming with rainwater. At last she picked him up. He was too heavy and slippery, though, for her to carry more than a few steps, nor even keep firm hold of his hand.

There was the sickening odor of wet skunkweed smashed underfoot. There was cold rain in her face and the rising roar of the creek, which she glimpsed through rain and branches and her own yellow-white hair grayed by rain and dirt. 'Nathaniel!'

Stumbling over Arthur, who had stopped short, Elspeth came so suddenly to the creek bank that her feet slid out from under her and she sat down hard in the mud, hurting her hip and likely ruining her frock. The mad thought occurred to her that if Nathaniel had seen that he'd have laughed at her, and she teetered on the verge of crazy laughter herself.

Arthur did not laugh. He cried out, 'There's Natty!' and there, indeed, he was, ten feet out in French Creek, the rushing water well above the small of his back, intent on the snakeskin he was prying out of the half-frozen muck on the bottom of the channel.

Floating around him, Elspeth swore, were body parts; she was sure she saw a severed hand, a leg.

'Nat! Come out of there!'

She feared he would not hear her over the rising storm and the swift noisy current, but he looked up. 'I almost got it!' he called gaily. Debris – scalped human hair – netted around him and then skimmed downstream.

Then the snakeskin let loose – broke, or finally came out of its entrapment – and Nathaniel fell backward into the water clutching a long lacy swatch of his treasure. Elspeth saw an arm under his head, but it did no good. His head went under and did not come back up.

Pushing her fists into the muddy slope, his mother slid down and went in after him. Arthur called, 'Mama!'

Elspeth flung back at him, 'You stay there!' but did not take time to see that he did. Nathaniel had disappeared.

Rain plummeted into the roiling surface of the creek and fountained up again, filming her eyes, stinging her face and arms. She aimed herself toward a spot a bit downstream from where she'd last seen Nathaniel, but the current twisted her heavy skirts around her knees. She'd lost a shoe, and both the stockinged foot and the one still shod slipped and stuck in the mud or the layered boneless bodies and body parts on the bottom of the creekbed. She fell, floundered, made another step or two of diagonal progress across the current, fell again, breathed in cold muddy water and gagged.

She could not find him. She found chunks of ice the approximate size of a boy, tree branches suggestive of a child's flung arms, the ballooning hem of her own skirt that she at first mistook for his shirt. She found handfuls of mud, mouthfuls of creek water thickened with floating weeds and hair, eyefuls of pouring rain. But she could not find her son.

It was not long before Elspeth and the son left to her continued on their way to Cussawago, but already the day was much too far gone. Her right foot, the one that had lost its shoe, was numb. The sensation of wearing only a single shoe was peculiarly disorienting. She found herself staring at her own feet, the left one with a shoe on it, the right with only a white stocking silvered by the rain and browned by the creek mud. They pressed against the front of the wagon box, and she could see but could not feel the toes of the right, indecently exposed through wet cotton.

She did not yet know how to think about what had just happened to her: an event among the events of her life, or the one true thing before and after which her life was to be forever divided. Either way, she did not know what to do about it, and it seemed to her that the event – unnameable, unspeakable – was rather like French Creek itself, at this very moment and the next and the next passing her by, but always with her, forever marking the edge of her world.

Almost dreamily, she began to notice that French Creek had risen over its banks in some places, as though from the addition of her son's small body. Before she could stop herself, she had a vision of Nathaniel being carried all the way downstream to Pittsburgh, to join up with his daddy where the salt barges docked. Once Frank had pulled Nat from the water – she could see him: dripping, cold, bruised and scratched, but not seriously harmed – the creek would return to its normal size and speed and both of them could come home.

More than once she was sorely tempted to leap out of the moving wagon and plunge into the current again – in this spot; in this one, which even as she thought about it, even as she would enter it, flowed downstream, altered and disguised itself. Had it not been for Arthur, would she have done so? Would she have knowingly offered her life for her son's? Would she have sacrificed herself in what would surely have been little more than a gesture?

That she could not say for certain horrified her, that she was thinking, among all her other thoughts: One loses one's children. It is a fact of life. The ways in which one might lose one's children are countless, unpredictable, and unavoidable.

Arthur, small and shaking on the high seat beside her, by his mere existence saved her from this bit of self-knowledge, one way or the other. There was really no choice to be made: Arthur needed her. It was foolish of him, for she'd proved herself unworthy of a child's need, but clearly he needed her. She must take care of Arthur until his Pa returned.

From the corner of her eye she caught motion through the steady motion of the rain. She turned her head, expecting to see nothing. But someone was there, a woman, gray as the rain, dark gray as the

240

woods. Elspeth all but raised a hand in greeting or supplication, but the woman gave no sign that she had seen them. Elspeth thought vaguely to offer a ride into town, but the woman, wet face lifted to wet sky, had backed into the woods and was gone.

Perhaps she ought not to have left the place where she'd last seen Nathaniel. Perhaps she ought to have waited out the storm there, or somewhere. With each hoofbeat, each slide and lurch of the wagon, each bend in the road, Elspeth understood again that by her actions she was abandoning one son and endangering the other. But she knew nothing else to do.

The wagon lurched. Arthur gave a little scream. Bobbitt leaned into the harness in the same direction the wagon was listing, thus adding to its off-balance weight, and for the next several minutes Elspeth was called upon to use all her driving skill to keep them from tipping over. By the time they were more or less righted, she was actively grieving Nathaniel's loss. Her throat was allowing only the barest passage of air to accompany the moaning of his name. Tears filled her eyes and fire her chest. Keenly, she yearned to think of nothing but Nathaniel, Nathaniel . . .

She could not have this. She must keep going. She reached behind Arthur for the horse blanket, thoroughly wet and exceedingly odoriferous by now, and insisted he wrap himself in it, though she was by no means convinced it would be of any benefit.

All along the slow journey then, Elspeth saw female figures. Their appearance did not baffle her as much as she'd have expected. She'd have assumed them to be products of her inflamed imagination, but Arthur saw them, too, and pressed harder and harder against her till she could scarcely stay upright on the seat and drive. He kept pleading, 'Look, Mama! Look there,' insisting his mother not only look but comment, interpret for him.

'Yes, Arthur, yes, I see.' Perhaps she should not admit to it, but it was the truth; she did see, more than he.

'Who is it?'

'Just somebody who lives here,' she'd say. Or, 'Just someone out walking. Hunting, maybe.'

But her explanations of this phenomenon, to Arthur or to herself, sufficed no more than did her explanations of what had happened to Nathaniel. 'Where's Natty?' Arthur wanted to know.

'I – believe he got lost.' Elspeth tried to keep her voice steady for him, a maternal falsehood. This truth was too much for a child to bear. Too much to be borne by anyone.

'Lost where?' he persisted.

'I don't know, Arthur. That's what "lost" means. Maybe in the creek.' Her throat closed over the words.

'Did that lady take him?'

'What lady?' Elspeth looked where he was pointing and saw something like a shadow fading into the trees, although surely there could not be shadows when the sky was so cloudy and the light so dim. 'I don't think anybody took him,' she managed to say, though actually it seemed to her as likely a possibility as any other.

The figures were decidedly peculiar, and Arthur knew that as well as did she. They showed themselves strangely, one instant not there and the next fully, vividly in this world. They did not seem to disturb or even to leave an impression upon their surroundings. They were in some way strangers, all of them, of this world but not of this time and place, somehow foreign.

For a time Elspeth entertained the notion that this must be but one person, vanishing and materializing, following her and her little boy. She might be able to fashion a suitable explanation for the presence of a single unescorted woman – like herself, in fact – but could not imagine sufficient reason in the course of ordinary life for several or more.

Life was, though, no longer ordinary. Elspeth could think about that only briefly, glancingly. Life would never be ordinary again.

These women were, undeniably, separate individuals, as unlike each other as they were unlike Elspeth herself, though she felt a queer sort of kinship with them. They were alone as she was, pioneers all. Before long she was anticipating them, and they did appear in all manner of places, whether she was looking there or not.

In the woods, resembling a just-leafing shrub until it moved in a certain way and revealed to Elspeth oddly bobbed hair and tight trousers of a strange, heavy, dark-blue fabric which, curiously, seemed untouched by the rain, though she'd have expected it to darken and drip.

In the road ahead of and then behind them, though Elspeth did not see her move; this one a woman of considerable girth in an ankle-length faded blue frock.

Then on the thin gravel beach of the island that, marking the approximate halfway point between Alden Mills and Cussawago, split French Creek into two channels, each still of respectable width. This figure had an Indian aspect, but was not – Elspeth did not know how she determined this – either a Seneca or a Delaware. On her cheekbones and forehead were red streaks, clearly visible even from across the channel, and Elspeth wondered nervously if that was warpaint.

These apparitions – for even if they were real flesh-and-blood women, which Elspeth did suppose them to be, they suggested ghosts, spirits – gave no sign of noticing Elspeth and Arthur, nor the horse and wagon, nor the woods nor the creek that had taken Nat nor the rain. The short-haired, trousered one in the woods and the stout one in the road were weeping. The Indian one on the island was too far away and indistinct for Elspeth to see actual tears, but her posture bespoke grief: head down, long tangled hair like sheets of dark rain, shoulders bowed, arms around herself.

Again, Elspeth was stirred by a sensation of kinship with these sorrowing women, of a terrible and powerful sisterhood. It frightened and strengthened her. Each time she looked away, looked back, the figure would be gone, but another would shortly present itself.

Nathaniel. Oh.

She raised the bundle of reins to press the fist that held them against her teeth. Obediently Bobbitt veered. Hastily she tugged to straighten him out again. Through an opening in the forest on her right, the creek flashed brown, and she raised herself to squint into it, but there was no sign of Nathaniel.

She would get them to Cussawago. Somebody there would help her. In desperate detail she planned what she would do: She would drive the wagon along the River Road all the way to Water Street, then turn eastward until she came to the diamond-shaped Common, where, if the weather was not completely foul, Mr David Mead might be drilling his militia. More than once Frank had assured her rather testily that the man was nothing remarkable, but he could not deny that David Mead was western Pennsylvania's leading citizen. Elspeth thought there was something quite remarkable about creating a town out of the wilderness, and some people did refer to Cussawago as Meadville.

Mr Mead would listen to her tale. She would stay in town with Arthur, awaiting news, or someone – the new Mrs David Mead, perhaps – would offer to keep Arthur for her and she would race with the rescue party north along the creek until they found Nathaniel. Alive, perhaps a little wet and cold and scared and in need of his mother but not hurt, or perhaps hurt just enough to persuade him never to do such a foolish thing again. He would even have his snakeskin wrapped around him like a shawl.

Elspeth smiled at the picture, recognized both the image and the smile as senseless. A sob escaped her before she steadied herself by vowing that, once she was assured Nathaniel was unharmed, she would give him a whipping, lest Mr David Mead think her a weak mother, his father not being here to do it as it ought to be done.

With a muffled crack, the front axle broke. The wagon sank forward and rightward and Arthur slid across the seat, reaching for her and missing, grabbing at nothing but somehow managing not to fall out. Elspeth heard herself rasp, 'Nathaniel!' before she came to her senses.

Stretching along the incline of the seat, she dropped to the ground and pushed Arthur, her surviving son Arthur, off with her. They backed away. The wagon teetered on an edge, spilling quilts and the clothing Elspeth had sewn for barter. The sight of those pretty things muddied and soaked, spoiled, was nothing short of tragic.

Then the wagon went on over, at first threatening to take Bobbitt with it – he reared and stumbled – but then snapping the harness and tumbling unfettered down the French Creek bank. The wood of it splintered; pieces flew off. Elspeth waited for the splash, as if that would settle something. Instead, she heard wet weeds and bushes breaking, some of them bent only and so able to rise again, rising already. That was not right. Given what had befallen them, they should be flattened. They should be destroyed.

Immediately the noisy, heavy wagon left him, Bobbitt settled. Now he was standing quietly in the rain, ears neither perked in alarm nor flattened in distress, tail swishing almost placidly. Elspeth forced herself to approach him, to extend one and then both hands. He didn't shy, paid scant attention of any sort to her other than to regard her whitely out of the corner of his eye. Taking up the broken harness, she announced, as if to the horse, 'There is nothing for it now but to walk.'

Arthur sank to the ground. 'I'm too tired, Mama! I don't want to walk!'

She made a decision with an alacrity that rather surprised her, even rather alarmed. 'Ride, then. Ride Bobbitt.' Slinging the piece of harness over her arm, she crouched to lift Arthur up out of the mud and onto the horse's bony back. Horse sidled and boy squirmed, but she managed to fit them together, to impose her will on them both.

And suppose she was wrong? Suppose, down the road, Arthur fell off and was crushed under the horse's hooves because of this very decision she was in the midst of making now?

They trudged along toward Cussawago then, she and Bobbitt, while Arthur bounced and complained at the level of her shoulder and Nathaniel floated somewhere in French Creek. The creek stretched on the right, which was west, a landmark to maintain their southward progress, since she now had no sense of direction of her own. There was a certain bitter comfort in the bordering steadfast presence of the creek; she might well not be able to distinguish south from east from north, all of them blurred, none with any innate characteristic different from any of the others, but surely even she, even now, would know if they crossed a bridge or a ford.

Her sense of time had also faded. It might be mid-afternoon, an hour when she had planned to be already well into the bartering with Mr Ross, with luck the transaction satisfactorily completed, the wagon stocked, she and both boys well on their way home. Darkness fell early and thoroughly on a rainy Pennsylvania spring evening. Now they would be lucky to be in Cussawago by nightfall. The thought of wandering in these woods after dark was so unpleasant that she forcibly turned her attention away from it, only to find herself thinking of Nathaniel, four years old and a-wander by himself in the woods after dark.

Her bonnet had long since slid off the back of her head, to hang against her neck like the body of an Indian child, sopping, limp, still close to its mother but for no purpose anymore. The uneven gait forced by her shoeless right foot and shod left foot suddenly became unbearable, and, almost without breaking stride, she loosened the remaining shoe and tossed it aside into the undergrowth, with the result that her balance was more or less restored but now both feet, both ankles, were cold and wet. Arthur's hands were bright pink and so cold he could hardly hold onto the horse's mane, and increasingly often Elspeth felt him leaning toward or away from her. Frantically, but also with less and less real interest, his mother reached up and reached up again to steady him.

In this way, they proceeded for a time. The woods blurred behind and ahead of them and on both sides, were no longer composed of separate trees, individual hillocks, clearings distinguishable one from another, but became one thing, and where she walked was not this spot or this but simply inside this great swallowing being, the Devil, or God. The rain was a steady downpour without thunder or lightning or wind. The sky neither darkened nor lightened. The road went on. Nathaniel was not dead.

Now and then Arthur whined or complained or asked when they would be there, but mostly he was quiet. His silence ought to have been alarming from a child his age and present circumstances; indeed, Elspeth was aware of alarm, very dim and distant, far back in her mind. Mostly, though, she was relieved to be thus left alone and absolved of maternal demands regarding her firstborn son, here with her, freeing her to concentrate on those of her absent second.

But she found she could not. She could think only, ferociously, about holding herself upright against the horse's steaming flank, about her freezing feet, about taking one step and then another that would lead them eventually to Cussawago. About going on, after.

The rain seemed to intensify, although she couldn't be sure. There was definitely snow in it now. The noise of the creek seemed to rise. Darkness seemed to be gathering. Arthur coughed, coughed again. Where could Nathaniel possibly be?

Some distance off the River Road, as though unrelated to it, she thought she saw a cabin. Then she was sure of it, untarred bark roof dripping, chinks of light speckling crooked walls.

In the doorway stood another female figure. Arthur murmured, as if to himself, 'Oh, there's another lady.'

'Stop! Come in!' the woman called with great, even excessive cheer. When Elspeth did not at once stop and it must have appeared that she intended not to, the woman stepped out into the sleet herself, beckoning with such eagerness that the motions of her hands and arms – reaching, hooking upward, wagging – would have been threatening had she been a step or two nearer. 'Weary travelers! Do come in!'

By herself, Elspeth might have declined, might have simply kept going. But Bobbitt had stopped, as if he understood the invitation – or, more likely, as if his small rider had given him a signal with knees or knuckles – and Arthur was whining. 'Oh, Mama, please, Mama, I'm so cold!'

By now the woman actually had come close enough to take the reins out of Elspeth's fist and lead Bobbitt to a slightly sheltered spot in a copse of trees behind her dilapidated little house. From a distance, then, Elspeth watched Arthur slide off the horse into the other woman's arms, and that seemed simultaneously the worst thing that could happen and precisely as it ought to be.

She could scarcely see her stockinged feet as she stumbled after the woman carrying her son, could barely feel them. The flickering yellow rectangle made by the opening of the cabin door caught and held her attention until she passed through it and the door was shut behind her.

Then she stood on the uneven dirt floor and could not think what to do next. The woman – muddy man's boots, soiled petticoat hanging under torn brownish hem, grimy hands – laid Arthur on a pallet which probably was no filthier than anything else in here. He tossed his head and whimpered.

Dreamily, Elspeth did know then what she ought to do, but she could not marshal the energy and attention it would have required to cross the tiny room and kneel beside her son, to speak to him, to comfort and minister to him. Especially if he was sick. If he might die.

'Where's your shoes?' The woman, busy with Elspeth's son, did not look at her, but had noticed.

'I – lost them.' For a moment Elspeth was confused by the vague sensation that this was a lie and that she ought not to be telling lies, but she could not place the nature of the falsehood or the reason it would matter in the least if she lied here and now. 'We're on our way to Cussawago.'

'No place else you'd be on your way to.'

'How much farther is it?'

'Two mile.'

'Not far,' Elspeth said, but two miles was very far to walk without shoes.

'Lost your wagon, too?' Elspeth nodded. The woman snorted. 'Bad weather for losing things in.'

Nathaniel, Elspeth thought miserably.

The woman gestured with her head. 'Barrel there behind the door's got Monongahela Rye in it. Help yourself. Best whiskey in the country. Cure what ails you.'

Elspeth shook her head. 'Thank you but no. I must stay clear-headed. We must go on to Cussawago.'

'Boy's asleep. Let him sleep.' She covered Arthur with a tattered blanket. As if her heart would break this very instant, Elspeth thought of her pretty quilts, lost to the French Creek freshet. From the clutter on the floor, the woman picked up another pair of boots, muddier even than the ones she was wearing and bigger, and held them out. When Elspeth did not move, she snapped, 'Put these on. Can't go stocking footed in this weather. Catch your death.'

'Thank you,' Elspeth said again, softly. 'But no.'

'Suit yourself.' The woman shrugged and tossed the boots aside. Their thunk caused Elspeth's heart to thunk inside her ribs, both noises accentuating the frailty of the structures that confined and created them, rotting wooden wall and bone. 'Come with me. Something I want to show you.'

'My son—'

'Right outside. Come with me.'

Elspeth feared that, if she refused, the woman would physically force her, and she vehemently did not want to be touched by her. She glanced at Arthur. He was entirely out of the lamplight and she could not see him clearly, but he did appear to be asleep. She had left Nathaniel floating in the creek; leaving Arthur warm and dry and sleeping peacefully seemed hardly worth notice. She slipped on the boots. They would fall off unless she shuffled. Her toes bumped against their toes, and then her heels against their heels, hard, ungiving. Water from her stockings, absorbed not at all by the hard cracked leather, pooled around her feet.

The rain was a shock when they stepped out into it, no matter that Elspeth had expected it. The door would not shut true. When she finally gave up on it, fingertips stinging, the woman had taken perhaps ten paces away from the cabin and was standing with her back to Elspeth. The sky was almost dark, the rain thick between them. Elspeth pushed through.

'There.' The woman pointed, indecently exposing her arm from wrist to shoulder where the sleeve fell away. 'There's my girls.'

Something white and rounded shimmered at her feet. Two white things, each with two rounded humps. For just an instant, Elspeth imagined them to be girls, or ghosts of girls.

But they were tombstones, and then Elspeth had the crazy idea that this woman had for some reason erected a tombstone for Nathaniel. Touched and enraged, she advanced to inspect them.

Heart-shaped tombstones, they were, points affixed to slabs set side by side in a tended clearing. The shoulders of the hearts reached barely to Elspeth's knees.

Kneeling, she was still too high to read the inscriptions, so she lay on her stomach and brought her face close to the wet stone. Wet and pliant, the ground rose like bread dough around her, folding her in.

'Here lies Lonely,' the one on the left proclaimed, and the one on the right echoed, 'Here lies Desolate.' No epitaphs. No names.

But there were dates. Awkwardly and with considerable trepidation, she raised a hand and traced them, as though to aid herself in understanding their sense: July 13, 1798, the same birth date on both – twins, then? – and death dates one day apart: January 10 and January 11, 1801.

The woman crouched beside her. Elspeth smelled her, the dirt of her, the long grief. 'Wanted to show you my girls.'

'Your daughters?' Elspeth managed to sit up. 'I'm so sorry. They were twins? And they died so young.'

'The typhus. Took 'em both. Just before midnight Lonely went, and just after midnight Desolate went, too, so they didn't even pass on the same day. Weren't right. Born on the same day, should've passed on the same day.'

'Their *names* were Lonely and Desolate?' Already cold and soaked through, Elspeth felt her skin crawl as though rain had sluiced down her back. 'While they were – before they passed? That was what you called them?'

In the other mother's laughter Elspeth recognized her own hysteria. 'Fine names, don't you think? For living in this godforsaken wilderness? Their father left us before they were born. Nobody else ever knew we were out here. Lonely, then, and Desolate. All I could give them, their names. But even their fine, fitting names did not keep them safe.'

Elspeth stared at the heart-shaped tombstones, gleaming in the evening rain, and at last it came to her unavoidably, the clearest thing in the world: Nathaniel is dead. Nathaniel, Frederic, Eileen, Lee,

Ian

my child is dead.

Chapter 22

It was early on a Saturday morning in May, not an anniversary of Ian's death except that every hour of every day could be regarded as an anniversary and would, then, require marking. Renata was, in fact, not directly thinking about him, not wholeheartedly mourning; that happened with increasing frequency and duration now, a few times a day for a few minutes at a time.

She was at the kitchen counter dicing chicken for dinner, thinking – with real if unsustainable interest – about a knotty situation at work and anticipating – with more anxiety than pleasure, but with pleasure, too – her planned excursion to the Botanic Gardens with Vanessa this afternoon. With more wonder than distress, she was thinking about Elspeth and her son, nearly two hundred years ago and two thousand miles away, another world and the same one.

A message came into her head, not voiced but clearly enunciated. 'Ian's with me. You and my mother take care of each other.'

Renata didn't stop what she was doing. But her mind swooped in from all the scattered places it had been and *focused*, a palpable sensation. At the core of the resumed activity of daily life was a waiting, a readiness, and, when neither a repetition nor an elaboration of the message came, a response. Something like, 'Yes.' Something like, 'Thank you.'

She didn't know what to make of it. As the laser of her attention began to diffuse slightly, she thought maybe she didn't need to make anything of it.

Many unfathomable things were happening to her these days. There were times when she traveled, she swore, in some underworld to which the bloody tunnel had led her. There were times when she lived the bereavement stories of other mothers at other times and

251

places. None of these, nor the message that had just now come into her mind, approached the mystery of her son's death. Believing that, as she was coming to do, she could believe anything.

She stood there for a few minutes, tingling, awed, aghast; she kept doing what she was doing. Cubed chicken heaped like stones into the crockpot, never quite enough so her husband and daughter would starve, always far too much so they wouldn't eat it and it would spoil. She chopped vegetables with a sharp knife on the little wooden cutting board. The carrots were more gray than orange. The crispness of the potatoes was different from that of the celery, and equally wrong.

Then she laid the knife down, put the lid on the crockpot and turned it on low, washed and dried her hands, and rang Althea. 'Do you believe in visions?'

'Visions. You mean—' She paused for a long moment, didn't go on at all.

'After Susan and Allen died did you ever have visions?'

'You mean like dreams? I had a few dreams about them. Not very many, actually. Not as many as I expected. Not as many as I wanted, I guess. I still do, now and then. I remember I had a dream about Susan being a cheerleader, which was something she always made fun of.'

'I just got a message from Susan.' Said baldly like that, it wasn't true. Or it was a metaphor, a synecdoche.

'What?'

'A message just came into my mind. "Ian's with me. You and my mother take care of each other."'

Althea breathed, 'Really?'

'Do you think that's possible?'

'Was it Susan's voice? Oh, you wouldn't know, would you? You never heard her voice.'

'It wasn't a voice, anyway, exactly. But it was a message, in words, and I knew it was Susan. Do you think that's possible?'

'Oh, I don't know.'

'I mean, is it real? Or is it just grief doing bizarre things to my head? Or does grief open up your mind to things that are real but we don't perceive most of the time? Is it real in some way I never knew about before?' Now she was getting confused, and upset.

Althea laughed softly. 'She did love children.'

Renata had nothing else to say. She did not want to break the connection with Althea; then she understood that, by hanging up the phone, she wouldn't be. She did not want to break the connection with whatever was the source of the message. Something approaching reverence suffused her, and radiance.

Followed by an explosion of equally radiant agony that flung her into a kitchen chair and pinned her there. *Ian is dead.* She couldn't breathe, must have been breathing because she didn't die or even lose consciousness, wept. Gypsy whimpered at her feet.

Time passed, apparently, because Vanessa came into the room with her sweater on, dirty at the cuffs but the right style and the right shade of pink. She glared at her mother. 'Aren't we going to the Botanic Gardens, Mom?' Always afraid, these days more than ever, that something was about to be taken away from her.

Glenn came in then, car keys in his hand, and looked at her inquiringly. She suspected he was worried not so much about her emotional state as about the possibility that she would disappoint Vanessa. In fact, the strong emotions with their colorful names – awe, radiance, grief, anguish, despair – had passed, leaving her dull, nearly blank, a condition to which he must by now be accustomed. He was trying to be gentle when he asked her, 'Did you forget, honey?'

She hadn't exactly forgotten. 'No!' she gasped, realizing as she did so that she could have spoken more or less normally. She got to her feet without a struggle, maintained balance without difficulty, said, 'I'll be ready in a minute.'

'Wait.' Glenn touched his fingertip to her side, which had been exposed when her shirt pulled up. 'What happened here?'

She peered down, rested her own hand there. The skin was red and swollen around numerous tiny punctures. She had the sensation that, just outside consciousness, she knew what had caused the wounds. 'Insect bites, I guess.'

'I guess!' He caressed her bare, inflamed skin. 'Are you allergic to something? Should you see a doctor?'

'It's okay. Really. I'll be ready in a minute.' She hurried to comb her hair and grab a jacket without losing track of what she was doing and also without inadvertently catching a glimpse of herself in any mirror. The insect bites neither hurt nor itched, and she supposed they would be gone soon.

Ian had loved going with her to the spring sale at the Botanic Gardens. He'd liked the sale better than the Gardens themselves. When he was six he'd pronounced the seedlings 'just my size.' When he'd first seen the mass of succulents on their plastic-covered table he'd almost not believed they were really plants. Last year he'd secretly bought her a potpourri pillow festooned with ribbons and lace, at a discount because he hadn't had quite enough money and he'd told the lady it was for his mom.

Vanessa, though, was bored before they walked in the door, and already starting to whine. 'It's *hot* in here!'

Trying to orient herself, Renata didn't answer right away. The big room was indeed warm and humid. It thrummed with the odors of plants, their shapes and textures and colors that, vivified and massed like this, seemed not so much unreal as over-real. The sounds of the crowd of which she and her daughter were parts – footsteps, voices, breathing, heartbeats – were absorbed and alchemized. A faint herbal taste limned the inside of her mouth. She missed Ian. She tried to think about the strange message, tried to elicit it again in her mind, could not.

'Mom, it's too *hot* in here! It smells disgusting!'

'The plants like it,' Renata said, mildly.

'Well, I don't.'

Ian would have left her side already, to wander among the scarlet and chartreuse geraniums and the African violets whose velvety leaves he'd known not to touch but sometimes couldn't help himself. She remembered him peering, leaning forward on the balls of his feet, head cocked and tip of tongue protruding, small rough hands behind his back. She wouldn't buy African violets this year. They never stayed alive more than a few months, and the idea of purposely acquiring something she knew she couldn't keep safe was intolerable.

Vanessa, predictably, picked up a small African violet with half a dozen purple blossoms on it and insisted, 'I want this one!'

'Honey, I'm not good with African violets.'

'They're really easy,' said the lady behind the table, helpfully.

'They always die.'

The lady took a breath and recited: 'They want a good northern exposure, and they don't like to get their feet wet. Water them from the top, being careful not to splash their leaves, and don't ever let them stand in water.'

'Last year,' Renata protested, more indignant than the situation called for, 'they told me to set the pots in trays and keep the trays full of water all the time.' Last year. Before Ian died.

'Nobody in our Society told you that,' the lady declared coldly.

Only barely did Renata manage to check herself from arguing back. She looked at Vanessa, who was regarding her balefully and clutching the little plant to her chest as though it were a doll, no doubt squashing its impossibly fragile leaves. 'See what I mean?' Renata said to her. 'You get all sorts of conflicting advice from people who are supposed to be experts.'

But the point was lost on the child. 'I want this one,' she insisted. 'It only costs a dollar.'

Foolishly feeling as though she were making – on the spot, at this very, irretrievable instant – a moral compromise, Renata surrendered and bought the plant. The lady behind the table, not looking at either of them, took the bill as though it had been hers all along, and almost immediately, Vanessa lost interest. She shoved the violet at her mother, who took it before she thought and now couldn't return it because Vanessa wasn't within reach. 'Vanessa, you carry it,' she tried. 'It's your plant. You insisted—'

The girl's face crumpled and her lower lip slid out, puffy and dangerous. 'I don't wanna carry it!'

'I need my hands free to look at other plants.'

'It's *hot* in here! It's *boring*!'

'You wanted to come.'

The resentment between them was escalating, the stakes somehow disproportionately high. Renata was thinking, though she didn't want to be, that she wished Ian were here instead of this unpleasant child. She turned away, but not before Vanessa demanded querulously, 'When's Dad coming to get us?'

'At three o'clock. You know that. You heard us making arrangements in the car.'

'I did *not*!'

'He's coming at three o'clock.'

'I did *not* hear you!'

'Vanessa, cut it out.'

'Well, what time is it now?'

Renata resisted the temptation to point out the prominent clock on the wall. 'Two-ten. We just got here.'

'That's almost an hour!' The girl was flouncing dramatically, and Renata thought she might even collapse on the floor. Of all things today, she did not want to handle a twelve-year-old's temper tantrum, but there was a cool pleasure in knowing that she could if she had to. Gritting her teeth and reminding herself that Vanessa *was* twelve, not two, and could be left unattended, she set the violet on a corner of a nearby table and walked away, all the way to the bromeliad display on the other side of the room.

There was nothing she wanted to buy, nothing she'd have dared to buy even if she'd been tempted. She'd long joked that her thumb was more brown than green, and there was no doubt that she'd be an outright menace to any living thing she took home with her this year. Any beauty or interest she might have found in the plants was pallid and altogether uncompelling anyway, not worth taking any risk for.

'Can I go wait outside till Dad gets here?'

Renata found the demand nearly incomprehensible. 'Outside? Where outside?'

'I don't know. Anyplace.'

'I – I'm not sure it's safe.' Renata scrambled to visualize where her daughter might wait outside, what the dangers might be (traffic? molesters? getting lost?). Furiously she resented having to make this judgment call. The excursion had been planned, just barely something she could handle. If she'd known Vanessa was going to force her into making an on-the-spot parental decision, she would not have come. In the midst of the gathering panic, it seemed important for her daughter's sake to appear decisive, competent. So she amended, 'I don't think it's safe,' which was only slightly less tentative.

'It's *boring* in here,' the child repeated ominously.

'It'll be a long wait out there, honey. Forty-five minutes.'

'I *know*,' Vanessa said, in that tone of adolescent contempt she'd just begun to affect before her brother died. They hadn't heard it again until now, and Renata supposed its resurfacing was a healthy sign, although she didn't like it much. 'It'll be forty-five minutes in *here*, too.'

'Okay,' Renata gave in, for no good reason, but she could see no good reason to deny permission, either. 'Wait on those benches right outside the front doors. I won't be long.'

Vanessa hesitated, looking a little surprised, a little hurt, and Renata guessed she'd committed some mysterious and irredeemable sin – letting her go, being reluctant to let her go, having the temerity to call herself her mother in the first place. The girl stormed off, and Renata thought she ought to follow her to the door and watch to make sure she went to the right place, stayed there, was safe. She didn't do it, and supposed bitterly that this was yet another choice she'd regret for the rest of her life, that any choice would have been.

She wandered around the entire room, forcing herself to look at every display. Memories of Ian lurked everywhere. Windowsill herb gardens: he'd loved food, had just been starting to cook. Cacti: One year he'd touched a little cactus that looked smooth and innocent, brought his hand away furred in hairlike spines, instinctively tried to pull them out with his teeth, then in horror put his other hand to his throbbing mouth – so that for a tearful hour or so his fingertips, lips, tongue were swollen and hurting although Renata still could barely see the offending thorns. Potpourri. For long minutes she held a lavender potpourri pillow in one palm and caressed it with the fingers of the other hand, dimly wanting to buy it, the very thought disloyal.

It was just after two-thirty when she maneuvered through the restrained, polite crowd and out of the stuffy room into the lobby, which was patched with rectangles of sunlight through its domed glass ceiling. She wished Glenn would come early but knew he wouldn't; he'd want to give her and Vanessa all the time together they'd planned on. When she pushed through one of the heavy outside doors, Vanessa wasn't on the assigned bench.

Bile surged into Renata's throat. She'd lost another child, and this one was her fault even less disputably than the first. This one she'd have to tell Glenn about. The scene had played itself out in rapid, obsessive detail in her mind by the time she got from the door to the bench, a few steps, a few seconds: Glenn would pull up, and she'd get into the car, and she'd turn to him and put her hand on his knee – or maybe she wouldn't touch him; maybe she wouldn't dare – and she'd say, 'Vanessa's gone. I've lost our daughter, too. I'm sorry, Glenn, oh, I'm so sorry. You have every right to hate me now,' and there was defiant relief in finally being able to say that without risk of debate.

She pulled loose from the self-indulgent fantasy as, somewhat sheepishly, she caught sight of Vanessa, just across the red-brick sidewalk. Crossing to her, she found herself thinking that grief was incredibly self-absorbed; for an instant, she was bored with it, but that was too terrible a thought to stay with for long, the possibility that this violent mourning for Ian to which she had committed the rest of her life would not hold her interest that long.

One hand clasping the other slender, pale forearm behind her back, Vanessa was staring at a little meadow of wildflowers in sturdy bloom. Renata intended to put her arms around her child, and, eventually, she did, but first there was a long elastic moment during which mother and daughter were connected by a third substance between them, a humming viscosity made of love and history and potentiality through which her yearning maternal touch passed and was transformed. Became both more intensely specific and personal and vastly more expansive than she'd ever known about before.

Grazed, stunned by the magic of it, she couldn't hold the apperception, and then her hands were resting on her daughter's strong and fragile shoulders and she was kissing the top of the small head in a sweet, ordinary caress, and Vanessa was leaning lightly back against her. 'Oh, Mom, it's so *pretty!*'

'Isn't it?' She ought to complain about her daughter's disobedience, minimal as it had been; now more than ever, Vanessa needed predictability. But – maybe she was wrong – it seemed to her more important right now to encourage Vanessa's delicate response to beauty. Maybe she was wrong. Maybe years later Vanessa would recall feeling cut loose and unattended after her brother died because her mother didn't bother to enforce the rules.

'I didn't know there was anyplace this beautiful.'

'There are a lot of beautiful places in the world,' Renata assured her, although she didn't believe it for herself. 'Still.'

'Can we come here again sometime?'

Renata took a deep breath and plunged into the future with her little girl. 'Yes. Sure.'

In the middle distance, between them and the buildings of downtown which created an almost botanical impression when they served as backdrop to the Gardens, a woman stood. Renata frowned; you were supposed to stay on the paths, and the woman was hip-deep in the meadow.

The woman saw them. Her head went up, and she moved toward them, although the size and angle of her didn't shift relative to the flowers and tall grasses in Renata's foreground or the buildings in the background. Her arm lifted, stiffly, as if maybe it pained her, and she stumbled, fell, got up again.

Renata was aware of perceiving more detail than she would have expected at this distance: saw the long dirty black coat too warm for the springtime weather, smelled booze and sweat, heard the rattling tubercular cough. A street person in the Botanic Gardens. Such a dissonant juxtaposition both pleased and dismayed her, the dismay clearer than the pleasure but both abstract.

She made to tighten her arms around her daughter and, unobtrusively if she could manage it, to turn them both away from the woman, out of her line of sight and, if they were lucky, out of the erratic trajectory of what seemed to be her approach. But Vanessa, whose usually hyper-alert attention the woman had apparently not caught, squirmed loose and ran along the path to the Alpine Meadow, a few paces away. Not wanting to interfere with the child's spontaneity, rare these days, Renata let her go.

'Fine girl ya got there.'

Renata couldn't tell whether the menace she suddenly felt was because of the thick unfamiliar accent, which made her unable to read voice tone or inflection, or because the woman had insinuated herself too close and kept coming closer even when Renata backed up, or because everything in the world had been shown by Ian's death to have menace about it, or whether there really was a threat here to another of her children. 'Thanks,' she said curtly, and moved so as to put her body between the woman and Vanessa.

'Fine girl. Fair girl. About fourteen, is she?'

'Twelve,' Renata said, unwillingly. If she walked in Vanessa's direction, the woman might well follow her. If she walked away, she would be leaving Vanessa undefended and the woman might not take the bait.

'Twelve. Had me a twelve-year-old girl once. Eileen, her name was.'

Renata turned slightly back toward the woman and was taken aback to encounter clear blue eyes, made clearer by tears. 'What happened to her?' she asked, not knowing whether this was a kind or sensible thing to do but wanting to know, suddenly, needing to hear.

'Died.'

'I'm sorry.'

The woman nodded. 'Lost all my young ones, I did. All seven of 'em.'

'Seven!' Renata breathed. Now she was holding the bereaved mother's cold hands, not knowing how their hands had happened to come into contact or why she allowed it.

'Far as I know, though,' the woman declared, 'far as I'll ever know, Eileen's the only one dead before her time. I lost 'em, but I saved 'em. That I did.'

There was a pause, and Renata was on the verge of saying she didn't understand, she'd like to understand, when Vanessa called to her. 'Mom, you got to see this! It's beautiful! Mom, come here!'

'I'm coming!' She pulled her hands away from the woman, who did not hold on. 'I'm sorry. I have to – My daughter—'

'Got a spare penny, mum?'

Now Renata knew where she'd encountered this woman before – on campus, in the park, a few weeks ago. She'd been panhandling then, too, with that same oddly inflected line.

Out of a discomfort equal parts suspicion and embarrassment, Renata had a personal policy against giving money to panhandlers. This time, though, she found a crumpled dollar bill in her jacket pocket and folded it hastily into the gritty palm. The blue eyes, dry now, widened, and the woman gasped, coughed. As Renata was hurrying along the path toward the Japanese Garden, where Vanessa stood awed before the lily pads and pebbled walkways, she heard a cracked, 'Thank ye, mum. I thank ye very much, mum. God bless ye, mum.'

260

Chapter 23

The toast popped up. The quick little motion was unpleasant, and she also didn't like the whole wheat crumbs on her fingers, under one nail. Anxiety roughened her breathing. Her chest hurt. Gingerly she laid the two pieces of toast, browned too much because she'd been inattentive, on a warmed plate and put two more bread slices into the toaster slots, pressed down the lever, hoped she could do it right this time.

She hadn't made cinnamon toast since Ian had died, and she didn't know how much to make now, but today she'd find out. Banana pancakes and cinnamon toast had been his two favorite breakfasts. Vanessa didn't like banana pancakes, so Renata wouldn't have to make them anymore. But cinnamon toast was one of Vanessa's favorites, too, and it wasn't fair to her daughter never to serve it again.

From the support group she knew that some bereaved parents did their best to create and maintain unadulterated associations with their dead children. One couple never went to the mountains anymore, a traditional family activity, because their son had loved going to the mountains; resentfully they reported their daughter's objections to selling their cabin as though she no longer had a claim on it. Patty Devereaux took pride in the fact that she hadn't allowed pizza or beer anywhere near her since Cory had died, because their last meal together had been pizza and beer. Rob Torres's wife had left him and their surviving children because the entire complex of maternity had come to belong exclusively to the children who had died.

The temptation was obvious, the ease with which one could follow that path and, indeed, the bitter gratification that would come from doing so. Renata indulged herself in a fleeting fantasy, breathtaking for the sick satisfaction it brought: I'm sorry, Vanessa, but we're never going to have cinnamon toast again, because your brother died.

The lightening of the southeastern sky – shell-pink streaks outside the kitchen window, clotted little clouds – had a sinister sheen. A bird chirping in the mock-orange bush was an evil portent. Something bad was going to happen today.

Something bad had already happened. Today was Friday.

As Renata was stirring cinnamon and brown sugar into melted margarine, Vanessa came into the kitchen. Her face and body registered surprise. 'Cinnamon toast,' she observed. Then, guardedly, 'Mmm.'

'I know you like cinnamon toast.'

Vanessa sat down at the table, hesitantly, as if not sure that was what she was supposed to do. She ducked her head. 'We haven't had it for a long time.' Her voice dropped off the way it did when she spelled a word whose ending she wasn't sure of, gambling that if she said it quietly enough the examiner would give her the benefit of the doubt.

Renata brushed a third and fourth piece of toast with the cinnamon mixture. She could make more if they wanted it. Maybe there would be too much, since Ian wasn't eating. Carrying the plate to the table and settling herself in her chair, she took a deep breath and looked squarely at her daughter. 'I haven't made cinnamon toast since Ian died, have I?'

Vanessa looked up, shocked, and then lowered her eyes again.

'Remember how he used to eat six or eight pieces at a sitting?' She braced herself for the bolt of anguish that would surely follow such a daring enunciation. What came, instead, was a bittersweet pang, and she could feel herself smiling a little.

'One time he ate twelve.' Vanessa allowed herself a chuckle. Renata didn't think that was precisely true, but she didn't argue. She took a piece of toast and passed the plate to Vanessa, who took four. 'I like cinnamon toast, too,' the girl reasserted, staking her claim.

'I know you do.' Once again, Renata thought, this child was teaching her how to do this right.

And at Tim's birthday dinner last week, he'd suddenly leaned out of the family conversation and into her misery to tell her, with uncharacteristic forthrightness, 'Mom, you've got to find something to fill the emptiness. If you don't, the emptiness will take over.' He knew something about emptiness, this troubled eldest child of hers, and about emptiness taking over, so his advice had seemed worth listening to, whether it turned out to be usable or not.

'When are Uncle Pete and Aunt Denise coming?' Vanessa wanted to know.

'They're at their hotel. Aunt Denise has her conference today. They'll come over here tomorrow and we'll have lunch and then we'll leave for the mountains.' The sequence wore her out.

'How come they didn't stay here?'

'I – don't know.' If she'd been privy to the making of the arrangements, it had slipped her mind. She could barely hold onto the simple, incredible information that her brother-in-law and his new wife were in town and a family excursion planned.

Vanessa stretched. 'Tired,' she yawned.

'Didn't you sleep well?'

'Jennifer's mean.'

Renata blinked. 'You're tired because Jennifer's mean?'

'I hate school.'

'What's going on, honey?'

But Vanessa wouldn't say. Fear lapped. Was she, at this very instant, missing something important in her daughter's life, committing an error with grave and far-reaching consequences? Had she lost one of the most basic parental skills – how to coax a recalcitrant child into sharing her troubles? Why was Vanessa – the least recalcitrant of children, expressive to a fault when it came to unhappiness – suddenly unwilling to tell her about this? Was Jennifer saying unkind things about Ian? The possibility chilled her.

Clumsily she tried, 'I don't much want to go to work today, either.' She waited for a reply, some expression of interest. When none came, she went on anyway. 'I'm sort of in the middle of a conflict, and it makes things unpleasant.'

'What do you mean?'

Encouraged, Renata elaborated. 'We caught this student cheating. So he flunked the test, and he thinks that's not fair.'

Vanessa was fidgeting with the curls of toast crust on her plate.

263

She didn't comment, but Renata could feel her interest now, perhaps as much in the rare phenomenon of her mother talking about something besides Ian as in the anecdote itself.

'He really makes me furious. He's just so obnoxious. We have another appointment today, and I expect it will get pretty nasty.' She glanced uncertainly at her daughter and risked confiding, 'Anger scares me now.'

'How come?'

'Because Ian was mad at Dad and me when he died.'

Vanessa scowled. Assuming this to mean discomfort with the turn the conversation had taken again, back to Ian, back to death, Renata felt chastened. But then Vanessa said, choosing her words with a care that was at once childish and sophisticated, 'But if he was happy when he died, would you be afraid of happiness now?'

Renata said, 'Oh,' and there was a luminous moment between them.

Throughout the day, then, she made note of pleasurable things. Red and purple petunias. A song on the radio to which she was singing along before she realized it, and which, wonderingly, she let herself finish. Getting a joke a student with cerebral palsy laboriously spelled out on his word board; laughing. On the way home, planning dinner. Cuddling with Glenn while they watched the news. Reading to Vanessa and rubbing her back. Finishing a story, the first whole thing she'd written since Ian's death; sending it out.

Life was good.

Ian was dead.

These things, both true, existed in the same universe.

That should have been incomprehensible, but it was not quite. Feeling herself on the brink of comprehension, Renata tried, futilely, to pull back, to stay rooted in the firmer, more familiar ground of despair.

After dinner she took a walk. Not long ago, she'd been too afraid to do that; tonight, she was only moderately anxious, and disoriented only half a dozen times. Painfully buzzing with awareness that this was Friday and eight o'clock was approaching (seven o'clock if you factored in the time change; so which hour, precisely, was the anniversary of the hour Ian had killed himself?), also aware of the rowdy flock of birds roosting in the neighbors' fat evergreen, also aware of her own footsteps, each of them one after another on sidewalk and grass, she could feel pressure at the edge of her consciousness. Something waiting. Something tugging at her, and her own resistance. Only days ago, the presence she'd felt grasping at her had been madness. Now it was, no less frighteningly, sanity.

The call to transformation, and her refusal of the call, and a recognition that she would not refuse it much longer. Soon, she would come to hold simultaneously the twin truths that Ian was dead and that life was good. She didn't yet; she was fighting, kicking and screaming. But she could tell that she would. Quite against her will, she was healing.

Knowing that, she couldn't tolerate more than once around the block. When she went back into the house, it was almost seven o'clock. She performed required tasks, remembering with no satisfaction the time when she couldn't. Clocks advanced, the red digits on the microwave silently and, as it were, linearly, her wristwatch in a ticking circle, the cuckoo clock with false cheer. Nothing she could do or refrain from doing would keep seven o'clock from happening. It was seven o'clock. Then it was a minute after seven. Nothing she could do or refrain from doing would stop eight o'clock on a Friday evening from approaching, staying its allotted span, and passing, every week, every spring, every March, every time March 18 fell on a Friday, forever.

Glenn came to bed shortly after she did, turned out her reading lamp and gently took her book away. Yes. She wanted him. Her husband. She took his dear, battered face in her hands and kissed him deeply. He swept his palm down the length of her arched body, lingering at her nipples, at the spot on her flank which had been and was no longer swollen, at the hollow of her hip. They made love with the abandon of lovers just discovering each other, with the profound and steady passion of lovers together for a lifetime. She fell asleep in his arms.

And woke the next morning into bone-deep sorrow. She reached for Glenn. His side of the bed was empty. She groaned and curled around a pillow. She stretched herself out flat and sobbed and called her son's name. She insisted, 'No!' But, suddenly as real and three-dimensional as the depression that leadened her limbs and propelled each thud of her heart to jar her brain against her skull, came the dreadful, liberating insight: Whether I accept this thing or not, whether I allow this thing fully into my life or not, Ian will still be dead.

The old yellow cat landed on the bed beside her, purring loudly, and stepped up onto her chest. Renata made to push her away but gave it up, and the cat settled herself squarely over Renata's aching heart. The warm vibration from the intent little body spread down into Renata's chest, loosening the tension, softening the pain. Cinnabar's claws worked in and out, kneading the bedclothes into a nest. The tip of her red-gold tail swished, and repeatedly she pushed her small triangular head against Renata's chin and cheeks, still purring. The comfort was enormous, and in an accessible form. Renata lay there for a while, crying, relaxing, and eventually was able to get up.

Someone ordered pizza for lunch. She must have eaten part of a piece, for remnants of crust and mushrooms splotched the paper plate on her lap. She was on the front porch swing with Gypsy as close to her as she could get, stretched out long and thin to fit between her ankles, breathing shallow and ears anxiously perked. Always a nervous dog – constitutionally unable or unwilling because of some canine neurosis to nurse the four pups in her only litter, she'd allowed them one by one to die – she'd been quite undone by Shaman's death, and Ian's. Whenever she sat or lay still now, even in restless sleep, her body shook.

Renata knew that since Ian died there had been discrete moments, moments strung together, when she had experienced something other than frantic sorrow or numbness. Just last night, in fact; distantly, she recalled acquiescing to the notion of healing. That had not been real, and would not happen again. This, now, was the way she would feel for the rest of her life.

The movement of the swing hurt her. Trying to stop it, she braced her toes against the concrete porch floor, but that hurt, too, and the swing kept moving – not much, not in any clear arc, but in response to the trembling of her body and the dog's.

In front of her, in the open rectangle framed by the wall, roof, and porch pillars, was a summer morning. Grass and leaves were green, the sky was blue, the house across the street was white, cars passing flashed multicolored. She knew the properties of the colors, but they had no personal meaning. Birds sang in the tree by the porch, and someone in the neighborhood was practicing a woodwind. She smelled mown grass.

Behind her was her house. People she knew were in it. Machines ran – the dishwasher, the refrigerator, clocks, the television. People were talking. From the small-talk tone of it, they weren't talking about Ian, and Renata didn't understand how that was possible.

She sat in the dim rectangular cube of the porch, half-enclosed, and sensations reached her but meant nothing. She trembled and missed her son. Missing her son pulsated with meaning and dimensionality as nothing else did.

She heard Tim laugh – not heartily, to be sure, but with some animation, and undeniably it was *laughter*, her son's laughter, welcome for its own sake, appalling in its strangeness here and now. She heard Pete's voice, its Southern timbre more pronounced than either of his brothers', and the unfamiliar voice of his wife. Renata supposed she was being inhospitable. The concept made no sense.

She didn't hear Vanessa. Or Glenn. Terror pinned her to the seat.

Glenn spoke to her from the screened doorway behind her, which would be dark and finely textured if she looked at it, the mouth of a tunnel leading somewhere she ought to know but didn't. 'Are you about ready to go, honey?'

She was shaking her head before the knowledge of where they were going had crystalized. 'I can't.' They were going to the mountains. They were taking Pete and Denise to the mountains, as if they were ordinary people hosting flatlander visitors from back East. 'I don't think I can go.' *And I don't understand how you can, either. Any of you.*

From the family room at the back of the house came another riff of Tim's laughter. Surely the burst of staccato exhalations with accompanying grunts was distorted by distance and perspective and by the fact that laughter manifestly did not belong in this house anymore; surely it didn't really sound like that. Renata tried to pull her feet up under her, to make herself a smaller target, but the slatted seat of the swing wasn't wide enough and its reaction to her movement was exaggerated, off-putting. Gypsy whimpered and sat up.

Glenn hadn't said anything either to convince her to go on the outing or to give her permission to stay home. But he was still standing there on the other side of the screen door. 'I'll go,' she said.

She sat in the back seat on the right. She turned as far sideways as she could manage, as if looking out the window at the scenery though of course she wasn't, and leaned her forehead against the pane. Glenn drove. Tim and Shauna weren't in the car. Where were Tim and Shauna? In the space between her realization that they weren't here and the emergence of the memory that they'd said they had to go somewhere, there was no fear or even sorrow, only a bitter acquiescence: of course he was gone. Of course she'd lost Tim, too. What else had she expected?

Foothills rose on both sides of the car, then canyon walls. With every curve of the highway, another vista opened, hills and peaks, clouds, brilliant sky, all of it beautiful in name only. The air was already noticeably thinner and cooler, and people were complaining about their ears popping.

Renata, though, was going down instead of up, through layers of water flowing into each other rather than cut strata of rock. Denise, on the other side of Vanessa, kept making appreciative comments about the mountains in Renata's general direction. Renata smiled faintly once or twice, the best she could do, and then surrendered to the striated undertow.

Chapter 24

She was at the edge of a fetid sea. Its brownish waves and ripples looked thick, like pudding, like mucus; they slithered instead of flowed, and stood peaked for long seconds as if hardly liquid at all. The stench nearly overpowered her: sour milk, spoiled meat, sick excrement. She covered her nose and mouth with a tattered sleeve, but the fabric had already absorbed the odor and made her gag.

The cesspool extended as far ahead of her and off to both sides as she could see, under a low, brindle-colored sky. The pool shone like dirty metal. She had to get across it. She didn't know why; certainly she had no idea what might be at its other edge, or why she would want to be there any more than here or anywhere else. But an urgent need to cross this disgusting body of water made her take a step into it.

The viscous matter parted for her and then rose around her like toothless gums with flesh half liquefied, smacking and slurping. Renata tried to change her mind, to extract her leg, but had no traction and was pulled farther into the mire.

She sank. It wouldn't be so offensive to sink to the bottom and die in this buoyant water. Even the odor didn't seem so offensive now, and the nausea rising in the pit of her stomach like the water itself foaming into the back of her throat was already so familiar that it was scarcely aversive. She leaned her head back. The surface of the water was filmed with a thin gooey layer that stuck the strands and clumps of her hair together.

A sluggish tide was pushing her out to sea. The undertow at her dragging feet was quicksand. Dully she wondered if what was happening to her could properly be called drowning, since

269

the medium wasn't precisely water, or whether she was inventing a brand new way of dying.

Something solid came up under her and raised her just above the surface, so that she breathed after all. She was propelled rapidly along. She thought of whales, dolphins. She thought of sharks. But then she recognized the broad arrow-shaped head of the serpent Belinda steadfastly parting the waves just ahead of her, and once again she surrendered, against what little she knew of her will, to being rescued.

Under the mottled sky, which exchanged useless brass-colored reflections with the sea, the snake carried her toward shore. Shore was slimy concrete, pocked and cracked. Renata readied herself for the unpleasant feeling of being deposited on something solid and relatively safe, but the snake turned with her and skimmed along a slightly curved wall, through the very edges of the water, through echoes of their swimming and of the coagulated sea.

A thin arch trembled both audibly and visibly ahead of them, a silver cut through fleshy yellow-brown. Belinda brought her to the tip of it, which would have fit into her cupped palm, where it vibrated against the concrete floor and wall. Still sprawled on the serpent's broad back, Renata leaned to touch the glittering span, and its razor edge sliced her wrist before she even realized she'd made contact. She yelped and made to bring her bleeding wrist back to her mouth, but the serpent's tongue intervened. Forked, flickering, it cleaned the wound faster than Renata could see or feel, and whether the bleeding actually stopped didn't seem important.

Belinda informed her, as though it meant something, 'You've come to the Sword Bridge.'

Renata shook her head. 'I've never heard of it. Should I have heard of it?'

'You've had no reason to know of it until now. But it has always been part of this journey.'

'From where to where?'

'Through the underworld.'

'Why should I even try to cross it?'

'You can't stay here.'

'My child is dead. Why not?'

'I won't allow it.'

The sharp span of the Sword Bridge sliced up through the dirty air like a rainbow through a sky still clotted with remnants of a storm. Renata forced her gaze to follow its glittering arc. It rose much higher than the lowering sky would have seemed to allow, and the end of it disappeared past the too-close horizon.

'Start now,' Belinda hissed.

Renata resisted, unable to think why she should start anything or how. She stood still, ankle-deep in muck and thigh-deep in the muscular coils of the serpent, and it would make more sense just never to move again.

Belinda insisted, 'Take the first step.'

Renata moved her foot as if in compliance, but she stayed where she was.

Belinda's coils readjusted themselves around her, forcing her to put one foot up and in front of the other if she was not to fall. Wondering defeatedly why she didn't just let herself fall, she climbed a reluctant step and then another.

The point of the sword screaked sideways across the concrete when she put her weight on it, and instinctively she caught herself, heart pumping, adrenaline gushing, terrified of falling off the bridge though it made no sense to her that she should be. The bridge swung wildly. She clung to the curve of it just above where she stood, feeling the flesh of her hands being scored, and waited for it to still. Then, more cautiously and precisely, she stepped up again.

She was not careful enough; the blade sliced through the sole of her shoe, and a wound opened in the bottom of her foot. The pain was so thin and sharp it could hardly be called pain, and she thought blood oozed, although it felt not much different from the viscous water and congealed air. Moving her foot around until she found a surface wide and flat enough, she stepped up again.

The sword swayed dangerously and twanged with almost no sound, sending vibrations through the bones of her feet and ankles, a painful itching. Again she stepped up, climbing, extending her arms for balance, trying to concentrate on the unlikely mass of her body ascending this oscillating arch. She couldn't imagine that it spanned anything, bridged anything, but by now it would be just as demanding and risky to retreat as to keep going up. The Sword Bridge made a polished silver path, very distinct, through the enveloping murk, and she stepped along it, one foot after the other.

She had climbed a considerable distance, high enough that the stagnant water merged with the stagnant air into an endless, featureless miasma, when she fell.

She plummeted through the brindle air, certain she would be crushed on impact with the brindle sea. Though she'd have thought it didn't matter if she died, now she shrieked in protest: *Not here. Not like this.* Vivid images accosted her of the things she had to lose: the spurting taste of a plum when her teeth first broke through the skin, Vanessa's pleasure at the Botanic Gardens.

With a thud that jarred the bones of her skull and made adrenaline pump painfully, uselessly, she landed on a surface that was both hard and springy. It gave under her impact and took on a few inches of greasy water, then dispiritedly bobbed up again. Breath was knocked out of her and she lost consciousness.

When consciousness returned, it had been altered. Her sensorium functioned, but was badly skewed. The range of her sight and hearing had been distorted, so that she was seeing clearly objects that barely moved far down in the murky ocean and hearing tiny sounds whose sources might not have been in this world at all, but she couldn't see or hear much of anything right around her.

Her sense of touch was erratic and acutely sharpened, thereby rendered virtually unreliable. Taste and smell had melded into a single peculiar sense whose information she didn't know how to interpret. The pervasive smell-taste seemed to be of the human body, blood and flesh, skin, bodily fluids.

Other senses, whose trustworthiness she had no way of gauging, told her that the surface on which she sprawled was wooden and more or less flat. She was floating on it. A gigantic raft, she decided, and she was not alone on it.

It was, in fact, extremely crowded. Trying to move, she could find no room for herself outside the space she already occupied. Even there, she might be lying on top of other bodies, pushing them aside. Her right shoulder was higher than the rest of her and her back was awkwardly stretched.

There was movement close around her and far away. Something was wrong with the movement; it seemed somehow abortive, as though each particular motion in the mass of motion started and stopped too soon.

A thick, soft cylinder nudged against the back of her thigh. Her first thought was of Belinda, but the thing wasn't the right shape to be a serpent. Her dulled and ungainly fingertips brought her data that seemed to indicate it was a human thigh, separate from her, separate from any body: hip joint to kneecap, bleeding sluggishly from both ragged ends, of a size and shape similar to her own.

Horror was slow in coming, but when it finally seeped through to her awareness she jerked her own thigh away from the insistent dismembered one. The sudden motion made the raft tilt and dip, causing an avalanche of foul odor-taste, thick water over the surface of the raft carrying countless other body parts into her.

A face like a mask flopped against her own face. It looked identical to the way she imagined herself to look, although it might not be the way she looked to anyone else. She struggled to sit up. The peeled face lay like seaweed in the spot where her face had been.

She pulled her knees up and hunched her shoulders, leaving as little body surface as possible available for contact. A hand crawled over her shoulder. Its little finger was crooked in the same way hers were and, a left hand, it wore a wedding ring exactly like hers.

On the raft between her legs, some sort of oval shell opened and closed. Then she recognized it as a mouth, and, when it screamed, the voice was unmistakably her own.

Renata screamed and flung the severed hand away from her. It caromed off the overloaded raft and skipped like a stone once, twice across the slicked surface of the water, then plunged beneath it. Renata felt a stab of loss so sharp and so surprising that her fists went to her heart, though she should have known by now that her heart could not be protected.

Something was nestled behind her. She could tell only that it was squishy, and that it fit into the small of her back. Warily, she eased one hand back there, wincing when the fingers came into contact with the object. Pliant, moist. She snatched her hand back. She cupped it, pressed it again over the aching spot in her chest. The object behind her moved of its own volition around her left side and into her lap. It was a heart, just like hers, torn open.

Steeling herself against the visceral horror of holding in her hands a beating, living, bleeding heart just like her own, Renata scooped it up out of her lap and flung it overboard. It punched down through the yellow surface slime and sank like a stone.

Then, as a great wailing and sussurating noise rose from the others who shared the raft with her, she became aware of who they were. Clones, replicas of her, dozens of them, milling, grieving aloud. Each of the throng by whom she was surrounded, in whom she was submerged, was identical to her, except that each was missing a part: This one wore a hole in her chest where her heart had been pulled out; the arteries and veins dangled. This one had no mouth, so that her mourning came out of her pores. That one, missing a thigh, stood crooked, resting a hip on a calf bone. This one had a dark, deep eye socket, with no longer any expression but emptiness, and one on the far corner of the raft held aloft, like a mast without a sail, an arm without a hand.

Abruptly the raft came to a stop. Only with the cessation of movement did Renata realize how rapidly and steadily it had been moving. There had been a nice wind; now they were quite becalmed. The metallic sky seemed to lower and the sheened sea to rise, so that the stranded raft with its bizarre cargo fit into a snug slot between sky and sea, and did not move.

Exhausted, Renata collapsed into the arms, onto the bellies, among the tangled hair and spread limbs of her tortured and deformed selves. This was as good a place to die as any. She waited. All the maimed versions of her waited.

Nothing moved. The world was completely without spirit or energy, which was as it should be. Nothing changed.

After a long time, Renata gradually and reluctantly became aware of motion through the brackish water off the edge of the raft. Any motion, any sound, was so startling and out of place that she'd turned her head toward it before she could stop herself, making her head throb.

Belinda's great head rose out of the water, a sea serpent whose body might well encircle the world. Renata's gaze was caught and held by the intent lidless gaze of the serpent, and then Belinda sank into the thick waves again, burrowed under the raft. Her head and a tremendous span of her body appeared underwater on the other side, while the length of her tail on this side stretched to the semi-liquid horizon. Then Belinda began to swim forward, carrying the loaded raft on her back, and Renata and the others found themselves paddling, kicking, taking up oars they hadn't known were there.

Chapter 25

This was the tenth or twelfth or twentieth dress Vanessa had tried on, in the fifth or sixth store. Renata sat on the floor at the end of the narrow corridor that ran in front of the fitting rooms. Whenever Vanessa came out – to model another dress, to get another armload off the racks – she'd roll her eyes and whisper loudly, 'Oh, Mom! How embarrassing!' But there were no chairs, and Renata knew she'd faint if she tried to stand so long.

The air was viscous and fetid, although nobody else in the crowded store seemed to be having trouble breathing it. There was a stench to which no one else was reacting. Her stomach was queasy as if from unnatural motion, and from this angle she couldn't avoid catching sight in one mirror or another of her own shoulder, the side of her head, her hand reaching out to her daughter, body parts cut off from the main body of her and sluggishly floating.

When Vanessa was eight or nine (*Ian was nine when he died when he died*), Glenn had taken her shopping for tennis shoes. They'd been gone a long time, but that had been back when Renata could still dismiss her nagging worry as neurotic and groundless, before she'd understood that every instant in the world without tragedy was a reprieve.

When they'd finally come home – Vanessa proudly showing off her new, plain white, low-top sneakers – Glenn had reported that she'd tried on twenty-six pairs. For days afterward, at odd moments, he'd wonderingly repeated, '*Twenty-six pairs!*' and Renata had laughed and hugged him and assured him he'd earned his daddy badge.

It had become a pleasant little collective family memory: 'Remember the time Vanessa tried on twenty-six pairs of shoes?' Now, of course, the memory hurt, because it was located in the family before Ian died, and she couldn't stop it from recurring and recurring like shotgun fire.

Any happy memory hurt now, because it was a fraud. Any happy anticipation hurt, because it was a set-up. Only the endless present, the *now* of Ian's death, didn't hurt, because it had gone well beyond simple pain.

'Mom?' Vanessa allowed the fitting-room curtain to open very slightly and stuck one finger through, from which dangled a dress on a hanger. Then her head poked out, modestly swathed at the chin, and Renata noted dully that her daughter's hair, fairly crackling with hairspray, hadn't been tousled at all by the afternoon of trying on and taking off clothes. There had been a time, not long ago but in a different life, when she'd have been amused by that. Now the thought of being amused by anything sickened her. 'Mom, could you go get me a smaller size?'

She struggled to her feet, sliding a palm hard up the wall and trying to breathe deeply until the worst of the vertigo passed. She couldn't tell whether she was breathing deeply or not. Vanessa's head disappeared back behind the curtain and her finger jiggled impatiently; the colors of the dress moving through the air left bleeding trails.

Renata managed to say, 'Okay,' she hoped loudly enough for Vanessa to hear. She reached out and took the dress. The weight of it, the peculiar shift of it across the metal arc of the hanger, came close to pulling her off balance. She made her way out of the dressing room, although it took long moments of fumbling for her to figure out how to work the latch on the half-door that led to the sales floor.

Randomly, she turned left, and was at once thoroughly lost, certain she'd never been in this place before. Racks of filmy pastel garments whose function she couldn't imagine covered a wall floor-to-ceiling on her left; pieces of them moved, swayed, fluttered in ways that disturbed her. Stretching interminably off to her right was a thick sea of inchoate color and shape and texture, no part of it relating to any other part and none of it having any meaning to her. Reds throbbed. Whites bled. Fluorescent lights skittered from floor and wall and ceiling, casting infinitesimal shadows that would never stop flickering.

278

'Can I help you, ma'am?'

No one can help me can't you see my son is dead? Renata managed to form enough coherent syllables to say, 'My daughter needs a smaller size,' and used both hands to hold up the dress on the hanger.

'Well, let's see what we can do here.' The clerk's motions as she took the dress were rough. Renata's fingers, hand, wrist tingled painfully. Her joints and muscles ached. Her skin hurt.

She stood still, not knowing where the clerk had gone or whether she'd ever be back, not knowing where Vanessa was or how to get to her, desperately wanting Glenn but not knowing why. She doubted he really existed except in her mind, which had shown itself to be utterly unreliable; Glenn, or at least her relationship with him, had to be a fraud and a set-up, too, like everything else that pretended to be happy. The sleeve of a delicate lavender nightgown drifted across her cheek. The pain made her gasp, but she couldn't think how to remove herself from its reach.

'Here we go.' The clerk was unrelentingly brisk and cheery. 'Here's one that might fit her. We're lucky. We don't get many in in those real small sizes. Your daughter must be nice and petite, is she?'

Renata nodded; she didn't know what it was she was agreeing to, but it didn't matter. Bracing herself, she accepted the dress from the clerk and, with enormous concentration, waded back to where she'd left her daughter. She used the rack of clinging pastel negligees as a guide, although their touch and odor stung; she turned right at the end of them, fumbled again with the latch on the half-door till she was sure her knuckles were bruised, and was back in the narrow airless corridor with innumerable mirrors and curtains arrayed in front of her and off interminably in both directions. Terrified, she realized that Vanessa could be behind any of them, or could have vanished. She was panting. Her heart raced in her ears. She couldn't feel her hands and feet.

'Vanessa?' she called, amazed that she thought to do it.

Just to her right a curtain shifted and a young hand stuck out. 'What took you so long? I'm in here half-naked, you know.'

Not knowing for sure that that was Vanessa, not knowing how to tell or whether it made any difference, Renata hooked the hanger on the impatiently wiggling fingers and watched, nauseous, as the dress was pulled back behind the curtain.

She sank to the floor at the end of the corridor again and began to wait. She had the sense that she'd waited here before, but she couldn't think when or why. She didn't know what she was waiting for now, or how long it would be. It didn't matter. Ian was dead. She could wait anywhere forever or for a split second without caring about the difference. She could wait for anything or nothing, because it was all the same.

'Does this look stupid? This looks stupid, doesn't it?'

Realizing the question was directed at her, and then realizing it was her daughter talking to her (*my daughter is alive my son is dead* and then another loud insinuating voice saying *you'll lose her too, you'll lose her too, he's more important because he's already dead*), Renata forced herself to open her eyes and to look up.

The dress had a short straight skirt and tight waist, shoulder pads in puffed sleeves, a big bow in the small of the back. Triangles of a bright white background blazed between splashy pink-and-scarlet flowers that had yellow centers and dramatically serrated green leaves. The neckline was straight across the collarbone in front, but behind it dipped in a very low V. Vanessa kept peering over her shoulder into the mirror. 'Is it too low, Mom? Do you think it's too low? Does it look stupid? Oh, God, it looks stupid, doesn't it?'

Renata shook her head. The motion seemed endless. 'You look lovely,' she said honestly.

I'll never go to Ian's sixth-grade continuation came naturally into her mind, followed just as easily and naturally by the other voice warning, *You don't dare go to Vanessa's continuation either, because she'll die someday, too, or you will. One way or another you'll lose her.*

Sternly, she brought as much of her attention as she could gather back to this living child, and said, 'You look very grown up.' Vanessa beamed.

Renata managed to pay for the dress without, as far as she could tell, making any mistakes, although neither the concept nor the details of money made any but the most distant kind of sense. On the way home she managed to discuss with Vanessa whether she could wear makeup for continuation, giving permission because it was a special occasion, bitterly wondering why parents spent so much time and energy trying to do the best thing for their children when the children die anyway. 'Tell Dad it's okay,' Vanessa pleaded. 'He's so old-fashioned!'

'Remind me,' Renata told her, because the only thing that would stay in her mind of its own volition was *Ian is dead Ian is dead*.

For her continuation Vanessa wore the flowered dress, white shoes with two-inch heels, pink earrings shaped like flowers, and her first officially sanctioned makeup, which she applied with suspicious skill. She tried to fix her hair in the style popularized by the Hispanic girls in her class: long and straight in back with a tight edge of curls, a huge pouf like a hat feather over the crown of her head. But her classmates' hair was much thicker and coarser than hers and, no matter how much mousse and hairspray she used, her fine soft hair fell gently over her forehead and temples, and it was only because she didn't want her mascara to run that she didn't cry.

Although she was afraid to, Renata watched Glenn as their daughter came downstairs. His face was open, vulnerable, proud. He was willing to keep loving this child. He would be hurt again. Renata could hardly bear the thought of Glenn being hurt again, and it enraged her with both of them. 'You look beautiful,' he was saying to Vanessa. His voice broke, but he cleared his throat and added, 'You're growing up, honey. You're not a little girl anymore.'

Flushed with pleasure and embarrassment, Vanessa shrieked, 'Don't ruin my hair!' but she allowed his hug. Against her will, Renata watched them. She was astonished, frightened, horrified by the faint happiness she felt, and fought it off. Then she took the few steps to her daughter and hugged her, too, being careful not to ruin her hair.

Vanessa went on ahead with her friends, and Glenn and Renata walked hand-in-hand through the June afternoon. 'This is the first time we've been to the school,' Renata observed, but could not say the phrase that made the rest of it make sense: 'Since Ian died.'

Glenn sighed and took his hand away to rub his eyes. The absence of his hand terrified her. In the bright sunshine, mottled by the shadows of the crab apple trees that had bloomed with such painful beauty a few weeks ago, she saw the lines in his cheeks, the

281

tightness around his eyes. She raised her hand to rest her fingertips on the side of his face, but he pulled away as if it hurt and said, 'I hope we don't see anybody we know.'

'You know we will. Teachers and parents. Vanessa's friends.' She swallowed. 'His friends.' It surprised her that, although she'd been unable to stop thinking his name, she couldn't say it aloud. A fresh loss. A fresh betrayal.

'I hope they don't say anything to us.'

'I hope I can get through this,' she said.

He looked at her in some alarm. 'Will you be okay? Maybe I should go alone.'

She stopped. He didn't, and after a moment she stumbled to catch up with him. 'Don't you want me to go? Doesn't Vanessa want me to go?'

'I don't want a scene,' he told her, staring straight ahead. 'I don't think I could handle a scene right now. I don't think Vanessa could either.'

Indignation and vestigial pride made her straighten her shoulders and breathe more evenly to keep herself from fainting. 'There won't be a scene,' she promised grimly.

'Good.' Then he said, 'Renata, I didn't mean—'

But they were at the front door of the school now, part of a small crowd of parents, and on their way in. She reached to touch his arm, to say with a gesture that she understood he hadn't meant to hurt her. But he didn't react, and she couldn't tell whether she'd actually touched him or not.

Besides, he had meant to hurt her. Everyone meant to hurt her. Ian had meant to hurt her when he hanged himself.

The school looked overwhelmingly as it always had, as all schools did. Though the floor and the walls halfway up were tiled gray, and though there were bright crayoned pictures all along the walls and a display about flowers in the lobby, the predominant impression of schools was always of browns – warm brown with a gold undertone, cool brown with an underlayer of gray, the shiny beige of hinged desktops, the almost-black brown of auditorium seats. Renata was flooded by browns, and by the fact that, although Tim and Vanessa had gone here, too, this now was Ian's school and *Ian was dead*.

She could have closed her eyes to keep out the browns, but

then she wouldn't have known where she was, and she'd have spun backward in time or spiraled underground, and Glenn would have accused her of creating a scene. Besides, the smells would still be there – the chalk-crayon-sweat-floorwax odor specific to elementary schools – and that would have invaded her mind and body with agonizing memories of Ian, too. Not full-fledged memories, not scenes or stories she could refuse to see through to the end, but snippets, flashes, a searing hailstorm, a strobe light spinning too fast to stop.

They sat toward the back of the little auditorium, though not in the last row because that would have made them too conspicuous. The principal saw them and raised his hand in greeting or salute but, mercifully, didn't approach them. Renata found Ian's class toward the front of the auditorium and stared at them for a long time, repeating their names to herself: Chris, Aisha, Pablo, Ryan, Eric. She braced herself for a rush of malevolence like that which had struck her when she'd come upon the little boys playing in the alley, but this time it didn't come. Ian's teacher sat with her class, and there didn't seem to be any empty seats. Why wasn't there an empty seat for Ian?

There were speeches – a welcome by the principal, a poem by one of the 'continuating' sixth-graders, an inspirational paragraph or two by a man from the local Optimists Club. It seemed to Renata that there was also a great deal of noise from the audience; her head buzzed with it and she couldn't filter it out, heard very clearly the grandmother three rows behind her scolding a small girl in Spanish, the large Asian family off to the left chattering like pigeons, the two high-school boys leaning against the back wall arranging a deal whose details she couldn't follow.

There was music from the school's band and choir. Not especially melodious, it nonetheless took Renata's breath away with pain; she understood then that she would never again be able to listen to music, because her child was dead. Then there was the calling of names.

Vanessa walked across the stage when her name was called. She was a little wobbly on her high heels, obviously a little embarrassed in front of all these people, obviously proud. She accepted her certificate of continuation and another certificate for good attendance, and then she turned and peered out into the audience for a moment.

Renata couldn't tell whether she saw them. The parents had been instructed not to applaud till all the certificates were awarded, but Renata clapped for her daughter anyway, only a few times because her palms hurt.

When the procession up the sloping auditorium aisles began, Glenn whispered, 'Did you bring the camera?' Trembling with remorse, Renata shook her head. She hadn't thought of it. It was just as well, she told herself through the waves of guilt. Photographs pretended to capture moments forever, and so, of course, they were fraudulent; they would only make things worse when she lost Vanessa, as, one way or another, she would. Vanessa smiled at her parents when she marched by. Renata intended to smile back, but couldn't be sure that she had.

There was a reception in the cafeteria after the ceremony. Everyone was taking pictures. 'Didn't you bring the camera?' Vanessa wanted to know, and Renata had to make a conscious effort to stop herself from repeating forever, 'I'm sorry I'm sorry I'm sorry.'

'Can I take a picture of the three of you?'

It was Wendy's mother. Renata stared at her, not knowing how to answer.

'Let me take a picture of your family,' she said, and Renata staggered under the weight of the word.

They stood together – the three of them, which was in fact some version of their family – and they put their arms around each other, and the camera flashed, two, three, four times. Renata wondered whether the pictures would be blurred by grief and, reluctantly, admitted they would not. Before the family grouping moved apart, she bent and whispered into her daughter's ear, 'I'm proud of you, Vanessa. I love you very much,' and Vanessa looked up at her with shining eyes.

Chapter 26

She'd awakened hard again, straight out of wrenching dreams that had everything to do with Ian although he was never in them himself. Ian's death. Violent shudders had pinned her to the bed, then driven her from it, and she had been able to eat some breakfast, which was a betrayal of Ian, but she hadn't tasted the food.

Sickened by any taste in her mouth including that of toothpaste, she'd lost track more than once of which teeth the brush had come into contact with and why. She'd had to clutch the edge of the sink and bend double when a memory burned through: Ian in his yellow windbreaker and hated brown corduroys, eyebrows puckered in puzzlement.

Vanessa had been up when she'd left, wan and small wrapped in her blanket on the family room couch. The frenetic chatter of cartoons was almost more than Renata could stand, especially after she'd kissed her daughter goodbye, reminded her to eat breakfast and not to wake up Dad, and retreated out the door, down the side steps, onto the hard sidewalk where the noise followed her like the ominous laughter of a gargoyle, leaning.

When she'd had to run for the bus, she hadn't even come close to falling. She didn't think she'd recognize her stop, or be able to pull the cord, but she did both. In the campus park she had to walk through to get from the bus stop to her building, the daffodils were gone and all but a few red tulips, but the rose bushes were crusted with pink nubs which, though she kept her hands well away from them, she knew were soft, ready to fling themselves open. It was their scent that would be painful; in a few days she'd be forced to walk through their scent.

In her office, she made it through the morning, though barely.

It struck her that that was nothing more than a mental posturing, fundamentally dishonest and self-indulgent, for what would it mean *not* to make it through a morning? The morning would go along toward afternoon whether she participated in it or not; her mere presence in it was participation. The morning would go along whether Ian was dead or not. Ian was dead.

Tension built, the backfill of horror behind her breastbone pressing ferociously outward. Theresa put letters, requisition forms, purchase orders, personnel forms in front of her – a stream of them; Renata had the impression Theresa was checking on her, bringing the papers in a few at a time instead of in a more efficient stack so that she could be sure again and again that Renata was all right, which was a good idea, since she might well not be from one time to the next. Renata signed everything without going through the motions of trying to comprehend any content; there was the vertiginous sensation of being in Theresa's hands, kept by her kindness and efficiency from sliding off the rim of the world.

She met with people, managed to focus enough, especially earlier in the day, to provide more or less what they wanted. She was aware of the brightening and fading of sunlight stripes between the slats of her windowshade, and the fluctuations didn't even come close to killing her.

Finally it was lunch time and though she couldn't eat, she forced herself to go outside. In the park she saw several people she knew, including the man from Physical Plant with whom she'd been playing phone tag for days about the hazards of the construction in front of the new classroom building. They engaged in a gratifyingly efficient little discussion right there and then, shading their eyes from the sun, and came up with a mutually acceptable solution. Renata went on her way pleased to have dispensed with something that had been niggling for longer than necessary, and with a startling sense of herself as more than just a grieving mother, more than just grief. If her colleague had noticed her emotional and physical dishevelment, he'd given no sign.

Across the park, blurred slightly as if from slanted twilight in this bright, vertical noon, she caught sight of someone who looked familiar although she couldn't identify her. The woman seemed out of place, even amid the diverse campus crowd: she wore a long dress made of what Renata guessed might be calico, and her hair, pinned up in a bun, was milky-yellow. She was staring straight at Renata, but when Renata waved – oddly, since she couldn't think where she knew this woman from and she decidedly didn't want to talk to her – she made no return gesture.

Someone hailed Renata, and she paused to exchange brief pleasantries with a professor from the physics department, then crossed the interior campus street between the end of the park and her building. At the sidewalk she turned to look for the strange woman again. There was some dim association in her mind between this person and Ian's death; maybe this was a parent from the support group, although that didn't seem likely. The woman with the pale yellow hair was nowhere to be seen.

In the grassy rectangle between sidewalk and building, a green snake crawled. Thin as the shadow of an overhead telephone wire to which it ran more or less parallel, it wasn't more than a foot long, and the small moving scallops of it might have been wind across grass. Renata peered over the railing to be sure what she was seeing, and a student hurrying with books, coffee, and backpack bumped into her, sloshed the hot liquid on them both, spat a hasty and unapologetic 'Sorry,' and veered around her, obviously not having seen the snake or not considering it worth being late to class.

The snake slithered over the lip of the sidewalk. Against the gray concrete, it was dense green, first its arrow-shaped head end, then the yarn-like length of it, in a split second its tapering tail. It crawled across her shoe, patent-leather green across shineless black cloth, across glinting buckle and the flesh-colored nylon trapezoid formed by the strap. She saw its scales, felt the scaleless caress of its underbelly. Then it looped into the grass again and vanished into the bushes under the classroom windows, opened to let in spring air, through which an introductory accounting lecture droned.

'Renata Burgess.'

Renata looked around. At the foot of the stairs stood a dapper old man in a powder-blue suit, tipping his soft gray hat to her.

'My name is John Brustein. I don't believe we've met.'

She knew who he was, though; everybody knew John Brustein. An architect and city planner, the genius and political savvy behind the creation ten years ago of this campus in the middle of the city, on his recent seventy-fifth birthday designated 'a living landmark.' 'Yes, Mr Brustein,' she said, shy in his auspicious presence and confused that he knew her name.

'John. Please.'

'John.' She nodded.

'I would like to invite you to join me for lunch at the Press Club. Perhaps sometime next week?'

She could not think when next week she would be free for lunch. She had, in fact, intended to spend every lunch hour crying on the floor again. 'Uh, sure,' she faltered. 'Of course. Sometime next week would be fine.'

'Thursday, then? They make a nice ratatouille on Thursdays. One o'clock? I'll call for you at your office.' He adjusted his hat on his thick white hair with the air of having settled something and came a step closer to search out her tremulous gaze. 'I have also lost a son, you see,' and her knees went weak with gratitude as she understood what he was offering. He gave her a courtly little bow and went off briskly in the direction of the new classroom building whose design he had commissioned and whose construction he was overseeing.

Deeply touched by the generosity of this genteel and revered old man, she watched him for a minute or two and thought: *He'll die soon. He's seventy-five years old. Surely he'll die soon.*

And then: *John Brustein's death will be no less premature than Ian's. They both will have, by definition, lived their full lives.*

And then: *It's okay. It's right. The profound sorrow of my nine-year-old son's death floats in an amniotic sac of rightness.*

The clock tower chimed the quarter hour. Already she was late for her one o'clock. But she couldn't bring herself to hurry. She could scarcely bring herself to perform the acts that would convey her into the building at all.

In the lobby she had to pass the waiting student. 'Sorry to keep you waiting.' Glowering even more than usual, he started to rise. 'I'll be right with you,' she told him hastily, and retreated down the corridor into her office, where she shut the door and sat at her desk for longer than she should have, thinking about John Brustein, about the milky-haired woman in the calico dress, and about the strange solace of the snake coiling across the opening in her shoe.

288

The afternoon closed in around her, and at five o'clock she was afraid to go home. Afraid to move out of the cubicle of space and time she occupied behind her desk. Afraid to get onto a vehicle which would move, into a vehicle which would enclose her. Afraid to impose herself on any more ground than she already had, to displace any more air.

She sat for a long time. The other offices around hers emptied. Co-workers waved, and a few, Theresa among them, stopped at her door. Theresa, though, came in. 'Renata, you look awful.' She knew better than to ask whether she was all right.

Renata drew a ragged, painful breath and tried to focus on her friend's kind face. 'I – I think I'm having an anxiety attack. I'm afraid to move.'

Theresa set her purse on the chair by the door. 'Should I call Glenn?'

Still dazed, Renata brought her shaking gaze to the phone on the end of the desk, its cord, the unlit lights for the three lines. 'I can call him.'

She wanted, yearned to talk to her husband, now that she thought of it, but she was afraid to touch the buttons on the key pad. Her fingertips curled inward and burrowed into her sweaty palm. But she was able to straighten out her hand. She picked up the receiver, wincing but holding on.

'I'll stay with you till he gets here.'

Some of the anxiety had faded already, dissipated by Theresa's willingness to face it down. Renata pressed the first digits of her phone number, forcibly swerving her imagination away from the picture of Glenn in the house where Ian had died, and shook her head gratefully to Theresa. 'I'm okay now. I'll be okay.'

Theresa looked skeptical. 'Are you sure? I can stay.'

'It's okay.' She'd apparently dialed all the right digits in the right sequence, although she'd lost track, because Glenn answered. 'Hi, honey.'

'Hi.' He sounded as if he'd been crying. He sounded as if he loved her.

She looked up at Theresa and said, 'Thanks,' and Theresa, with a last worried hesitation, went away. Renata bent herself around the mouthpiece. 'I can't come home.'

'What do you mean?'

'I have no place there.'

'You do. You live here. This is where you belong.'

She was crying now. She couldn't breathe, and she certainly couldn't speak.

'We need you.'

'No,' she said, but she knew it wasn't audible. *Don't need me. Ian needed me.* 'No.'

'You have to come home,' Glenn said, and Renata, thinking he was about to remind her of spousal or maternal obligation, was readying herself to answer – coldly or harshly or hysterically or whatever it took – that she refused all obligations now that Ian was dead. But Glenn said, 'You have to come home. We're having spaghetti for dinner.'

The dazzling preciousness of the everyday whirled in upon her. It returned her breath, steadied her heartbeat, and brought its own tears. 'Oh,' she said in awe. 'Oh.'

But there was something she had to do before she could leave. Something she had to receive. She made arrangements for Glenn to pick her up in an hour, not knowing how much time she would need. Then she turned off her light, shut her door and window blinds, and rested her head on the desk.

Chapter 27

In Morning Sun's dreams was rain, and she awoke rejoicing. But there was no rain. The pre-dawn air was dry and broken as a skeleton rearranged for burial, and, already so early in the season, cold.

On the other side of the canyon – behind the cliff house abandoned now for the second summer but where she could sometimes still glimpse people moving, still hear voices that had always sounded closer than they were – sun was not yet visible above the jagged horizon. The dry purple sky showed no clouds.

From the balcony where she stood, what she'd once thought was the world swept in three long directions. Morning Sun still had difficulty really believing anything existed beyond this mesa and the high plains that abutted it, but she knew that everyone but the inhabitants of this single balcony house had gone somewhere else. South, somewhere, where there was rain and the growing season was as long as it needed to be, and beans and corn would grow.

Here, no rain had fallen since long before Morning Sun was born. A few times there had been rain in the sky, like streaks of holy ochre gray-blue instead of the red for streaking cheeks and foreheads in mourning and for sprinkling over the bodies of those mourned. Her mother, dead now, had been a babe on her board the last time real rain had fallen here, so hadn't remembered it either. Her father had been a child; not knowing at the time that that particular rainfall was the last he'd ever see, he'd taken no special note of it, and so had had to make up things about it later in order to tell her and her brothers and sisters about it, a storyteller though he was not good with tales, a storyteller about this one thing, rain.

For her part, Morning Sun wasn't sure she believed in rain. Like the hump-backed traveling fluteplayer she'd never met, either, the one who was supposed to bring good luck and fertility, rain was a legend, perhaps never intended to be taken as fact, and a fickle stranger.

Shadows skittered like rabbits across the canyon walls, and Morning Sun was angered; there was no sense in running and no place to hide when the enemy was the world itself. Shaggy junipers in the growing light made her think of shed antlers, dried and brittle past any use. Cracks slithered across the hard tan earth like snakes unable to slough dead skin.

As far as she could see, a long and wide view, there were no people in the world anymore. Many had died, and she could at least imagine where they had gone: Bodies bent and arranged to be lightly buried in the long slope below her, where disposal of garbage had loosened the soil enough to dig, spirits returned to the underworld through earthenware vessels opened at the base. Only lately had she realized that the sipapu at the back of a kiva was not really the hole through which spirits passed on their journey to and from the underworld. It was a symbol. Which was to say, a lie. The sight of a sipapu now, along with many other things, enraged Morning Sun.

Death she understood, at least generally. People died. Many people she'd known and many she'd loved had died. Her father would die soon, before the next spring if they stayed here, before they got to the mythical southern place if they moved. He was sick and frail, very old in his thirty-eighth year; she'd have thought him ready to go, but he often told her wistfully that in his father's father's time, when the people all lived on top of the mesa, it hadn't been unusual for men to survive into their fifties.

Morning Sun herself would die. At seventeen she'd almost certainly expended half her life, maybe much more. The baby about to be born, through her as if through a sipapu, would die – before it reached its first birthday like most babies; as a toddler, like her sister's two daughters; as a young woman in childbirth, pulled back through the passageway by her infant who would know better than to be born, or, if this unborn child was a son, he would die a young hunter captured by his prey; or as an elder, in some distant unimaginable future. Sooner or later, in one way or another, everyone would die.

Morning Sun was saddened by death, and sometimes frightened

when there seemed more of it than of life in this world. But it was not unnatural. Those who left the canyon alive were forever lost – some every spring and summer she could remember, more and more until now the dozens of dwellings she could see from here, and dozens more obscured by the morning mists and the twists of the sandstone walls, were all abandoned.

South, they said. Morning Sun turned south now, to her left, and leaned out dangerously over the thigh-high parapet built to keep small children from tumbling off the cliff, although some still did every year. She sighted south along the sweeping wall of the canyon until the canyon turned westward and her gaze kept going south, out over the high wooded plains. Nearly bare rectangles showed where the juniper and pinon and mountain mahogany had been cut and burned to make way for the crops, but – ungrateful, mysteriously unsatisfied – the corn and beans and squash would no longer grow anywhere.

Morning Sun mused grimly that those barren spots wouldn't look ominous from up here unless the observer already knew what they meant; they could be just part of the landscape, endlessly diverse, every part altering the whole. A light bright brown, almost white, where the subsoil had been laid open like skin under skin, the plots glittered almost prettily as the rising sun caught them. Morning Sun narrowed her eyes.

Smoke was already rising from the fire pit to join the dark brown winglike stains on the ceiling from generations of fires. Women were grinding corn for breakfast; the harsh swish of mano on metate made small echoes under the ledge. She ought to be with them, but instead she leaned out over the wall again, recklessly challenging the canyon to take her and her child *now*.

She could see much farther both south and north than she'd ever traveled, and she couldn't imagine a country so far away that it was different from here. Many days south, they said, to the home of the traders who brought cotton and redware pottery. South, to a place where sky and earth had not hardened against the people. South, they said, those who urged exodus, who said they all should have left a year ago or five, who did leave, without the family but diminishing the family with their going, and were never heard from again. Those who argued against this radical, not to say heretical, idea insisted that the people had lived *here*, in *this* place, since they'd emerged from the underworld, and would vanish as a people if they tried to transplant themselves elsewhere.

It was clear to Morning Sun that they were vanishing as a people anyway, even here in this ancestral place which, of all places, should have been safe. Her baby would be like a tiny gray puff of smoke squirted into a great gray cloud.

She rubbed her arms. The baby inside her shivered, cold as she was. Sighing, she went to take her place among the women who – however pointlessly, however ineffectively – were doing what they knew to do to prepare the village for another day.

As she settled down to her bowl and griddle, her unwilling glance caught the flash of brilliant red where, so fleeting that she almost missed it and desperately wished she had, the sun shone through the tail feathers of a sailing hawk. Pierced by the unfair beauty of it, she resolutely turned to face the blackened rock wall at the back of the alcove, protecting her unborn baby from the sight. The sun had risen now, but without a prayer from her. She would not salute the enemy.

For whatever reason – and Morning Sun was bitterly convinced that it was merely force of lifelong habit over too many generations to count – a day begun without a few moments of prayer in the kiva seemed not truly to have begun, seemed like still part of its preceding night. So this day, feeling bested already by some force she didn't bother to contest, when the corn was done she lowered herself carefully into the kiva farthest away from the parts of the cliff house still inhabited.

The ladder shifted and bowed under her weight and she had a fantasy about losing her balance, but in fact the weight of the baby was insignificant and always would be. At summer noon, being underground soothed, but now, with fall coming on too fast and the corn reaching not even to a man's knee, not even tasseled, it was unpleasantly cold down here.

When she sat down on the narrow stone bench against the curved wall, one of the hooks for fastening the straps of the loom pressed into her shoulderblade, and irritably she shifted position. Although somebody up on the plaza had closed the roof of the kiva, an edge of sunlight shot through, annoying in its irregularity, in the fact of sunlight itself. She was annoyed by the muffled sounds of footsteps and voices overhead as people went about their morning tasks. The bench was too narrow. There was too much dust and ash in the air. The ladder leaning against the wall was supported on only one leg. Though it wouldn't hurt anything if it toppled, she was seized with an urge powerful as an itch to get up and straighten it, but she didn't want to move.

She sat for a while with her feet up under her. Then she lowered one foot to the floor. All positions were equally uncomfortable. Finally she lay down on the bench, which was, of course, far too narrow for both her and the baby. After only a few minutes, she sat up again, then got to her feet, and saw a woman in the kiva with her.

She was taken aback. She hadn't heard anyone come down. She hadn't seen the light change as the roof was opened and then closed again. She hadn't felt the presence of another human being – in fact, she realized, she still had the distinct impression of being alone in the kiva. There was only the visual image, and that was translucent, no less substantial for allowing shapes and colors to be seen through it, but oddly half-dimensional.

The other woman saw her. If she thought there was anything strange about being in somebody else's kiva, she didn't show it. Her entire face, her entire body, her entire physical and spiritual aspect were like the wheel of life that was carved into rock, woven into baskets, formed in the shapes of clouds. Four-limbed with a hole in the middle, the figure created an emblem of things going on and on. This woman was like that, suggesting frantic motion that would never stop. Arms and legs cocked, giving the impression of spinning almost out of control. A mouth at the center of the figure, howling, a black spinning hole like a sipapu.

Morning Sun had seen that expression in the face of many a parent, lover, child, elder when someone was dead, another of the People. They kept looking that way, even though so many died and so many were on the verge all the time. Who would look like this when all the People were gone?

The revolving aspect of profound grief hadn't stopped, had, if anything, intensified, as if to spin out one individual sorrow among communal grief, worldwide grief, grief through the ages. The wheel of life, which was the strange woman who was the wheel of death, rolled rapidly on its edge past the place where Morning Sun sat, past the fire pit still warm and sending up motes of ash from the men's three-day vigil, and down the small incline to the dimple in the hard floor that was the sipapu. The spinning wheel-woman stretched herself out, first into her four pronged limbs joined at the center by the wailing mouth, then into a single long tube, and disappeared into the sipapu like a snake into its hole. Morning Sun hardly even paused to watch, hardly took time to be surprised, before she had followed.

Morning Sun doubted that distances through space or time were measured in the underworld the same way they were measured up above. The last time she'd been here, before her birth, she hadn't noticed time or space in any way she could remember. But it didn't seem that she followed the woman far. She heard a chittering as if of insects in dry branches. She flinched away from strafing and suckering along her arms and legs. She caught a glimpse of what appeared to be a severed head, an amputated hand. Then she was back in the kiva, and the phantom woman gone.

Morning Sun stood up. The hubbub of the village overhead was clearly audible again. Her baby was not moving; she realized that she hadn't seen her baby in the underworld, and wondered sadly where it was. She positioned the ladder and climbed out of the kiva.

'Good morning, Morning Sun,' several women said, and she replied cursorily. 'Did you learn anything in the kiva?'

'Nothing useful.' Wishing bitterly that her name were something else – though she couldn't think of any name that wouldn't make her bitter in the midst of hostile and alien nature – she set herself fiercely to stirring the batter in the bowl, which was thinner than it ought to be because the corn meal must be made to last longer and longer. Children chattered like squirrels. Babies shrieked, and echoes from the close rock faces could deceive the unwary hearer into the illusion of more babies than there were, more hope than there was.

She was a bead on a thong. Ahead of her, the thong had broken, or had never been properly knotted. Behind her, though, it was endless, and sometimes a motion she made with her hand, a pattern of light and shadow across the cliff, the way wind dropped and rose could pull her back generations.

This morning her mind flashed vividly, in and out of ancestors' lives, before they had traded with anyone else, before they had even known that anyone else lived anywhere else and would have things to trade. With the exception of cotton, which by now had become as much a natural part of life as yucca fibers, she didn't see that much would be lost if they disconnected themselves again. Isolated, life would be a great deal simpler and the People a great deal safer.

While she was eating, or pretending to eat, Raven came to squat beside her, spooning the watery mush into his mouth without comment and gnawing on a jackrabbit bone. Morning Sun hoped this was the last of the jackrabbit, though that was a risky wish when it was unclear when the next meat might be snared; this one had been stringy and tough in the first place, and there was hardly anything edible left. She was tired of being hungry. The baby must be hungry, too. Like the land on which the corn couldn't grow, she had not much from inside herself to give for the life of anything else. Raven said, 'We'll finish the turret on the east wall today. It's beautiful.'

Morning Sun flung her own rabbit bone over the wall. A few scraps of fat and sinew still clung to it, making her gesture wasteful but not nearly shocking enough to suit her. She shouted at him, 'How do you know? How do you know when it's finished? How do you know if it's beautiful? Why is it worth risking your life to build a Great Temple that the gods probably won't even notice, if there are any gods? How can you be so sure of anything, Raven?'

She could have shouted many more things at him, and she started to. But it would have been just more of the same, and she stopped herself, resentfully.

Around them, people took notice. Morning Sun tried not to care. Some people glared. Some made a show of moving to the other side of the plaza. Some grinned and waited with obvious glee for what would happen next.

Raven regarded her calmly and answered. 'I'm not sure. But I think I'm risking my life, and yours, and our baby's, and everybody else's, if I *don't* help to build the Great Temple. I believe it's what the gods require. I believe it's our last chance.'

Morning Sun had, of course, heard all this before, from him and from the other men who'd been laboring for years on the Temple, which was being constructed on the highest, sheerest cliff face in the canyon, as though difficulty and sacrifice made it more holy. She spat in derision but said no more, gathered her bags and sticks and left the house.

After wandering half the day, she bitterly considered dumping the few pitiful little lumps she'd collected out onto the ground, where, after a day or two, nobody would even know they'd been disturbed and they might make a light meal for a squirrel. But prudence kept her from it. Six or seven pine nuts and a handful of shriveled berries and a branched root with a little fibrous moisture still left in it were better than nothing, though she wondered at the expenditure of energy required to find these few things compared to the amount of energy they would give. Her bags hung limp at her waist, and her basket hardly registered the weight of the food.

When the sun was high and hot, she found parsimonious shade under an oak and sat down to rest. She was more exhausted than she'd ever been in her life. Every day she said that, 'I've never been this tired,' and then the next day found herself a little more exhausted, a little weaker. She had stopped thinking anything like, 'A human being couldn't be any more tired than this and still survive,' which seemed true but every day was not.

The underbrush, most of it dry and brown, buzzed with insects that she kept seeing one or two at a time, but never in the numbers that would account for this much noise. She could eat them if she could catch them, but she doubted she could move that fast anymore. The baby inside her hadn't moved. Suddenly, cold racing through her like flame, she couldn't remember the last time the baby had moved.

Hearing a song that was neither birdsong nor human singing, she roused herself slightly. It was chilly in this shade, noticeably warmer but no more welcoming when she moved out into the sunshine. For a while she walked bent over like a branch about to break but still pitiably clinging to its trunk, dimly hoping that in that position she would be able to feel the baby. She could not.

She did, though, spy a cache of sweet pulpy bark stripped and stowed inside the hollow of its tree. She meant to take it all home in her bag, but much of it she ate, unable to stop herself until only a mound the size of her fist remained. That she stowed in her bag, where it bulged only very slightly. Her stomach was less empty than it had been for days, although the hunger pangs persisted. She would not have seen the bark if she'd been walking upright. Perhaps this was a gift from the baby, or from the gods. Or from the gorgeous, poisonous creature from which the world had been suspended.

She pushed her way through a long thicket, across a sandy open space. Off to one side, a woman was standing.

This woman was not from here. She wore clothing Morning Sun had never seen before, and her hair was fashioned strangely. Her face had few lines, and her body, her hands and fingers, were straight and unswollen. But Morning Sun, stopping, looking closer, did not think she was young; the face, the hands raised to it, the writhing body bore signs of age, and Morning Sun concluded, with an unpleasant little shock, that this woman must be more than thirty years old.

The old woman did not seem to be aware of Morning Sun. She was saying something that sounded like, 'Ee-an! Ee-an!' which could have been any of a number of common words, none of which made sense coming from this person at this time and place.

Maybe this woman of such peculiar age and dress and demeanor was from the south, where it rained.

There were plenty of enemies in these canyons – poisonous snakes, the occasional wild cat, lightning, avalanches. Drought. Not human enemies, though, until the argument between that faction which wanted to stay and that which wanted to migrate south had grown so vicious: enemies now within the family.

If this stranger was an enemy, bent on doing harm, Morning Sun didn't quite know how to respond. She flailed around in the powdery underbrush for something she could use to protect herself and her child, something that would drive the woman back to wherever she had come from. Whoever she was, she did not belong here.

But Morning Sun did not belong here, either. Her baby, certainly, did not, unborn, perhaps forever unborn, but inside her so not really belonging in the underworld, either. Apparently none of them belonged here now; though it was such an alien thought that there scarcely were words or images for thinking it, this place did not seem to be the People's home any longer. So the woman was no more a stranger than Morning Sun herself. She had no real sense of being in the presence of an enemy. She had no sense of this woman, really, as even a stranger; she had seen her before, been in her presence somewhere before. Morning Sun tried to bring her into focus, now and in memory. Then the woman disappeared. An after-image hovered in the still air. Then it was gone, too, leaving only dust.

Morning Sun moved on. She did not know why. She could have stood there, staring at the place the woman had been. She could have tried somehow to follow her, or to hear a lingering cry. Instead, mysteriously and much against her will, she was inspired to move again, to make an effort again, and especially to care about her baby again.

The baby was not moving. Morning Sun was sure it was dead, but she didn't know whether her certainty was born of actual knowledge or of the kind of magic that led some of the People to draw pictures on the rocks – not propitiating pictures of rain and of corn growing tall, but visions, maybe, to give substance to the worst fears: straight-line barren landscapes with nothing growing and no People. The hump-backed fluteplayer without his flute.

Morning Sun made her way through the woods, talking to her baby who, even if dead, needed her. Singing. Teaching it things: how to make a path through the shattering woods. How to distinguish plants that would nourish from those that would neither harm nor nourish from those that would sicken or kill. How to live in the face of death.

Thoughts of Raven came into her mind as she pushed aside a curtain of brush so dry it crumpled before her hand. Thoughts of Raven often came into her mind. She was fonder of him than of others, liked the way dust etched his sweat-glistened skin, the rough and slick way his feet felt when she wiped him down.

Morning Sun stopped suddenly and made a mark with the edge of a white stone into a soft red sandstone outcropping of which there were many along this and other paths. She gouged deep, not because it occurred to her to try to make her mark last, but out of some hard fury that came out through her fist through the stone. She chiseled and pounded, knuckles bloody and breath coming short, light through the not-dense-enough woods flattening and the sounds of the woods changing as afternoon lengthened into another evening. When she left that spot she left on the sandstone an etched figure of a lizard with the world in its maw.

As she straightened, her glance caught the pale yellow glimmer of bearded grass. She accepted the bounty – not gratefully, exactly, but she was willing to pick it up, lay it in the basket, note its texture, and carry it home.

The baby had not moved.

She ate a root thick as her tongue, and made a face at its tastelessness. It was pithy, without much fiber or grain, and she doubted it would give much to either her or the still baby.

A decision came to her, an impulse born out of anger but given shape by some other emotion, some other need. She would go to the Great Temple. She would see for herself what this place of worship was, this place of sacrifice and beauty, and decide whether it would please the gods. If she, herself, determined that it would, then she would stay here. If she, herself, determined that it would not, then she would leave. Tomorrow. Tomorrow, she and this baby, live or dead, would go south.

Morning Sun knew exactly where the Great Temple was, even though she'd never been there. The whole village knew where it was, although only the handful of men building it – among the handful of men left to the village – were supposed to have been there, on pain of what? Abandonment by the gods? Cataclysm? Death? It was hard to be frightened anymore by any cosmological threat, and none that specific had issued out of the kivas, only vague warnings about the need for secrecy until the right moment. Most adults, like Morning Sun herself, had cared little about the Great Temple. A few children had spied, but they weren't even reprimanded, and no one took much interest in their tales.

One or more of the gods was adjudged to have been offended in some way known or unknown to the People, to have, in fact, taken enormous offense, and the Great Temple was the latest attempt at propitiation. Morning Sun was more than a little bored. There had been other buildings. There had been other kivas. There had been dances and songs, wonderful baskets, perfect white pots with perfect black designs, and paintings so high on such sheer cliff walls that it seemed the gods must have painted them for the People rather than the People for the gods. As well they should. It was, in her mind, the People who needed to be propitiated, the People who had been grievously wronged.

As she approached the Great Temple, the construction noise was familiar; she'd heard it all her life, mixed with other everyday sounds, and most of the time hardly noticed it.

Without warning, she was weeping. Frightened by the noise of it, she buried her face in her arms in the dusty ground cover, but not before two or three great sobs had burst out of her and into the hot arid air. They echoed; she heard the echo of her sorrow from the opposite canyon wall, then again, diminished, from the curved walls of the Temple, and it seemed to her such a natural sound that she rolled over onto her back, bared her face to the blank heavens, and cried aloud. While she wept, clouds passed over the sun, without bringing rain, and the sun dropped behind the high ridge.

A bullsnake parted the grass in front of her, and for some reason she let it go, didn't catch it with her forked stick and wind it into her bag. It was not from sympathy for the creature or reverence for its life over any other life that she allowed it to live, but more out of an indolence, a lethargy born, she knew, out of despair, heavy as bread but not at all nourishing. She watched the snake go.

To get to the overlook which provided the clearest view of the Temple construction, she had to climb up and around a ridge. It wasn't a very long climb, not more than the length of a dozen tall men head-to-foot, and the path didn't go straight up its face. But she was tired and weakened from insufficient food, and she was carrying a child. All these she gave to herself as reasons for her short-windedness and trembling muscles after only three or four steps, but the real reason was a dangerous lassitude, for she had to fight as hard against the urge simply to let go and fall backward off the cliff as against the cliff itself. She would be just one more dead person, with her baby two. There would be some time of fear and pain, but no more than now, the exchange of acute fear and pain for chronic anxiety and illness and discomfort. Then it would be over.

Her foot cramped, and she couldn't stop to massage it. Her fingers were scraped, there was virtually no pain but a line of blood oozed out across the first knuckles where they tried to find purchase in the shallow handholds. Her mind flashed on the spinning wailing woman, she missed a handhold, grabbed the root of a scrub oak which held, and went into labor.

The baby was born quickly, with little pain or effort, and dead.

She lay on her back in the dry afternoon and held the child. Its skin against her breast was neither hot nor cold; it would be cold soon but for now it was the temperature of her own body, and they both smelled spoiled, like old meat. It was hardly separate from her, though the cord had broken with no help from her.

The baby was not fully formed. It had been born too early, though Morning Sun didn't believe it would have been any more complete if it had stayed inside her for the right amount of time. It was a girl, which seemed a cruel thing to notice one way or the other, like the fact that she had all her fingers and toes. Something was wrong with her head. For one thing, the fuzz of hair on the crown was milky white. Morning Sun stroked it with just the tips of her fingers. Something was wrong with the baby's chest.

Sorrow kept her on the ground longer than was wise, holding her dead baby to her, sorrow and overwhelming fatigue, and hot dry despair. The extent of her sorrow surprised her. She'd known this baby was dead long before it had been born dead. Long before that, she'd known that it was going to die. More babies died than lived these days. There'd been no reason to suppose hers would be any different. Still, she wept, and lay in the sun holding the baby, who was getting cold. When she told Raven, he wouldn't even be surprised.

The noise from the construction of the Great Temple hadn't changed much during the time it had taken her to have her dead baby. Sometimes it sounded closer than she knew it to be, sometimes impossibly far away. No single man's voice separated from the others'.

Stretching the baby along one forearm and feeling its small warmth leave both their bodies, Morning Sun sat up. She lowered her head and waited for the dizziness to pass. There was very little pain between her legs or inside her anywhere, and that seemed wrong; there ought to be pain. There was, however, a great deal of blood, and nothing to clean herself with.

The baby, cold now, was coated with blood, which had caked and darkened like a shell. Morning Sun wiped at herself with handfuls of pine needles so dry they crumbled on contact with her skin, but didn't even try to clean her daughter.

She didn't bury her, either; the ground was too hard. There was no time to set out the body and wait for the turkey vultures to take the flesh so she could properly arrange the bones, and she had, of course, brought no red ochre with her, no beads.

She had no energy to spare, and it didn't matter anyway. This little body had never been of much use, and it was of no use now. And she was not sure the child had had a soul.

Morning Sun laid her daughter's body on the open dry ground, deliberately seeking no shelter from the high sun. She gazed down at the little face. Something was wrong with it.

It was too easy, she reflected. Birth and death were too easy, and the span of life between them, however long or brief, too hard.

There was, though, something she could do. She had no pottery vessel, but she had the skin pouch in which she'd have stored gathered food if there had been any to store. With the point of the knife from her belt she punctured the bottom seam of the pouch, then turned the blade into the skin to slit it open. She'd allowed the blade to dull and the skin to stiffen, so the task took more time and considerably more energy than she'd anticipated, and several times she thought to give it up as both pointless and too difficult. But for no good reason she persisted, and finally, sweating and shaking, managed to open the bottom of the bag all the way across. It was a narrow opening. Maybe it would be wide enough to allow the baby's soul to escape. If the baby had a soul. If anybody did.

As she walked away, she was still bleeding. The juniper bark she'd folded to staunch the blood kept slipping when she walked, and she hadn't brought a thong to tie it in place. Finally she just let it drop. Some hungry creature would find it. The blood trickled and clotted down her legs unimpeded. Cleaning dried blood from her skin when she got home would require more water than probably would be available, and she thought briefly of the trail of blood she was leaving through the crackling woods.

Her foot came down beside the corpse of a squirrel. Busy activity teemed inside the carcass. So the impression she carried for her next few steps, before it faded and she forgot the squirrel altogether, was not of death but of life, and she didn't like it.

Pain made itself known in the lower parts of her torso, but not much and it passed. Clouds were gathering along the slash of sky between the canyon walls. When she was a little girl she'd known, for a very short time, an ancient woman whom clouds had

304

always excited when their bases were heavy and dark gray like these. Reverently, she had talked of slow, steady rain showers that soaked the ground and made brown green for a little while. She'd talked about thunderstorms. Morning Sun knew what thunder and lightning were, but in her experience they were always dry. The old woman had insisted that rain could come from clouds.

Morning Sun rounded a stand of serviceberry shrubs, looking in passing for edible fruits and finding none, and was at the overlook above the Great Temple. The workers would be able to see her as clearly as she saw them if they glanced this way, and she tried to crouch, but her thigh and pelvic muscles wouldn't allow her to spread her legs that way and so she just sat, hugged her knees, and watched.

The canyon wall bent here, one sheer face of it set against another sheer face like the corner of a constructed house, a pit house sunk in the world. Slightly below and facing her, the Temple wasn't very big. She was shocked, then mocked herself: Why had she thought the gods would want something enormous? Who in this world had any idea what the gods wanted? Perhaps now her baby knew.

She was sorry to discover that the flow of blood from the place the baby had pushed through had slowed to a dribble. It would have been good to bleed to death here, out in the open like her doomed child, looking down on the Great Temple, which was not very big and not very elaborate and could not possibly convince the gods to right the world soon enough to make any difference.

The Temple was composed of four interlocking semi-circular kivas. There were turrets, as Raven had described, and she was sure they were placed in some sort of exact pattern in relation to the sun or the lay of the land or the envisioned shape of perfect life, but she didn't try very hard to make out the design. Wide notches had been fashioned in the curved walls, which of course would not have been feasible if these had been underground like ordinary kivas, and Morning Sun wondered angrily what the notches were supposed to be. Regarded as a whole, the Temple was an attenuated circle, the north side straight. Doubtless that also meant something arcane.

She could not imagine why this structure was taking so long to complete. It was true that the masonry looked highly skilled, the stones rounded to fit precisely together, outer surfaces dimpled for, she supposed, aesthetic interest, unless there was some function she didn't know about for those little depressions. The design features built into the structure – shape and color and texture of rock against rock – were subtle and complex.

But many a cliff house was larger and more complicated than this, and Morning Sun didn't think any of them had required three generations to construct.

She must have slept, for she awoke. Disoriented, she struggled to gather her thoughts, which were scattered wide and thinly and of which only a few were usable.

She was hungry. Her body hurt, especially in her lower belly and between her legs. She was bleeding; there was a little shock when she saw the blood.

When she sat up she was dizzy and nauseated. Hungry. Chilled. Her child was dead. Distantly, she did not want to die. She lay back down on the open ground, which retained a small amount of heat from the day.

She swooned back toward sleep. But it was not sleep that claimed her. She left her body and entered into a vision.

She stood in soft gray rain among a crowd of weeping women. They were all, she understood, mothers who had lost children. Among them were women she knew, for almost every mother she knew had lost at least one child. Among them, too, were strangers to this time and place: the wheel-woman she'd met in the kiva, still turning around a center hole of sorrow; the woman she'd glimpsed in the woods, still calling, 'Ee-an!' which Morning Sun now understood to be her dead child's name. One with hair the color of milk. One stout, the knuckles on her right hand badly scraped.

Stricken, all of them. Some emitting sounds of mourning, wailing and keening and screaming and hoarsely chanting their children's names; some terribly silent. Milling in the steady gray rain, outlines blurred by moisture. Holding hands in a long misty line which stretched far on both ends, toward what Morning Sun understood to be the distant past on one end and the distant future on the other; she could see neither end, and the line was infinite. She took her place in the infinite line and clasped the hands of those on either side of her; their fingers, palms, wrists were dewy and solid, and she held on.

306

Light like a bone needle pierced her. The morning sun aligned and concentrated through the openings that had been fashioned for just this purpose in the walls of the Great Temple. Embraced from all sides, watching the sun slip out of the long labor tunnel of sipapus, Morning Sun lost and gained consciousness.

Chapter 28

Belinda swam out from under the raft, leaving Renata and the crew of her maimed doubles to propel it by themselves. For a while it was an adventure, gratifying, even exhilarating. They plowed steadily across the water, cutting through the palpable surface tension and creating a lugubrious wake behind them.

Renata was able to forget that she had no idea where they were going or why. There was a certain giddy pleasure in being able simply to move, to exert directed force that caused a more or less predictable reaction.

She'd grown fond of her traveling companions. She could tell them apart now, and by more than just their deformities.

The one whose hand Renata had herself tossed into the ocean rowed more expertly than any of the others. Subtly or dramatically, she could alter the course of the raft to avoid floating debris and rough water. The stump of her left hand played the oar, not as though it had fingers but in its own way, palming.

The bald one, whose scalp was bloody and pocked where the hair had been torn out by the roots, then scabbed like freckles, then scarred in a glistening pattern that in certain angles of the strange light was beautiful, also had a beautiful voice. Sometimes her songs were laments, heartbreaking and ageless. Sometimes they were chants which the others, including Renata, took up to establish a rhythm for their rowing. Sometimes they were love songs.

The one with the amputated thigh, whose hip connected directly to her knee giving her a lopsided stance, was a storyteller. Her stories were lopsided, too, middles tending to be more fully developed than either beginnings or ends. Frequently the tales themselves didn't make sense, though the telling did.

The one without a mouth, whose mouth Renata had tossed away as though it had been hers to do with as she pleased, couldn't get enough hugging and kissing. Time and again she would climb into Renata's lap, making it impossible to row. She demanded kisses, which Renata was loathe to bestow because there was no mouth. The same height and weight as Renata, she pinned her where she sat. Renata chafed and fidgeted and protested, but when the other one moved, huddled in another spot on the crowded raft looking hurt, Renata herself felt cold.

So the entourage traveled. For a long time there was no wind, and they struggled for every bit of progress. Progress was hard to measure because they could detect no shore, no end or edge to the spreading sea or river. They were exhausted. They were hungry and thirsty. They were cold at night and hot during the day; though the sun never shone directly, the brassy cloud cover heated up and the water steamed. The stench became multi-dimensional; they could see, taste, feel it as well as smell it. But one could become accustomed to anything.

Then a breeze stirred. At first it moved only the air; the rafters felt it across the backs of their necks. Rapidly, though, the wind picked up, both the clouds and the water began to move, and now there was no more need for the passengers to propel their craft. It lumbered through the sticky waves, its speed increasing, and before long was fairly shooting across the water. The travelers, who at first had been so relieved to give up their strenuous efforts, now clung to whatever protrusions they could find or create on the raft and to each other, struggling not to be thrown overboard.

Wind pushing her, wind in her hair and harsh light in her eyes, one of many grievously injured selves, Renata said to herself experimentally: *Ian is dead*. The thought brought with it a terrible, wild exhilaration, far more disturbing than the anguish she'd come to expect. *Ian is dead*, she told herself again. Wind gusted. She gave herself over to it.

The sky darkened. There was no storm, but there was also very little light. The strong steady wind seemed to have thickened the slimy cloud layer. Before long, the raft was catapulting through almost total darkness, and Renata was afraid. Frightened, too, the

310

others closed in against her from all sides until they might all, herself included, have been one creature.

Then, with a lurch and a drawn-out thud, the raft ran aground. In the darkness Renata could just see an even darker darkness that suggested land.

The raft broke apart, and its passengers were flung onto a gritty beach where they lay, jumbled together or so separated that they couldn't find each other and were as if alone. Some were injured. Some had been killed. Renata had struck her head on something hard and sharp; she lay stunned and, gradually, aching.

Eventually the sounds of the wreck subsided. Shrieking faded. Even the moaning had dwindled to an occasional whimper and sigh. The wind, having succeeded in bringing them to this place, stopped now. Dawn began to lighten the sky until it and the water were a yellow-gray.

They were on an island. While the solid ground of it remained densely shadowed, the ocean surrounding it continued to lighten with the sky until both had achieved a venomous brindle-yellow. Halfheartedly trying to make some sense out of her circumstances, Renata was confusedly noticing tangled trees and brush, boulders and pebbles, sand, waves like the dirtied yolks of eggs, when the attack came.

Rats. Easily three feet long and forty pounds or more in weight, with long hairless tails and lean bodies covered with rough fur, hordes of rats bounded across the beach and set upon Renata's companions. Bones crunched like glass. Flesh ripped with a moist slurping sound. Cries were cut off by the noisy spurting of blood. Squealing, claws clicking on rock and trenching wet sand, tails looped like thin banners in the air or slithering along the surface of the water, the rats swarmed over Renata's friends and devoured them.

Sorrow over the terrible loss of these poor other selves was, to her surprise, overtaken almost immediately by terror for her own life. *Not here*, she thought frantically; *not like this*. She burrowed into the sand as far as she could and curled into a tight ball, knowing how exposed she still was and, finally, giving up and waiting for the huge rodents to find her.

Only one came. A gigantic red-eyed beast, it straddled her. Thick saliva dripped from its gaping mouth onto her face. She winced and gagged.

The enormous head descended abruptly. Fangs pierced the soft spot at the base of her throat and embedded themselves in the flesh; she could feel poison pumping into her. The animal buried its long snout in the hollow of her shoulder like a lover or a beloved child.

Pain coursed through her, but was followed almost at once by an intense spreading sensation of peace and wellbeing. She understood that it was artificial, induced, only for a fraction of a second before pleasure overcame her and quite willingly, even eagerly, she relaxed under the rat's spell.

After a long time the rodent stirred. Renata didn't want it to leave and she tried to get her arms around its furry haunches to hold it to her, but it extracted its fangs, now bloody, from her neck and bounded away. Renata knew she had been poisoned, and the pain was sweet.

She was adrift on a sea of forgetfulness, the only one of all her companion selves still alive and in any sense whole. Dreaming began. As the poison coursed through her veins, arteries, capillaries, arterioles, she plunged inside herself and rode on its sweet, savage current. Torpedo-shaped, sleek and pointed and flanged, she dived into her own circulatory system, entering through the break in her heart.

Though her heart had been torn open, it continued to pump, a stubborn muscle. The bloody sides of her wound glistened like wet canyon walls, rose around her, swallowed her up, and the relentless pulsing of her bloodstream took her downward and inward, past her own center toward the molten core.

Thick tunnels, thick-walled, branched off from the pounding heart. Every heartbeat pulled her closer to the pain, *My child is dead*, made her gasp and gulp her own poisoned blood and cry out, then pushed her farther out along the branching and branching system, into uncharted though not undiscovered territory, downward, both forward and backward, through finer and finer vessels. Their walls, pressing in on her, bowed out around her. The force of the flowing blood, the force of the poison, swept her along.

Beside and outside her, the huge rat hunkered. Sentinel, monitor, guide, it kept its feral red gaze on her, ready with another injection should she show signs of regaining her ordinary senses.

As she traveled through channels of diminishing diameter and thinning walls, she herself became smaller. The span of her arms shortened. Her body length and girth shrank, so that everything around her was thrown into exaggerated relief. Her skull contracted around her brain, the bones eventually spreading open at the top.

And she was simplified. Interpretations fell aside, layer after layer, because she had less and less experience, then no experience from which to interpret. Names of things, their histories and uses and meanings beyond use, were peeled away, leaving a sense of loss burning and hollowed out but with no identity anymore, no comprehension of who was gone, just: *gone*.

She didn't know what lay beyond the tips of her fingers and toes, or that anything did. She understood only dimly, and then not at all, any boundary between *me* and *not-me*, between *me, with something gone* and *not me, not me*.

There was hurt. She didn't know why, didn't know that it hadn't always hurt her and wouldn't always.

The rat lowered its massive head. She felt a surge of intense comfort, and stopped crying.

Deeper she swam, no telling whether backward or forward, downward or upward. Her perception branched and she followed it, into a consciousness both buoyed and limited by the pouch of viscous fluid in which it was now suspended.

Thick watery impressions presented themselves: warmth; the dangers of heat and of cold; food free-flowing, undemanded, scarcely noticed; cushion against blows, against even the possibility of blows or of jostling which hurt, might hurt; darkness, threat of light, threat and promise of light; breath through gills, threat and promise of lungs. Intimations of birth: being sent away, emerging. Intimations of death. Preverbal fear, primal sorrow.

The fluid in which she floated suddenly glowed. False comfort passed through membranous barriers, and she forgot what she had known.

Burrowing beneath human awareness, sloughing it off. Smelling. Detecting heat. Gathering information on long forked tongue, curling, depositing into roof of mouth. Knew how to eat, mate, migrate, die. Knowledge filled entire perception; did not know knowledge, no shadow or reflection of knowledge, no space around it. Sorrow passed like the need for sleep. Fear subsided, vanished. But still, memory.

Poison was injected and seeped in, sweet and fatal. Instinct obscured. Organism in mortal danger, but did not know. Forgetfulness filled entire perception. Forgot.

Was taken farther down.

Grow toward light. Find water. Surface open to nutrients. Surface open to oxygen. Surface open to carbon dioxide. Air exchange; no loss. Roots, root tendrils. Stem. Leaves. Flowers, fruit, pollen, seeds. Sweet poison: Brighter flowers, bigger fruit, shallower roots.

Done. Death. No loss.

And farther.

Single

cell.

One.

Nucleus.

Splits.

Two

single

cells.

No

connection.

No

differentiation

Chapter 29

'Renata Burgess.' John Brustein said her name as if it meant something. 'Tell me about yourself.'

Renata was shocked. He'd invited her here because he already knew everything there was to know about her: her son had died. 'I – I'm a bereaved parent,' she managed.

He inclined his head and sat back in his chair, which did not alter either his erect posture or his firm, direct gaze. He was a slight man, dark-eyed, white-haired and -moustached; they'd walked here from campus, and she'd noticed that, although he was not much taller than she and probably weighed less, he was far more solid and surer on his feet. She wondered whether that had always been true, whether, if she'd had lunch with him before Ian's death, she'd have felt the same potential from him of guidance and protection. But she hadn't known him before Ian's death. If Ian hadn't died, she would most likely never have had lunch with him at all. She passed an unsteady hand over her eyes.

The Press Club, like John Brustein, exuded dignity and solidity. The square tables and square chairs were of heavy blond oak. The background music was classical, uninterrupted by commentary. Half a dozen other tables were occupied, most by pairs or small groups of men of John's generation; although at a back table was one other woman, elderly, elegant, white-gloved. As they'd entered, John had introduced Renata to the steel-haired man sitting alone across the room: the poet laureate of the state. Each occupied table was surrounded by empty ones, as though the Press Club had no need or taste for crowding.

The waiter was a man perhaps twenty years younger than John, which made him still a generation older than Renata. He and John

315

spoke to each other by name, and she was duly introduced. John ordered for her. The waiter brought wine, which she didn't dare drink in the middle of the day, especially not in her present mental state, but she was, dimly, glad for the red wine in clear goblets against white cloth.

John asked, 'How old was your boy?'

'Nine.'

'How did he die?'

'He hanged himself.'

John had no greater or lesser reaction to that detail than to any of the rest of it, and so, in his company, neither did she. 'And how long ago did he die?'

'March 18.'

'Of this year.'

'Yes.'

'Not quite three months.' He nodded, then patted her hand, a gesture of surprising intimacy. 'Ah, my dear, you are at the very beginning, aren't you?'

'How long has it been for you?' She took as deep a breath as she could and forced herself to ask, because it seemed important to enunciate all the words although she couldn't have said why, 'Since your son died?'

'Thirty-one years this fall.'

She whispered, 'My God.' He withdrew his hand to reach into the inside pocket of his suit coat for a monogrammed linen handkerchief, and she realized his eyes had filled with tears. 'I'm so sorry,' she breathed.

'Stephen was nineteen years old, a freshman at Yale. On a Friday evening in November, his mother and I received a telephone call from the campus infirmary informing us that our son had been taken suddenly and seriously ill and that we must come immediately. We were on the first flight out the next morning, but he had died in the night. Spinal meningitis.'

She had covered her mouth with her hands. Now he reached across the elegantly appointed table and took them in both of his. He was weeping freely, this genteel and accomplished old man, here in this public place where he was well-known, thirty-one years after the loss of his child. She was stunningly grateful.

316

'Stephen's death hasn't destroyed your life, has it?'

'No. My life since then has been rich and rewarding in ways I never would have dreamed.'

'I live in terror that my life will, after all, turn out to have been ruined. I keep thinking of words like "barren." I can't find myself anymore.'

He tightened his grip on her hands and gave them a little shake before releasing them as blue bowls with thick yellow chowder were set in front of them. He dabbed at his eyes, discreetly blew his nose, replaced the handkerchief in his inside pocket, straightened and smoothed his jacket, and set about the business of eating, an activity he clearly enjoyed.

Renata took a spoonful, swallowed. Obviously the chowder was good; she could tell there were interesting spices in delicate balance, and the vegetables were just slightly crisp. She could barely taste it, though, and wouldn't be able to get much of it down; her stomach was closing like a fist. She took a sip of water, held it in her mouth for a second or two to keep from spitting it up.

John motioned and someone came to refill her water glass. 'I feel so alone,' she said.

'Ah, my dear, you are alone.'

'I have friends,' she protested weakly. 'My husband and children are there for me. I have a good support system—'

He set his empty bowl aside as the salads arrived; the waiter removed Renata's barely touched chowder without comment. John drizzled homemade house dressing onto his greens before he continued. 'It's important to have friends and family at a time like this. But I believe it to be even more important not to let them overwhelm you. Most of the time in this life we are alone, and we must come to terms with our loss alone. Too much kindness and loving support can interfere with that.'

She laid her fork, on which she'd speared a slice of cucumber she could not then force her lips to accept, on the edge of the plate. 'I can do this,' she said wonderingly. 'I can do this, can't I?'

John nodded gravely. 'You can,' he told her. Because he said so and manifestly knew what he was talking about; because he still wept for his lost child thirty-one years later, had not had to give up his grief in order to have a good life; because he'd brought her to the Press Club for lunch – she believed him utterly.

They walked together back across the bridge onto campus. 'Thank you, John,' she said as he left her at her building.

He tipped his billed cap. 'My pleasure. We will do this again,' and she knew they would.

The giddy excitement – 'I can do this!' – lasted through the afternoon and into the evening. They went out for pizza. She and Vanessa chatted about Girl Scout Camp, coming up next month, and she knew she was considerably more animated than usual. Vanessa kept glancing at her appraisingly, and Glenn seemed to flinch away as though from grit blown into his face. When Vanessa left the table with a handful of quarters for the jukebox, Renata laid her hand on her husband's arm. 'How are you doing, sweetheart?'

He looked at her hollow-eyed. 'Hard day,' he said, finally.

'About Ian?'

He nodded once, broke contact with her to press the heels of both hands against his eyes. When he lowered his hands, his face looked exposed, as if he'd removed eyeglasses, and there was distance between them that she didn't try to close.

'I'm sorry.' Her own happier state of mind was assailed by his distress. Maybe he'd cried today for Ian; she couldn't bear to imagine Glenn crying, although she'd have worried about him if he hadn't. She'd thought to tell him about John Brustein, but now didn't dare. 'What can I do?'

He shook his head. 'Nothing. I have to do this myself. I'm okay. I'm supposed to be feeling like this.'

'You know, I've had such a stake in being happy, noticing beauty, being open to love. Not missing a moment. So it pisses me off that I'm missing so much now because of grieving.' She paused, waited. Glenn said nothing. A disco song one of Vanessa's quarters had paid for burbled out of the speakers. Renata said, 'But actually, I guess I'm not missing anything. I mean, happiness and beauty aren't all there is. Pain is an honorable thing to feel, too, isn't it?'

'I don't know about "honorable,"' Glenn said, with an edge of what she took to be impatience. 'But it's what's real.'

'Glenn,' she heard herself say, 'I've been thinking—' This was

318

not the right time. But she finished, because it seemed coy not to, '—I'd like to have more children. Adopt again.'

'I can't think about that now,' he said at once.

'I don't mean now. It's too soon. In a year or two, maybe.'

'I can't think about that now.'

Unwisely, perhaps unkindly, she persisted. 'Do you think you'll ever be able to think about it?'

Very deliberately, Glenn said, 'I can't imagine ever getting past this pain enough to be willing to start over with another child.' He got up then to go to the bathroom, and Renata let it go. A few steps away from the table he hesitated, turned. 'I'm sorry, honey,' he said, miserably.

They didn't leave the restaurant until well after eight o'clock, and Renata was aghast that the hour had passed without her quite knowing. She was afraid to go in the house. She was afraid to check for phone messages, more afraid not to. There were no messages. She wished she would dream about Ian tonight, but, again, she didn't.

The next morning she was mowing the fescue between the sidewalk and the street, trying to keep her mind on the task at hand. The therapist she was seeing now, an existential social worker she'd admired since she'd taken a class from him in graduate school – she remembered thinking at the time, 'I have more to learn from this man, someday' – had taught her how to calm herself when panic swooped in: Take a step, pause, ask and answer out loud, 'Where is happiness? Right here.' Then take another step, pause, ask and answer again, 'Where is happiness? Right here.' That answer was meaningless; there was no happiness here. But the acts of questioning and answering, she'd discovered, were not.

So behind the noisy mower, whose plastic-sheathed handle sweated and vibrated in the tunnel of her loose fists, she was taking one step, pausing, asking herself aloud and answering aloud under the machine's obscuring whine, 'Where is happiness? Right here.' The early summer sun was warm on her shoulders through the T-shirt, which smelled of cotton. The ground was bumpy through the soles of her tennis shoes. Something sweet was in the air along with the fragrance of mown grass. Ian was dead. A van went by on the side street. A dog barked in the alley. A small blue car pulled up to the curb on the other side of the street and a young man got out.

Ian was dead. Oh, Ian was dead. She took another step. 'Where is happiness? Right here.' Her mowing progress was slow and jerky, and none of the sensory impressions she catalogued meant anything to her except Ian is dead, but the grass was getting cut.

'Renata. Hi.'

She let go of the mower, the lever swung open, and the machine shut off. She didn't know who the brawny young man was, except that he was the one who'd gotten out of the blue car.

'It's Rudy. Remember me? Rudy Van Nuys.'

She recognized the name; she would never have recognized him. Rudy Van Nuys had been their babysitter for a while when Ian was maybe five and Vanessa eight, a shy, scrawny, and unhappy young teenager. This kid was a head taller than she was, with the triangular torso of a bodybuilder and a direct, appealing gaze. He was extending his hand. She didn't want to take it. Ian would have been blond and fair, not dark like this, if he'd lived that long. A memory flashed: she'd sat beside a distraught Rudy on the bench in the family room, arm around his thin shaking shoulders, making encouraging neutral comments while he'd sobbed about his abusive father. Here was Rudy Van Nuys now, grown up, alive, while her son was dead. Rudy's abusive father hadn't lost his son. She'd lost hers.

She took the big young hand, intending the handshake to be brief. But his other hand came up in a practiced charming gesture, and he was clasping hers. 'Hi, Rudy. How are you?'

He told her in a rush, 'I'm going to college back East on scholarship. I'm going to be a doctor.'

'That's great.' Panic exploded. *Where is happiness? Right here. Where is happiness? Right here.* But it was not. She was touching a boy with a future. Hers had none.

'Yeah. Thanks. So how are you? How's Glenn? How are Vanessa and Ian?'

'Ian died.'

The brilliant smile clung to his handsome face even after the horror had reached his dark eyes. His hands flinched around hers, but now she didn't want to let him escape, and she was the one holding on. 'What?' he gasped.

She nodded. 'Almost three months ago. March 18. He hanged himself.'

320

'Suicide?' Now blood had drained from his face, the high cheekbones hollowing its chiseled planes. 'He committed suicide? Oh, my
God. Why? How old was he?'

'Nine. We don't know if it was suicide. Maybe it was an accident.
Maybe he killed himself without really knowing it would be forever.
He was only nine.'

'Oh, my God.'

He had to know the details. Unkindly, she pressed. 'He made a
noose out of the rope he used to walk the dogs, and tied the other
end around the post of his top bunk. Remember his bunk beds? Then
he jumped or fell. Glenn found him when he went to call him for
dinner.'

'Oh, my God.' Rudy had somehow freed himself from her. She
watched him retreat, take a few clumsy steps backward, stumble
off the curb, then turn and hurry to his car and slam the door and
speed off without another glance at her. She was not ashamed of
the mean satisfaction his discomfort gave her. Served him right. If
he was going to be alive while Ian was dead, the least he could do
was know it.

By the time she finished mowing the parkway, on the south
side of the house and on the west and on the corner where it
was hardest to get to – property the city owned but homeowners
were responsible for, an aspect of the social contract that she now
bitterly resented – rage was making her reckless. An eyeball-sized
stone she'd purposely steered over cracked and whined under the
blade, but nothing broke and the stone bounced harmlessly off
the fire hydrant. A chattering group of kids cavorted past on the
sidewalk, and the temptation to drive the mower through them was
acute, equally acute her resentment at having to restrain the urge.

She left the mower out while she went back to the garage, grimly
hoping somebody would try to steal it and she could apprehend the
asshole. She dumped fertilizer into the inverted pyramid of the
spreader too hard, and the eye-stinging grit puffed. Furiously she
pushed the spreader in zigzags the length of the parkway, swung
around and went back the other way, not knowing whether she was
overlapping or not, hoping she was, hoping she was killing all the
fucking grass and, even better, poisoning herself.

She stayed out until the twilight was deep, which was not an anniversary time of day since this wasn't a Friday. Angrily she pushed the mower and spreader back into the garage and stuffed the empty fertilizer bag into the trash. Glenn's longstanding disinterest in yard work suddenly made her livid; how could she have married a man who wouldn't mow the lawn? As she stalked around the back of the lot she came upon a spot she'd missed, a square foot of ankle-high growth, and, nearly roaring with fury, she flung herself onto her hands and knees and pulled the stand out by the roots, wrenching and tearing handfuls of living grass, gouging up clods of earth, leaving as much evidence of her wrath as possible. Not that it would do any good. Not that anyone would even notice.

At the dining-room table Glenn and Vanessa were immersed in algebra homework, a little diorama of father-daughter partnership in misery. Renata stormed past them. 'I'm going to bed.'

'Are you all right?' Glenn asked after her, alarmed.

Of course she was not all right. Their son was dead. With difficulty she managed not to scream that at him. 'No,' she snapped, already nearly to the top of the stairs.

'What about dinner?'

Fix it your fucking self. Or starve. 'I'm not hungry,' she called down, and shut the bedroom door just in time, as the tidal wave of fury rose and rose and broke.

She threw herself onto the bed. It wasn't hard enough. She crawled to the edge and threw herself onto the floor. She plummeted through it, through the solid outlines and connecting spaces of her house and on into the time and space and interconnecting dimensions beneath it, hoping to find there the means of her destruction.

Chapter 30

drifting shapeless no center formless no pain no edge to hold the pain

'Renata.'

space

between molecules pressing them apart farther apart drifting propelling thoughts apart allowing thoughts not to touch each other not to touch anything

nothing touching anything no pain

'You are Renata.'

no

formless nameless no history or future no present

no nucleus no pain no core

'You have lost your son.'

Ian.

Drifting in the space, which is made to appear limitless, where nothing touches anything and there is no self, nothing personal. *Ian.* No.

'Your child is dead, and you are still Renata.'

No.

But yes. Organization again now, shape and substance. Time again now. And space: a medium for form to float in but not taking up all of it.

Form not the same as space.

Shape not the same as space. Shape of body, shape of mind, and shape of soul, different from the space they float in.

'Renata.'

'No.' But answering. Answering to her name.

'Renata. Go on.'

Renata dragged herself together. Maimed parts of her struggled, weeping, to stay separate, to stay here floating on forgetfulness, but she gathered them together as if on a beach, lashed them together as if to the hull of a boat.

The giant red rat stirred in dull alarm. Its naked tail looped in the sand like a parody of a serpent. It heaved itself to its feet, lumbered over to her, and lowered its massive head.

Renata understood that the rat was a danger. She should stay away from it. She should trap it, kill it. But the heady fragrance of the venom dripping from its yellow fangs tempted her.

'Renata.'

The rodent's long soft whiskers caressed her cheek, brushing away the ache in the bones of her face. Its so-sweet breath puffed into her face, and she inhaled it like an addict. The rat made her the lulling offer: 'Forget. Stay here.'

Two drops of the pearly poison beaded on her skin. There was a long sting, muted, and then the awaited rush of wellbeing, the gorgeous flush and fizz of forgetfulness that had become so welcome. Belinda's sibilant voice, insisting, 'Remember,' was very far away. Renata swooned with craving which was readily satisfied.

But forgetting wasn't enough. She remembered. *Ian.*

Belinda gave the command again. 'Go on.'

Belinda's broad patterned back materialized under her, a surface not exactly solid but capable of supporting her weight. She flattened herself along it, spread her arms and clawed her fingers into the cool pliant flesh. The rat called to her and tried to fix her with its red eyes – pleading, demanding, mesmerizing – until she wrenched her gaze away from it and hid her face in the snake's silk-leather back.

The serpent rippled, and Renata was transported by her internal motion as well as by the progress of the huge body through external space and time. At first, her yearning for the false bliss of forgetfulness dragged at her, threatening to slough her off Belinda's back like dead skin, but by fastening her fingertips under the flanged scales she was able to hold on.

Gradually the serpentine undulation itself became addictive. Renata discovered that she was able to think, *Ian is dead. My child died*, the words, without actually encountering their meaning.

They had a hallucinogenic quality, like a mantra or a magic spell. *My child is dead.*

Belinda halted. It took some time for the shuddering set up by the abrupt cessation of forward motion to travel the length of her body. Renata felt it pass under her, like a separate creature being devoured whole.

She waited for Belinda to explain to her why they'd stopped, or for the slithering travel to begin again. Instead, the thick snakeskin shimmied sideways, and Renata slid off onto the ground.

The serpent vanished.

There was a thundering silence and aloneness. Then Renata found herself staring into a cave so immense she had thought it was simply the whole world, and, far back in the depths, into a pair of huge, glittering, malevolent eyes.

Chapter 31

Renata sat in the back seat with the squarish black dog who hadn't stopped growling and trembling since they'd first glimpsed her in the cage. The dog's eyes bulged. The deep wrinkles around her neck and along the muscled little flanks quivered like quills, and she kept her rather impressive teeth bared. She leaned against Renata, though, repositioning herself whenever the motion of the car separated them. The continuous low growl was both warning and plea.

Vanessa peered over the front seat again. The growl rose a notch. 'They kept her in a cage *all the time*?'

'That's what Althea said.'

'Why?'

'They just said they didn't like her.'

'That's mean.'

'Yep.'

'Hopefully,' said Glenn, 'it hasn't made her mean. We can't keep her if she's dangerous.'

Vanessa started to object, but Renata said over her, 'Dad's right, Vanessa. We talked about this. That's the deal. We'll try, but we can't keep her if she's going to hurt somebody.'

Her daughter's face was turned in silhouetted profile against the bright windshield, and Renata, seeing her jaw jut stubbornly, braced herself. The dog edged closer. 'We don't give up in this family,' Vanessa pointed out. 'We didn't get rid of Tim when he was bad.'

The dog punched a paw onto Renata's thigh. The force and sharpness of it, not to mention the claws, caused more than a little discomfort, but Renata only squirmed under the hard foot, didn't dislodge it. Glenn laughed a little. 'We're talking about a damn dog here. Not our son.'

327

'What kind is she again? She's funny-looking. She's all wrinkly and her tail's curly like a pig's.'

'She's a Shar-Pei. That lady supposedly paid fifteen hundred dollars for her, although why anybody would pay that much money for a dog is beyond me.'

'Why anybody would pay for a dog, period,' Glenn said, 'when the pound is full of perfectly good dogs who need homes.'

'But we got her for free, right?'

'The lady wouldn't give us her papers. So we wouldn't be able to prove she's purebred, which is what would bring that much money.' Renata rested her hand lightly on the dog's back. The animal flinched but didn't entirely pull away. Her fur was like the short bristles of a soft brush.

'That's stupid,' Vanessa observed. 'Spike is a stupid name, too.'

'I wonder if they tried to use her for fighting.' Glenn sounded worried again. Glenn sounded worried much of the time these days.

'Maybe she wasn't fierce enough and that's why they didn't want her,' Renata said hopefully.

Glenn asked Vanessa, 'What would be a better name for her?'

'Jade,' Vanessa said promptly.

'Oh,' Renata said, pleasantly surprised. 'I like that. Jade.'

'Why Jade?' Glenn wanted to know.

'Shar-Peis are Chinese dogs, right? So I thought of Jade.'

'Very good.' Renata smiled to see the motion of Glenn's head and shoulder as he reached to pat their daughter's hand.

'Jade.' The dog was preoccupied with staring out the window at the blur of potential attackers, intent on keeping herself ready. Her ears went up, but it could not be in response to her new name yet. Renata stroked the velvety head. The dog leaned harder, muscled shoulder into her upper arm.

It occurred to Renata that here they were, having an extended conversation, following a rather expansive family activity, that was in no way related to Ian, neither about him nor studiously not. And then that this whole thing – Althea telling her about the Shar-Pei that needed rescuing, Glenn's reluctant and conditional acquiescence and Vanessa's excitement, driving out to the seedy trailer court, interacting as minimally as possible with the gravel-voiced woman, the eruption of the frenetic little dog when the gate of the big wire cage was opened, her racing in gradually diminishing circles around the dirt yard until finally she would approach Renata's patiently extended hand, this ride home through rush-hour traffic with Mozart on the radio, their anticipated efforts to integrate Jade into the family and whether or not it would turn out to be possible – all of this was a new experience that would be a new memory with Ian nowhere in it. He wasn't part of this. He would not know this new dog. He and Jade would not be part of the same life.

He was, in fact, steadily moving into the past. Renata sat very still to consider this.

Ian, her son, was becoming part of her past. Which was, of course, where he belonged, no matter that the sudden concept of it set her teeth on edge. Her present and her future didn't include him.

This seemed nothing less than an epiphany. She waited for the pain, and there was some, but mostly there came a kind of radiant understanding: When she was able to let Ian go, this was where he would go to. Into her past. Fleetingly, it seemed a safe enough place for him.

'Gee, Renata,' Glenn said amiably as they passed their house on the way to the garage. 'You really did a number on the grass, didn't you?'

Indeed, the parkway between the sidewalk and the street might have been stitched with bright yellow rickrack where too much fertilizer had dropped from the spreader. Vanessa squealed, 'Dad!' in indignation that might declare itself mock or real depending on her mother's reaction.

This wasn't the first time the sight of the flamboyantly dead fescue had caused Renata's stomach to churn. She considered allowing Glenn's teasing to upset her, which would have been easy and genuine. Instead, she said softly, 'I kind of like that shade of yellow myself,' and the three of them chuckled, and she let her breath out, feeling adventurous and triumphant.

It took about ten minutes, and no overt interaction that Renata could detect, for Gypsy – by nature the underdog and deprived of domination since Shaman had died – relievedly to subordinate herself to Jade. It took the rest of the day for the cats to find high or hidden places from which to survey this abrupt and unpleasant alteration in their circumstances and then gradually to redefine how they would live here from now on: The skittish white cat slunk against the baseboard, back and forth and around corners more often than necessary, as though Jade wouldn't notice; in fact, she apparently didn't. Cinnabar strode past with ears and tail straight up; for some reason this evinced from the stocky little canine a rear-end-up, front-paws-flat-on-the-floor invitation to play, which Cinnabar regally ignored. The tabby puffed herself up and issued a strident back-of-the-throat challenge, which Jade rose to, and the two of them raced around the back yard a few times before the cat leaped onto the garage roof and hunched at the very edge, glaring and hissing. Jade barked and stood up on her bowed back legs, front paws scrabbling on the brick. Then she sank back on her haunches and stared up for a while, snuffling. Eventually, she wandered off around the yard, found an incipient opening under the back corner of the fence, and wriggled her way through, forcing Vanessa to search the neighborhood for her, coming, though, when she was called by her eight-hour-old name. By suppertime, the impact of this one smallish animal on the household had begun to be assimilated – an enormous impact, and impermanent, for they would assimilate her absence, too, if it came to that.

In Glenn's arms to say good night, Renata told him, 'I'm glad we got Jade.' 'Glad' might actually be too emphatic a word, but she did have a mild positive feeling about it, and she supposed that Glenn, of all people, would understand how remarkable that was.

'I hope it doesn't turn out to have been a mistake,' he said.

'She seems to be doing fine so far.'

'Yes,' he allowed. 'She does.'

'She's a funny little thing.' Renata didn't laugh; the very prospect of ever laughing again made her chest ache even more than usual. But she did acknowledge that amusement could be found, by someone who hadn't lost Ian, in this situation, and that was risk enough. 'In any case, I think today was good for us.' She felt him nod. 'Part of getting used to this new life. Life without Ian.' Now she felt him flinch, and was sorry, and tightened her embrace around his ample striped shirt. 'Oh, honey, was that the wrong thing to say?' She felt him shake his head. 'Glenn, I'm scared. Most couples don't make it through losing a child. Something like seventy or eighty per cent split up.'

'We won't.'

'But our life together is ruined.' Renata knew she said this so that he would tell her it was not true, because she could believe him more than she could believe herself.

'Not ruined. Changed.'

She waited, breathless, for he was about to utter magic words. But of his own volition he didn't go on, and if she pressed he might well shy away, withhold the magic from her. She pressed anyway. 'What do you mean?'

He sighed. She thought he wasn't going to give her what he had, and anger began to gather. But with obvious effort he said, 'There are a lot of lives a person could live, a lot of forks in the road. When something like this happens, you have to make other choices.'

That was right. That was revelatory. The world shifted. Renata couldn't say things like that to herself with any authority, couldn't generate her own magic spells. But for a few hours now, maybe the rest of the day, she could use incantatory power borrowed from these words of her husband, of Ian's father. So she unlocked her embrace and let him go, aware that she had taken – at some cost to him – what she required in order to survive, hoping that was all right.

'Have you heard anything about that adolescent grief group for Vanessa?' Glenn wanted to know.

'It'll start next month.' He nodded. Chilled, she asked, 'Why? Are you worried about her? Is something going on I don't know about?'

'No, no, I just think it will be good for her.'

'What about you, honey?' She put her hand on his arm. 'What about some kind of therapy for you? Do you want to come to the adult grief group with me?'

He shook his head and sighed and regarded her with a wan calm. 'I've thought about it. But I think I have to do this myself.'

She was lying across the bed watching the six o'clock news, taking in almost none of its content but absorbing the repetitive pattern of field story and Dan Rather's anchor and commercial and Dan Rather again that was very nearly liturgical in its rhythms, wondering if Rather and the others had any inkling of the healing properties of what they did, when she felt the heart attack start.

Her chest seized. Her head bucked and swam. Her vision

331

blackened and her ears rang. She couldn't feel her hands and feet. Her heart surged, beat very fast and very hard, internal pressure ratcheting wildly up toward explosion.

She thought to call out for Glenn, but Vanessa, in her room at the end of the hall, would know soon enough that her mother had had a fatal heart attack. Renata pushed herself off the edge of the bed, then up onto all fours, and crawled out of the bedroom still rumbling with the six o'clock news. Something – a shoelace eye, a protrusion from her flesh – snagged on the old red carpet with a tiny tearing noise. Her shoulder grazed the wall, staggering her. She caromed around the corner to Glenn's closed office door, through which came his music and the click of his keyboard. Her chest was on fire. She couldn't feel her arms and legs. Her brain was full of the eruption of her heart.

She scratched like a cat, like a wolf, at Glenn's door, feeling ridiculous, worried that Vanessa would come out of her room and catch her. She managed to slap the flat of her hand against the knob and, wildly dizzy, huddled toward the brief, faint rattle, chasing it as it faded away.

Glenn called, 'Yes?'

She couldn't answer out loud. Her heart was a siren without a destination, no longer in the service of anything.

Glenn opened the door, looked down, saw her, gasped, crouched. 'My God, Renata, what's wrong?'

She let him grasp her forearms and raise her to her feet. 'Sorry,' she rasped. 'I'm sorry.'

He lowered her into his desk chair, which swiveled under her uneven weight, then went to shut the door carefully, no slam. 'What's *wrong*?'

'I think I must – be – having a heart attack.'

'What? What do you mean?' He had her clammy face between his hands.

'I – can't breathe. My heart is racing. I'm going – I'm going to faint. I'm going to die.'

His hands moved to her shoulders, leaving cold burning swaths on her cheeks. She could barely feel his grip, although she knew he was holding her hard. 'Breathe deeply,' he commanded.

'I can't.'

He shook her a little. 'You're hyperventilating. Take a deep breath. Come on, honey. *Breathe.*'

'My heart—'

'It isn't your heart. You're having a panic attack.'

'How do you know that?' she cried, but the instant he had named it, it began to subside. She risked opening her lungs, because Glenn told her to, and air settled in deeply; it hurt, but bearably. The fluttering blackness began to clear from her vision, and her heartbeat to recede.

'I've had three,' he told her.

'Panic attacks? Like that? Where you thought you were dying?' She did not now think she was dying. Sensation in her extremities was close to normal, and the cold sweat was drying on her skin. Her heart was still beating too hard, but steadily now, and she could see and hear clearly. Glenn's hands rested gently on her shoulders; she leaned her head back against his belly.

'So I did some reading. Panic attacks are pretty common when you've been through a trauma.'

'I – I didn't know you were going through that. Oh, Glenn.'

'It's okay. It passes.'

'Why didn't you tell me?'

'There was nothing you could do.'

'You helped me.'

He was stroking her hair. 'Everybody's different. That isn't what I need from you.'

'Don't leave me, sweetheart. Don't go away from me.'

He bent and kissed the top of her head. 'I won't. I couldn't. We're in this together.' His arms came around her, palms warm on her chest, and she turned her face into him, both of them breathing deeply, breathing in peace.

The next day, after her usual lunch hour spent weeping on the floor of the empty room – the chrysanthemum blooming and the apothecary jar newly filled with just the kind of candy you'd expect an apothecary jar to be full of, butterscotch lozenges wrapped in butterscotch-colored cellophane – Theresa came into her office. With an air of resolution, she shut the door, sat down and leaned forward, elbows on knees. 'Renata, I need to talk to you for a minute.'

Before Ian died this would not have been unusual, but in their

333

relationship now the sheer oddity of it snagged Renata's attention through the murk of pain and release and pain already coalescing again until it could be released on that chrysanthemum-room floor tomorrow at noon. She felt hunted down, treasure and prey. What could Theresa need to talk about that was worth rooting around in this murk to find her?

She said nothing either to invite or to rebuff. She just sat still, struck by how prepared Theresa seemed to be, how much care she'd given this. How important it was, then, to someone. 'I really admire how you're doing this,' Theresa began earnestly. 'Facing it head-on every minute. You're so brave.'

'I'm – not sure from one minute to the next that I'm – going to make it.' Renata clutched the edge of the desk.

It was a measure of their friendship that Theresa offered no reassurances. Instead, she nodded. 'I know. That's what I mean by brave.' Her gray eyes suddenly glistened with tears, which she made no attempt to conceal; this, too, was a measure of their friendship. 'But, Renata, I can't find you anymore, and it's been almost four months, and I *miss* you!'

If Tim or Vanessa had said something like that to her, she'd have taken it as further proof of what she already knew: She was a terrible mother, and, apparently, always had been. If Glenn had said it, she'd have been outraged that he'd dare to expect anything of her now or devastated that their marriage was, in fact, in ruins because she wasn't the partner in grief that he needed her to be. But nothing about Theresa's plea was threatening. 'I'm sorry. I know this has put a lot of responsibility on you.'

Theresa shook her head. 'It's not that. I don't think I'm really asking you to be any different. We're okay. The office is okay. I just wanted you to know that I miss you.'

'I think I will come back,' Renata said, tentatively, testing this bizarre new perception. 'I don't think I'll stay away forever.'

Theresa nodded. For a few more minutes she sat there, smiling, eyes welling. Then, rising, she said briskly, 'Your two o'clock is here.'

'She's early.'

'Been here since noon.'

'Great.'

334

'Shall I tell her she'll need to wait till the appointment time?'

'No,' said Renata, suddenly eager to meet this new student. 'I'll see her now.'

'I'll go get her.'

After her, Renata said, 'Thanks, Theresa,' and Theresa flashed her a smile.

The two o'clock was a very young, very schizophrenic woman who didn't take meds because she *admired* the way her mind worked. 'Reality flows,' she explained somewhat dreamily to Renata, 'and every now and then reality puddles.' It was hard, though, to take notes in her accounting class since that particular reality didn't happen to puddle and stay puddled every Monday, Wednesday, and Friday evening between six and six-fifty. She liked accounting – 'all those beautiful little numbers, and, you know, they aren't the same any two times I look at them. Isn't that fascinating?' Musing that she would likely not have understood the concept of occasionally-puddling reality before the madness of grief had caused everyday reality to plunge and flow and geyser, Renata gave her a ream of self-carboning paper and told her how to find a notetaker from among her classmates. Imagining what that conversation could be like gave them both some pause.

Renata finished her column for the student newspaper, which she'd started the week before Ian died. It wasn't hard to write now, required only a modicum of updating. At the Affirmative Action Council meeting, she managed to follow most of the discussions about the search process for the Director of Business Services and the discrimination complaint filed against Public Safety. Pain filled her chest and abdominal cavities like illness, did not require its host to acknowledge it or its source in order to sustain itself; it wasn't quite that she could ignore the pain, but rather that she could let it proceed on its own, without her active participation.

A fruit tray had been ordered from Food Services. Absently, Renata took a plum. When her teeth pierced the firm purplish skin and the sweet juice spurted into her mouth, she tasted it. Lost in the astounding sensation, she missed the next several minutes of the meeting, and bit attentively into the plum again, awestruck.

As she gathered up her papers after the meeting, carefully because her sense of touch might still be muted and roughened and it would be easy to drop things and not be able to pick them up again, someone commented genially, 'We saw you and your family down here at the Fourth of July celebration.'

Renata's immediate response was *I don't have a family anymore.* She managed to keep it unspoken, and of course it wasn't true.

'We called to you a couple of times but I guess you didn't hear us,' he said, smiling, faintly accusing.

She couldn't think what to say. *All I can hear now is grief. All I can see is grief. All I can taste is grief.* But, because of the plum, that was no longer true.

'Were those your daughters?'

'My daughter and her friend. The lighter-haired one is my daughter. Vanessa.'

'She's a beautiful girl.' Renata nodded, pleased and frightened. 'How old is she?'

'Thirteen. We just celebrated her thirteenth birthday.' *She was twelve when Ian died. Now she's thirteen.*

'Oh, boy. A teenager. You're in for it now. I swear, all girls are completely nuts when they're thirteen and fourteen. Maybe there's something in the water. They're a lot like two-year-olds, except they're bigger and they know more ways to say "no."'

He chuckled fondly. Renata guessed his daughter or daughters must be well past the crazy stage, but she didn't remember and she didn't ask.

'It's not easy being the parent of a teenager.' He seemed to be pressing some particular point, but it was lost on her.

'It's not easy being a parent, period,' she said, and was both relieved and insulted when he rolled his eyes in wry agreement. He had no idea that she meant it was impossible to be a parent, given that your children could die no matter what you did.

'Did you enjoy the festivities? The fireworks were pretty spectacular, weren't they?'

Renata finally brought her gaze up. The man was smiling at her, being friendly. 'No,' she had to say, because it was true. 'I didn't enjoy it. I'm not enjoying anything yet.'

Clearly it took a beat or two for her meaning to register. He looked baffled, then shocked, then embarrassed. But he collected himself.

'Of course,' he said, nodding, not backing away though she guessed he'd have liked to. 'Of course you're not.'

'But I'm glad we came,' she said, thinking how strange that was. She remembered lying on the grass – first warm, quickly cooling once the sun had set – next to Althea, while Vanessa and Wendy had run off to buy hot dogs and watermelon, run off to listen to the concert up close, come back, run off to get a better view of the fireworks. She remembered the conviction that this would be a pleasant memory, although the primary experience of it wasn't especially pleasant. She remembered watching Althea, fourteen years past the death of her second child, to see how it could be done. She remembered Vanessa's face, glistening with excitement in the red and green showering light from the flares and starbursts in the night sky. 'I'm glad they had fireworks for the Fourth of July, and I'm glad we came.'

Sunday was her parents' wedding anniversary, and the first time they'd been to her house since the week after Ian had died. Then, she'd lain on the couch howling, and her father had advised, though from across the room, 'That's right. Let it out. Don't keep it in,' and her mother had visibly shied away from her, and Renata, she thought, had moaned, 'Don't be afraid of my pain.'

This time, Vanessa was setting the table, taking care, when her grandparents arrived. The roast, waiting to be sliced, looked moist and tender; roast beef with onions, potatoes, and carrots had been her mother's favorite meal since Renata was a little girl. The rolls had risen nicely and were almost done baking; Renata grinned inwardly at her own insistence on baking bread when her parents came to dinner, given that bread had been her mother's specialty for a good thirty years and she couldn't hope to compete.

Because she'd rearranged the table, there was no glaring empty place, and nobody mentioned Ian; Renata tried to find a way to bring up his name casually, but it seemed to be too soon for that. Occasionally pain flared. Occasionally she saw acute mourning on her husband's face, a peak on the high plateau of sorrow that was always there, and Vanessa was alternately edgy and more affectionate with her grandparents than usual.

'School starts pretty soon, doesn't it?'

Vanessa rolled her eyes. 'A month or so,' Renata confirmed.

'What grade will you be in?'

'Seventh.' *Ian would have been in fifth.*

Renata's mother smiled and nodded, paused, smiled and nodded some more. The girl giggled and looked away. Neither of them seemed to have a clue how to continue the conversation. Renata prompted, 'Middle school. Junior high.'

'Oh, will you change schools then?'

Vanessa glanced at her mother. They'd had this conversation before; Vanessa had even pointed out her new school to her grandmother one day last spring. Renata recognized that they were likely to get the same few queries about school again and again, because they represented to her mother known, relatively risk-free territory, though only within a very limited range, never to include learning disabilities or spells of weeping in class or those difficult early days when Vanessa had hysterically resisted going to school because her birthmother wouldn't know where to find her. Unable to come up with a signal that would tell her daughter just to answer what Grandma had asked, not to make a big deal, Renata was vastly relieved when Vanessa said simply, 'Uh-huh.'

'New school,' Renata said, doing her part to preserve the appearance of a normal conversation, 'new teachers, lockers, changing classes, being the youngest instead of the oldest class in the school. Lots of changes. It's a big step. But she'll do fine.'

'My goodness.'

Vanessa smiled with nervous pride and seemed to be waiting for more. But Renata knew that was her mother's way of seeming to comment without actually doing so, and was intended to end the topic.

Indeed, her mother reached now, not for the first time this afternoon, to pat her father's hand. 'Forty-two years,' she said again, again tipping her head with exaggerated coyness to look into his face.

'Seems like a hundred,' he muttered gruffly, as he was supposed to.

She gave his hand another little slap. 'Do you suppose we'll make it to fifty?'

No matter how many times or in what context she asked this unanswerable question, he never replied. After a moment, Renata

338

filled the uncomfortable silence, as if that were her job. 'It's a long time to be married to the same person,' she agreed, as if that had been her mother's point.

'Mr Walton, our neighbor? He had a massive heart attack last week. We saw the ambulance while we were out for our walk.'

Renata had never met Mr Walton, but lately both her parents had brought him up often and with animation. Reputedly, he had plenty of money, a much younger wife, and generally bad luck. 'Is he okay?'

Her mother shook her head, whether in negative response or in appreciative dismay, it was hard to tell. 'He's had so *many* things. He's had heart problems ever since we've known him—'

'Since well before we knew him,' Renata's father cut in.

'—and then last summer he had that car accident, and before that there was a fire at his home. Just one thing after another.'

Before she got up to get the pie, Renata said somewhat tentatively, 'That's too bad.' This was leading somewhere, but she had no idea where.

Then, from the kitchen, she heard her mother say, apparently to Glenn, 'I was just telling Les the other day, I'm so grateful nothing bad has happened to us.'

Coming through the door with pie in one hand and ice cream carton in the other, Renata actually staggered. She hadn't heard what if any reply Glenn had made to this outrageous comment, but apparently no one had called much attention to it, and now the conversation turned quickly and smoothly to how good the pie looked and whether or not her mother ought to eat ice cream.

Renata's hands were trembling too hard to cut the pie or serve the ice cream, so she asked Vanessa to do it. Vanessa looked alarmed, but agreed. Afraid to look at Glenn, Renata was even more afraid to stay in the room lest she shriek at her mother, pointlessly, 'Something bad *did* happen to you! Your grandson hanged himself! Didn't you notice?'

She hurried into the bathroom, shut the door carefully, and leaned against the counter. In a few minutes she was able to go back into the dining room and help Vanessa serve dessert. She still did not dare to look at Glenn.

'Pretty soon it will be your anniversary,' her mother said cheerily.

Renata longed to tell her mother how frightening that prospect was. She managed to smile and affirm, 'Nine years.' Then she risked adding, 'A lot has happened in those nine years.' Neither of her parents picked up on the reference, but when she caught her husband's eye, he was smiling, too, apparently genuinely, and her heart seized.

Chapter 32

'We're sorry that you have to be here,' Rob Torres said again. Renata was touched again by the graciousness of the man and, newly, by the seductiveness of the ritual words. 'We're so sorry that your children died. But we welcome you here with us.' Rob's deep breath then was part of his established rhythm. 'My wife and I lost two daughters. Cassie was four days old. Amanda was four years old. They both had a hereditary lung disease.'

Brenda Henneman was sitting next to Rob tonight, and, after a suitable pause, she took up the torch, telling the story of how Colin had been the victim of a hit-and-run accident on a mountain road on his way back to the dorm from an evening class, ending with, 'His roommate's mother thought it was her son who had been killed, but it turned out to be mine.'

Renata had a place here. Her hand on Brenda's knee covered by Brenda's small hand, she began. 'My son Ian died.' She stopped. There was much more she ought to tell, was expected to tell. She didn't want to, not because it was too awful to say but because the details, the *story* of it, tonight seemed dangerously irrelevant.

Everyone waited. She shook her head and lowered her eyes to signal she was finished. The chorus resumed at once, the call and response. Brenda squeezed her hand in support and comfort, which did not seem to be what she needed.

'Until Bill, I didn't know children died,' Jean McIntosh said, as she always said, and there was the usual ripple of assent around the circle, bitter chuckles and stunned inhalations and exhalations.

'Children have always died,' Renata said, not meaning to sound argumentative but knowing she did. Her place in the millennia-long line of parents who had lost or would lose children steadied her, and

341

she wanted to tell these parents in this room about all the others, but couldn't think how to do that.

'We have four other kids,' Jean's husband Arnie said.

'And four grandchildren.'

'But we never got over Bill.'

'You don't. You don't ever get over it.'

Renata squirmed in her chair. Brenda tightened her grip knowingly. *They're stuck,* she was thinking, and the judgment seemed both uncharitable and important. *All they are is bereaved parents.*

She thought of John Brustein's invitation, 'Renata Burgess. Tell me about yourself,' and how she'd been taken aback, even offended, that he could imagine there was anything worth telling other than that she'd lost Ian.

Brenda leaned to whisper, 'Are you okay? I know it's hard.' Renata nodded and gently, as if meaninglessly, withdrew her hand.

'We don't criticize each other's grieving.'

'Whatever works for you is okay. Whatever you need.'

'Nobody knows how you feel. Nobody can tell you how to do this.'

'There's no right way or wrong way to grieve.'

Patty Devereaux – one high-heeled cowboy boot across the other tensed and tightly-denimed thigh – shook her ringed fist above her head. 'Grieving for Cory is the best thing I've ever done in my life. I'm better at this than I've ever been at anything. Hell, I'm not about to give it up!'

'Good for you,' murmured Brenda. Renata, shocked, restrained herself from glancing her way.

A father new to the group, whose son had died in a car accident almost a year ago, said, 'I know it doesn't make any sense, but I can't shake the idea that if I let loose of the pain and start to heal, even a little bit, then I'm letting the demon in to hurt somebody else I care about.'

Around the circle came nods and small noises of agreement, and Arnie said, 'Makes perfect sense to me.'

'The thing is,' someone else added, 'anything any of us feels makes perfect sense.'

It's magical thinking, Renata thought to say, but was afraid she would seem to be discounting this father's feelings. *It makes sense that we'd think that way, but we have to see it for what it is.*

'Grieving is the only way I can be his mother now,' Patty went on animatedly. 'If the pain ever stopped I wouldn't be his mother anymore, and then what would I be? Nothing.'

Althea spoke up thoughtfully. 'Well, you know, we're really *not* their parents anymore, in that way. But I've been reading Viktor Frankl, and he talks about other ways of loving people who aren't present anymore.'

Renata felt something in her rise, and with a certain excitement she waited for her friend to go on. But Jean said, 'Such a waste, you know? To die so young. Before their time.'

Renata wanted to object: *Ian's life wasn't a waste. And it was as long as it was supposed to be. By definition, it was his time.* The thought so startled her that she longed to sit in its presence for a while, get to know it, but someone else was talking.

This was the young mother whose two-year-old had drowned, here the last two or three meetings without her husband. Sobbing and shaking, she spoke unnaturally loudly, as though to be sure she could hear her own words. 'Somebody told me, "When you lose your parents, you lose your past. When you lose your children, you lose your future." It's true, isn't it! I've lost my future, haven't I?'

I haven't lost my future. It was less a voice in Renata's head than the pealing of a bell.

'I've lost my whole life,' Brenda said, matter-of-factly. 'Everything that was important to me, everything that made my life valuable to me, died two and a half years ago on that mountain road with Colin.'

'We've never been the same since Bill died,' Jean agreed.

'We never will be,' said Arnie.

'None of you will be, either.' Jean fixed her sad soft eyes on one person after another around the circle, meeting and then dropping Renata's gaze. 'It changes you forever.'

What had begun rising in Renata now shot upward some more, and with it flowered a joyous claiming she would not, just minutes before, have thought possible: *This is mine, too. This loss. This grief. This belongs to me. This is who I am now, and it's not the same, and that's the way it should be.*

Rob said, slowly scanning the circle, 'This is the most important thing that will ever happen to any of us. Maybe the only important thing,' and Renata silently responded, *No*. Not long ago, she would have thought, greedily, *Yes. Yes.*

'I don't think I can come here anymore,' she told Althea in the car on the way home.

'Oh,' said Althea. 'Why? Doesn't it help you?'

Renata frowned, trying to be clear. 'There's a lot of support for how terrible it is, and at the beginning I really needed that. But I don't think the group really supports healing. And I want to heal.'

After a moment, Althea said, 'You know, I don't think I've really gotten anything for myself out of the group for some time. I guess I go for other people. For newly bereaved parents.'

'I don't think I can go anymore,' Renata repeated, and noticed her arms were wrapped around herself. 'It feels dangerous.'

Althea nodded.

Renata hesitated only briefly before she asked, 'I can still see you if I don't go to the group, can't I? We can still be friends?'

Althea pulled the car up to the curb and turned to smile at her. 'Oh, of course. We have more in common than just our children who died.'

Ian died, Renata thought experimentally, and was able to say it aloud. 'Ian died.' For a long moment she looked at Althea, who was smiling at her fondly. 'My son Ian died. Isn't that amazing?'

They hugged good night and Renata made her way through the summer evening – in which, among many other things, existed the truths of Ian's life and Ian's death – up the steps to the back door of her house. She was not, tonight, afraid to go in, and there flashed through her mind some of the many things she'd found herself afraid of since Ian had died: Standing up when she'd been sitting down for a while. Leaving her house. Writing new words on blank paper. Going into her house. Reading anything she'd written. Looking in a mirror. Looking into Glenn's eyes.

It was not, now, that going into her house had shown itself to be perfectly safe, but rather that the dangers there and elsewhere were not, for the moment, enemies. Were not friends, either. Were simply present among a host of other real and present things.

The house was quiet, but not completely so. As she passed the ajar door of Vanessa's room, she heard Glenn talking, and she glanced in to see Vanessa on her father's lap on the bed, lanky legs dangling, head on his shoulder and fingers to her mouth. Glenn was recounting to her the story of the first time they'd met her at the foster home: 'You were such a tiny little thing your feet stuck straight out in front of you on the couch.'

'Really? I was seven and I was that little?'

'Yes, ma'am, and your eyes were huge. Mom and I knew the minute we saw you that you were our daughter.'

That was true. Renata pressed a fist to her mouth, awestruck, remembering.

Vanessa said something. Renata couldn't make out words, only the urgent need and the interrogatory inflection. She thought Glenn hesitated. Then he said, very gently, 'The first time we saw Ian he was playing on the sidewalk outside his foster home. He was riding a Big Wheel. The minute we saw him, Mom and I knew he was our son.'

He was crying. For long moments Renata leaned against the wall, weak from the pain and beauty of the memories but, more, from wonder at this man, willing to do what his child needed even when it caused him such anguish.

She was awake when Vanessa came in to say good night. The child lay on her mother's stomach for a few minutes, head tucked under her mother's chin, the way she'd done when she was much smaller and her tummy ached. 'I love you, Mommy,' Vanessa murmured, and Renata, who'd thought nobody in the world would ever again dare to call her Mommy, drank in the marvel of *this* child and whispered, 'Oh, Vanessa, I love you, too.'

When Glenn came to bed, she snuggled against him. She'd just begun to absorb the warmth and comfort of him when she remembered she had something to tell him.

'The detective called today,' she said into his shoulder, and felt him tense. She pulled back a little but didn't look at him to continue. 'She says she's followed every lead to try to find Vanessa and Ian's birthmother, and all the trails are cold. I guess women are a lot harder to track down than men, when they get married and change their names a lot.'

'So,' he said flatly, 'what happens next?'

'She says she'll keep the file open and maybe something will turn up. She says sometimes you can try the same things you tried a year ago and this time you get lucky.'

'I hate to think of Vanessa having to tell her about Ian's death someday.'

Again, the phrase 'Ian's death' sent a searing buzz like nerve pain through her chest. 'I know. And I guess I was hoping – and dreading – that we'd find out some clue about – about why he killed himself.'

They were silent for a while. Then Glenn asked, 'How much do we owe her?'

'Nothing. She says it's the least she can do.'

'That's nice.'

She kissed him and told him she loved him, how much she loved him. He said he loved her, too. She fell asleep while he was still reading.

Ian doesn't belong to me anymore. He belongs to the universe.

She shot awake out of dream darkness into late-night darkness in the room. Glenn's bedlamp sent a conical light across his sheeted shoulder and hip. She got out of bed, leaving him asleep or awake, and staggered the length of the hall to the bathroom. Got lost. Got back into bed, did not dare to touch Glenn, and went back to sleep.

Something was inside the cave. Renata was assaulted by the impression of monstrous hidden life.

She heard, felt, smelled its breath. The rhythmic inhalations and exhalations were alternately fetid and fragrant, rasping and sonorous, sheets of fire and a chill mist. Each enormous in-breath threatened to suck all the air out of the world. Every out-breath was an explosion.

The reptilian chill of it swooped out of the cave and radiated through and around her like a negative image of body heat. She was reminded of Belinda, the beautiful serpent, but Belinda was not here.

Pearly luminescence swelled like music out of the dark cave mouth. Renata lurched sideways and shielded her head with crossed arms. But the light caught her.

346

Her eyes adjusted to the radiance, which at first had been so painful, and now she yearned to see more and more of it. Layer after layer, she probed toward its source.

An immense object. Curved. Globular. Glimmering, with a solid and opaque seed at its core the size of a human being. A pearl.

A perfect enormous pearl, and she *wanted* it.

The setting of the pearl was a nest of grainy, fleshy wrinkles. These folds were higher by far than her head and deep and wide enough to swallow her. Surrounded by scales of rigid armor tipped razor-edge out, so sharp they seemed not content to wait inanimately for her to blunder into them but actively reached for her, quivering, possessed of both individual and collective purpose, eager to draw her blood.

There was dull movement, drawing her eyes, and she saw:

Long pulsing throat. Chin stretched out to form a narrow isosceles triangle, flesh and horny skin stretched taut over bone and cartilage. Jaw hinged so as to spring open into an obtuse angle, to swallow whole prey considerably larger than itself. Red forked tongue, long as a noose and sticky, curling upward from the tip like a gaudy party favor and inward, like a rolled map, from both cracked edges. Snout elongated across the ground, its end flat and smooth as a wall, high arched nostrils ringed by whiskers stiff as quills. Eyes closed.

'It's asleep,' Renata whispered. Coveting the magnificent pearl, she gathered herself to tiptoe closer.

'No, that's a trick,' hissed Belinda, and showed a part of herself. 'A lure. This dragon closes its eyes while it's awake and sleeps with its eyes open, to deceive you. Be careful.'

'What should I do?'

The dragon raised its massive head. There was no longer any need for camouflage, and its eyes – open or closed – glittered as if they were scaled like the rest of its body.

It heaved itself up onto its huge front legs. Its scrabbling claws shook the ground. As it made its way, slinking and lumbering, out of its lair, the wings on its shoulders unfurled; thick and leathery, they did not lift it in flight, but their flapping stirred the air into a storm. The rest of its body emerged, a mammoth slithering, and its tail like a thick serpent with shards of armor set in rows along the whipping tip.

347

Renata turned to flee. Sorrow for the magnificent pearl she was abandoning weighed her down, made her clumsy and slow. The footsteps of the dragon were heavy, long, and very fast; they made the earth and the sky tremble, and the air in between. The pearl no longer shone to dissipate the darkness. There was no light and no shadow.

The dragon roared, spewing cold flame. The icy, fiery net descended over her. The long jaws sprang open many times wider than the enormous head and body, and the tongue shot out and wound around her. She was swept backward into the dragon's maw, and the long jaws snapped shut from above and below.

She was inside the belly of the dragon. The acute and merciless knowledge of where she was and what had happened to her was as horrifying as the experience itself, a doubled-back twist of suffering and awe.

The cavernous space teemed with noises. Rumbles, hisses, squeaks of the beast's bodily systems, she supposed, especially its digestion, which would break her apart. She was immersed in a murky, wet, reddish gleam, and something came to rest against her cheek.

Renata wrenched away, lost her balance, and toppled onto a pulpy pillow-like mass. It shifted under her weight, ballooned between her fingers and toes. She slid down its spongy slope and tumbled against something hard and pointed, the inside surface of a great rib. Fluid spurted onto her skin, and burned.

The acid was wiped away. Hands helped her crawl to a relatively level and sheltered place. But the entire enormous cavity pulsed and thundered and gurgled, tipped and swayed, secreted.

'Make yourself bigger,' instructed a calm voice. Renata was just able to discern the figure of a woman in a shawl, regarding her from some distance away.

Pain seared the tender hollow of her left ankle. She cried out and looked down, could see almost nothing of her body through the blood-colored miasma. She managed to bring her foot up and saw that her flesh was pocked and bleeding, had been smeared with a liquid that was visibly eating into the bone.

She shook her foot violently to rid it of the viscous acid. The acid sprayed up onto her calf and knee where at once it bored agonizing pinprick holes. Frantically she tried to wipe it away, thus brindling her palms with it, too.

The woman cleaned her efficiently and gently with the end of her shawl, which was damp and slightly abrasive. The worst of the torment subsided as the liquid was removed, but the holes and trenches in her skin, flesh, and bone still ached and burned.

Because the woman had kept herself wrapped in the shawl while she used it to tend to Renata, the two of them had been brought very close, bound together. Now her firm hands cupped Renata's head and she said urgently to her, 'The dragon will eat you alive if you do not make yourself bigger.'

'I – don't know what you mean,' Renata choked out. 'Who are you?'

'My name is Margaret. I have been swallowed by the dragon myself, and I've helped countless others on this part of the journey. I know whereof I speak. You must make yourself bigger. You must make yourself huge. You must break free of yourself in order to break free of the dragon.'

'But how?'

Margaret took both Renata's hands, placed them over her own heart, and held them there. She felt the woman start to grow. The pendulous breasts swelled until her arms to the elbows were swaddled in them. The ribs under her fingertips spread apart. The belly puffed out and rose around her like bread dough. The woman's body elongated, widened, deepened, and Renata sank into it. Her arms came around Renata in a suffocating embrace.

Then Renata began to expand. Bigger and bigger she grew inside Margaret's guiding body, until the top of her head, the soles of her burned feet, her shoulders and hips and breasts pushed against the walls of the dragon's belly, at first lightly but with ferocity rapidly intensifying. The dragon shrieked but had no way to fight against this enemy it had meant to trap inside itself.

Renata's internal organs swelled until they burst, split through her flesh, splintered her bones, shredded her skin, and her voice scattered into anguished shards, but she did not die. Thus both dismembered and protected, she broke out through the skin, flesh, bone, and armor of the dragon.

Even more immense than she, Margaret opened the billows of

her body and let Renata go. The dragon had exploded; its spinning razored scales caught the light like prisms and broke it, and its wings lay in dreadful stillness flat on the ground. She didn't see the pearl anywhere, but she had destroyed the dragon.

He doesn't belong to me anymore. She hurtled awake into sunlight, alone in bed, arms wide open, buoyant with loss and release. *He doesn't belong to me anymore. He belongs to the universe.*

Something left her. Something entered her. Both were excruciating. Both brought joy. As if she were once again scattering that first unbelievable handful of his ashes among the pines, there was terrible, immediate loss, and at the core of it a holy rightness. *He belongs to the universe.*

She sat like that, amazed, opened, until she could get up.

The amazement lasted through the day, much of which was spent getting Vanessa ready for Girl Scout Camp. There were lists to check off: clothes to launder, cosmetics to buy and assemble, the sleeping bag to learn again how to roll up and tie. There were stories for Renata to tell, as she did every year, from her own summers at Girl Scout Camp. About the horses; Vanessa, who didn't much like horses, hardly listened to these. About the evening around the campfire when somebody had stupidly swung a forked stick and the hot gooey marshmallow had flown off and stuck, burning, to the back of Sue Fargo's wrist; Vanessa expressed suitable chagrin. About the morning they'd awakened early to banks of fog, rolls of fog, the first time Renata had ever really been aware of fog rolling, the first time she'd understood about fog coming on little cat feet. Vanessa knew the poem, but the image obviously meant nothing in particular to her. The shared memory did, though, and the act of sharing it with her mother. She smiled.

Noticing that the blue plush pig Tim and Shauna had given Vanessa for her birthday was in the pile of things to be packed for camp, Renata touched the child's hair affectionately. 'You like that pig, don't you? I don't blame you. It's a great pig.'

'Tim's nice. Sometimes.'

'I guess you could say that about anybody.' But she knew what Vanessa meant, and she forced herself to give a real answer. 'I know. Sometimes he acts as if he doesn't love us at all, and other times he

350

acts as if being part of this family is really important to him. He's a hard one.'

'He talked about Ian on my birthday.'

'Did that bother you?'

'No. It was nice.'

Renata swallowed. 'It will be good when we can all talk about Ian easily. They tell me that can happen, although I have to admit it's hard to imagine now. When his life and his death will be a natural part of our lives and our conversations.'

'Do you think Ian was with us? In spirit? Do you think he knew it was my birthday?'

'Oh, honey, you know as much about things like that as anybody in this world.' That was the best she could do.

It seemed enough, for the moment, because Vanessa said, a little shyly, 'I'm a teenager now.'

'That's right. You have lots of adventures ahead.'

'Boys.'

'For one thing.'

'If I ever sneaked out to meet a boy, Dad would have a heart attack.' Then, 'He was never like that with Ian.'

Renata forced herself to explain, because it was the truth and important to say to her daughter at this exact moment, 'He never got old enough for us to worry about things like that with him.'

Vanessa said, 'Oh,' easily, and then went on chatting. Renata, riding the pain, hardly heard. But she was grateful to her daughter, who had made her take another step.

In Vanessa's underwear drawer were three of Ian's socks. A red and two blues, the blues not mates. Vanessa bit her lip and didn't look at her mother. Steeling herself for the stab of sorrow that would surely come, Renata plucked them up and deposited them into the bag of outgrown clothes they were getting ready for donation.

There was no stab, only the calm recognition of limitations: she couldn't throw the small grimy things away herself, never mind the negligible chance that somebody would be able to use three unmatched socks. Let the sorters at the warehouse do it; they wouldn't know the socks had once belonged to a little boy with blond hair and crooked eyebrows named Ian Burgess.

When the moment had passed and they were going down the camp list again, Vanessa observed, 'I need a backpack.'

'You have a zillion backpacks. Don't you?' Rather vaguely, Renata glanced around her daughter's disheveled room. Various styles of bags and packs hung from straps from doorknobs or bulged among stuffed animals on the floor, all of them full of something.

'They're too small. Or they're worn out. Or they're ugly.' Vanessa allowed herself a grin.

'Well, okay, I guess we could spring for a backpack.'

'Ian had that purple one.'

Renata nodded. 'Okay. Sure. You can have that one. Do you know where it is?'

As Vanessa scampered out of her room and into his, Renata was struck by the realization, stunning but without pain in it: *My God, we're talking about Ian as if he were dead.* Leaving Vanessa happily loading the purple backpack, she went outside to weed the petunias for a while with the thought in her mind, getting used to it.

After supper and the passage without much note of eight and then nine o'clock, after Vanessa was in bed, Glenn and Renata took the dogs for a walk. They didn't talk much. She wondered – at first sadly, then with some panic at the thought of his pain – what he was thinking. She kept her eyes down.

She looked up, and was struck hard by the beauty of the evening sky.

She had no time to dodge it. Anyway, there was no place she could have gone where the beauty wouldn't have pursued her, wouldn't have already been there lying in wait for her.

She lowered her head and hunched her shoulders. She steeled herself. But she kept on walking. It seemed important to keep on walking, and the sturdy little dog at the other end of the leash would have it no other way. Jade was in characteristic high spirits, snuffling determinedly at spots in the grass that held some real or imagined messages from other dogs who'd passed this way before, uninterruptedly wagging her curled tail whether there was any particular reason for wagging or not, tugging Renata along in search of squirrels and cats. For Jade, the world was now unremittingly abundant.

352

The world is abundant. Very cautiously, Renata held the explosive idea in her mind. *Even without Ian, the world is abundant.*

The hazy moon, nearly full, was dappled by blue-black clouds, and the sky around the moon was both bluer and blacker than the clouds. Glenn walked beside her with the larger and more skittish Gypsy, who'd followed Tim home from the park one summer and never gone wandering since.

The whitish moonlight and the pinkish glow from the streetlamps gave texture and dimension to the strands of Glenn's hair and beard, the folds of his shirt, the bones and tendons in the back of his hand. He was not a silhouette, not a shadow, not something she'd made up to fool herself into happiness. He was, no matter how Renata struggled to deny it, real.

Gypsy suddenly pricked her ears and trotted faster. At the same moment, Jade lunged diagonally, intensely interested in something Renata couldn't see in the dark. The leashes tangled. Both dogs whimpered and looked back in confusion. Glenn chuckled.

Chuckled.

Renata stood still in amazement. How *substantial* he was. When he died – and of course he would die; everything died; one way or another she would lose everything she loved – the substance of this moment and of all the other myriad moments of their lives together would be proved false. A trick. The thought of it made Renata furious, and she stood still while Glenn untangled the leashes, trying not to take in the familiar beloved sound of his voice scolding and quieting the dogs, thinking to move back out of range of his body heat, but staying where she was because she was afraid that any motion would bring her into contact with more beauty, more things to love and lose.

Glenn and Gypsy resumed their walking. Jade tugged at the leash and whimpered, but Renata resisted. She watched the big, plaid-shirted, blue-jeaned figure of her husband striding along the moonlit sidewalk, and thought clearly, deliberately, 'When he dies, this is one of the things that will hurt.'

Gypsy looked back anxiously over her shoulder to see why she wasn't following. Since Ian had been big enough to handle them, it had been his job to walk the dogs. Now, already, there was a new tradition, precious despite the fact that its source was in Ian's death and Shaman's death: Glenn walked Gypsy, Renata walked Jade, Gypsy looked back anxiously if she didn't keep up, Jade tugged at the leash.

Standing still in the midst of ephemeral beauty was no safer than walking toward it. Moving or stationary, she was a target for great loss.

Up ahead, Glenn and Gypsy had stopped to wait. Jade was dancing and snorting at the end of the leash. Renata took a hesitant step and then another, and then was walking fast while Jade trotted faster, keeping the leash taut.

A row of Russian olives, just past the peak of their bittersweet fragrance, leaned over the sidewalk like cupped hands. They had thorns. Ian's friend Eric had once lived in this house with the Russian olives, she remembered suddenly, willingly. The summer evening air, soft, made her skin crawl. When she caught up to Glenn, he asked, 'You okay?'

'Jade saw a cat,' she said, by way of not answering.

'Come on, Gypsy, let's have a race!'

They were off then down the sidewalk, Glenn lumbering a little awkwardly from the old knee injury, Gypsy's raggedy tail floating nearly horizontally behind. Jade tensed, trembled in such excitement that the leash vibrated, yipped frantically. Renata was able to hold back only for a moment before the dog's strong shoulders and absolute concentration won out, and they were chasing the other two, who had already turned the next corner.

Renata shrieked with unaccustomed laughter and held onto the leash with both hands. She stumbled over an uneven crack in the sidewalk but easily righted herself, and the disequilibrium made her laugh even more. An evergreen branch trailed across her neck, every one of its long soft needles tickling. A car went by; its tires sounded deliciously different through sprinkler puddles than on dry pavement.

They caught up to Glenn and Gypsy and started to pass them. Glenn yelled indignantly and blocked Jade's path. The dog hesitated, then feinted to the right and angled back hard to the left, through the corner of a yard, pulling Renata ahead. Renata whooped. Gypsy, old and nervous enough that she almost never saw reason to move faster than a slow trot, now broke into a run.

They raced, two teams, down the Irving Street hill to the light at 23rd Avenue, picking up speed, jockeying for position, shoving each other off the sidewalk and into the arcs of sprinklers going full force. When they stopped for the red light, Glenn and Renata leaned against each other for support, panting and sweating, but the dogs wanted more. Gypsy wagged her tail, pressed against Glenn's knee, and gazed soulfully up at him. Jade pranced and kept her leash stretched taut.

Ian hadn't known Jade. Jade didn't miss him. Renata stared at the exuberant little dog, trying to comprehend how it was that life went on.

Still laughing, still spurting into a race now and then, they went east on 23rd to Federal Boulevard, where the heavier traffic made both dogs uneasy. Gypsy wedged herself between Glenn's and Renata's thighs. Jade charged ahead as usual, but kept up a very quiet growl in the back of her throat that made the leash tingle across Renata's palm.

As they walked back along their street, past the neighbors' tiny yapping dog and the house on the corner where someone was, as usual, practicing a flute, Renata gasped with the force of the understanding that came again: *He belongs to the universe. As do we all. As we always have done.*

Chapter 33

She had had to make herself huge in order to escape from the dragon's belly. Unimaginably huge. Unbearably huge. Bigger than the pain. She had had to make herself limitless, in a peculiar way to surrender, to allow the boundaries of what she'd regarded as herself to be destroyed in order to keep from being destroyed.

It had been worth it. On balance, barely but undeniably, it was better to have survived the loss of Ian (*Ian is dead*) than not. Shocking as that realization was, she tried to face it squarely, but it kept glancing away like an electron under a shaft of light.

Escape had exhausted her. She yawned, stretched, resettled herself to sleep. The surface on which she'd collapsed seemed infinite in both depth and surface area, and was springy, firm enough to support her and malleable enough to accept her shifting position and considerable weight. Her body ached. Her mind was numb with fatigue and with the memory, fading already, of incredible exertion.

The ache, the numbness, the memory were hallucinatory and lulling. A scented breeze wafted across her skin, which was stretched and marked as though she'd given birth. Birdsong and another, deeper melody floated in and out of her consciousness. Delicate mist limned the air in rainbow colors, in silver and gold. The edges of things were pleasantly blurred, and shapes were altered and altered again, including her own.

She drifted through sweet sleep and sweet wakefulness. Willingly, she moved toward the source of the mist and the mesmerizing song.

'Be careful,' Belinda hummed, as though from somewhere in Renata's inner ear.

But Renata was eased away from the warning by some sort of current – gentle, insistent, seeming to cajole rather than to insist and certainly not to coerce. Resisting it, though, would have required great sustained effort and a sense of clear purpose, both of which were beyond her. She couldn't have gathered herself enough to hold her ground, and she had no wish to do so.

Instead, she was buoyed by the song. It was three-dimensional, textured, shadowed and brilliantly thatched with crisscross strands of melody and rhythm. It was sung by a powerful voice made soft just for her.

The serpentine warning came again. 'Renata, be careful. Your dragon has more than one head.'

Renata opened herself to the mist, which was warm now and sparkling, and to the song. But she couldn't help hearing and understanding what she was being told.

'Your dragon is not dead. You have more to do.'

The music swelled, grew not louder but more intense. Surely it was irresistible. Surely, a creature who could emit such spellbinding substances was not to be feared or denied.

Renata was dancing. There were not discrete movements, but an evanescent undifferentiated tide of motion and energy. She bent and stretched to the sensuous, demanding rhythm, arched and curled and spun. With gathering momentum, she slid toward the singing, gaping maw. She couldn't stop herself, and wouldn't have if she could.

'Renata.' The snake's hiss saying her name could have been part of the dragon's song, was at least in counterpoint to it. Renata thrilled to hear it, and it said her name again. 'Renata. Save yourself or the dragon will devour you.' The forked tongue that folded up around her could have been Belinda's. The delicious poison of the mist – denser now, wetter – needled through her pores and into her bloodstream, into her heart and brain. She knew she was in terrible, sweet danger. The song mutated into a guttural roar, and the gentle tugging became fierce. Fangs appeared above and below her, set into the wedge-shaped darkness of the dragon's mouth. The mouth would close, and she would be inside.

Something hard and cylindrical was thrust into her hands. The whispering of her name had risen to a shriek. Perhaps it was

Belinda, or perhaps it was the dragon, or perhaps she was screaming it herself.

She closed her hands around the object she'd been given, which she understood to be a weapon. A spear: Shaft thick enough to fit comfortably in her grip; fluted, razor-sharp, triangular edges; long sharp tip. She felt a line of her own blood spurt from her scored palm, and the sting of it jolted her.

The dragon sang gloriously. Renata trembled in the face of such evil beauty. The mist coalesced into clouds, settled over her like bees, each drop a glistening note of music that stung, spread sweetness, spread death. The dragon sang, and Renata could feel herself forgetting again that she was in the presence of a vicious predator, for she yearned not to know that so that she could succumb to the magic of the song.

'Renata!' and she thrust the spear deep into the dragon's throat.

Blood and music drenched her. Suddenly she understood what the dragon had been singing, and she huddled on the red soaked ground, arms over her head, until the dragon died, the air cleared, and she was alone.

Chapter 34

'I want to stay home alone.'

'Are you sure?' Glenn had been right to be skeptical; until today Renata had refused to be home without someone else in the house, even for as long as it would have taken for Glenn to go to and from the grocery store. For fear, she guessed, of Ian's ghost. It had shamed her to be thinking in such reductionist terms, and she wasn't sure it was precisely accurate, but certainly she'd been afraid of something like that, some encounter, some haunting.

'I need to start getting used to how my life in this house is going to be from now on,' she'd said to Glenn on this Sunday morning while Vanessa was at camp. 'This new life. This alien life.' She'd smiled – wanly, she was sure; perhaps ironically.

So Glenn had gone off to his writers' convention, which would keep him away till suppertime or so, and here she was, alone in her house for the first time since her son had died, contemplating the possibility that it was her own ghost she didn't want to encounter.

She didn't know what to do, exactly. She went and stood in the foyer. The staircase was dappled by sunlight through the ivy outside the tall windows, by sunlight through the leaded glass like embroidery and lace across the tops.

By sunlight as if through a lid and she at the bottom of a jarlike space, the stairwell, a rounded and lidded underground room. She was spinning with grief. She saw someone else in the striped dry shadows of ivy, leaded glass, dust and ash, as she spun around a hole at her center, a tunnel to and from the underworld. But then she came to rest again in her own foyer and nobody else was there.

She took a chair at the dining-room table. She sat there. She placed her hands flat on the polished surface. She laid her cheek

361

down, listened to the minuscule creaks and groans of the wood, listened to her own breathing slightly amplified in the little pocket between her lips and the table, slightly distorted. As if from a great inner distance, she felt sobbing, but she herself wasn't making that noise, though it echoed from her pelvis and ribs as if from high red canyon walls.

She walked to the kitchen and stood there. The refrigerator hummed. A hidden bird chirped. Two squirrels scolded on the fence. She felt rather than heard the undertone of the dragon's song – not a dream, in any common sense of the term; not a vision; but an experience under this one, parallel to it and concurrent.

On the counter was a very faint stain where someone – Ian, most likely – had spilled and incompletely cleaned up grape juice. This was not the first time she'd noticed the stain, but it came as an unwelcome surprise.

She walked outside and breathed the summer air. She walked back inside and breathed the inside summer air, closer, threaded with house rather than city smells, seeming to require more to fill her lungs although probably, since it had respirating house plants and no highways, it actually contained more oxygen for her use than the air outside.

She placed herself in each room of her house, one after another starting with the attic and working her way down. Ian was not in any of them, and never would be again. She paid attention to that.

In each space she spoke aloud, to hear how her voice would sound. Sometimes she said Ian's name. Sometimes she said to him things like, 'I love you. I miss you.' Sometimes she said nonsense syllables, or sang, or commented on what she was doing: 'Now I'm in the hall. Now I'm in the furnace room.' At first she was composing journal entries and repeating them so they'd be intact when it came time to write them down, but there was a small keen triumph in the fact that she didn't need to write in her journal several times a day anymore in order to calibrate meticulously every nuance of her grieving.

She could not sustain this intense *being in her house* for long. Nothing unpleasant happened – nothing much happened of any sort – but profound uneasiness allowed her only to make a beginning this morning. It was not yet noon when she'd had enough, and, vastly relieved, called Jackie.

'How are you?' Hearing Jackie settling in for a long talk, the kind of nesting noises they'd both been making on the telephone with each other for a good twenty-five years now, she felt cared for across the miles.

'I'm okay. I've had a pretty good week.'

'Really?'

'I think I'm going to make it. I'm still fighting off the acceptance of this thing, resisting healing, but I seem to be accepting and healing anyway.'

Thoughtfully, Jackie said, 'It's too soon, isn't it? It's only been four months. This can't be real.'

Renata didn't know what to say.

'And I can sure understand why you're fighting off acceptance. I think if I were in your place, I'd feel that a loving parent couldn't possibly feel that way.'

A high, hot wave of rage thundered over her. Did Jackie think she hadn't loved Ian enough, didn't love him enough still?

Maybe that was right. Maybe she hadn't loved him enough, and that was why he was dead.

Her thoughts were racing, spinning, close to out of control. She saw no point in trying to control them. Madness was a perfectly appropriate response to what had happened to her. Sanity, peace, wholeness were illusion.

Didn't Jackie want her to get better? Of course not. She didn't deserve to get better.

They said she couldn't control what happened to her, but she had some choice about what it would mean to her life. Like a child given a 'choice' between punishments – spanking or grounding; more lashes with a thin belt or fewer with a thick one – she would be made an accomplice to the fraud if she even considered the proffered alternatives: Be destroyed, or heal.

If she got better, if she allowed anything good to come out of this, she would be saying Ian's death was acceptable, tolerable. Which it could not be. Jackie was right.

Dimly through the noise and skyrocketing pressure of the building rage, Renata was aware that Jackie had said almost none of this, had probably intended none of it. But she could not talk to Jackie anymore. By the time she got off the phone, fury had taken her over.

Taken over her body: She raced down the rickety basement steps, slammed her fists into the concrete walls and opened the flesh, raced upstairs again, falling, wrenching herself to her feet. She screamed, roared, shouted obscenities, whispered curses.

Taken over her thoughts: Viciously she wished the colleague who'd rolled his Jeep in the mountains last month had *died*. Wished a sniper would, *right now*, take out all the children in the neighborhood. Reveled in hatred of Tim and Vanessa and Glenn, especially Glenn, for not grieving right.

Just last night Glenn had said he was tired of being a bereaved parent, and at the time she'd thought she understood what he meant – he was tired of the pain, tired of defining himself that way, tired of obsessing. She'd even said herself, tentatively, 'Lately it's seemed that talking, reading, writing, even thinking directly about Ian's death gets in the way of living it.' He'd nodded. They'd been sitting at the kitchen table, holding hands. 'And, like C.S. Lewis, sometimes I'm assaulted by the *idea* of my own suffering, not so much by the suffering itself. Maybe there is such a thing as a too-well-examined life.'

She'd said that. They'd stopped talking then and held each other's hands.

Now, though, throwing a pan and then its lid against the kitchen wall, she raged: What right did he have to be tired of it? A bereaved parent was what he was and what he always would be, because Ian, Ian would always be dead.

She flung herself onto the living-room floor. Gypsy and Jade came to investigate, Gypsy anxiously and Jade out of curiosity. She pushed them away, yelled at them fiercely, and they backed off, Gypsy slinking, Jade dancing and feinting.

She'd been set up. Life – God, fate, the universe – had allowed her to feel good about her life for a long time for the express purpose of beating her down. That meant she didn't dare ever feel good again, because it was a trick, it was all a trick. Allowing herself to appreciate life – to love, to have fun, to experience beauty – was playing the game, setting *herself* up. She was damned if she would ever do that again.

But if she were to succeed in never loving or feeling happiness or noticing beauty again, nobody would lose but her. The

364

universe – God, fate – wouldn't care. So, either way, she was a sucker.

She didn't dare stay inside any longer, for fear she'd damage the house, for fear Glenn would call to check on her and she'd say something awful to him on the phone. Her marriage, she realized, was at this moment in jeopardy. This was how relationships were destroyed by the loss of a child.

Outside, at least, was more room for the fury, but the instant she left the house the fury expanded to fill this larger but still finite container, and now she suspected she would damage the world, destroy the world, which seemed only fitting.

The geraniums in the planter on the back patio were doing well, though she'd hardly thought of them since she'd set them out. Bright red, bright pink, bright green fuzzy leaves with purplish fluted markings. She snapped the heads off one or two of them and hurled the blossoms, now become gaudy debris, into the lilac bushes, but it was such a paltry act of violence that she gave it up scornfully and let the rest of the geraniums be.

Glenn had pointed out that she loved flowers whilst knowing they wouldn't last forever; Renata had until now been unable to articulate why that was a specious comparison. Now she stood still in the hot sun and formulated a bitter, detailed rebuttal which she hoped she would never say to him:

One marigold is essentially interchangeable with any other marigold, at least from a species-centric human point of view, but Ian is irreplaceable, people I love are irreplaceable, my life is irreplaceable. I will never live this moment again, never draw this breath again. It's a cruel and false choice: I don't dare allow myself to engage fully with anyone or anything because I'll lose it all.

Or, for the very reason that this is the only moment I have and everything is transitory, I *must* fully engage here and now or not live at all. I don't like either alternative, and that's at the heart of my rage at the way things are – a pointless rage, I grant, but consuming. The choice is either to love and therefore to be terribly hurt like this again and again, or not to love and therefore to live always on the surface.

She glared around her. The brown patches in all the lawns – this was, after all, midsummer in a semi-arid climate – were hideous and comical. The white plastic grocery sack that had lodged in the top branches of the catalpa tree was obscene. Jade's drool and Gypsy's loose flying fur disgusted her. The sun on her skin felt acidic, and under it her skin smelled spoiled.

A terracotta flowerpot full of last year's caked potting soil sat by the back door, testimony to the ridiculousness of engaging with anything alive. Renata grasped it by its rim and hefted it over her head. Dirt sprinkled onto her shoulders and hair. She flung the pot onto the patio and it broke, the bottom popping out as if perforated to expose tubers and tendrils of the roots of plants that had died there over the winter.

She lowered herself onto the ground. Pain at her navel hardly surprised her. The sun was in her eyes, creating visions, after-images, access to a common pain.

Glenn came home from the convention early. He said he hadn't been enjoying himself, and Renata wondered nastily how he'd ever thought he could. He mentioned, too, that she hadn't answered the phone, he'd called home twice, and Renata was enraged that he'd been checking on her, enraged that he'd imagined she'd want him here with her if she were in trouble, would have been enraged if he had not.

'What happened to your hands?' He reached for them but she stayed out of his reach.

'I punched the basement walls.' Her lip curled.

His eyes widened and he said, but mildly, 'Honey.'

She managed to avoid him for most of the evening, which she knew must be hurting him and did not care, was even glad. Just before she went to bed – early; hoping she'd be sound asleep before he came in – he yawned with what gave every appearance of peacefulness, smiled at the three cats asleep in yellow, gray, black-and-white puddles on the couch, and observed gently, 'It's a sleepy time in the Burgess household.'

Already livid, Renata felt a surge of hotter anger. There *was* no Burgess household anymore, no Burgess family, no Burgess life. How could he pretend otherwise? Was he deluding himself or deliberately deceiving her?

The next morning she called in sick. There'd have been no need to lie or explain to Theresa, but a student work-study employee answered the phone, so Renata just said she wasn't feeling well and wouldn't be in. 'I'm sorry to hear that,' the girl said perkily. 'I hope you feel better soon,' and Renata hung up hastily before she said something pointed and pointless about stupid remarks.

The instant the offending connection had been broken, she dialed again, this time the number of the therapist she'd been seeing for a month or so now. He answered. It was an emergency, she told him through gritted teeth. He could see her in an hour.

By the time she got to his office, she was shaking violently, bones rattling like a funhouse skeleton, eyes wide and empty as sockets, skin crawling in prelude to peeling off. Breathing fast and hard, she could not force air past the constriction in her throat, and her head spun, her hands and feet tingled, her heart was everywhere and nowhere in the cavity of her body.

He said, 'What's going on?'

She said, 'I'm dying.'

He said, 'I doubt it. Here, sit down. Take a deep breath.'

'Why would I want to do that?'

'To get more oxygen into your lungs. Take a deep breath.'

She did her best to shriek at him, 'I don't *want* more fucking oxygen in my lungs!' but she did, in fact, on his instruction take a deep breath, and then another, and she did eventually let him guide her to a chair, where she closed her eyes and leaned her head back and took another deep breath.

At some point he urged, 'Go into it. Don't push it away.'

'The pain will burn me up,' she moaned. 'The rage will devour me. I'm in real danger here.'

'I know,' he agreed softly, which startled her a little.

'I'm going to lose this battle.'

'I don't think so.'

She wasn't entirely aware of having started railing, but now she was whispering hoarsely, furiously, 'I lie next to Glenn, listen to him breathe, watch him across the dinner table, and I imagine him gone, myself without him. For a long time I've done that, trying to live with the knowledge of loss, and apparently through this first half of my life I thought this knowledge would protect me from experiencing actual loss. Ah, the constant search for magic, for amulets and spells to keep me safe in an unsafe world.' Still in an undertone, she barked a harsh laugh. 'What a fool.'

'We're never safe,' he said, 'if by "safe" you mean protected from things happening to us that we regard as bad.'

'Well, it's a shitty system, if you ask me.'

His laugh was not harsh, nor, surprisingly, did she interpret it as mocking. 'Nobody asked,' he pointed out gently.

They were quiet for a while. 'I suppose,' she said suddenly, shifting in her chair, 'someday someone will be mourning me like this.'

'No doubt.'

She sat still a moment, then slammed her fist into the hard padded arm of the chair. 'God*dam*mit, I don't *want* to find that comforting!'

'Being part of a larger process,' he said, agreeing or simply restating and reflecting.

'I've lost all my memories, too!' she wailed.

'Do you mean you can't remember things?'

She was shaking her head vehemently. 'No, I mean because they're too painful. Not only have I lost my son, I've also lost all my memories of him, because they hurt so much. And all my memories that aren't directly of him, too, because they're either from before he died or after he died, and they all *hurt*.'

'Burn your memories,' he told her.

'What?'

'Write your most painful and important memories on slips of paper and take them out into the back yard with a book of matches and burn them. Watch the paper turn black and disintegrate. Watch the smoke drift away. It's really quite beautiful.'

She was shocked, indignant. 'I don't want to destroy my memories of Ian. I just want them to be bearable.'

'The burning doesn't destroy them,' he said quietly. 'It cleanses.'

She sat for a while then, visualizing herself writing some of the most painful and most important memories of Ian on little pieces of blue paper.

'His yellow windbreaker.'

'The way his eyebrows got crooked when he was puzzled.'

'Laughter like seashells.'

'Playing a trivia game: "What sound does a bat make?" "Wap!" and the rest of us insisting he was wrong until it dawned on me that he meant a baseball bat, and of course he was right, a baseball bat does go "wap."'

The blue papers filled her lap. Striking a match, she smelled sulphur, felt the tiny heat flare between her fingertips. She held up one paper by its end, the one about the bat, which she could hardly bear to write, could hardly tolerate reading, but could touch. She brought the burning match to it. It caught. Fire swelled, small and strong. The paper charred and vanished, hardly even any ash. A thin wriggle of gray-white smoke drifted up toward the bluer sky, dissipating long before it had risen even above her head.

She was crying. She was freed. The memory remained – 'What does a bat say?' 'Wap!' – but it was sweet now, bittersweet, and clean.

In the last few minutes of the session, the therapist offered to do a guided visualization with her, a relaxation exercise she could use herself when the next panic attack came on. When she'd shifted position and made herself more or less comfortable, he started with what she knew to be the standard invitation to visualize herself in a safe place.

'There is no safe place,' she said at once.

'A mountain meadow, maybe.'

'There's a vulture circling.'

His voice betrayed no impatience, though there might have been a light patina of amusement. 'Imagine the vulture gone, the sky blank. Put yourself in the safest place you can imagine. A mountain meadow. A forest clearing.'

Psycho mountain men came unbidden. *Cougars. Lightning storms.* But she recognized these images as in some way perverse, refrained from telling them to him, and did her best to feel safe, all things being relative.

'You find a key. A gold key, just the proper size to fit in the palm of your hand. Feel the weight of it, the warm metal. Feel the ridges on the side.' He paused. 'Can you feel it?'

She'd never lied to him, could see no point in dishonesty now. 'No,' she said. 'I'm sorry.' When he didn't say anything, she repeated, 'I'm sorry, but I don't have a key in my hand—'

And then she was floating face-down in a wide deep river. The current carried her swiftly; she couldn't touch the banks or the bottom, and she had no wish to do so. She was breathing easily, though her face was submerged. Her back, her hair were warm and moist, though they were exposed to the night air. The water was black, silky. The black air was silky.

She was in the midst of a school of luminescent creatures, fish or birds or something else. It was they who carried her along.

She tilted, head down. The V-shaped luminescences carried her down. Torpedoing cleanly, smoothly, with no wake and no splash and no sensation of danger although her life might well be over, not exactly in silence for there was sound as soft and flickering and buoyant as the lights. Down, farther down than she'd ever known a river could flow, and she was perfectly safe although she might drown, perfectly accompanied although she was alone, perfectly loved and known although she was no longer who she had started out to be.

Then:

She was inside the tall bloom of a tulip. The glowing red petals curled around her and touched their fluted tips above her head, making an egg-shaped space, placing her in it. She was bathed in a silky red glow. At the base was black, silky dense glowing black, the heart of the flower, her heart. She was safe.

Chapter 35

'The dragon encircles the world,' Belinda informed her. 'You cannot escape the dragon.'

'The dragon told me that,' Renata realized, 'but I didn't believe it.' The secret language of the dragon was obfuscated again as the splatters of blood dried on her skin, were absorbed or sloughed off, and she couldn't be sure anymore of anything she'd thought she understood.

'The dragon is the foundation of the universe,' Belinda declared. 'You can never defeat the dragon.'

Renata made an expansive, weary, and bewildered gesture that took in the scene of devastation around and inside her. As she did so, she saw the dragon forming itself again out of chaos, pieces of it fusing into new but recognizable shapes, bloody limb joining to great bloody tail melding to headless torso and severed head in unexpected ways. 'Then why have I done all this?' Renata demanded to know, but, in the small span of time between forming the query in her mind and uttering it, its meaning had altered.

'The dragon girdles the world. The dragon is the force of creation, gnawing at creation's frame. The dragon gives birth and death to everything, eater and eaten alike.'

A sinuous shape had settled around her, coils upon coils. Out of the half-light appeared a long triangular head, studded above and below with double rows of dripping fangs. As the head rose higher and higher, towering over her and rising higher, the thick neck accumulated substance from below, from where she stood.

Under the long throat, among the leathery folds of skin and the scales that bristled razor-sharp and perpendicular to the surface, a spectacular luminescence now showed itself. Once Renata had

371

seen it she couldn't imagine how she hadn't been seeing it all her life; its presence usurped all her attention, and its brilliance so diminished the visibility of everything else that nothing else might have existed, including its host dragon. Blue and green, yellow and pink and silver, mother-of-pearl and pearl itself, glowing and growing, already immense.

Renata backed away.

'The pearl is yours for the taking.'

Renata was shaking her head, flinging her hands in front of her, shaking her head. But as she retreated, the pearl grew in both size and luminosity so that the physical distance between her and the sensuous curve of it quickly became infinitesimal. Its extraordinary beauty titillated her almost beyond bearing, and now, as though she'd never known anything else, she knew she must have it.

'Without this pearl,' the snake confirmed, 'you will never leave the underworld. You will never go home. Your child's death will have destroyed you.'

The yearning to go home sprang from her full grown, and with it the need for the treasure which would give her passage. With both hands she reached for it, imagining she could simply pluck it from the pocket under the dragon's jaw, for the fearsome creature gave every appearance of offering it to her.

The dragon roared.

Renata screamed in response, equally without words, an expression of mortal fear and fury, and an acceptance of the challenge. Others gathered, not to help her because they couldn't, but to bear witness: a woman with white-blonde hair, a woman whose face was streaked with red, a woman in a long black coat, a stone woman, a woman whose scraped knuckles smeared blood across her mouth.

The beast lowered its mammoth head, but the treasure was too big and too bright now to be hidden in the caves of its body, however deep and dangerous it could make them. The pearl showed clearly around the sinister outline of the dragon's jaw, curved against its angularity, shimmering inside its darkness.

Desperation made Renata reckless. She flung herself at the dragon's red eyes, hoping somehow to blind or dazzle it by the sheer force of her determination and desire. The monster swiped at her with a huge taloned forepaw and lashed its razored tail. The tail missed her and shattered the air instead, booming like thunder. But she was raked by the claws, long bloody furrows down her chest and belly and a luminous pain.

She lay still, catching her breath, finding a way not to ignore the pain but to incorporate it into her experience of the world, plotting. The dragon was enormous. The pearl was enormous, and glimmering made its boundaries unclear. There was nowhere in this dark place untouched by the pearl-light.

Renata flattened herself on the ground, as though she could get under the light and under the dragon's line of sight. She slunk toward the beast from its side this time, knowing she was laying down trails of her blood, wondering if the dragon could smell or in some other unfathomable way sense her approach.

She came up under the pearl and actually had her palms on its sleek surface when the dragon shrieked and contorted itself, tossing her into the air. The dragon rose with her, screeching and flapping its great wings, caracoling, spewing fire. Scarlet, cerulean, jade-green talons of flame engulfed her, and in the stench of her own searing flesh Renata longed for water to quench the fire.

But there was no water. There was fire. There was the fire of the dragon, cascading from the sky, and there was her own fire, coming out of her mouth somehow, coming out of her heart and loins, shooting up to meet the dragon's fire.

Fire met fire and exploded. Deafening noise and blinding light, a cold burning heat, and then the fire went out and the dragon plummeted. Out of the sky, pulling the sky with it. Past her, and she lunged for the streaking pearl, had it in her grasp but could not hang on.

Down into a bottomless river, dark and deep but entirely clear, and now the pearl lit it from within. Renata flung herself toward the shore, but misjudged its distance and its incline and slid into the water. She floated face-down and gazed, transfixed, at the underwater scene.

Palaces had been fashioned from stone so lucid that all life in and beside the river could be seen by those who lived inside the pearly walls; she knew they were watching her now. Ornate columns of jade were adorned with glistening filigree. Doors and friezes of ivory were inlaid with shell. Rosy coral branches made staircases, banistered with gold.

In the shimmering light, like liquid mother-of-pearl, the shapes of the dragon-folk who lived there appeared to Renata in one form flowing into another, now horned and crested, clawed and scaled, and now as the most beautiful of children with Ian's face, his wide brown eyes become ancient, wise and sad and merry.

'Ian,' she breathed, and his name sent bubbles down into the dragon kingdom. The children smiled at her and changed into dragons again.

Renata arched her back, scissored her feet, and dived for the pearl. The river blackened and grew dense. The underwater kingdom had vanished because the pearl had vanished, leaving no color, no shape, no movement, and no way home.

Abruptly, Renata's lungs screamed for air. She couldn't get to the surface fast enough. She couldn't find the surface. She kicked and clawed at the endless suffocating liquid, struggled and seemed to be moving but couldn't tell whether she was moving upward toward breathable air or downward toward the magical drowned kingdom or in any direction at all. Made a sound of anguish which only served to bring water into her lungs; the water tasted sweet and was smooth going down, but it would kill her. She spat it out, not knowing, because she was immersed in the same sweet smooth water, whether water was still inside her or not.

Then she burst through the surface tension of the water into luminescent air, breathing again, gasping. She was wrapped in a striated, turbinate tunnel of coils that had rippled to push her upward. With a final fierce constriction, she was disgorged from under the long jaw. In her arms was the pearl. Its cool glow suffused her flesh and bones. The air hurt in her lungs, but she kept breathing.

The mouth of the dragon swung open. The tongue forked. Fangs as tall and thick as she was spouted iridescent poisonous nectar. The dragon screeched. The watchers sighed and faded.

It was Belinda who said, 'The pearl belongs to you.'

Renata was hanging up a dress in her closet, wondering if she could get away with not ironing it; thinking that Vanessa's first day of school had, unexpectedly, been harder by far than her and Ian's birthday or Mother's Day or any of the other holidays she'd braced herself for; fearing that she wouldn't be able to celebrate her marriage to Glenn on their anniversary tomorrow because, although there was plenty to celebrate, there was also within this marriage the fact of their son's death; missing Ian—

—she was inside the coils of a snake. At first she was afraid.

The coils cast a cool interior shade of concentric ripples. The undulating cone of them was wide enough at the base to encircle her snugly without pressure, though simple rearrangement could have squeezed her to death. Like the plastic stacking rings a toddler plays with, the cone of the snake funneled into a narrow apex just above her head. Above that rose Belinda's long wedge-shaped head.

The soft sibilant voice exuded from everywhere. 'You are safe.'

She was not protected from storms. Rainwater sluiced through the spaces between the fleshy coils, and she could feel fierce wind, buffeting the serpent, making it tip and slither, driving debris painfully into her face. Thunder roared, and lightning slashed patterns like the patterns on Belinda's great back.

But she was safe. 'You are safe with me.'

She was not protected from monsters. Giant rats' claws skritched, and the segmented leg of a huge red roach insinuated itself toward her. Sweet and rank odors, subtle and almost overpowering, and a motley taste at the back of her throat warned her of monsters she had not yet met.

But she was safe. 'You will always be safe with me.'

She was not protected from the pain of injury or loss. Ian's death was not the last hard thing that would ever happen to her. She was not protected from death. Everyone she loved would die, and so would she. But she was safe. In the midst of anything that could happen to her, she would be safe.

Belinda began to glide upward, carrying Renata with her. The space inside her coils, where Renata traveled, changed shape as the serpent moved, from conical to spherical to tubular to flat. It was not precisely a shape at all, but the inverse of form.

The serpent rippled upward, through rock and water and air, through time and space. The pearl had dazzled, but the sudden breakthrough into the expansive sunlight of the upperworld made Renata gasp, although she did not look away. Belinda the beautiful serpent fell away from her, though she would always be there.

—she was hanging up a dress in the closet, missing Ian, loving

Ian. The light in the closet was pearly. The hanger was solid in her hand, one end of it in the shoulder of the dress. Joyous, she slipped the other end into the other shoulder, fastened the top button, hooked the hanger over the rod, smoothed down the skirt, stepped back and shut the closet door.

I am to bear witness, she understood. I am to say, with words and without: This is agonizing. Yes, this is a dreadful wound. But, see, I can bear it. We, all of us, can bear it. And acknowledgment of life's abundance can mean acknowledgment of it all. Her spirit rose and deepened to meet Ian's.

From across the hall Glenn called to her, 'Come see if this is where you want your computer.' This weekend, Ian's room was becoming her office, a practical expansion of the cubbyhole she'd been using and an antidote to haunting. They'd both anticipated this project would be fraught with emotion and meaning, but, when they got right down to it, mostly it was labor-intensive and detail-oriented.

Standing in the doorway, she was pleased, even excited. The red and blue wallpaper, red carpet, blue window blinds made a whole new context, and the murderous bunk beds were gone, along with all other evidence that this had been a small boy's room. It was a cheerful and efficient workplace now, and his spirit was no more or less here than anywhere else. 'That's fine,' she told Glenn, and went to kiss him.

In the morning she woke to find an envelope propped against the coffeepot, where she would be sure to see it. She touched it. It burned and she snatched her hand back. She used both hands, then, to pick it up and open it, withdraw the card.

'Happy Anniversary to My Best Friend,' the outside read. Tears blurred her vision. She opened the card.

The verse inside was from Robert Browning: 'Grow old along with me! The best is yet to be.' The sheer brazenness of it, its gutsy affirmation of life's abundance, tore her heart open.

The best is yet to be? Without Ian?

Renata took a deep breath and acknowledged that it could be so.